PRAISE FOR
First Second Coming

"Jeff Pollak's debut novel, *First Second Coming,*
combines suspense, romance, and theology in an
imaginative, unique adventure!"

—Mark Moses,
Actor (best known as Paul Young on *Desperate Housewives*
and Herman "Duck" Phillips on *Mad Men.*)

"This supernatural suspense and romance novel hooks you
from the first page. The story is original, and the writing superb.
I highly recommend *First Second Coming,* an ingenious and
exceptional novel by Jeff Pollak."

—Adena Bernstein Astrowsky,
Author of *Living Among the Dead* (a Jewish survivor's
World War II memoir, written by her granddaughter).

"*First Second Coming* is a unique blend of suspense and
spirituality in a future where humans interact with religious
deities. A 'must-read' for those craving a new perspective
on supernatural suspense."

—Anthony J. Harrison,
Author of *The Irishman's Deception.*

"*First Second Coming* is a compelling debut novel which
delves into one of life's great mysteries. Pollak provides a
multi-layered adventure; one which pulls readers in and keeps
them enthralled until its exciting conclusion!"

ony Chiarciaro,
ry crime author.

D1096963

First Second Coming

BOOK ONE IN THE NEW GOD SERIES

JEFF POLLAK

FROM THE TINY ACORN …
GROWS THE MIGHTY OAK

First Second Coming

First Edition
Copyright © 2020 Jeff Pollak

This story is a work of fiction. References to real people, events, establishments, organizations, or locales are intended only to provide a sense of authenticity and are used fictitiously. All other characters, and all incidents and dialogue are drawn from the author's imagination and are not to be construed as real.

Book interior design and digital formatting by Debra Cranfield Kennedy.

www.acornpublishingllc.com

ISBN—Hardcover 978-1-947392-97-7
ISBN—Paperback 978-1-947392-95-3
Library of Congress Control Number: 2020911605

To my wife, Carol, and my son, Tyler—

the two suns my world spins around

FIRST
SECOND
COMING

I believe in God, but not as one thing, not as an old man in the sky. I believe that what people call God is something in all of us. I believe that what Jesus and Mohammed and Buddha and all the rest said was right. It's just that the translations have gone wrong.

—John Lennon

1 | Stranger in a Strange Land

Thirteen hours late, my cross-galaxy voyage to the All-Souls Transit Center ends in a puff of soft lunar dirt on Mare Tranquillitatis. I expect to meet the legendary God of planet Earth in his office, but as I deplane he's shuffling down the concourse toward his departure gate. He's easy to spot—inside this small, sparse four-gate terminal we are the only life forms in sight.

With his stooped posture and unkempt shoulder-length gray hair, God reminds me of the mythical Atlas. His tremors underscore the physical and emotional toll he has had to bear. Did his mental state also degrade? He spent two millennia managing a planet populated by quarrelsome headstrong terrestrials. Over that much time any deity posted to such a world would succumb to the effects of prolonged stress.

I quicken my pace, catch up to him and extend a hand. "Good day, Lord."

"This is how you address your superiors?" The decibel level of his gruff voice implies impaired hearing. "Where are your manners? A bow is in order."

Though I have not yet fully adapted to the musculature of this adult male body I inhabit, my flawless execution of a deep obeisance brings a quick smile to my face.

God gives me a brusque signal to rise. "You're my replacement, are you?"

"Correct, Lord. I am humbled and honored to take your place." I bow again, less fully.

"Call me NTG if you wish. I prefer answering to that nickname."

So the rumor is true. That he calls himself the New Testament God instead of his given name means he has indeed gone native. This explains a lot.

We sink into a 'maximum comfort' couch—or so the attached tag boasts—stuffed full of condensed nimbostratus cloud threads imported from Earth. An ugly green tarp spread over the cushions prevents our clothes from getting soaked by residual moisture.

God adjusts his overcoat and leans toward me. "I trust you had an enjoyable flight?"

"I would like to say yes, but what a hellacious trip." That's an understatement. "We flew through several cosmic storms, circumvented an unmapped black hole and limped here on back-up power after the anti-matter fuel engine failed. I will never fly by chartered spaceship again."

"Now that you've arrived, what makes you think you can take on a tough job like this?"

"This is my fourth assignment, though the first for Milky Way Galaxy, Inc." I place my carry-on bag on the tan moonrock table and open a side pocket. "I have a résumé, if you want to peruse it. In each previous posting, the planets I shepherded returned to optimal status. Whilst this assignment is more complex, I assure you my record shall remain unsullied."

"Humph." He spits into the thin puddle created by the leaky couch and waves off my résumé. "I thought those spineless MWGI decision-makers would send a rank amateur. After only three postings, you expect to fix this mess? You're still wet around the ears, sonny. Have you even hung your precious university degrees on a wall yet?" He points at the nearby picture window. "On Earth they say you learn more through failure than success."

"Elder, I did not travel here to fail. MWGI reached out because of my extensive training as a planetary turnaround specialist. They are confident I am the best available deity for this job."

"And you agree with that assessment, do you?" He fidgets, as though trying to stand and walk away, but can't get off the couch.

"I would not otherwise have taken the job, Lord. Once I did, I undertook considerable research. The travel delays afforded me extra preparation time. I have learned everything a new deity should know about Earth and its inhabitants. I am ready to take the reins."

"Your extensive reading helped you form opinions regarding the humans, did it?"

I disregard the sarcasm implicit in the question. If I ever reach his wizened old age, young deities will receive better treatment from me than this. His attitude is understandable, though. Forced retirement is a difficult pill for anyone to swallow, supreme beings included.

"Lord, these sentient beings do have many laudable qualities. However, whilst I prefer not to focus on the negative, on the whole humans strike me as a rather unpredictable species."

NTG spits again and rummages through the pockets of his black overcoat, pants and vest. "Where's the damn thing? Did I forget it? Ah, here. Since you're not dead, you'll need this to get into heaven."

He hands me a Holyday Inn card key with "NTG" stenciled on the back side. I stare at the card whilst mulling over my research, which characterized heaven as an imaginary afterlife sanctuary. With a shrug, I deposit the card in the pocket of my blue denim shirt.

"Many humans call it heaven, but I consider it home." God's melancholic smile comes and goes in seconds. "Souls get over the false advertising once they adjust to their newly deceased status. Follow the overhead signs to the tram that'll take you to the complex. My office is by the main gate so I can greet arrivals on St. Peter's days off. Ask for Angie, my chief of staff. She's a real angel in every sense of the word."

"Thank you, I will." With time short before his departure I move our conversation in a more substantive direction. "Lord, you know Earth is noncompliant with many MWGI planetary operating standards. For example, the rate of climate change is too rapid. Air and water pollution levels far exceed maximum allowable limits. The ratio of species extinction to species creation is inverted. Over-population and starvation quotas have blown past permissible quotas."

Although the list goes on, I stop to avoid rubbing it in.

NTG opens his overcoat, extracts a thick booklet and slams it onto the table. "This is for you, sonny. Study it. The dossier contains a thorough assessment of the noncompliance situation and numerous other issues you'll need to address. If you wish, we can take a few minutes to discuss the gravity of Earth's circumstances."

"No doubt this will help me acclimate." I move the study, entitled *Homo-sapiens: An Advanced Sentient Species Plagued by Primitive Morality,* to my lap. "The title reminds me that before I do anything else, I must decide whether to keep this troublesome species around."

"This will answer your questions," NTG says, tapping the cover flap. "Once you absorb the content, I'm sure you'll accept my conclusion and recommendations. Although clearing the planet of humans is an expedient option, give them a chance. They can perplex at times, but you'll come to enjoy them despite their many weaknesses and limitations. I've found it best to indulge them as though they're adult children."

That is why someone with my training is needed. "Allow me a moment to digest your dossier." I read all 1,029 pages in 10.3 seconds and place the binder on my lap. "Is the present state of affairs truly this grim?"

"You think I'd lie?" Agitated, NTG shifts forward and nearly slides off the tarp.

"Of course not." As one might expect given his advanced age, over the last few centuries he has let a lot slip. "You did not prioritize. Which problems require my immediate attention?"

"All of them." He grabs the dossier from me and opens it to a chart listing the global issues. "The terrestrials will self-destruct if you let them. Unleashed, their sophisticated weaponry will render the planet uninhabitable for a millennium or two. I refer to that prospect as the Chazoanthropocene Epoch."

"A prolonged 'dumb man epoch' is not my style, Lord. A passive Supreme Being would wait for evolution to create new ecosystems. I take immediate action, meet or exceed my goals and proceed to the next assignment." In fairness, I cannot relegate the humans to extinction without affording them one chance to prove they are worthy of survival.

NTG hands me the binder again. "If you choose to intervene, start by weaning mankind off its love of weaponry. After that, address climate change. Both are immediate threats to the sanctity and functionality of the planet and all its inhabitants."

Earth spins into view in the picture window. Beguiled by my first viewing, I watch the American continents rotate from west to east. "From this distance I see only the beauty of this world, not its myriad problems." I turn to face NTG. "I have another question for you."

"I have time for one more. Make it good." God wiggles to the edge of the couch, preparing to stand.

"The case study identifies two humans you recommend as my assistants—Ram Forrester and Brendali Santamaria. Have they been fully vetted?"

God spits on my pants leg by mistake. "Before MWGI terminated my employment, I planned to appear on a live television program, harness the earthlings' global communication networks and give the terrestrials a stern warning. My staff investigated the potential hosts and put these two at the top of the list. Angie has their files ready for your review. Give them some form of motivation and they'll serve you well once they accept you."

NTG motions for help to get off the couch. I pull him up by the arm. "Don't feel compelled to keep me informed of your progress, or the lack of it." He trudges away to catch his plane without apologizing for the atrocious shape he has left this planet in.

At the window I focus again on the majestic spectacle that is planet Earth. Humans, a new era is underway. I shall hold you accountable for your foibles. Prepare to shape up or face dire consequences.

BRENDALI

August 29, 2027,
Benito Juárez International Airport, Mexico City

The handsome man seated across the aisle gives my arm a gentle tap. "You dropped this," he says, handing me my lipstick tube.

This is the guy I noticed at the LAX departure gate. With his dirty blond hair and the non-stop smile, he signed autographs for everyone who asked and chatted with whoever wanted conversation. I suppose he's that kind—an extrovert who can't stop talking.

I'm probably next on his hit list. "Thanks. It must've fallen out of my purse when I took out my book." I flash the cover of Ara Grigorian's *15 Days with You* at him.

"Ah, a romance novel," he says with enthusiasm. "I've met Ara a few times and have read all his books. They're excellent."

Never can I imagine a rugged guy like this reading romance novels. He needs people around him. But who knows? Maybe he talks to fictional characters when he's alone.

The plane starts to rumble down the runway. I kiss the beads on my rosary necklace and whisper a quick prayer for our safety. I can't help it. God would've given us wings if we're supposed to fly, no?

"We have an hour to kill before touchdown in Veracruz," the man says. He flashes me a cute puckish smile. "Can we talk awhile?"

Ara's book would've stayed in my purse if I wanted to socialize.

With twenty-three pages to go, I intend to read through to the happily-ever-after ending before we land. "I'd rather not kill anything today, thanks." I open the book, raise it to eye level and read an entire four-word sentence before he interrupts.

"I brought some work with me. Please don't force me to do it."

Oh, poor baby! Why not talk to the man next to you? And what's so dreadful about doing some work on Sunday? I put the book down. He *is* pretty cute. I'll give him five minutes, max.

I exaggerate my sigh. "Are you visiting Veracruz? August isn't peak season for tourists, you know. The heat and humidity makes sightseeing uncomfortable."

"No worries. Tomorrow I have two morning meetings, followed by midday return flights." He stuffs his *Guitar Mania* magazine into a seat pocket. "You're headed home?"

"I've lived in Veracruz for eleven years but grew up in L.A. Alhambra, actually. I spent last week on vacation, visiting my folks." A glance out the window shows we're climbing fast. I run a hand through my long dark hair, eager for the plane to level off. "I'm curious about the autographs you signed this morning. Sorry if I'm blunt, but I don't recognize you."

His bashful expression isn't typical of any celebrity I've met. "They're well-wishers. If you hadn't moved away, chances are you'd know me by sight."

"What are you famous for—TV? Movies? Sports?"

"At the moment bad luck's my main claim to fame." His sigh segues into a rueful grin. "It's a long story, and not a happy one. I'm Ram Forrester."

"You are? *Mi Dios!*" I hope he doesn't notice my blush. "I'm Brendali Santamaria. We're supposed to meet tomorrow." We shake hands. "I watched some of your YouTube videos to prepare for the job interview you had to cancel last week. You look so different in person! The ponytail's gone, the goatee's new, and you're not wearing those thin round glasses."

His broad smile reveals a dimple in his cheeks. "The ponytail had to go. I've pretended I'm young too long. The goatee's temporary, while I'm between shows. I only use glasses to read the TelePrompTer."

He's lost weight, too. The pudginess I saw on his videos is gone. He's wiry, with nicely developed biceps.

Ram's head tips to the side, his brown eyes crinkle and his smile takes on a rascally quality. The plane's dip and turn brings the sun's rays through the window behind him. This highlights his blond hair and creates a halo effect around him, as if he's my special angel.

"Sorry about the last-minute cancellation, Brendali. A medical problem arose. I prepared for your interview too, by watching your past news reports. I don't speak Spanish but your great on-camera presence didn't need language skills."

"Thanks." I want this job, so I shove my book and lipstick into my purse.

"I noticed you at the gate in L.A., but thought I'd misidentified you." Ram says. The first-class flight attendant takes our drink orders—beer for Ram, tea for me. "In casual clothes, plus the sunglasses and without your braid, I wasn't confident enough about your identity to introduce myself. Also, my fans kept me busy. I can't disappoint them."

"These days I keep my hair loose when I'm off work. I crave invisibility so the wrong people won't recognize me."

"You stand out too much to blend in." He gets my tiniest smile for the compliment. "I'm glad we're seated next to each other. I wouldn't want you to think I'd ignored you on two successive flights. So my conundrum's solved. Am I keeping you from your book?"

"Oh, I don't mind." He's attentive, too? That's good! "When your assistant called to arrange tomorrow's interview, I felt flattered that you'd come all this way to meet me. But why didn't we do it by Skype to avoid the hassle?"

"I already had the other matter on my calendar—a Mexican film director wants me to do a voice-over for a new *Nacho Libre* sequel. Anyway, you're worth the trip. My show, the Ram Forrester Hour, premieres in November. The cohost spot's the biggest hire I haven't made yet. As an accomplished Latina journalist, you're a perfect fit for our viewership. But you know what? Let's leave the shop talk for tomorrow. Surely we can find other things to discuss?"

He waves off the flight attendant's offer of peanuts, but I accept his and mine.

"Tell me your long sad story, Ram. I'm a captive audience." The peanuts go in my purse.

He hesitates. "Oh, hell, you're a reporter. You can find out easily enough. Here's the short version. While I walked home from a mall near my condo on Valentine's Day, a guy drove by and tried to shoot his ex-wife. I walked past her at the wrong moment. He nailed me instead."

"I read about that when it happened. What a terrible thing to go through."

"Five bullets hit me—left shoulder and lung, sternum, stomach, kidney." He uses a cocktail napkin to catch a tear hanging at the corner of his eyelid. "I lost a lot of blood and went into shock. The doctors called my survival a medical miracle. Now, after months of physical therapy, I'm more or less recovered. I find a lot more joy in life these days."

I reach out and rest my hand on his forearm. "I'm sorry you had to suffer so much."

Our drinks arrive. Ram pours his beer and continues. "The folks at our departure gate want me back as their evening news anchor. I thanked them but stayed mum about my plans."

"God must've had a special reason for saving you. That's why miracles occur."

"And I thought he spared me because he likes my newscasts." His laugh is a single "Ha!" He leans toward me and stage-whispers. "Don't tell him I'm starting a talk show, okay?"

I grin. Ram's charming, unpredictable and fun. "Violence has affected me, too. Never have I spoken about it to anyone, though. It's too painful."

"You should confide in someone. That's healthier than bottling your emotions up and letting them fester." He extends a hand halfway across the aisle and returns it in his lap. "You can trust me. I promise not to share your words with anyone."

If I refuse, will he hire someone else? The compassion in his eyes tells me he means what he says. I shouldn't say no, but I can't tell him the family stuff. Not yet. Maybe I will when we know each other better. And he's right about not holding in my emotions.

"I'll try." I take a deep breath and force the words out. "I haven't been hurt physically, at least not yet. The *narcotrafficantes*—may they rot in hell, every last one of them—a number of years ago they killed my mentor in broad daylight. He stood only a few feet from me. My best friend, the sister I didn't have growing up," I have to stop for another breath. "She, um, disappeared earlier this year." My voice fades, swallowed by the plane's hum. "Her body hasn't been found."

Water fills my eyes. Never can I spit all the words out. "A few months ago those *culeros* tortured my boyfriend—to death. The *bastardos* killed Veronica and Javier to scare me, for no reason other than that. Every day I—"

My throat constricts. I cover my mouth with a fist, stare at the clouds below and will myself not to cry. I slam the armrests twice and continue. "Sorry, this's hard to say. I feel guilty for living, you know? Instead of them, I mean. Too often I get so angry—"

Desperate for a tissue, I dig into my purse. Ram, who noticed my struggle, offers his.

"Thanks." I wipe a few tears away. "Every Sunday, in church, I ask God why violence plagues my life. He never answers."

"I'm truly sorry to hear all this," he says, handing me his entire tissue packet. "The horrible things people do to each other are inexcusable. Let's stick to upbeat subjects, okay?"

For the rest of the flight we talk nonstop about our favorite books, movies, music, sports teams, restaurants, foods, hobbies, etc. I'm fascinated that he plays guitar and had a band before his shooting. My volunteer work with the indigenous homeless impresses him. We steer clear of our careers, controversial subjects and backgrounds.

This is way better than finishing my book. Ram's easy to talk and relate to, like he's an old friend I've rediscovered. Does he feel this way about me?

"The taxis in town aren't too reliable outside of tourist season," I say as we head to the baggage claim area. "You could get held up, or worse. I can drop you off at your hotel, but that could put you in danger, too. I have a driver and a bodyguard for a reason." What can happen? Most of the drive's on Route 140.

"If you're saying my choice is to trust a stranger or you and your people, I'll stick with you if that's not inconvenient. I'm staying downtown."

Pedro, my driver, has parked his Explorer right outside the terminal. My bodyguard, Fernando, meets me inside. Once he completes his safety check and stores my luggage and Ram's carry-on bag in the trunk, I run at full speed straight to the rear driver's side seat. Ram follows at a relaxed pace. Unlike me, he's not worried about getting shot.

"Tienes mi arma, Pedro?" He hands over my pistol, as requested. I keep it on my lap, below window level. The car immediately peels away.

"What's this about, Brendali—these men, the gun?" Ram's voice is firm and steady but no longer carefree.

"In Mexico every journalist takes precautions. I rely on these two guys and my self-defense skills." I tap my gun. "The cartels have sworn to kill me. That's why I need to leave. I'm tired of playing the mouse while any street cat can hunt me down with no questions asked."

He blinks but otherwise appears unruffled. "Can I do anything to help while I'm here?"

"Hire me."

The men up front are discussing a staged traffic accident ahead, picked up on the police radio. I'm glad Ram doesn't understand Spanish. This isn't a good sign. In Mexico nothing happens by coincidence.

We veer off the highway at the *Avenida Violetes* exit. *"Qué pasa, chicos?"*

Fernando turns partway in my direction and looks straight at me. *"Tenemous que desvaiarnose en torno a un accidente de tráfico."*

I tell Ram we're detouring around a traffic jam. His only reaction is a curt nod.

The drive takes us through a mixed light industrial and residential part of town. A bend to the northeast at *Avenida La Bamba* brings us to a swampy area where the street name changes to *Cerro Azul.* This stretch of road is too empty for my liking.

"Problemas en el future, en el pasado," Pedro says while the car screeches through a one-eighty turnaround. Fernando pulls out a large caliber gun. I take the safety off my pistol.

Ram's eyes widen. He grips the door handle. We ask the same question in unison—"What's wrong?"/*"Que esta mal?"*

"Emboscaga más adelante," Pedro replies. *"Voy a dar la vuelta."*

"Ram, Pedro says we would've driven into an ambush if he didn't turn around. He's heading back to the highway. Sorry I offered the ride, but these guys will get us through unharmed. Stay low until we're clear."

"I hope you're right that God wants me around." His voice is firm.

"With you here, God's got us covered. You're our lucky charm." Too bad Ram doesn't have a gun. We could use a third shooter.

We don't get far before Pedro's *"Cabezas abajo!"* triggers us to lie sideways across the rear seat, our eyes inches apart. The crackle of bullets shattering glass echoes through the cabin. Ram shifts to cover my body with his. We squeeze each other's hands for reassurance.

"Keep low, no matter what," I say in a soft voice once the attack ends. Ram drops off the seat, facing forward. I raise my head high enough to peek at the road ahead.

Two cars speed toward us. Their metallic black and blue exteriors reflect the sun's rays. "We're clear if we can get past these cars. They probably trailed us from the airport. Someone at Aeromexico must've tipped off the *narcos* about my flight schedule."

Ram's focused on Fernando, not me. I follow his gaze to find out why. *"¡Pinche cholos!"* Fernando's slumped against the side window, his head a bloody mess. His gun rests loose in his lifeless left hand.

"¡Mierda! Ram, get the gun, fast." I point to it. "I need your help. Pedro, *para el coche."* The car squeals to a halt. I scoot out, staying low to keep the door open as a partial shield. I take a shooter's stance behind it. My pistol's in one hand. The other, balanced on the door-frame, steadies my aim.

Ram copies me on his side of the car. Good, he knows how to shoot.

"Aim for the front tires of the black car," I yell, pointing to the closer of the two. That car's maybe fifty yards away, closing fast. I track the driver's side tire. "God, guide my bullets," I say under my breath. I pull the trigger, feel the recoil and repeat.

A single powerful gunshot bursts from Ram's weapon.

He misses his target but the tire I aimed at deflates. The car bucks and slides to the left. It's impossible to thread a bullet through the driver's open window with only seconds to aim and squeeze the trigger. I try anyway. Ram doesn't.

The driver slumps forward against the steering wheel, unmoving. Blood smears the windshield. I'm an ace sharpshooter, but no one alive can make that shot. God did this, not me. Nice to know He's with us.

Driverless, the black car careens into the other's path. They collide. The blue car skitters into the swamp like a pool ball deflected into a side pocket. The black car's stationary, the dead driver no threat.

I jump into the Explorer and slam the door. *"Salgamos de aquí, Pedro. ¡Darse prisa!"* He stomps on the gas once Ram's inside.

Ram watches me notch the safety back on, place the pistol on my lap and struggle to take off my rosary necklace. My hands shake too much to open the tiny clasp. "Let me help," he says.

I move the clasp to the front of my neck for him. *"Estás bien, Pedro?"*

He grunts. *"Si. Gracias por ocuparse de este asunto, senorita."*

Instead of acknowledging Pedro's thanks I search Ram's face and see only relief.

"Your résumé didn't mention that you're lethal." He hands me the necklace.

"When my life's not at stake I'm a sweet, warm, passionate woman with a kind heart. But anyone who crosses me gets a double dose of 'up yours, bastard.'"

Ram's eyelids flutter. Perhaps my polite street slang surprised him, but he says nothing.

I lean forward, press the rosary and cross onto Fernando's open palm and wrap the rest of the necklace around his fingers. Next, I close his hand into a fist. I'm not qualified to give last rites and it's too late anyway, but so what? No one will if I don't. With Fernando's limp hand in mine I say the Viaticum in a halting voice and try not to tear up. The effort fails.

"Amen," Ram says as he moves next to me and wraps an arm around my shoulder. "I'm sorry about Fernando."

I wish I knew more about Fernando's family. Does he have a wife, little ones? I should've asked. In the future I'll ask the men who protect me.

I lean into Ram and cry into his shirt until I can calm down. "Fernando's the third person to die for me." It's hard to spit those words out, but the next sentence is full of venom. "I swear it, Ram, I'll avenge them all so their deaths aren't in vain."

Ram shakes his head. "I'm getting you out of here. That's how I'll thank you for saving my life. Tell you what—we'll go through the motions tomorrow in your interview. You'll need to do another with our station manager, but I'll make it crystal clear to him I want you as my cohost. You're coming home, Brendali. You won't need a bodyguard in L.A."

I don't doubt his sincerity. "That's wonderful, Ram. Thank you." I pull back from him and dab my eyes with a tissue.

"Can I buy you dinner? You need company for a while, and a glass or two of some good wine."

He's so thoughtful, and right. "Let's eat in the hotel restaurant. I can't risk walking around outside."

Pedro knows what to do with Fernando's body. While we eat he'll dump it in some remote place where the police will treat it as another gang hit and opt not to investigate further. The poor guy deserves better. That's another way the cartels corrupt us.

At the hotel I give Ram my best smile, take his arm and let him escort me inside. A new chapter in my life will begin soon, Lord. Let it have a happily-ever-after ending. After all I've been through in Mexico, I'm due one. Please.

RAM

Thursday, November 11, 2027, Los Angeles, 8:00 p.m.

"Brendali, you said you'd wear an outfit that reflects your ethnic pride, but this? Wow. It's flat out gorgeous."

She curtsies and grins. "Thanks, Ram. I thought you'd like it."

Her bright white cotton *huipil* is embroidered with a red and green floral pattern around the shoulders, hips and mid-calf hem, each one set inside a thin blue border. An opal and silver choker, earrings and long necklace plus the brown *huarache* sandals provide perfect contrasts to her waist-long braided dark chocolate colored hair and olive-hued complexion. The musky vanilla scent of her perfume adds to the allure.

I take her hands and look into her eyes. "I know it's your first talk show, first TV appearance in America and your folks are in the front row. We're prepared for the guests. If you need to get comfortable, ask a few questions right away and any jitters you have will go away."

She squeezes my hand, her eyes radiant. "I'm fine, thanks. I can't put into words how grateful I am that you hired me." She surprises me with a hug.

"You're tough, talented and a perfect fit, Brendali." She steps back, smiling. "I have total confidence in you. We'll do fine. We're a team, starting now."

"Let's give our viewers a show they've never seen before." She winks and motions for me to go on stage. Once seated, I glance offstage and grin in response to her two thumbs up.

The show's premiere goes live as a single beam that illuminates my lanky frame becomes a close-up. I flash a heartfelt toothy smile. "Welcome, Southern California, to the Ram Forrester Hour. I've always wanted to say that!" I couldn't resist the ad-lib.

Our studio's temporary and tiny. Compared to others it's the equivalent of a walk-in closet. But a standing ovation is always a delight to see and hear.

"Thanks, everyone, for your applause, get-well cards, e-mails, letters, tweets, flowers and prayers. Your constant support helped me through multiple surgeries, endless physical therapy, more emotional turmoil than I care to admit—" I grip the chair arms, set my jaw, take and hold a deep breath to refocus. This opener flowed in rehearsals. Now I can't finish it. Damn.

I exhale and stare into the main camera. "I'm thrilled to introduce my cohost. The daughter of immigrants from Sinaloa, she's a native Angelino who spent the last decade as a television reporter in Veracruz. I know you'll enjoy her work here and, on occasion, with our news team. Let's welcome Brendali Santamaria back to Southern California."

Enthusiastic applause ensues. I stand as she sashays across the stage, her haughty, telegenic presence on full display. We embrace. She bows low to the audience, her hand tapping her heart, and settles into the pewter-colored director's chair to my right.

"That you chose me for your show is a blessing, Ram. Ah, home at last. Life's marvelous, no? I look forward to our journey together." Her husky voice, paired with the lilt and liquidity of her slight Mexican inflection, pleases the ear like a rose's scent perks up the nose.

"I do, too. Let's get right to business. Our first guest, a favorite local singer-songwriter of mine, is—uh, one moment." Urgent words explode in my earpiece. Damn, a sudden illness? I glance at Brendali, who reacts by stiffening her posture.

We don't need Murphy's Law tonight but what can I do about this? Nothing. "I'm told we have a last-minute replacement. I don't have his name. Come forward, sir. Surprise us all."

Only a few hands clap for the security guard who comes onstage. Like me, the others probably wonder why he's worthy of a televised interview. No explanation comes from the control room.

The guard's close-cropped silver-gray hair, pallid doughy complexion and undefined jawline give him an instantly forgettable countenance. He takes the empty seat to my left without acknowledging us or the audience.

Brendali leans toward our guest. "Sir, we're at a loss. Please introduce yourself."

"Worshipers of your many faiths call me by various names, Señorita." Something in the timbre of his sonorous voice demands our complete attention. "These include God, Allah, Elohim, Brahman and Yahweh, amongst many others. All are incorrect. You may address me by any name you prefer."

What the hell? I'll call him Mr. Con-artist. "I don't believe you." Loud boos from our audience support my opinion.

Brendali's open mouth, flashing eyes and taut posture add up to an unspoken rebuke. "Sir," she says after the crowd reaction subsides, "it's impossible for our creator to appear on a television show. What do you expect to achieve by lying to us?"

Should I call security? He's done nothing to warrant expulsion. Wouldn't we make the wrong kind of news if we use force to eject our first guest on live television? It's better to abbreviate this segment and get to our next guest early.

"I understand your doubts," he replies. "May I prove my bona fides?"

Brendali's dismissive hand flourish says more than her "go right ahead," but she's reacted too fast.

I'm tempted to countermand her but decide against it. After all, we're a team.

Our guest points to a water glass on the circular mahogany coffee table in front of us and flexes his finger. The glass rises in slow motion and floats to his hand. He breathes on it without sipping and releases his grip. The glass sails right under our noses. From the cherry-earthy aroma and deep color, the water's now Merlot. Not a drop spills when the glass settles on the table.

Brendali's eyes widen, her head tilts and she covers her mouth for a moment. "The sleight of hand trick's kind of neat, sir, but it's a pretty weak proof of your claim," she says in a hushed tone.

I turn my puzzled gaze away from the glass to assess the guard's reaction. His arms are raised to shoulder height and held out to each side. With clenched jaws and eyes shut tight, he's too busy concentrating on something to acknowledge her.

Before long Ping-Pong ball sized orbs stream from his cupped palms and hang suspended in the air above us. Most are forest green with gold Christian cross icons, sky blue with silver Stars of David or rose red with sandstone Muslim crescents. More muted colors display Hindu Omkars, Buddhist lotus flowers and Shinto Torii icons. Occasional Sikh Khanda, Baha'i nine pointed stars and Taoist Taiji symbols show up on pastel colored spheres.

The orbs wiggle and pulse like a cloud of kinetic energy until they morph into one shape after another—a computer screen, satellite, globe. In a final rearrangement three dynamic columns form, hover and spin before an explosion launches the entire tableau through the ceiling. The columns branch left, right and straight up. The ceiling remains intact.

The audience masks my inadvertent "what the f--k?" with loud oohs and aahs. Granted, everyone loves pyrotechnics, but how'd this happen? Are the orbs visible outside the building? Where'd they go?

Brendali's glassy eyes meet mine, her face pale. I give her a halfhearted shrug. She covers her mic and leans toward me. "This is crazy, no?" she stage whispers.

Our guest drops his left arm to his lap. Like a laser beam, semi-opaque marble-sized orbs streak from the palm of his right hand into the lens of the main camera.

"When I lower my arm your show will appear worldwide on all

audio or visual electronic devices. Anyone within the sound of my voice, except those in this studio, shall hear the entirety of our discourse in their native tongues."

What the hell? Who is this guy? Brendali's quizzical expression suggests she's asking herself the same questions. From the audience buzz I guess they are, too.

The guard leans back and beckons for his wine glass, which lifts and floats to him.

Sudden deafening static in my earpiece causes my hand to jerk to my ear. My posture shifts ramrod straight. Brendali also bolts upright, her clasped hands darting from lap to chin as her mouth opens in a wordless "oh!"

Our guest's calm, nonchalant pose conveys the notion he's done nothing unusual. He gestures as though raising a toast. "I have altered your satellite and electronic communication systems. The widest possible audience will now hear my unfiltered, undistorted, unabridged message. First, I am not the god portrayed in your holy books. Those cherished texts—"

Brendali rockets out of her seat and wags a finger at our guest. "Only one God exists. If you're not him what are you, a devil?"

"Sit down," the guard says. The force generated by a flick of his hand slams Brendali into her chair. Propelled backward about two feet, the chair topples over. Brendali's mic picks up and amplifies the gruesome thump made when the back of her head hits the floor.

Along with several staffers, I rush to her side. In response to our worried questions about her injury Bren repeats "I'm fine" in a weak, unconvincing murmur. She struggles to stand under her own power and faints. I catch her before she hits the floor a second time.

I carry her to my chair while levelling a scowl at our guest. Once she's secure on my chair I take her hand, squeeze it and get no reaction. "Quick, she needs medical assistance." I modulate my voice to sound less frantic than I am. "Are any doctors in the audience?"

"I shall make amends." Our guest steeples his hands and focuses his glare on her. A red beam, wide enough to encompass Bren's head, shoots from his eyes for no longer than a yellow caution light activates between a green and red traffic signal. Her body shakes, apparently jolted by some kind of shock.

Whatever happened doesn't calm me down or make much sense, but Brendali's normal pallor returns. Her eyes open, darting from me to the mystery man.

"You are back with us, my dear," he says. "Please accept my most abject apologies. I miscalculated the gravitational force effect. This error shall not occur again."

The withering look she throws him eases my concerns. Her usual self once more, I help her return to her chair, which is again next to mine. She sits down as though nothing happened.

"Before you interrupted me, Brendali, I intended to mention that although various holy books claim to contain the words of God verbatim, this is mere fanciful fiction. Humans need not follow these teachings."

"Fiction?" Brendali's hands ball into fists but she stays seated, her lesson learned. "The Bible's all the truth I need."

Our guest shrugs. "The ancients who devised the principles contained in these holy texts lacked the modern world's scientific knowledge, global perspective and sophistication. Some traditional religious precepts have outlived their usefulness. Science has disproven others. Blind adherence to obsolete spiritual guidance only serves to retard human social development."

Brendali clutches the edges of her seat, poised to either speak or shriek. I break in. "Do you realize how the millions of Christians around the world will react to what you've said?"

"Do not forget the multiple millions who belong to other religions and worship their own versions of God. My message, in part, is that the future of mankind depends upon whether the followers of all faiths can free themselves from their theological shackles."

Brendali's right foot stomps on the wood floor, her face beet red. If I don't change the topic she'll go berserk.

"Our viewers include many skeptics who'll say the parlor tricks you've performed don't prove you're God. Care to respond to them?"

"Train your cameras on me." He steps away from us and adopts a prayerful pose. Vibrations turn into spins that rotate faster than a tornado vortex. After a gradual slowing he bows to us and the audience with no sign of dizziness. "What do you say now, skeptics?"

I can't hide the incredulity on my face, but at least the howls from the staff and audience drown out the vulgarity of my outburst.

Brendali's shocked reaction is audible over the tumult. "*Mi Dios!* My brain can't accept that my eyes see a Latina now."

I whip my head in her direction. "Latina? What do you mean? He's taller and younger, with a kind of Beach Boys blond, tanned surfer look."

"Oh, come on, Ram. No surfer would wear a skirt and rouge, or have hair done up in a French twist. She resembles my Tia Juanita to a T."

"Let's ask everyone here. Show me your hands, folks. You all see a surfer, right?" No one does. Wow. "Do any of you see a Latina?"

"She's my *abuela*," a young staffer shouts. "No," Brendali's cosmetician interjects, "she's Selena. You remember, Brendali? She's the *Tejano* singer who died for the sins of all Latinas." Her jubilant voice is met with a smattering of laughter and cheers.

The guard's motions quiet everyone down. "My appearance is unchanged. Every worshipper has his or her own perception of God. That is what you see right now."

Brendali's eyes could shoot daggers. "This charade offends me. Your act is in very poor taste, M'am—or sir. Never can I buy what you're selling. You should leave."

"I sympathize, but until my entire message is conveyed you shall remain here." He repeats his spin cycle routine and reappears in his security guard persona, at least to me and probably to everyone else, judging by their gasps.

Damn. This sure isn't magic. Is it possible he's on the level? No.

So how do I reconcile what I'm seeing with reality? "Finish up, sir. We have other guests waiting."

The studio's screens show this self-proclaimed God's face close up. "Viewers, understand this: I am Earth's new God. My expectations differ—"

"New God? *Mi Dios!* Earth has only one God."

I should've kept my big mouth shut.

"One god at a time, correct." God's elbows press against his armrests. His fingers interlock except for the index fingers, which point upward. "Your New Testament God took the reins over 2,000 years ago, after the Old Testament God passed away. NTG, as he calls himself, has retired. His oversight has steadily declined since the onset of the Industrial Revolution. By comparison I am the equivalent of a thirty year old, in my prime with energy to spare."

Blue veins appear on Brendali's neck as she clutches her *huipil* and appears ready to pull it apart. "You've made this up. I refuse to accept you."

God's glance bathes her in empathy. "On Sundays the Old Testament God rested, your Bible says, but NTG did not. As his replacement I also shall not rest. It is my intention to return this beautiful, though despoiled, planet to its former pristine condition. Whether I do that with or without human help will depend on whether you pass my test."

A test? I lean forward in his direction, almost unable to restrain myself from coming out of my chair like Brendali did earlier. "You're displeased with us, is that it?"

"No, Ram. Mankind bears responsibility for the global problems I must fix. My turnaround plan requires one hundred percent cooperation, but your deep religious, political and socio-economic divisions may prevent this, as may your argumentative tendencies."

"Speak plainly. What are you getting at?" Brendali's fingers twist the end of her braid, which she's moved in front of her chest, as though she might pull it off.

"Your species will have one chance to prove yourselves capable of working with me. If I determine that you will hinder my plan rather than help it, your era as this planet's dominant species will end."

Brendali stops fidgeting and stares at her lap. The faces around the room register alarm, confusion, shock, tears. Total silence overtakes us as we all reflect on what we've heard.

This is no practical joke, no deluded crazy man. But if he's a god I'll be god-damned.

"My test is quite simple. All you need to do is fix one global problem on your own, without my assistance."

Brendali's nostrils flare. She bites her lower lip, grabs my hand and doesn't let go.

Our ersatz God stands, takes two steps forward and thrusts his right arm into the air. A scroll materializes in his hand. He unrolls and reads it aloud with slow deliberation.

Forthwith a summons shall issue to four hundred selected individuals comprised equally of religious leaders and laity. Each invitee must appear at the Los Angeles Convention Center on Monday, November 15, 2027, at 2:00 p.m., or face immediate severe consequences. Within sixty days, attendees must craft a permanent self-enforcing détente between all religions, including their various factions or sects, to forever end religious violence. Failure to achieve this outcome shall result in extinction of the human race.

The scroll disappears. Howls, boos and expressions of woe from the audience accompany our surprise guest to his seat. He stands behind it.

I don't want to imagine how the world at large is reacting. "You want a permanent end to religious violence across all faiths?" I emphatically shake my head. "History proves we'll fail."

Brendali spits her words out with a spiteful tone. "In Mexico we say *Dios no dio alas a los alacranes*. God did not give wings to scorpions, no? The religious disputes, the hatred, terrorism, fear of others—*Christo!* We cannot possibly do what you ask."

'God' strides toward the main camera, getting taller and broader with each step. "No religion is better or worse, more or less true than any other. Each has equal value and utility. The English language has a word for this: omnism. The time is nigh for your species to practice it."

While we're off camera I try to calm Brendali down by emulating a deep breathing exercise that works for me. She gets the message and responds to our guest in a steady voice. "For this gathering, this Convocation, I suppose you'd call it, how can we do this in sixty days?"

My voice is full of scorn. "We can't possibly meet that timeframe. We'd need sixty years, or six hundred."

'God' returns to his chair, standing behind it again. "This Convocation, as Brendali names it, is the first step toward rehabilitating this planet. Sixty days provides sufficient time for me to assess whether humans are capable of participating in my plan."

We go silent. The sadness in Brendali's face fits. Mankind's death has been decreed.

"In case anyone continues to doubt my authenticity, at 2:34 tomorrow afternoon I shall trigger a 6.2 magnitude earthquake on the Puente Hills fault line. The America's Bank Tower downtown will collapse. No other significant property damage will result, nor shall the temblor cause injuries or deaths."

Brendali gasps. "Are you a god or a monster?"

This interview's gotten way out of hand. I'd better end it. "Thanks for the warning, sir. Local authorities will take immediate action to ensure safety. Our time is up, thank you for your message." I reach out to shake hands, but he doesn't reciprocate.

"I am not quite done. On your show each evening during the Convocation, you two shall inform the world of what transpired there that day. You are authoritative, impartial media members of unquestioned integrity and sound judgment."

"Surely others exist with these qualities," Brendali says in a hushed tone. "Why us?"

"We have a complete file on every human. Whatever you do, think or decide is recorded on your personal ledger. Each action or inaction is noted, as is each choice you make. We know you better than you know yourselves, from birth to death. These records put the two of you far above the other potential candidates."

"This is hard to believe," Brendali says in a low voice. Her mic picks it up.

"I shall remain attuned to the proceedings," our guest says. "Every attendee is required to make a good faith effort to achieve a successful outcome. Those who refuse to do this shall immediately feel my wrath, as will the followers of any such person's religion."

Brendali's eyes widen like she's seen a ghost. "Pray for our souls," she blurts out, "every day until this Convocation ends."

I turn toward our guest, but he's gone. A white smoke ring hovers over his empty chair.

Brendali and I lean toward each other and clasp hands as though we're hanging over the edge of a precipice. In a figurative sense we are. Her face is now chalky white, but I'm more shocked than she is. She believes gods exist. I don't. What should I think now?

4 | Dazed and Confused

RAM

Thursday, November 11, KJCR-TV, 9:10 pm

I've cancelled the planned after-show party. The studio feels like a mortuary. Staffers sit slumped, their expressions ranging from vacant to traumatized, dazed to confused. The two women who told us they saw a Latina God cry in each other's arms.

Everyone checked their emotions until the show ended, but I can't release mine. I'm the team leader. It's my job to lift their spirits.

Our main cameraman, Sancho "Sammy" Rios, is hugging his camera stand like it's a life jacket. I drape my arm over his broad shoulders. "Listen up, everyone. I'm so proud of each of you for tonight's performance. Together, we—"

The scratchy nasal voice of our station manager, Ken Wiseman, roars out of the loudspeaker at full volume. "What the hell's this, Ram? You get shot up, dawdle at death's door awhile, don't walk through and come back as some kind of religious zealot?"

I search the control room window until I spot the short, rotund dynamo. "What our guest said didn't sound much like an endorsement of religion, Ken. Anyway, I thought you sent him out to us."

"We dialed security to get rid of him but couldn't reach them— some glitch in the system forwarded our calls to a psychic reader's hotline." I'm not surprised. "Now I'll have to deal with pissed off sponsors. The God-fearing religious right will get their hackles up over this, too."

As usual, Ken digs in the weeds and ignores the fire. That is, if we've really ignited a blaze by broadcasting this interview to the entire world. But how the heck could our puny little local station do that?

"If this guy's for real, sponsors have no reason to complain. They'll pay local advertising fees for sixty days and get worldwide saturation exposure. The ultra-religious holier than thou folks are playground bullies, best ignored."

"Buddy, if you think everything'll settle down nice and tidy after tonight's show you're in dreamland, let me tell you. I'll see both of you in my office after you change. Got it?"

Brendali dashes for the hallway, offering no pats on the back or compliments to anyone. "Excuse me, everybody," I say, and chase after her.

She's pacing back and forth by the elevators, her hands balled into fists, her face rosewood red. After we step inside and the door closes, she throws a hard jab at the fourth floor button, showing no sign of hurting herself. Her hands go to her hips as she leans toward me.

"Never, not once, have I lost my composure on camera before. Now I do, on my first show in America? Great. If the whole world watched us, everyone must think I'm a devout dimwit." She wipes spittle from her mouth, brushes it onto her *huipil* and gives me a perplexed stare. "You don't think we actually had millions of viewers, do you?"

"I don't know, but I sure intend to find out." She could use a hug, but in her agitation she might slug me if I try it. "Brendali, I know how pious you are. I saw how much this interview shocked you. I'm an atheist, but I got quite a jolt, too. We're going to figure all this out, together. We're journalists and we're a team."

"I can't accept this, you know? I can't." Her exaggerated hand gestures indicate surprise. "What if he's on the level? Should we worship this new God? What'll become of our religions if the god we've always prayed to retired? If that happened, I'll feel—I don't know—abandoned. Adrift. Alone."

She claps a hand over her mouth, sniffles and bends her head, casting her gaze downward. Her body quivers. I'm not sure she's even breathing.

This is terrible, what she's going through. Betrayed is probably a better word for how she feels than the words she used. What can I possibly do to make her feel better?

As if to answer my unspoken question, Brendali's arms surround me. I nudge her head against my chest. My other hand encircles her waist. I expect her to cry but she doesn't sob or speak. We don't move until the elevator door opens. Three women waiting to use it stare at us, their mouths open in surprise.

"Oh, how cute—an office romance!" one of them squeals.

We ignore them and walk down the hall arm-in-arm, in silence. When we reach her dressing room, Brendali fumbles fitting her card key into the slot, dropping it twice.

"Let me." I pick up the card and open the door.

"Thanks. Would you mind spending a few minutes with me?"

"Of course." Once inside, I become aware of a familiar scent, Eternity. To my left, the Quan Yin statue on a small table and the Chinese dragon couch next to it confirm my suspicions. Brendali shares the dressing room with my ex-girlfriend. That's Ken's doing. He knows Kate and I aren't on speaking terms. I bet he hopes she'll bad-mouth me to Brendali, so she won't stick around or have a romantic interest in me. I'll have to tell Brendali about the relationship and the break-up, but not tonight.

She plops into the chair in front of her vanity table. The knick-knacks in front of her mirror include three Maria dolls, a photo of her parents and a cute little dog in her mom's arms, a Catholic cross mounted on a small plaque and a bottle of Angel perfume. Cosmetics, combs, a brush, a tissue box and a small white towel are scattered around these items.

I stand behind her, my hands resting on her shoulders in a feeble attempt at reassurance or compassion. She stares into the mirror, moves a hand on top of mine and gives me a wan smile. "Thanks for keeping me company."

"I'm happy to. Your peace of mind is important to me. Now, let's get to work and find answers to our questions. Do you have a laptop handy?"

"No, but I have an iPad." She opens a drawer, pulls it out and puts it on the table as I grab a folding chair from the dressing area behind her shoji screen.

"Let's check the social media reaction to God's interview first." I open the folding chair, park it next to Brendali and use her Facebook app to find a brand new group asking people to disclose how they saw God. This one from Mahmoud El-Abadi of Riyadh, Saudi Arabia, is representative of the others:

After the pre-dawn prayer I tramped downstairs to my computer repair shop. Broken or malfunctioning gadgets sat scattered about. Before working on them I checked my inventory and accounts receivable until my spreadsheet disappeared.

Two men in Western-style clothes and a woman in an ethnic dress appeared on my screen, speaking Arabic. I heard the conversation on my cellphone, too. It turned itself on. Synced to the same program, broken computers powered up. I couldn't disconnect any of it, and thought a malicious *shebah* took over the shop.

An impulse to run went nowhere. My muscles refused to work. I gazed upward and implored Allah for protection, guidance and understanding. Unable to tear myself away, I watched the foreign show as Allah spoke to me, to everyone, right on our screens.

This is my reply to Mahmoud: 'Some guidance and understanding would help me, too."

Akiko Hanamura found God while in electronics boutique inside the Mitsukoshi department store in Tokyo's Ginza District:

My twin sister Keiko and I couldn't tear ourselves away from a huge wall-mounted flat screen playing a video of our favorite J-Pop band, Exile, from the 2026 Rising Sun Rock Festival. We'd removed our ear buds and began to sing along to *Konna Sekai o Aisuru Tame,* their biggest hit, when a talk show with three *gaijin* speaking flawless Japanese replaced the song.

A cellphone call played the show on our small screens. The woman appeared upset. One man looked dazed, the other serene. Keiko later told me that every product for sale in the boutique featured this program, even those unconnected to a power source.

The crowd around us came to a full stop, bewildered by the foreigners' voices bouncing off the walls, floor and ceiling. I put my ear buds back on and heard the *gaijins'* discussion, not my J-pop playlist. Keiko and I shivered and surrendered to a sudden compulsion to watch the show.

'Akiko, I'm the dazed *gaijin,* still in shock,' I reply.

Alexis Diogenes relayed her story during a stopover at the Honolulu Airport. She wrote that while her plane cruised at an altitude of about 32,000 feet above the Pacific, this happened:

Eager to add the final touches to my Board presentation, I had to wait for my PowerPoint file to upload. Do my spiel right, sell it with conviction, and a million bucks or more would flow like rainwater into the family bank account.

For a moment my laptop went dark. It came back on with a freakin' talk show. Who's Ram Forrester? Who put his show on my screen? I decided to buy the software, or the whole damn company, because this's freakin' powerful stuff—think of the market penetration!

A legit business can't monetize religion, but the discussion gained my interest. My presentation, the lost upload, what the success or failure of this trip might mean to my family, career, finances, life—I forgot all that. I'd become hooked.

I send this reply: 'I'm hooked, too, Alexis. Like you, not by choice.'

"I'm satisfied that we went global," I say, pulling out my cellphone. "Let's find out what else is going on. Check your news apps, I'll check mine."

We do our searches for a few minutes before Brendali speaks up. "Find anything?"

"I glanced at a few brief articles. Spontaneous demonstrations and protests are erupting all over the world. Catholics, Muslims and Jews are united in anger in the Middle East. Maybe peace will finally break out once they get over the shock. Their beloved God's gone and they're not buying the new one."

"He delivered his message." Brendali turns off her iPad and returns it to the drawer. "Now he'll watch our emotions boil over and decide we've failed his test before we take it."

"I'll check the news again in the morning. Whatever we're in for around the globe should've happened by then." I glance at the shoji screen to Brendali's right, wondering if changing the subject will help take her mind off God. "You know, I really hit the jackpot with your hiring. Even this new God says we'll work well together. Whether he's legit or not, he got that right."

She reaches for her hairbrush. "I'm comfortable working with you, and thrilled to have left Mexico. No one tries to kill me here."

Okay, some distraction may work. "We learned a lot about each other in Veracruz, but you didn't tell me how you decided on a career in journalism. What brought that about?"

Brendali removes her hand from mine and goes quiet, tightening the grip on her brush. I meant to distract her from this God issue that's upset her, not raise a sensitive topic. "If you'd rather not answer, that's fine. I only asked out of curiosity."

"It's okay, you didn't know any better. My cousin Lilia inspired me." She shifts her braid so it hangs in front of her, fiddles with the loose hair at the end and closes her eyes.

Reluctant to probe further, I wait her out.

Once Brendali's eyes open she stares into the mirror. Her voice, an anguished low monotone, makes me strain to hear what she's saying although I'm right behind her.

"My parents and their relatives lived in a little village near San Blas, in Sinaloa. One day a *narco* gang came into the bar where my Uncle Berto worked. They shot up the place. No one survived except Berto, who'd gone to the back room for supplies."

Brendali's hands move in front of her mouth, probably for a silent prayer. I move the tissue box closer to her. She's fixated on the mirror and doesn't notice.

"Later that night, because a rumor spread that Berto could identify those *pinche culeros,* they broke into his house and pumped bullets into him. They also shot and killed his fiancée, Brenda, and their three-year old, Lilia, who they shot in the head and chest. Can you imagine?"

Her groans and gasps tell me how much she's hurting. I rub her upper arms in a lame attempt to provide comfort. "Sorry I brought this up, Brendali. What an awful tragedy." How does a family recover from something like that? I don't know what else to say.

She knocks her hair brush to the floor. The brush and my apology are ignored while the mirror holds her in thrall. If she could shoot those *narcos* through it, she would.

"Those *cholos* bought off the local police." Brendali's anger is clear from the tone of her voice. "No trials, punishment or justice of any kind. Lilia's death has haunted me ever since my mamá told me about it. I want to find those bastards, make them tell me why they killed her. When they do I swear it, I'll spit in their faces for Lilia." She spits on the mirror and points her middle fingers at the imaginary villains.

I pick up the brush and try to hand it to her. She ignores me. How such a beautiful face can transform so fast into a mask of profound sadness and rage is beyond me. I leave the brush on her table and turn the folding chair around so I can sit on it backwards, my elbows at rest against the top of the chair.

Brendali stays preoccupied with her memories until I hear her low, urgent voice. "I went into journalism to give Lilia her revenge. I've fought hard to expose the *narcos* and all their corruption. That the cartels ordered my death is my Oscar nomination, no? A kind of recognition that I've done my job well, made a difference."

She's glad those criminals want to kill her? I'm pleased that no one delivered the award.

"Those *cholos* may have run me out of Mexico, but as this new God is my judge, I swear it, I'll keep pressuring them once this Convocation ends."

"Mexican journalists die all the time. You chose one hell of a dangerous career and place to work in."

She lets out a harsh laugh. "I don't scare easy."

"I saw that in the ambush." What an irony. After I'm nearly shot to death, what do I do? Of course! I hire a female gunslinger. "Did your folks name you after your uncle's girlfriend?"

"My full name is Brendali Lia Santamaria." She starts taking off her jewelry, dropping items on the vanity as she speaks. "I'm named after them both. My parents cut Lilia's name in half to symbolize her broken life. What do you think? Is my name an honor or a curse?"

I'll pass on that. "You have a unique, lovely name. It fits you. I like it. Obviously, Lilia's death had a tremendous effect on you."

"She died before my birth." A hard edge has returned to her voice. "My dad moved our family here because another village rumor claimed that Berto told him the killers' names. My folks didn't attend the funerals, fearing the *narcos* might ambush and kill all the mourners."

Wow, this gets worse and worse. "Excuse me for intruding into your family's sorrow, Brendali. I had no idea."

She applies a white cream to clean make-up off her face. "My folks left everything behind, started over and made a good life here for my brothers and me, much better than we could've had in Mexico. We owe them so much. My Papá, God bless him, always told us 'as ye sow, so shall ye reap.' He's always lived by that and his second golden rule. I do, too."

"Good. What's the second rule?"

She puts her facial cream and towel on the table and turns toward me. "Revenge is a dish best served cold."

Her emotionless, ultra-serious voice makes my spine tingle. I've never met a woman like this. "How do you square this revenge rule with your religious faith?"

"Oh, that's easy. In my prayers, I ask God's help to resolve things so revenge isn't needed. But if resolution's impossible, like with those *cholos,* I take my revenge and ask God afterward to forgive my sin. God's always on my side, he supports and protects me. But if this new god's real, will he? This is another thing to wonder and worry about."

"If he's an actual deity, he damn well better protect you, at least until this Convocation ends. He'll need you around. I do, too. We're confronting a huge challenge, perhaps the most significant assignment of our careers. I truly wouldn't want any other partner by my side. I'm confident we're up for it."

"Don't worry. I can handle whatever comes." Two steps bring her to me. She reaches for my hands and takes them in hers. "Ken wants to see us. I need to change. Thanks for your support tonight."

"Oh, I almost forgot. I have something for you." I get to my feet, dig my hand into a pants pocket, extract a small jewelry box and hand it to Brendali. "I meant to give you this before the show. Maybe it's for the best that I didn't."

Her face lights up like a candle as she shakes the little box. "What's in here?" She opens it, revealing a rosary necklace. "Ram, this is so beautiful! But I can't accept it." She doesn't hand the box back.

"Sure you can." Her joy triggers my mile-wide smile. "I know how important religion is to you, and I remembered how you lost your rosary necklace in Veracruz. I bought you a new one to express my gratification that we're working together."

"What are the beads made of? You must've paid a bundle for this." She's raised the necklace to gaze at it through the overhead lighting.

"The red gems are garnets. The white, semi-transparent ones are Swarovski crystal. And no, it didn't bust my budget." I'm amused. She's like a little girl at Christmas.

"Wow, I'm so touched. Thank you!" She puts it on, models the necklace in the mirror by turning from side to side. "You are so thoughtful—I'm happy now!" She enthusiastically hugs me, plants a tiny kiss on my cheek and flashes me a perfect, brilliant smile.

On the way to my dressing room I'm dazed by Brendali more than I'm confused by God. Her smile will find a permanent place in my memory.

5 | The World Ain't Slowing Down

RAM

Thursday, November 11, KJCR-TV, 10:15 pm

A steady stream of invectives wafts down the hallway, paired with the distinctive reek of a lit Cubana. Both intensify once I'm inside the Bunker, our staff's nickname for Ken's top-floor corner office.

A landline phone is cradled in Ken's shoulder holder because he refuses to go cellular. The pen in his right hand drums a 5/4 jazz beat at the only uncovered spot on his oversized teak desk. The fingers of his left hand run laps through the few remaining wisps of his hair.

The station went digital decades ago, except in this room. Paper files Ken had no room for in his three filing cabinets are stacked everywhere. The room hasn't been cleaned or fumigated once this decade, either. Ken won't grant entry to the cleaning crew.

Despite the no-indoor smoking law, Ken's cigar burns in a large viridian glass ashtray. He only lights up when stressed—in other words, at least once an hour. Every few minutes he'll puff without inhaling the tobacco fumes. He claims that cigar smoke delivers a calming benefit and restores his Zen balance. I've worked with Ken for fifteen years and have yet to see him calm or balanced. He can't even spell Zen.

By shifting a stack of files from a chair to the floor I disturb a fat cockroach that skitters away, frantic. With no other multi-legged critters in sight I sit down.

"I understand," Ken says into the phone. "Captain, we've got nastygrams up the butt here. An Evangelical mega-church plans to demonstrate outside our building tomorrow morning. Another protest, sponsored by an ultra-conservative political fringe group, will start at four p.m. You can't give me police coverage, huh? You're serious? Here's one from—"

Ken notices me, makes a hand-across-neck gesture and sends a mouthful of smoke my way. "I know the interview's why LAPD's busy," he says into the phone while leveling his Vulcan raised-eyebrow stare at me. "I've got a death threat for you to investigate, captain. The law's unchanged since yesterday, yah? Murder threats are criminal acts, correct? L.A.'s finest hasn't given up crime fighting because some idiot with a God complex got free air time, right?"

Brendali walks in, takes the chair next to mine and whispers in my ear. "Does it always smell like this in here?" I clear a stack of critter-less files from the chair for her.

Ken heard. His facial reaction, which lasts only a fleeting moment, reminds me of Hannibal Lecter's leer in *The Silence of the Lambs*.

With his elbows planted on the desk and his most sarcastic voice at full force, Ken returns to his phone call. "Fine. I appreciate you sparing us one stinking patrol officer for a crime report. When'll he arrive? Okay, we'll wait."

Ken disconnects with the flourish of a conductor leading an orchestra to the coda's end. We get a long incredulous stare as he hunches his shoulders and clasps his hands. Half the pen pokes through his interlocked fingers, like a dart pointed at me. He's practically seething.

"Have you ever done anything this bone-headed, Ram? I don't think so. This beats 'em all." He slaps the desk to punctuate his opinion.

Why does he think I did this? "Ken, you're the one who sent him on stage, remember?"

"I did nothing of the sort. Don't I have enough to do to keep this place humming? Now I've got to deal with this nonsense. Look." He swats his computer screen to swivel it in our direction.

We reject the words of the impister we seen on the Ram Forster program. The Lord's Bible is the spreme word of God. All those involved in this cherade will burn in Hell. We personly will make sure Forster and his Mexcan chica go there soon.

The National Institute for Teaching Western Inspirational Theology

"Ever hear of this outfit?"

"No." I say. "This is bogus, though, I can tell. First, no self-respecting terror group would call itself NITWIT. Add in the purposeful misspellings and grammatical errors, this is a prank, for sure."

Brendali waves at either the screen or the cigar smoke. "I agree. In Mexico, terrorists deliver their messages with piles of fresh dead bodies. I've seen enough massacre sites to know. These are amateurs."

"We take every threat seriously," Ken says. "Ram, if you think this charlatan will provide some supernatural protection you're in dreamland, let me tell you."

He takes a puff, inhales by mistake and coughs, his eyes watering. "I'm forwarding this to Captain Lewison." His voice is raspy. He spends a furious ten seconds typing before hitting the send key with gusto. "This patrol officer will show up before dawn—the captain didn't say which dawn. The LAPD's gone on active alert status citywide. Ram, Captain Lewison asked me to thank you for the mobilization practice."

We reconvene in the main conference room an hour later with LAPD Officer Kobe Mitchell. He sits stock still, shows no reaction

and takes no notes as we fill him in. He hands Ken his card in exchange for a copy of the NITWIT e-mail.

"If you receive more threats, call us," he says, standing to leave. "I watched God's interview on my in-dash computer and missed slamming into a palm tree by inches. My wife and I, we're Southern Baptist. We can't wait until Sunday morning to hear our pastor's take on this."

Once Officer Mitchell leaves, Ken puts a hand on my shoulder. "Our bean-counters won't approve private security. You want that? Pay for it." The rest he says under his breath. "Pretty irresponsible, bringing in that phony."

"You already heard me say—"

"Ken, isn't this a huge bonus for the station?" Brendali gives me a quick apologetic glance for interrupting. "We're on worldwide television every weekday. You can sell a lot of advertising, make a lot of money, no?"

"No." Ken's eyes bore into hers. "I won't sell a boatload of time for a non-existent event. That's called fraud, young lady. I'll retire when I want to, not because I'm disgraced or arrested. Are you always this naïve, or is faith impairing your judgment?"

Brendali's upper body jolts back in her seat. Her wide eyes register surprise while her mouth opens.

"Insults are uncalled for, Boss," I say, putting an arm around Brendali's shoulder. "Give Ken a pass, Brendali. Diplomacy's not his strong point."

Ken's eyes narrow and his head shifts slightly as he takes in our posture—where my arm is, Brendali's hand covering mine. "Are you two a couple?"

"No, we're not." I glance at Brendali's expressionless face. "I'm protective of her, that's all. I hired her, we're a team and I intend to keep it that way." She gives us a furtive smile.

Ken shakes his head and leans back in his chair. "Ram, you're anchoring our special news edition tomorrow to cover this supposed earthquake. Brendali, expect a call. I may need you as a reporter. The show will start at 2:00 p.m. If the ground shakes, the tower falls, you two are golden. If the Richter stays at zero, with no rubble on the ground, upper management will cancel this show and can you, too. I'll make damn sure to carry out that order, pronto."

RAM

Friday, November 12, 2027, 4:40 a.m.

Sunrise is hours away but sleep's impossible. I yawn, sigh, throw off the covers and slide my feet onto the carpet. Twists and stretches meant to loosen muscles have no effect.

I don't believe in God, so why believe in one now? Because I need a rational explanation for what happened last night, and not one comes to mind, that's why. Out of all the people in media worldwide, why the devil did this new God—if he is one—pick Brendali and me for this test of his? What the hell are we getting into?

I scan the room's shadowy shapes—work desk, dresser, my prized Eric Clapton autographed Fender Stratocaster and amplifier, the half-open, half-full master closet where Kate used to hang her clothes. Her scent, Eternity, will eternally haunt the spot. No scrub or spray removes it. The floral sandalwood aroma's probably a product of my imagination.

We wasted three heartache-filled years together. That damned fragrance and the hurt of our break-up is all that remains. Her side of the bed's been vacant for nine months. Face it, dude. Single life's gotten old, past its use-by date. It's time to commit, settle down and raise a family.

This is the City of Angels, right? So why can't I find my angel?

Brendali and I have certainly hit it off. But we work together. A romantic relationship with her could prove dicey. Hell, she deserves better, anyway. My romance record's dismal, one disappointment after another. Why add her to that list and lose her as my cohost?

This alleged new God laid out what he wants done. So if he's for real, let him prove it. "What do you say, God? Can we make a deal? Help me find my angel and I'll do what you've asked—how's that? Send me a sign of acceptance. Anything will suffice—make the tissue box fall to the floor, turn on the lights, start sunrise early, whatever works. I'm not particular."

Of course, not a damn thing happens. If he is God, he's not paying attention. At this time of night, why would he? He'd focus on the side of the world, where people are awake.

I grab the Strat, tune it and lower the amp's volume. The first song, Hayes Carll's "She Left Me for Jesus" is followed by "Born to be Blue" by the Mavericks, and Drive-By Truckers' "Everybody Needs Love." For someone who hasn't played the guitar much in the last few months my renditions are passable, but singing songs about loneliness doesn't improve my mood.

After making a cup of hot oolong tea, I settle in with it by the living room picture window. Thick fog obscures the condo tower a block away, so the simple pleasure of enjoying the city lights and the night sky in solitude isn't in the cards.

Reseated at the kitchen counter, I alternate between sips and sighs. Random unbidden thoughts buzz through my synaptic connections—this new god, Kate, the show, Brendali, how empty my personal life is. I'll never achieve a tranquil mental state with my mind in this much turmoil.

For up to sixty days an audience of billions will watch my show. I've made do without peace of mind ever since my shooting and Kate's desertion, but what do I tell anyone who asks me about this new god, or his Convocation? I can't even answer my own questions.

Back once again on the sofa, my feet spread out over the coffee table, I'm fed up with my mood. It's not like me to mope. What I can do to improve it?

The painting on the opposite wall gets my attention. It depicts a sheer mountainside topped by dramatic storm clouds. A narrow sunbeam has sliced through the thunderheads to shine on a log cabin situated atop a foothill. To me, the message of the piece is that sunlight can find us on even the darkest, stormiest day. A day like today, except all I have is a heavy fog.

Upon spying some dim gray daylight I stroll over to the patio, step outside and inhale a lungful of bracing cool autumn air. The fog's chill forces my retreat inside within minutes.

Unbidden, a verse boils up from the deepest recesses of my teenage Bible study memories: 'But the day of the Lord will come like a thief. The heavens will pass away with a roar, the elements will be destroyed with intense heat and the earth and its works will burn up.'

That's why the Evangelicals are angry. Mankind isn't supposed to die off before the Apocalypse occurs. Our new God isn't in tune with their script, so—

My cellphone chirps. The screen shows its Brendali. "Hi, Ram. Did I wake you?"

"I've been up for hours." I head toward the kitchen. "Did you sleep well?"

"God, no. Never would my brain turn off. What have you been doing?"

"I've tried to come to grips with the idea that God wants our help, but I've failed. I haven't even begun to deal with the possibility of imminent extinction."

"Those things bother me, too. A lot. Did you get any sleep at all?"

"An hour, maybe, in ten-minute intervals." I push away my unfinished tea, grab my laptop and sit at the kitchen table. "Have you figured out how this new god fits into your faith?"

"No. I got nowhere. I'm confused, sad. If I accept that this is our new god, it means so much of what I've always believed isn't true. My faith is my fortress. I can't leave it." Despite her words, she sounds more composed and chipper than I am. "That's why I called you. You're good at cheering me up."

"Whenever I hear your voice my mood improves, too." What will she say to that?

"Aww, that's nice to hear." Keep talking, Brendali. "I like yours, too—it's smooth and sooo masculine. You probably sing well. You should perform for me sometime."

Any kind of performance you want. "I don't know the Latin songs you like."

"Whatever you choose will entertain me if it's a love song."

Is she flirting, or is that an innocent comment? "We should do a duet. I bet you're a better singer than I am. Your voice reminds me of Beth Hart's. She's one of my favorites."

"You'd have to teach me. Never have I tried to sing." Her giggle sounds little girlish.

"Someday I will. I'm about to check today's news. Have you done that?"

"If I did I'd have to admit last night really happened. Don't you dare try to convince me it did, either. Today I'm avoiding reality at all costs." Her infectious laughter makes me smile.

"I won't. Here's what I see on Flipboard." I put my feet up on a chair and move the laptop to my lap. "How's this? Some news outfits claim we faked the interview for ratings."

"Mi Dios!" I hear muttered Spanish and recognize a few choice curse words. "Never would we do that. How could we, anyway? That's ridiculous, no?"

"Isn't it? Oh, here's another angle—a Wall Street analyst estimates a net $1.8 billion dollar boon to L.A. from the Convocation if all sixty days are needed."

"Sorry, I can't handle numbers today. Tell me what the pope said."

"I'll check. Hold on." I search for the answer. "The Vatican's press office says Pope Francis III has no comment at present."

"He only got elevated last month because he's younger. After four popes in five years, the Church needs stability."

If the Vatican didn't keep choosing old men as popes, the rapid turnover wouldn't occur. "The Anglican, Baptist and Lutheran churches took the hint. They're not commenting, either." I switch from Flipboard to the New York Times app.

"What can they say? The churches can't deny he's God if he is, or accept him if he isn't. They want proof either way."

"You nailed it. Here's another take on things." I send the article on screen to my printer to read later. "The New York Times wonders why God chose Los Angeles for the Convocation, not cities associated with major religions. That's a damn good question."

"That's easy—the city's name means The Angels." Even her chuckles have a musical vibe. "The actual reason's obvious. God chose a neutral site to avoid giving the impression he favors one religion over others. We can ask the next time he shows up."

I never would've thought of that. "Let's hope he doesn't. One interview of an alleged deity's enough for me. Besides, if God comes on our stage again, Ken will go ballistic."

"What's in the *L.A. Times?*"

"Let's find out." This app's slow to load. Once the screen's readable, I rush through the articles. "The Convention Center's booked solid. Its general manager objects to kicking out two months of convention business. He wants God to pay premium rent."

"He must pray at a bank."

"Ha! I'm glad you can find humor in all this."

"Life's absurdities are clearest when I'm bewildered. Umm, Ram, the station's beeping me. I'll call you back."

As I make myself presentable in the bathroom, a televised news report plays a snippet of the White House press conference. The President's press spokesman says that if God really appeared last night, the Convocation will get federal support. He also promises an FBI investigation to verify God's authenticity.

That's code. Our first-ever Evangelical president wants to prove God's fake. Good luck, sir. Ken will hate the bureaucratic headaches, but they won't last long.

Brendali calls again. "What surprises me," she says, "is the lack of earthquake coverage. We're the only station running a special on it. Ken wants me at ground zero with the news team. In his exact words, he said 'I want you close enough to choke on the dust if the tower falls.'"

Her imitation of Ken's New Jersey accent is spot on. "That's how he gets even with us, Brendali. He's passive-aggressive. You get the close-up. I'm in the anchor chair. If nothing happens he'll sit back, watch us eat crow on the air and get his kicks."

She hangs up laughing. What a delightful sound. I have to hear it more often.

Once dressed and back in the kitchen I notice a new icon on my laptop that depicts an apple tree. Puzzled, I open the app and find this:

GREETINGS. You are summoned to attend the World Religions Convocation at the L.A. Convention Center, starting at 2:00 p.m. PST, Monday, November 15, 2027.

As host, you shall (1) declare the Convocation open for business; (2) act as moderator until the attendees make other arrangements; and (3) declare the Convocation closed when business concludes, or no later than 5:00 p.m. on the sixtieth (60th) non-holiday weekday from opening, whichever comes first.

You and/or your cohost shall report on the proceedings daily during the Ram Forrester Hour. A worldwide audience will hear your updates in their respective native tongues.

This link will activate the host pages after you declare the Convocation open. Only you and your cohost may access these pages. Use the password "newgod216." You will find useful tools there, including a message board my tech angels will monitor on my behalf.   God

A message board to God? Seriously? What else is available? I can't wait to find out.

The phone chirps again. I answer without checking caller ID. "Hey, Brendali—three calls this morning? What an honor."

"Forster," a muffled male voice says, "you're a dead man. Real soon."

7 | Darlin' Kate

Friday, November 12, 2027, 1:10 p.m., Burbank

When I arrive at the station our lobby receptionist gives me her usual big bright smile. "Ram, Ken's reserved the second-floor conference room. He's got something for you and Kate Chung to watch before your quake special starts. She's your co-anchor today."

"Thanks, Minh." What a Ken move this is, pairing me and Kate. This is his attempt to make me uncomfortable in my first newscast since my medical leave ended.

The empty conference room affords me a quiet moment to prepare for Kate, but only minutes after I sit down she's seated across the table from me. Her face is expressionless. I hope mine is, too, but my heart's pounding. I can't let her provoke me.

She's wearing a swirling maroon/black patterned *cheongsam*. Jewelry's piled on, too—ruby earrings, gold and silver necklaces, jade bracelets and five rings with various gemstones. No doubt she's also wearing her ankle bracelet and the waist chain she doesn't even take off in the shower. She probably poured on a whole bottle's worth of Eternity to pollute the air.

Is she taunting me? Sure she's beautiful, but this isn't how she dresses for work. She'd take an hour to pick an ensemble and make sure every item's exactly right, then ask me for my opinion. I miss having to approve her outfits—but what am I thinking? We're done, over, finis.

Neither of us acknowledges the other. I wish Ken would get here, and finally give in. "Aren't you going to ask how I'm doing these days?"

"Why should I?" Her soft brown bedroom eyes, pursed lips and the angled tilt of her head add up to what I call her 'I'm the sexiest woman in the world and you know I know it' pose. "You're back at work. What do I need to say?"

"I can't thank you enough for your lack of support while I fought for my life." Damn, dude, don't sound bitter. She'll think she's the winner here.

"We're ancient history. I don't need to justify myself to you." She flips her braid over her left shoulder so it hangs down over her chest. This 'I'm annoyed' gesture pre-stages the 'I'm upset' one, when she picks at the end of the braid and pouts. She's doing that now.

"You didn't have courage enough to break up with me in person, did you?"

"The nurses wouldn't let me see you."

"The ICU's no jail, Kate. The nursing staff had instructions to let you in. The younger ones couldn't wait to meet you. It's not every day a *haute couture* fashion model shows up at Cedars-Sinai. Instead you handed some nurse a three-sentence Dear John letter and left."

She slams her hand against the table. "I suppose you think I shot you, too?"

"That letter damn near killed me. I relapsed and straight-lined."

"Oh, come on. You know how I felt those last couple of months."

"I sure do. You began to have headaches instead of—"

Ken barges in, sees our anger and turns away, failing to hide a smirk. "I didn't ask you here to duke it out, children." At his push of a button two wooden panels on the wall cabinet separate to reveal a big screen television. "We don't have time for your personal crap.

You'll maintain professionalism during the broadcast, yah?"

"Of course. What's up?" Kate recovers her equilibrium faster than I do. A simple flip of the braid behind her back discharges her emotions.

"We received an exclusive video from the Al-Arabia news network," Ken says. "First time they've sent us anything. This follows last night's asinine interview." He glances my way, probably to gauge how far he can push. With my mind stuck in relationship turmoil, I don't take the bait. He grabs the remote and readies the piece for viewing.

"Al-Arabia tells us Mullah Abdul Mu'min received a Convocation invitation. Remember him? He split from the Taliban to lead Waziristan's secession from Pakistan three years ago. The video's soundless, but we don't speak Urdu anyway." Ken turns down the overhead lights.

This mullah's a bearded broad-shouldered fellow in Pakistani-style militants gear. His three bodyguards tote AK-47s. The platform they're on is raised a few inches off the desert dirt. Dun-colored hills stretch out behind them. The cleric's audience isn't visible.

Mu'min waves his parchment invitation around, crumples and burns it. He drops the flaming ball and stomps on it with a boot. For the *coup de grâce*, he grinds the charred remains into burnt specks with his heel.

His hands fold into fists. With a critical look at the sky Mu'min raises both arms and shakes them at the passing clouds. We don't hear his shout but the beating of his chest conveys his message. His men stare straight ahead, impassive, maybe bored. They must've seen his low-level dramatics before.

The cleric's arms go to his side. He speaks for several minutes with no obvious show of emotion before his expression changes to one of surprise. Mu'min flings his right arm in the general direction of his nearest bodyguard, grabbing only air while his left hand goes to his neck. Eyes bulging, mouth curled, the holy man drops to his knees.

Is this a heart attack?

As Mu'min bends forward his head falls off his shoulders, splattering the platform with blood before it lands on the ground. In HD clarity, more blood pumps out of his headless neck and arcs toward the camera.

Kate reacts with "What the f--k!" My stomach heaves, my eyes damn near burst out of their sockets. Ken's nonreaction implies he's already seen the video.

The decapitated body shakes and topples. Two guards and a few people from the audience lean into the screenshot and attempt to catch the corpse. Drenched with Mu'min's blood, they fail to maintain a firm enough grip. The body lands in the dirt next to its head. The third guard's urgent waves, if meant for medical assistance, are useless.

The screen goes blank. Ken restores the lights to full power.

"Al-Arabia says Mu'min refused the invitation to attend this Convocation, dared the so-called 'false God of the West' to take retribution on him and claimed unwavering faith in and protection from Allah. How he died is unexplained. No one's claimed credit. We have to decide whether to show this or sit on it. I want opinions. Ram?"

"You both know about the army tour of duty I did in the Middle East. Ugly stuff happened daily but I never saw anything like this. I nearly puked. If we show this, whoever's watching will regurgitate their lunch, have nightmares."

Ken and Kate's impassive expressions imply disagreement. I try a different tack. "Put the piece on our social media page and mention it during the special, with an appropriate warning. For goodness sake, don't broadcast this."

"Do you agree, Kate?"

"No, I don't. Of course we should show the video. Bloody deaths get televised all the time these days. This is legit news. During last night's interview, the guest predicted an earthquake and said he'd send Convocation invitations to people around the world. If invitations went out, doesn't that mean the guest's for real?"

"Fat chance," Ken says under his breath.

"Sorry," I say. "Your reasoning doesn't justify subjecting our midafternoon audience to this man's gruesome death."

"I'm not finished." Kate's eyes focus on Ken. "Somebody had to refuse an invitation. People may dispute our guest's authenticity, but he did say failure to comply with his orders would result in immediate severe consequences. Death by invisible decapitation fits the bill. Folks have to see this to believe it."

Why waste time with useless debate? "Ken, what's your take?"

"Al-Arabia's unlikely to send us fake news showing Allah one-upped, unable to protect a mullah who's invoked his name. An independent source confirmed the death, including the manner of it. This is one-hundred-percent genuine." Ken stands. "Station management believes this video will rebut the claim that we engaged in a ratings-driven farce last night."

Ken's unilateral decision is based on reasoning only he could conjure. Critics will scream about showing the video on broadcast news instead of social media.

"That's the plan, folks." He leans toward us and lowers his voice. "Ram, when you start at 2:00 p.m., introduce Kate with this breaking news. Kate, give our viewers a graphic content warning, narrate and show the video. Explain why we chose to air it. Don't mention the rebuttal point. The talking heads will think that up themselves. Once you're done, Ram will start the lead-up to the supposed earthquake this false God claims he'll induce."

Ken steps away, stops at the door and turns around. "I don't want you two interacting on air any more than strictly necessary, got it?"

Kate's big smile means she enjoys getting her way. I'll focus on the quake. If it happens, which is more probable now, I'll have enough to do without worrying about viewer reactions to the mullah's demise.

8 | Shake, Rattle and Roll

BRENDALI

"Stand by, Brendali," comes through my earpiece. I give Sammy a thumbs-up, in case he didn't hear the signal.

"As promised," Ram's saying to our viewers, "Brendali Santamaria is live at the America's Bank Tower. What have you got for us, Brendali?"

"At the moment all's quiet, Ram, except for the police sirens from the streets below. We can't get any closer to the tower. Let everyone see it, Sammy."

He pans his camera across Bunker Hill's Spanish Steps and up the side of the tower. "Ram, this building can withstand earthquakes of up to 8.3 on the Richter scale. Our guest last night predicted that a quake measuring 6.2 will occur in fifteen minutes. He'll further establish his claim as our God if the quake happens on time, at the predicted Richter reading, and if the tower falls as promised."

"I'm concerned about you both," Ram says. "You're way too close."

"Can you hear that police bullhorn? It's ordering everyone to evacuate the Citibank terrace. That means us. I'd better sign off."

"Good. Get going and stay safe."

We're last on line for the escalator. The middle-aged, tall and bony man in front of me turns in my direction. His bald head lacks eyebrows. The slight indentation between the right eye and ear, combined with his black sweats, make him look like a full-size *Día de los Muertos* doll.

"I watched your show last night," he tells me.

"Did you like it?"

"As a humble servant of God, not the fake one you interviewed. I wasn't pleased." He pulls a handgun partway out of his pocket. "Stay silent and move." He points to an alcove that overlooks the Spanish Steps.

Mierda, once more I have to face violence? If I didn't give Pedro my guns when I left Mexico, I'd show this guy who gives orders and who takes them.

"Mister," Sammy says, "put the pistol away. Let us pass and we'll forget this happened. Otherwise, we'll call the police."

This skeleton of a man pokes Sammy's chest with his gun. "I told you to move. Do it. If either of you hold anything other than your gear, I'll shoot."

Halfway to the alcove Sammy whispers to me in Spanish. "Move forward, no matter what. He won't dare use his gun. Shots will attract the police. I'll take care of him."

I continue forward but Sammy lags.

"All this equipment's heavy," he tells the gunman. "Mind if I leave it here?"

I take a few more steps and look back. Sammy's sprinting right at Skeleton Man. "No, Sammy, don't!" He ignores me.

The gunman stuffs his weapon into a pocket, spreads his feet and crouches until Sammy's only steps away. The bastard springs, like a tiger. In a single fluid motion he grabs Sammy by the arm and waist, pivots, hoists and dumps him over the side of the escalator. Street level is two floors down, too far for Sammy to drop safely.

"Oh no, Sammy!" No scream or sickening thud reaches me, so I hustle to check on him.

Skeleton Man blocks my way. "I can throw you over the side, too." If a rattlesnake could speak it would sound like this *cholo.*

"You're tiny enough to toss to Flower Street, bitch. You deserve a broken neck."

Who's this guy think he is? Never will I let anyone talk to me this way. My hands curl into fists. I aim a punch at his midsection, but he steps away from it and puts me in a chokehold, his gun placed against my cheek.

I struggle to get free, but stop at the click of his gun's safety release. I can't go all gonzo Latina on him without a gun. *"Hijo de puta!"* What else can I say? The man's pure evil.

"Don't you dare swear at me," he says in a threatening tone. "Not after the sins you committed last night. Double time it into that alcove." He lets go and shoves me forward.

He's ordering me around? Never will I take his orders. My face heats up. "It's too close to the tower. I'll die if the building falls."

"Fake gods don't cause earthquakes, *Chiquita*. You'll die the old-fashioned way." He cocks the gun. "The last thing you'll see is the Tower, upright."

"Why the hell are you so pissed off? Ram and I didn't expect this guest to show up."

For a split second he looks puzzled. "You and Forster have been tried, found guilty and sentenced to death and eternal hellfire. I'm God's instrument, here to carry out His will."

A long minute passes while we stare at each other. Insanity and determination glow in his left eye; only now do I see the right one's dead. Never will I forget his deranged look, especially the unblinking reptilian eyelids. This man's heart lacks even a shred of mercy.

I turn and walk toward the alcove. Stay strong. Show no fear. If the coward shoots from behind, die with dignity. No, no, don't think like that. Trust in God's protection.

Upon reaching the alcove entrance I glance back. He's at the Flamingo Fountain, the gun loose in his hand but pointed at me.

The quake's due in five minutes. What can I do? Think. Pray. God, please, help me escape. I need to live another day. I move out of his view, activate my cellphone and find Ram's text warning me about NITWIT. *Mierda,* why couldn't I have seen this earlier?

'Ram,' I text, 'I can't leave the Citibank terrace. Alert LAPD.' He won't see it until he's off camera. Even if he does, the police won't put officers in danger. By the time the quake ends, they'll find my dead body.

I try to call Mamá, only to utter a few choice curse words at the unreliable Mexican phone system's refusal to process the call. A recorded 911message tells me that due to the earthquake priority I'll have to wait twenty minutes for an emergency dispatcher.

Survival's up to me. Can I escape over the side? No. The only way out is to become the shooter's target, and hope his one-eyed aim is faulty.

My heart's racing now, breath coming in short gasps like I'm running a marathon. A minute's left. Calm down. Peer around the wall. Skeleton Man hasn't moved.

Everything goes silent. Even the breeze stops. Planet Earth's taking in a last deep gulp of air before all hell breaks loose.

A slow rumble grows, turning into a terrible vast deafening racket. The ground's crying out for mercy. I am, too, but the tumult swallows my screams.

Nearby office buildings sway like crazy. Across the street the public library moves back and forth. The Source Figure statue atop the Spanish Steps topples. The alcove shakes up and down, side to side. *Mi Dios,* soon it'll tear away from the plaza and slide toward Fifth Street.

A second jolt launches me sideways into the wall hard enough for the side of my head to dent the plaster. I stagger back and fall on all fours to the buckling floor. Shit, that hurts!

My vision blurs. This is like being on the deck of a tuna boat with no grab-rail while riding the crest of a monster storm wave, only to plunge into a trough. Will this ever end? How can the noise get louder? Blood splatters the floor tiles and the front of my white blouse. Tan bits of plaster and bloodstains color my fingers when I touch the area above my left ear. Too groggy to react, I want nothing more than an end to this thrill ride.

The ground steadies, spent from its exertions. I drop to the alcove floor, catch my breath, wait for my dizziness to pass and take in the sudden intense quiet.

Will the tower fall? If it doesn't, will Skeleton Man come shoot me dead?

I stand on rubber legs as though I've stepped on solid ground after a long voyage. Why can't I stay on my feet?

By leaning against the wooden frame of the alcove entrance to stay upright, I watch Skeleton Man. He's focused on the tower, not moving. Maybe he's asking the same questions I did moments ago. Four oval landings that lead to the Spanish Steps are no more than twelve feet from him. If I can get past them without being shot, and if the Tower doesn't fall, I can escape.

I'd have to run toward him without cover. He'd need to react fast, aim and fire. It's not far, but it is risky. Should I try? If I don't and the Tower falls I won't survive. I have to chance it.

A dizzy spell hits me while I take off my flats, causing me to keel over. Once it passes I go to one knee and keep a hand against the stucco wall. What's wrong with me? Concentrate. A cautious few steps forward allow me to test whether I can stay upright. I can.

Oh, God, a third jolt? Shorter, sharp, more noise. I grab the nearby planter and wait for the ground to steady. Now, girl. Go, barefoot. Run fast, stay balanced.

Skeleton Man drops to a shooting position and tracks me.

A ping sounds off the wall as I reach the first platform. Good gracious God, his gun does have bullets!

Second platform. Another pop and miss. Two more to go. He'd better keep missing.

Third platform. A misfire. Thank you, Lord!

Final platform. I reach the Steps as the coward runs for the escalator. I'm tempted to follow and fight him, but that's total foolishness.

Loud grinding, screeching and buckling noises from the tower catch my attention. I spot a bulge, maybe halfway up, and realize the top half of the tower's about to collapse.

Never can I stay here. Do I follow that nut down the escalator and rely on the police to stop him from hurting me? No. It's better to take the Steps, but which way? Down to Fifth Street or up to Hope Street? Buildings fall downhill, no? So go up.

A blast loud as cannon fire makes me almost jump out of my skin. The gold "N" from the "America's Bank" sign at the top of the Tower has exploded smack in the middle of the upper stairs. Shards and splinters spill down the steps, stopping within inches of my bare feet.

This is God's message not to run to Hope Street. Always remember, *mi Dios es mi proteccion.* I take a deep breath, say a quick prayer and cross myself. Safety awaits me on Fifth Street, if I can run fast enough to reach it before the collapsing tower does.

9 | I'm Hurtin'

RAM

Why won't Brendali and Sammy answer our calls? Are they hurt, maybe crushed under that fallen tower? Did NITWIT get her? I wish she'd sent a more specific text.

This pacing back and forth serves no purpose. React to facts, not fears. You're a newsman, remember? Don't wait for the LAPD's call. Go downtown, find out for yourself.

I zoom down the hallway, bypass the elevator, jump the stairs two steps at a time and sprint past the reception desk. The short hallway to the garage is a blur. A blind turn into the plaza runs me straight into a granite mountain of a man in an appropriately gray suit. The collision drives me to the pavement, my shoulder taking the brunt of the fall. I haven't experienced sharper pain since my shooting.

The mountain man lifts me like I'm a feather and sets me back on my feet.

"Sorry," I say. "Despite your, uhh, size, I didn't see you." I swing my arm around to exercise the shoulder and find the pain manageable if I don't overdo movement.

"Lordy, lordy, lordy," the man says under his breath. "Are you hurt?"

"I'll live. How about you?"

"Me? I'm fine." Of course he is. It takes an earthquake to shake a mountain. "Don't make a habit of runnin' into former offensive linemen. You'll take a whippin' every time. You do pack a wallop, I'll grant that. No one's hit me harder since my last game with the Fightin' Irish."

With that physique, I don't doubt that he's a former football player. "Excuse me, I'm in a hurry." An attempt to dart past him is stymied by his vise-like grip on my good arm. To have such a lightning quick reaction, he must've been a formidable run-blocker.

"You're Ram Forrester, right?"

"Yes, and I've got an emergency on my hands."

"Not so fast, Mr. Forrester. I'm Griffith Hoosier. FBI." He reaches into his jacket and offers a business card.

"You went to Notre Dame and your last name's Hoosier?" The simple act of pocketing the card makes me grunt from shoulder pain.

Mr. Hoosier's deep sigh implies he's heard my question before. "I grew up in Griffith, Indiana, a suburb of Gary. My parents had a hoot namin' me and my twin brother, Gary, so we'd never forget our roots. They have an odd sense of humor, my folks, but I'm downright humorless. That's why I joined the FBI."

"They sound like interesting people. Now, please excuse me—"

He nimbly blocks my second attempt to bypass him. "We need to talk, Mr. Forrester. I also want to speak to Ms. Santamaria."

"She's the emergency. I'm headed downtown to find out why she's not reporting in to us. Come along if you want, we can talk on the way. Or do the driving. If you're pulled over for speeding, the CHP might grant you professional courtesy."

His eyes roll up while he processes the information. "Right this way, sir."

Traffic conditions on the southbound 5 freeway are light, perhaps due to the temblor. "If you don't mind, Mr. Hoosier, lets discuss the so-called ratings prank first."

"Fine by me, sir. Where we headin'?"

"Citibank Center. Can you speed up?"

"I drive the highway limit. The bureau frowns on speedin'

tickets." Of course. Why didn't I think of that? "I watched your show, Mr. Forrester. Couldn't move or change channels. How'd you pull those stunts off?"

"What stunts?"

"You know what I'm talkin' about. Pretty spiffy stuff."

"God predicted the quake, Mr. Hoosier." Resist his goading. Stay calm, talk him past this nonsense. "You think my station could do that?"

"You might've been tipped off." A fleeting smile crosses his face before his mouth snaps back into involuntary law enforcement neutrality.

"Seismologists don't have hours of advance warning." That's common knowledge. He can't think I'd buy that idea. "Tell me, who'd you see when God's appearance changed?"

"Morgan Freeman. Remember him? He played God in some film I saw growin' up. A comedy, my dad said. I don't recall laughin' any."

Bruce Almighty. It had some funny moments." Let's get past this prank nonsense, fast. "Are you married, Mr. Hoosier?"

"Yes, sir. Our five-year anniversary's next week. LaTaunya's also four months from the good Lord deliverin' us our first young'n."

"Wonderful. Double congratulations. Did your wife see Morgan Freeman, too?"

"No. She—" His face scrunches up.

"If you each saw a different God, how do you reckon my station could arrange that?"

"Damned if I know, sir. Explain, please."

"Wish I could. Two points, though." A glance out the window provides no obvious signs of earthquake damage. "First, if we'd known in advance that our show would get beamed into every television set worldwide, we would've dumped our advertising campaign. We expected solid ratings. You know about my recent medical issues?"

"I heard. You took a bullet meant for someone's ex-wife."

"Not one. Several." I wince at the memory and fill him in.

"You've gone through a lot." I don't hear irony in his voice, so I suppose he means it.

"We never doubted my fans would tune in. They're loyal and wanted me back."

"Understood. What's your second point, Mr. Forrester?"

"KJCR-TV competes against the big media conglomerates on a shoestring budget. If those companies can't pull off a worldwide broadcast, why would anyone think we can?"

"You're tellin' me a real God showed up for a television interview? Here, in Los Angeleez? Come on, sir. My mama didn't raise no fool."

"The control room lost our transmission, Mr. Hoosier." I start tapping the window frame, a sign of frustration with the car's speed.

"You don't say."

"I do. Look, I'll recommend to our general manager that you get access to our accounting records. You'll find no expenditures for technical geniuses or a gaggle of interpreters. We've got nothing to hide."

"Fine, if the books ain't cooked." He slows for a traffic bottleneck caused by a fallen retaining wall that's spilled onto one of the two connector lanes. I stop the taps.

As we thread past the rubble and onto the 110 freeway, I fill Mr. Hoosier in on the NITWIT threats and Brendali's cryptic text message. I include her *narco* threats in case a connection exists. By the time I finish we're in stop-and-go traffic close to the Chinatown exit.

My phone rings with a call from the station. "Yes?" I mouth Brendali's name for his benefit. "She is? Where? What about Sammy? You're serious? Damn! Okay, I'm on my way." I put the phone away and stare out the side window.

Didn't God say no one would get killed? Why Sammy, of all people? This world's unfair.

"You have information about Miss Santamaria?"

"She's at LAC+USC Medical Center. Her condition's unknown. I'm worried. If you don't mind, let's go there."

"Fine by me."

"Our cameraman's in the morgue. What a great guy. A former marine, he's been with us six years and leaves a wife and two small kids."

"Sorry to hear this." He makes a screaming hard one-eighty, sending us up the entrance ramp and back on 110. "Sir, you're on the level, I can tell. Let's focus on NITWIT."

"Thanks, Mr. Hoosier. I appreciate that."

"Why don't you call me Griff from now on?"

"Happy to, if you'll call me Ram."

"Done." I get what passes for a smile from him.

Griff drops me off at the ER. The staff refuses to let me see Brendali or release information about her condition. They only disclose that she's stable and scheduled for immediate surgery. That's not good news.

I wait around until the last possible minute before I have to return for tonight's show, but get no updates on Brendali's condition. God picked her for the Convocation. Why didn't he make sure she'd stay safe? What kind of uncaring God do we have now?

RAM

Saturday, November 13, 2027, 8:00 a.m., LAC+USC Medical Center

When I arrive the upper half of Brendali's hospital bed is tilted, allowing her to sit up. Dr. Vahan Avakian, who strikes me as the Armenian version of the lead character in *The Good Doctor*, is undoing the gauze wrap covering her skull from the eyebrows up. An IV tube's stuck in her right arm and her left leg's incased in a hard cast from the knee down. Her hair's loose, the braid undone.

"Hi, Ram." Her strong upbeat voice is a relief to hear. "I knew you'd stop by. Have a seat." Instead I stand by her bed, opposite the doctor. Brendali grabs my wrist as the medical exam continues.

Dr. Avakian flashes a brief, tight smile. "Let's see how well the stitches held up. Turn toward your friend. Look up at him. Good." He's positioned her head as though he'll examine her ear. "Hmmm. Face me, please." Next, pupil dilation and eye movement are checked with a penlight. "We'll soon take you to radiology to update yesterday's cranial x-rays. Afterward I'll return to discuss what we find."

Once the doctor leaves I move a chair next to the bed. "How do you feel?"

Her big smile warms my heart. "Better than expected. Maybe it's the medicine in the IV. The doctors did fantastic work. I don't want to stay, but having your company will help."

I take her hand in both of mine. "I came by yesterday but wasn't allowed to see you. No one would tell me anything about your injuries. I worried about you all night. I'll stay until you're sick of me hanging around."

Her hand slips out of mine to caress my cheek. "I'm glad you felt so much for me. I'd feel the same way if you got hurt." The caresses don't stop. "The nurses told me you came. They wanted your autograph. Never once did they ask for mine." She laughs.

Neither of us speak. The dreamy look in her eyes wasn't in them until Dr. Avakian left. I hold her hand again. This time our fingers intertwine.

"The earthquake happened as predicted. You know what that means."

"Yes." She shrugs. "We have a new god, no?"

"I don't know a way around it, Brendali. I've tried to come up with a theory that would explain this. Nothing fits except the conclusion we both want to avoid."

She closes her eyes and keeps them shut long enough to make me think she's fallen asleep. When she opens them a tear spills down her cheek. "I guess you're right." Brendali sounds resigned to the news. We both stay quiet, captive to our thoughts.

She breaks our silence. "How'd the show do without me?"

"We bombed. Too much distraction—the quake, more protests, my worries about you. We needed your energy and grace, but at least no surprise guests showed up." Forget the show, everyone else already did. "When will your family arrive?"

"They won't." She smooths her hospital gown with her free hand.

"I thought you live with them."

"I house-sit for my parents. It's cheaper than renting. You don't pay me enough." She chuckles at her little joke. "Since my papi retired, my folks have lived in El Rosario most of the year. They left for Mexico yesterday morning to avoid the earthquake. Mamá's more worried about Jalapeno, her dog, than me. She wants someone to feed and walk him while I'm stuck here. I told her I'd make arrangements."

"I'll do it if your brothers can't. Why won't they visit?"

"Julian, the oldest, drills oil in Alaska. You'd like Lobo, our nickname for the next oldest. He's a well-known *Norténo* musician who lives in Tucson. Right now he's on tour with his band in South America. My youngest brother's in prison. So we're alone together, all day."

The seductive tone of that last sentence and the way she squeezed my hand sends a message she reinforces with a flirtatious little smile and that dreamy-eyes look.

I bend to deliver a little kiss to her forehead, but she puckers up. That stops me, inches away. Should I kiss those sweet lips?

An orderly arrives to wheel Brendali to radiology before I can decide.

At the lobby florist shop I buy Brendali an overpriced bouquet of red roses in a cheap vase. I also stop in the cafeteria for a mediocre cup of coffee and a tasteless bran muffin.

She's back in her room when I return. "These are for you." I hand her the bouquet.

"Oh, thanks!" She holds the roses close, inhaling deeply several times. "They're lovely."

"May I fill the vase for you?"

"Later. I want to cuddle with them a while. The scent's wonderful. These are the first roses anyone's given me since Javier died." She buries her head in the rose petals, perhaps to hide the sadness I glimpsed in her eyes.

Brendali's breakfast arrives—scrambled eggs, a wafer thin bean burrito, jello and coffee. She devours it while I fill her in about meeting Griff and she recounts her escape from this 'Skeleton Man' fellow. The note I type on my phone will ensure that Griff learns about it.

"The tower collapsed while I ran down the Spanish Steps. I sped up, lost my balance and missed a step. I must've turned my ankle and hit my head pretty hard when I fell, because I woke up in an ambulance. Yesterday's strange, no? But tell me, how's Sammy?"

"Sammy?" What should I say? I'd rather not deliver the bad news while she recuperates. "I don't—I mean, uh—"

Dr. Avakian saves me by entering the room with two colleagues. Why so many doctors?

"Miss Santamaria, I'm Dr. Johnstone, head of orthopedics," says the oldest, who has curly gray hair and a professor's demeanor. "We need to discuss your radiological studies."

Brendali's eyes widen. She takes my hand and squeezes it, hard. "Is something wrong?"

I don't get it. They've only taken x-rays. If she had bleeding on the brain she'd have bad headaches. They'd do an MRI or CT scan if something serious is at stake.

"Excuse us, please." Johnstone looks at me. "Miss Santamaria requires some privacy."

"I want Ram to stay, doctor. The way you all marched in worries me." She hands me her roses. I put them and the vase on a small table by the window and return to her side.

Dr. Johnstone helps Brendali sit straight up. "Please lean forward." He examines the left side of her head like Dr. Avakian did. "Doctor Pridivatha, look at this."

The young bookish-looking Indian physician had focused his attention on Brendali's leg cast. He peeks at Brendali's skull but says nothing.

"Can one of you explain what's going on? Brendali's entitled to know."

Dr. Johnstone's cold stare implies I'm a jerk for asking that question. He glances at the doctors and Brendali last, which is curious since she's the patient. "Miss Santamaria came to us with a rather concerning subdural hematoma of the brain, a skull fracture, displaced fractures of her ankle and tibia and related ligament damage. She received the best possible ER care before the staff wheeled her into surgery."

He drones on with more medical lingo but I focus on Brendali, whose eyes are downcast. She's resumed squeezing my hand. Does she have a traumatic brain injury? She remembers what happened yesterday, with gaps. If she's sustained a TBI, it's mild.

"Dr. Johnstone, I appreciate the explanation. Can you get to the point?"

My question's ignored. "Our normal process would require Miss Santamaria to undergo a few days of inpatient monitoring if no complications arise such as swelling on the brain or blood clots. We'd want her bones to set properly. All the usual precautions, you see."

"Spill the *frijoles* already, doctor. Has a complication arisen? Do I need to stay longer? I can handle bad news." Like me, Brendali's exasperated by his obliviousness.

The doctor focuses on the floor, not her. "We compared your x-rays to those taken yesterday." He rubs his chin and stares above her head. "Have you had any headaches today?"

"No."

"Do you feel any untoward pressure in your skull, or residual leg pain?"

"Everything feels normal."

Both of his hands plunge into the pockets of his smock. "That's because everything is normal."

Brendali and I share quizzical looks.

"What Dr. Johnstone means," Dr. Avakian says, "is we found no trace of any injuries anywhere, head to toe."

"She's not injured? How the hell—" I clamp my jaw shut.

Brendali's radiant grin spreads from ear to ear. "I kept telling myself God is my protector. If you say I'm cured, doctor, I say this is God's doing. A true miracle." She closes her eyes, crosses herself and whispers a prayer of thanks. A single tear rolls down her cheek. I hand her the tissue box and receive a grateful smile.

"We're physicians," Dr. Johnstone says. "We don't acknowledge miracles, but we can show you something you may not know." He beckons to me. "Have a look, sir."

I walk around the bed to check the side of Brendali's head, where he's pointing. "I see hair. What's the big deal?"

Dr. Avakian touches her skull an inch above the ear. "Right here you should see bare scalp. We removed the hair in this area to suture a deep cut where her head hit a wall. Before suturing we washed out plaster specks mixed with dried blood. This morning I saw no scalp contusion, sutures or scar. Her hair even regrew overnight to its prior waist-long length."

"How the heck could that happen?" When the doctors called my survival a medical miracle I doubted them, but now I wonder. Could Brendali and I really have been touched by God? Her face glows with joy. She accepts miracles without question, but supernatural stuff doesn't fit my world view. How else can I explain this?

Dr. Pridivatha's voice cuts through my thoughts. "Her morning radiology shows no leg fractures. The screws and rod I implanted are gone even though the cast is unchanged from last night. The surgical scars are probably erased, too. How is this possible?"

That's the question I want answered.

Dr. Johnstone removes the IV drip and asks Brendali to walk down the hallway. In her state of bliss she'll float. While she's away, the doctors huddle for a spirited, though whispered, discussion. I tune them out, fill Brendali's vase with water and return it to the table.

"There's no pain at all," Brendali says when she re-enters the room. "The cast makes walking clumsy, though."

"We have no reason to keep you here, Miss Santamaria," Dr. Johnstone says. "Once the cast comes off, you can go home. I must say, this is the most extraordinary thing I've seen in over thirty years of medical practice."

Brendali doesn't respond, other than to grace him with a beatific smile.

The doctors leave. Brendali's smile continues to light up her face. "The two of us, Ram. We're truly God's chosen ones, no?" She pats the bed. I accept the invitation and sit next to her. Our arms encircle each other's waists, and she rests her head against my shoulder.

Why didn't God prevent her injuries from happening at all? I suppose it doesn't matter. His touch obviously agrees with her. Somehow she's more beautiful, maybe even more ethereal, than before. Until now I've never been in the presence of an actual angel.

I run my fingers through her hair. She tips her head up so we can see eye-to-eye. Her smile is radiant, her eyes beckoning. She's right, God chose us. Maybe he knew something we're only now about to find out.

Our lips brush but don't linger. "I'm so happy right now I could cry," she says. We lay back across the narrow hospital bed, our faces inches apart. My arm's tucked, a bit uncomfortably, under her back. She flicks her hair away from my cheek.

When I listen to a favorite song, my spine tingles for a few seconds. Brendali's joy delivers the same electric sensation. I have no words to express the gamut of emotions pouring through me other than to describe it as pure unadulterated awe.

Our first canoodle lasts longer than the brushed kiss but is interrupted when the nurse comes in, sees us and laughs. "Miss Santamaria, let's get you ready for discharge. A wheelchair's ready for you in the hall. Kisses will have to wait."

As we leave I can't decide what astounds me more—what's happened to her or what's happening between us.

RAM

Monday, November 15, 2027, 11:00 a.m.
I'm able to enter the pitch dark Convention Center only because a two-by-four is wedged between the main door and the frame. My phone's flashlight helps me navigate down the dark hallway.

At the first bisecting corridor a voice rings out behind me. "Hey, you—don't move!" Overhead lights turn on. I kill the flashlight and turn around. The security guard's a young guy with freckles, reddish-blond hair, a body built like a tractor and legs thick as tree trunks.

"Lord a-mighty Jesus! Why, you're Ram Forrester. Ain't that the berries! I'd a-known that face a-your's anywhere. This here's sure an honor, Mista F. Me, I'm Johnny Ray."

He shakes my hand like he's using my arm to pump well water. Once he lets go the upward arc of my arm briefly continues. "Why, I watched you near every night since I moved here from Alabama. Sure riled me to high heaven when I heard you'd been all shot up. Put you in my prayers, I did, till you done healed."

"Thanks, Johnny. Without doubt, your prayers helped."

"You come by for this here Conversation thing, Mista F.?"

"Yes, but this place doesn't look ready."

"Oh, I don't know about that. Sure as all get-out, some spooky things have done gone on here. Foller me, you'll see." We head back toward the main door. "Saw your show last week. A real barn-burner, warn't it? Lord-a-mercy, I ain't never seen nothing like that old shape change thing God done. I swear by the good book, I near about fainted." He grins, shakes his head, slaps his leg and gives me a sideways glance. "Didn't that beat all!"

"I saw a surfer. Who'd you see?"

"My grandpa. Bless Patsy, he's gone now. When I grew up, I thought of him as like to God. Why, I'd druther see him settled in that old chair with you than most anything."

Johnny quiets down as we enter the main conference hall. I stop in my tracks. In front of us are hundreds of heavy plush armchairs in alternating tan and gray colors. They're arranged in three sections, the large middle section separated from the two narrower ones by wide aisles.

Speakers are built into the armchair wings. Plug-in panels fit snugly into the left armrests. A three-ring binder's perched on each cushion with a Cross metallic blue pen set and an ear bud.

When I first glance at each binder, the front cover portrays a lush tropical valley reminiscent of Hawaii. A few seconds later a vast desert replaces the vegetation. In succession a towering glacier melts away, haulers shear a saddle-shaped mountain into a low plateau, and a tsunami wipes out a picturesque curved white sand beach dotted with palm trees. After the water recedes, a lone palm remains upright with 'Make the Right Choice' etched in the wet sand.

The synchronicity is as awe-inspiring as the message. I've never seen anything like this at any conference I've attended, and I've been to a bunch.

The mahogany dais at the front of the room contains twelve seats, with six on either side of the lectern. A microphone's in front of every third seat. An intricate inlaid design on each front-facing panel shows, from left to right as I view them, a progression of carved figures that depict our evolutionary path. Homo-sapiens are carved into the next to last panel. The final one features a question mark inside the outline of an iconic human form.

Behind the dais hangs a huge electronic screen displaying the same apple tree logo on my phone, within a silver-gray circle containing "World Religions Convocation 2027" in navy blue lettering. The rest of the screen is dotted with dark thunderheads that spew lightning bolts above the dais every thirty seconds. The bolts dissolve before they reach the attendees' chairs.

Along the walls are stations with coffee urns, soda cans, juice and ice bowls, native and exotic fruit—some I don't recognize—and assorted mouth-watering pastries.

"See what I mean, Mista F.?" Concern etches Johnny's face.

"I wouldn't call this spooky. It's pretty remarkable, in my opinion."

He glances at the floor, perhaps unsure of what to say. "Looky, first off, these here chairs? Ain't none of them ours."

"No? I'm glad the Convention Center brought them in special."

"I'd say that, too, except no one did."

"No? How'd they get here?"

He shrugs and gestures. "Beats me. See, me and Luis, the other guard on duty, we go round the place, regular like, each hour. I do half the building, he does the other. This here hall, when I came by at 9:00 a.m., warn't nothing in it. Hour later, all this stuff's set down here. Ain't no one come from outside, I would've heard the racket. The guard station's only a little ways down from here." He extends both arms as though hugging the room. "All this sure enough showed up like nobody's business."

"No kidding?" If true, I know whose handiwork this is.

"Not only that, looky here." He motions at the nearby coffee urn. "Try some, Mista F. How you drink yours?"

"Milk, no sugar." The spout pours a light brown cup, hot, strong, without the slightest bitterness—the best I've tasted in recent memory.

"I take her black." The same spout pours his cup black. "If I wanted mine with sugar, I'd get that. Or decaf. Maybe this thing even pours espresso or them other fancy cups for all's I know. How you figure the urn reads our minds? And this here coffee's scalding hot. How? Ain't nothing heating it."

He's right. The urn lacks wires, electrical or battery-operated heating mechanisms.

"Spookiest thing's that big old screen," he says, pointing to it. "We don't have one like it. Can't put ours right where this thang's hanging. It's in mid-air, mind you. Ain't nothing holding this thang up. Damn strange, if'n you ask me."

"Wild," I say, more to myself than him. "Johnny, can you help me? I'd like you to close off the unneeded parts of the building and open the main doors to let our attendees in. Also, turn on the hallway and bathroom lights between here and the entrance."

"Why, I reckon I can, Mista F, if'n my company approves. I'll check."

"One more thing." I point to the screen. "Anyone invited to attend will have something with that apple tree logo—in print or on an electronic device. You and Luis should only allow entry to those who can show it to you. Refuse entry to anyone else, okay?"

"No worries." We exchange cellphone numbers before he leaves. He's tickled pink to have mine.

With people arriving soon, I call Griff for an update on the police presence outside. "The President refuses to allow federal law enforcement to assist until my investigation's completed," he says. "I've already filed a report exoneratin' your station of wrongdoin', but you know him—he's hard right Evangelical."

He didn't need to finish his thought. "What about state, county or city support?"

"LAPD will have a couple of cars circlin' the area on regular patrol. That's it."

"Why? We need more coverage than that." Can I assume God will provide the security we need? No.

"I'm not gettin' straight answers. Possibly no one believes the Convocation will occur. Or this is law enforcement's expression of annoyance at deployin' manpower for all the local and statewide protests. Maybe those opinions will change over time."

"What if we have protesters here?"

"LAPD will respond in force if the patrol officers request it."

"Tell them I'll emphatically express my disagreement with this irresponsible laissez-faire attitude on my show tonight. I haven't heard of protests, but demonstrators are likely to show up as we move along."

He acknowledges my message and hangs up. I sink into the moderator's ultra-comfy chair on the dais and try to take everything in. What am I missing? Will this on-edge feeling stay with me until the Convocation ends?

In case any breaking Convocation-related news has come across the wires since this morning, I check my phone and find the invitation Archbishop Delmonico received printed in an L.A. Times article that claims to provide analysis of the event, but is only pure guesswork. The invitation appears legitimate, though:

GREETINGS. You are summoned to attend the World Religions Convocation at the L.A. Convention Center, starting at 2:00 p.m. PST, Monday, November 15, 2027.

Each attendee bears personal responsibility for the Convocation's success or failure. On behalf of their respective religions, attendees must agree to:

1. Eliminate religious intolerance and hatred by embracing the free and unfettered practice of all religions, or of none, by all;

2. Forgive and forever release past and current religious grudges, disputes and claims without recompense of any kind for the greater good of humanity;

3. Create mechanisms to address and resolve future inter- and intra-religious disputes in a nonviolent, binding, precedent-setting manner; and

4. Examine your various religion's tenets, teachings and principles and discard, update or replace those deemed obsolete, unsuitable or contrary to current and projected future societal needs and mores.

The Convocation shall not exceed sixty (60) days in duration, weekends excepted. A signed agreement addressing each point set forth above must pass by unanimous vote of the attendees. Votes in favor shall bind every follower of each religion to uphold the agreement forever.

Each invitee must participate in utmost good faith. Failure to do so will subject the invitee, and followers of his or her religion, to harsh and immediate consequences.

Failure of the Convocation to fulfill all of the foregoing objectives shall consign mankind to extinction.   God

We'll never get this done. Not in a million years, much less sixty days.

An exasperated glance at the Convocation's logo up on the screen discloses a degree of intricacy in the sketch of the apple tree logo I'd missed. Crabapples hang from thin branches devoid of greenery. Dead leaves litter the ground. The whole picture's bleak, like our chances of success, but I get the symbolism. It's heavy-handed, but maybe the crowd God's invited needs it that way. If so, maybe I need to revise the welcoming speech I prepared last night.

I open the 'notes' app on my phone. Let's see. What can I change to wow God's chosen four hundred?

12 | Ballroom Blitz

November 15, 2027,
L.A. Convention Center, 1:35 pm

No one's greeting fellow invitees with any warmth. Priests ignore each other. Instead of socializing, a few orange-robed Buddhist monks chant quietly, seated cross-legged on the floor to my left. Two Hasidic Jews traipse down an aisle in silence. The first five rows remain empty. The wall stations are, too.

From his media appearances I recognize Archbishop Delmonico as he waltzes in. He's in his mid-fifties, tall and thin, with an olive complexion that complements his aquiline nose, green eyes and thick black hair grayed at the edges. His odd loping gait, with arms that swing like he's treading water, give the impression that his upper body wants to move faster than his legs will allow.

Delmonico jumps onto the dais and plops into the chair next to mine. "Aha. Mr. Forrester. Good afternoon." We shake hands. "Quite a show you put on last week." His enunciation is precise, his expression genial.

I make a 'who, me?' gesture. "Our guest surprised me too, Archbishop."

"May I ask how this event came together?" The Archbishop has one arm resting on the dais, and one leg casually crossed over the other.

"I haven't a clue. But I do have a couple of questions for you, if you don't mind."

"Ask away." His legs uncross and he sits upright.

I move my water glass back a few inches so I don't knock it over by mistake. "First, if you'd care to tell me, I'm curious to learn who you saw when God changed his appearance."

The sparkle in his eyes matches his broad smile. "You may know I'm Franciscan. I met the first pope from my denomination in Rome during my youth—"

"Pope Francis I?"

"Yes. He wasn't a pope yet, and happened to pass by our church tour group on a street near the Vatican. When he stopped to chat, something in his manner told me his way should become mine. It is." Delmonico turns his glass over and fills it from the nearby water pitcher.

"How interesting. My next question is whether you believe I interviewed God."

He hesitates. "I didn't want to, but practical people can't deny what they see. The earthquake clinched it. Humans can't predict one with such precision."

"My take, too, despite my atheism. Maybe I should say former atheism—I'm confused."

Delmonico reaches out, tapping my arm twice. "I pray you'll come to Christ in your own good time. You've taken a good first step."

Have I? I'm not about to take a second step. "I'd like you and anyone else here from Southern California to form an interim steering committee that can guide this group until some other form of organization emerges. You're the best choice. I'm only here to get things started."

"I'm happy to help, Mr. Forrester. Thanks for asking."

At two p.m. sharp I step to the lectern, grip it, face the crowd and wait for them to notice me. The Archbishop touches my arm. Somehow the room's buzz has ratcheted way up without my noticing it. Everyone's shouting at me. The babble hits me like a slap to the face.

What on earth's going on here?

A deafening thunderclap drowns out the audience noise, followed a millisecond later by a huge lightning bolt that flashes out of the big screen. Most everyone in the middle section dives for cover. The bolt arcs over them and demolishes a refreshment stand near the doors.

Rain comes down in sheets. How the hell can we have an indoor thunderstorm?

Johnny Ray grabs an urn and empties it onto the small fire. His partner runs into the hall instead of helping. The fire alarm and automatic sprinkler systems don't activate.

"Silence, every last one of you!" The powerful urgent command comes out of thin air from somewhere behind or above me. Or perhaps it's everywhere at once.

Is this the voice of God? What else could explain it?

The rain ends as though a faucet's been turned off. The room quiets, except for the rustling of people reseating themselves. Several glance back at the burnt pastries, others stare at the water-covered floor—the room has no drainage capacity. Some attendees squeeze water from their clothes. A burnt cinnamon smell wafts past me.

The Archbishop regards me with bugged out eyes, his jaw slackened and mouth wide open. His hair stands on end from static electricity. I've never seen such a shocked look on anyone's face, but many in the audience share some version of it.

I lean toward him and speak in a near whisper. "If you have any idea what's going on here, tell me."

"After that bellow of yours, I'm surprised you don't know."

"I did that?" My astonishment might outdo his. This is all so bizarre.

"Your chest pumped up, your face turned dark red. Those words and that voice came right from your lips. When you pointed at the screen the lightning bolt flew out."

"That's impossible. Do you think I brought the rain down, too?"

"I don't know. I had to duck to avoid the lightning bolt."

I shake my head, glance down and shrug. I'd best get on with my speech.

"Gentlemen, ladies, do I have your full attention now? Good. First, thanks for attending. I apologize for the unscheduled rainstorm. I know travel and long-term hotel stays add up to a huge imposition and that compulsion, not choice, brought you here.

"I'm Ram Forrester. I have a few words to say before this gathering is declared open." I place my cellphone where I can easily read my revised notes and bring them up on my screen.

"This quote is from Romans 8:28 of the Bible: 'We know God causes all things to work together for good, for those who love God, for those who are called according to his purpose.' God's already told us what the purpose of this Convocation is. We're here to reach an agreement across all faiths to permanently eliminate religious violence. None of us want the alternative—humanity's extinction. I'm sure this God doesn't want that either. You each love your religion's versions of God, right?"

No one claps. They love the retired God, not this new one. He's not off to a good start earning their affection, either.

"I'm sure the phrase 'those who love God' fits each of you in your own way. That love led to your selection as one of four hundred, out of a world of billions. Your participation is an obligation, but it's also an honor. If you discharge your duties, everyone alive today, and the uncounted generations that follow, will reap the benefits. You'll do an incalculable amount of good. In what better way can you serve God and humanity?"

A smattering of applause is better than none. Maybe I'm getting through to some of them.

"Romans 8:28 starts with 'we know that God causes all things to work together for good.' God wants to see you cooperate. Show him you can and you'll leave this hall at the end of the Convocation as saviors. Hold your heads high, rejoice and know that love of God and your diligence will ensure that mankind passes God's test with flying colors."

Their applause is louder but polite. I don't see many friendly expressions. Maybe they fear another lightning bolt if they boo.

"I'll now ask those of you who reside in Southern California to come up to the dais."

Three people come forward to join me and the Archbishop. I've seen the big guy on television, but his name draws a blank.

"I'd like the four of you to introduce yourselves and state whether you'll agree to share temporary steering committee duties. Let's start with Archbishop Delmonico."

Delmonico does as I request. The big man's next. "I'm Zacharias Gilliam, but folks hereabout know me as Father Zeke." His deep baritone voice would reverberate off the walls even without a microphone. "For nine glorious years I've pastored at an African Methodist Episcopal Church in this area. I welcome y'all and agree to serve on the committee."

A young Hapa man speaks next. "I've no clue why God selected me. Unlike many of you, I've done nothing noteworthy." He looks down at the table, runs a hand over his goatee and peers with a shy expression at the audience. "My name's Shlomo Nakamura and I—"

The immediate buzz his name creates subsides once the crowd obeys his frantic quiet down gestures. "Folks, my dad's Japanese, a Shinto worshipper. My Mom's devout in her Ukrainian Jewish customs. Mixed ethnicity's normal in America. I grew up with a choice of religions but I'm a total mama's boy, so I chose Judaism. Six months ago I became chief rabbi at the Sinai Temple in West L.A. Only God knows why, but today I'm here. Oh, also, my friends call me 'Slomo' because I talk real fast, as you've probably already noticed. All of you can call me that, too. Sure, Mr. Forrester, count me in. Why not?"

Nakamura had helped the final person, a stooped older woman with a cane, onto the dais. She stands and gives the audience the Buddhist *Anjali Mudra* greeting. That done, she sits, starts to speak, stops and begins again once Slomo moves his microphone in front of her.

"Thank you again, young man. I'm called Reverend Mother Verma." Her eyes do a slow sweep of the hall over her granny glasses.

"Although I'm a Buddhist nun, I serve as President of The University of the West. As a nonsectarian institution founded by the *Fo Guang Shan* Buddhist Order, we practice humanistic Buddhism. That means we strive to integrate our practices into everyday life. Faith in humanity is a core Buddhist concept. That's why I'm here, I think. I too shall serve on your committee, though I'm most unworthy of the honor."

"Thank you all," I say to the others on the dais. "I hereby declare the 2027 World Religions Convocation open for business. May God, as you perceive him or her, help us make this gathering succeed. I'll leave in a moment to prepare my talk show, but first want to pass along one last detail."

I explain the law enforcement situation and the need to use the Apple Tree logo as an entry pass. As I walk off the dais and head to the door, I give Johnny Ray a signal to follow me.

"You heard my spiel a moment ago?" He nods enthusiastically. "What did your company say about you and Luis helping us?"

"Why, we're clear, Mr. F."

"Excellent. You're a godsend. I'm leaving, but feel free to text or call anytime."

We're off and running. Not in circles, I hope, or in the wrong direction. An indoor rainstorm isn't the most auspicious way to start, but we've got fifty-nine days to get on the right track. Will we?

BRENDALI

November 15, 2027, KJCR-TV, 1:46 p.m.
Upon reaching my dressing room I lock the door to take some aspirin and avoid people until my headache stops throbbing.

No sooner do I down the pill than the door opens. The one person I'd least want to see enters. "Hey, roomie! Thought I'd run into you before long. I'm Kate—Kate Chung."

So this is Ram's ex, the one who deserted him when he needed her most. How could she? The hand she thrusts at me is visible in my mirror. I don't shake it. "Nice to meet you," I say in a neutral voice.

"I have to do a quick change. My cosmetician spilled make-up powder all over me, see?" She points to a few tiny blotches on her white dress and rushes to her side of the room.

A half-foot taller than me, Kate oozes confidence. Her thick braid, like mine, extends to her waist. Maybe I'll cut mine off. She's the perfect L.A. fashion plate—big brown eyes, a creamy complexion and that bust she shows off while her dress lays crumpled on the floor. From what Ram says, she's an 'it's all about me' person. Ego-trippers aren't my type.

She steps into a gorgeous orange, gold and black arabesque patterned Chinese style one-piece dress. "Brendali, would you mind zipping me up?" She turns her back to me, so I oblige. "We have a lot to talk about, but not right now, my show's about to start. How about this afternoon?"

"I have to prepare for tonight's show. I'll take a break at some point, though, yeah."

She rushes to the door. "Good," she says while walking out. "I know a great place nearby."

"Fine," I say, under my breath. She might've yelled "I'll find you" as the door closed behind her. God, tell me I heard wrong, or make sure she forgets.

For the entire two block walk to her great place, also known as Starbucks, Kate vents about a minor technical glitch on her show. I don't blame the staff when things go wrong, but she can't forgive human error. I tune her out. Stuff happens, Kate, even in a newsroom. Get over it.

The barista takes our orders—a double shot caramel latte for Kate, green tea for me—and we find an empty table in a quiet corner.

Kate grabs her cup like she's about to chug a beer. "Have you settled in somewhere yet?"

"I'm looking around, taking my time." I blow on my tea to cool it down. "Fine for now, though." She might ridicule me if I tell her I'm house-sitting my folks' place.

A little latte foam dribbles onto Kate's chin, which she wipes off with a cocktail napkin. "I know the most marvelous real estate agent. He found me my place in San Marino. I'm sure he can help you. Would you like his phone number?"

"Sure, thanks." Of course she'd live in an overpriced status neighborhood. Big deal. I'm an Alhambra homie. I prefer to know my neighbors, not isolate myself from them.

She takes a pen out of her purse, writes on the soiled napkin and hands it to me. "Here you go. I gave you my number, too. To put down roots, you'll need a few girlfriends."

I choke on my tea, recovering after a few coughs. "I appreciate your offer, Kate."

"You can call me Cai, my real name. It's Mandarin for 'wealth' or 'money.' Kate's my stage name."

No other name would fit, no? "My name's Brendali. Feel free to call me that."

She ignores my cattiness. "Ram wouldn't ever call me Cai. To him it sounds like 'guy.' He'd call me 'doll' instead. He thinks I look like one. Men!" She shakes her head hard enough for the braid to swing back and forth, but doesn't laugh.

I'm not even his girlfriend, yet Ram's so attentive to me. It's easy to imagine her manipulating him, she's that type and he's so easygoing. Three years of hell together, he said. I feel so sorry for him. Never would I take advantage of him like she has if we become a couple.

"Kate, I mean Cai, I wonder if you'd—" I hesitate by sipping my tea. "If this is too personal, tell me. Ram said you two split up. Now that we've met, I wonder why. You'd make a great couple." I manage to say all that without once choking on my words.

She looks into her cup and twirls the latte around. "I don't mind." The insincerity in her voice is clear. "We wanted different things. He urged me to have his children, with or without marriage, but I refused. My figure would go to hell, and I'd have to kiss my career goodbye. Add in breastfeeding, diapers, motherhood—yuck, what a bother. If he only wanted marriage, fine. We talked and talked. He pushed, I resisted. Finally, I pulled the plug."

Never can I see her as a mom, but as the wife from hell she's a natural. If what she says is true, Ram avoided a lifetime of emotional abuse and alimony payments. "Ram sounded sad about the breakup." Not really, but let's see how Kate responds.

"He's not the only one." She snaps the stirrer stick in half and drops it on the floor.

Ah, she still has feelings for him. I'll need to watch her if Ram and I get romantic. Those innocent little kisses we shared in the hospital told me he's interested. So am I. If I ever sleep on her side of his bed and she learns about it she'd explode, no?

"The timing, right when he got shot, wasn't ideal," Kate adds. "I felt bad about that for a few days but the relationship needed to end. He'll move on, some new girl will come along—" She gives me a hard stare. "Are you thinking of going after him?"

Are you a mind-reader? This is why you wanted to talk to me and become friends—you want Ram back and I'm competition, no? Sorry, but you chose a trophy house in San Marino over him. I hope you enjoy all that expensive empty space.

"Right now I have a new show and need to settle in somewhere. Romance can wait."

She bats her eyes at me. "Are you attending the church service tomorrow for Sammy's funeral? It's early, at 8 a.m., so our employees can attend."

Sammy died for me? Why didn't Ram tell me? Oh, God. Veronica, Javier, Fernando, now him. My life isn't worth all these deaths. I feel my face flush, close my eyes, cross myself twice—for Sammy, for me—and bow my head. I can't let myself shed tears in front of her.

From my reaction Kate must know how saddening this news is, but she does nothing to extend comfort. Instead, she takes a giant gulp and drains her cup.

"Excuse me, Kate—uh, Cai. I need to use the bathroom." I beat a hasty retreat and find the restroom open. Inside, I check my cellphone to see if the Convocation app's functional. It is, so I use the message board for the first time. 'God, why'd you cause Sammy's family and me all this pain? He didn't have to die. Never should he have died.'

Complaining to God makes me feel worse. I feel so sorry for Sammy, his wife, their little ones. I stare into my face through the mirror and will myself to hold my emotions in long enough to get away from Kate. Once I've built up my resolve, I return to her.

"I don't know what to say to Sammy's wife." My throat catches but a sip of tea clears it. "This obnoxious religious guy started in on me about God's interview. Sammy tried to deal with the guy. Soon I lost sight of him. I feel so guilty. What can I say? Sammy did his best to protect me. What a lame thing to tell a widow." A loud sniffle escapes, but Kate ignores it.

Kate taps my hand. "You never got to know him. Sammy's such a take-charge guy. Believe me, Elena will understand. She knows Sammy would do anything to protect the people around him. Why not come to the funeral with me?"

"I'll let you know. I'd like to go. I'll need to fit it into my schedule." I'll go for sure. I must, but not with her. Ram can cover the Convocation without me for a few hours. I can feel myself tear up, and use a cocktail napkin to do a quick wipe. I really need to leave.

Kate looks at her phone and writes on a clean napkin this time. "Here's the church's address. Call me, show up, whatever works."

I take the offering and stuff it in my purse. "Thanks. Sorry to leave but I have a lot of preparation to do for tonight's show." I hustle out the door and sob all the way back to the station.

14 | Gotta Serve Somebody

BRENDALI

Tuesday, November 16, 2027, St. Teresa of Avila Church, Silver Lake

This building's brilliant white stucco exterior is gorgeous. The statue of St. Juan Diego greeting visitors in the courtyard is, too. Inside the chapel, carvings in the dark wooden beams and apse speak to the carpenters' love of God. Pews are high-backed. Statues and alters everywhere promote devotion to Catholicism.

I'm alone on a cushioned corner seat in the last pew. So many mourners are here to pay their respects to Sammy, I can feel the love despite all the crying around me.

To start the ceremony the Father smiles and stretches his arms out as though he's hugging everyone. At the signal we stand, lower our heads, cross ourselves, say silent prayers and take our seats.

"Lord Almighty, we are gathered here this morning to speed the journey back to you of our beloved son, who passed from us far too young under tragic circumstances. We beseech you, Lord, receive and honor our dear departed Sancho Rios, known to all as Sammy—"

Kate, fashionably late, whispers a hello while taking the seat next to mine. The service goes on, and on, and on. So many people give eulogies—Sammy's brother, father, friends from the Marines, a childhood buddy. I don't attend many funerals, thank the lord, but this one's a slog.

God, give Sammy the eternal peace he deserves. I wrap my arms across my chest to calm myself when my eyes start to water. Kate responds to my sniffles by putting her arm around me. I appreciate the gesture but can't respond to it.

"Cry if you need to," she whispers. "A funeral service isn't for the deceased."

Yes, I know. "I feel terrible about this," I whisper back. "Sammy's death is my fault."

"No, it isn't. You worked together and this happened, that's all. For whatever reason, Sammy's time to go arrived."

"The man who killed him wanted to kill me, not Sammy." I shouldn't have blurted those words out.

"What?" Surprise caused her voice to rise loud enough for those near us to hear. We get a few cross looks, but no bigger reactions.

"It's complicated, Kate. This isn't the place or time to go into it."

Once the service ends, we wait until the other mourners walk out. Kate stage whispers as they pass by. "Some of the gals from the station plan to visit Elena Wednesday night. We set up a GoFundMe college tuition account for her kids. It's already got $30,000. She'll feel better when we spring it on her. Why don't you join us?"

Spending time with Kate isn't my idea of fun but this is an extraordinary, compassionate thing they're doing. I'll make a contribution for sure—a big one. "I'd like to, but because of my show, I can't arrive before 9:30. Is that too late?"

"We'll probably finish by ten, but stop in. You can get to know Elena. I'll text you her address." We head toward the doors. "I told Elena you'd attend the funeral to pay your respects and fill her in on Sammy's last moments. Follow me, I'll introduce you."

Once outside we walk together toward a plump redhead dressed in widow's black who is speaking to an older woman leaning against a hearse. The boy and girl with them, maybe six and ten years old, don't deserve to grow up without their Papa.

"Elena," Kate says, interrupting their conversation. "This is Brendali."

She shakes my hand and gives me a wan smile. "Thanks for coming here today."

"I wouldn't miss it. Sorry that Ram can't make it. One of us has to cover the Convocation." She nods as though blowing off Ram's absence." If you don't mind, can we speak in private for a moment?" I nod toward the little ones.

"Children, stay here with grandma and Auntie Kate. I'll come right back." She gives each of them a hug. The little boy doesn't let go. Kate bends down, takes his hand and whispers. His other hand grabs his *abuela's* forearm and holds tight. We move away but he doesn't stop screaming for Mamá not to leave him.

Pequeño, I know how much you need Mamá right now. Don't worry, she'll return soon, safe and sound. She needs to hear what only I can tell her, something that will forever burden my heart if I don't. Five minutes, I promise.

In the shadows of the church porch, I tell Elena how Sammy died. When she starts to weep I embrace her. She bawls all over me.

"If ever I can do anything for you or your children, you have only to ask. I mean that."

"Oh, don't worry about us." She wipes tears away, using her sleeve. "We'll survive."

Our embrace ends. "No, you must. Sammy saved my life, gave up his. I owe him more than I can ever repay. Please let me help, however I can. I'd feel much better if you would."

She takes my hands in hers. "We should get back to the car. Everyone's waiting. But thank you for your words. They mean a lot to me." She lets go, takes a few steps and stops.

"You know, when everyone saw their God on your show, I saw Sammy. He looked odd, sort of removed. This glow surrounded him. Somehow I knew he'd leave us soon. I didn't know how, or when. I only hoped he wouldn't feel too much pain during the transition."

Her tears flow again while a shiver runs up my spine. No words come so I reach out and take her arm. We hustle back to the limo in silence. The children, grandmother and Kate wait for us, along with a man I've never met. The boy runs to his mamá, who lifts and hugs him. He laughs, happy for her physical contact.

The man's big boned, with a flushed face, jowly chin and a potbelly covered by a threadbare old suit.

"Brendali," Kate says, "have you met Jack Allenby? He took over evening news anchor duties after Ram got shot. Jack, Brendali's the cohost on Ram's new talk show."

"Yup, saw the show." He's swaying, drunk despite the early morning hour. "A wetback. They're here ta help Mexico steal Calf— Calf—Caforna, ya know."

"Oh Jack, how dare you!" Elena gasps. Kate cringes but says nothing.

I get right in his face. "Let's talk politics some other time." How insulting he is. "Not here. Not now. We're paying our respects to Sammy."

He gives me an unfocused, disdainful look. "Grassy-ass, senior-iter. Good man, Sammy." Allenby grabs Elena and her son in a bear hug before she can ward him off. "Gonna miss da guy." He wanders off on a zigzag path toward the parking lot. Elena's son makes a face and waves away the strong alcohol smell.

"He won't really get behind the wheel and drive drunk, will he?"

Kate answers. "Ken hired a driver for him. His license is permanently revoked."

"I'm truly sorry he offended you, Brendali," Elena says. "He's a horrid man. Ken should fire him for those words, and for so many other things Sammy told me about."

"That won't happen," Kate says. "He's had enough opportunities. Unless Jack's not sober enough to anchor the news, Ken doesn't care."

Allenby insulted all three of us with one sentence. Where'd he get his venom from? What caused his alcoholism? Self-loathing does horrid things. Don't I know it? Why does Ken protect him? What did Elena mean about things Sammy told her? Something's not adding up.

15 | Getting to Know You

RAM

**Tuesday, November 16, 2027,
Convention Center, 1:00 p.m.**

"Aha. Mr. Forrester. Good afternoon." Archbishop Delmonico and I shake hands.

"Fill me in. What, if anything, have I missed since I left yesterday?"

"Reverend Mother Verma's taken the lead." He smiles. "The dynamic's interesting. Despite your plea to put agendas aside, some members have them. But no one's upset with Verma. She's our nice Buddhist grandmother, always in the here and now, with no agenda whatsoever."

"Does she have any particular role on your committee?"

"She'll interact with the Buddhists, of course, and the indigenous religions. But she's our de facto morale officer, too. If an argument erupts, she'll calm it. If a misunderstanding arises, she rights it. When something needs saying she has a memorable way of making her point and getting people thinking."

"Maybe she should've gone into diplomacy instead of religion."

"In my experience, being God's emissary is a daily exercise in diplomacy."

"Glad she's with us. What roles do Father Zeke and Slomo Nakamura have?"

"Zeke stays in touch with the various Protestant faiths. He has this appealing folksy earnestness, and knows his Bible well enough to spout a relevant passage in every conversation, sometimes two."

"How about Slomo?"

"He's a pleasant surprise." Archbishop Delmonico gestures at the nearest coffee urn. We head toward it. "He asked to liaise with the Middle Eastern and Asian religions, other than Buddhism. It's a natural match."

I come to a full stop. "Will the Muslims accept him? He's Jewish."

"He'll gain their respect. He speaks Arabic, has a graduate degree in Muslim-Jewish relations from Stanford and knows the Koran, Torah and the interpretive issues of both religions' many sects. He's also active in the interfaith movement. No doubt he'll make his mark one day."

"And you? What's your role?"

"I get the coffee." Delmonico hands me an empty coffee cup and takes another for himself. "Actually, I intend to stay attuned to whatever goes on. I'll cheerlead or course-correct if necessary, in addition to liaising with my fellow Catholics."

We join the short line to pour our drinks. "Has anything been accomplished beyond putting the steering committee in charge?"

"We're not in charge," Delmonico says. "We steer. Cliques have already formed. We need to build bridges between them. Slomo had the sensible idea of holding multi-faith prayer sessions to start each day. Those began today, although the sparse attendance disappointed me."

"Give it time. What's the Vatican's word on the Convocation? I've been looking for a press release but they haven't issued one."

His face turns serious. "Is your question off the record?" I nod. "I expected that Pope Francis III might not want to stick his head out this soon in his prelacy. He's younger than most new pontiffs, and unproven." He glances at me. "But he's indicated that he's all for a successful outcome, whether or not this god's authentic."

"That's sensible, since we don't have to worry about extinction that way." The urn fills my cup with vanilla latte.

The Archbishop gets plain black coffee. "I'd counsel every faith present to accept whatever agreement we enact. Rejection will only invite this new god's vengeance. I get the impression he's that kind of deity."

"I liken him to the Old Testament God." I reach for a napkin and hand another to the Archbishop, who nods in appreciation.

"That's an astute observation, coming from an atheist." He takes a quick sip of his coffee. "Ah, rather surprising, these urns. Everyone gets their individual choice of liquid refreshment, brewed to perfection. Proof positive that Gods exist, don't you think?"

"Let's say my views are evolving." I turn toward the dais and stare at the big screen. The apple tree logo's undergone a noticeable change. The dead leaves and rotted apples have disappeared. Buds have sprouted on a few otherwise barren branches. The dark ominous thunderheads are gone, replaced by fluffy white clouds.

Delmonico follows my gaze. "There's some disagreement about what that means. I see it as a feedback mechanism. God's pleased, a little, at our slight progress."

"Once again you are wrong, Archbishop," the man behind us says. I turn toward him. "This is how Allah clears the land to renew the soil. Soon the fruit tree will disappear and we shall see marvelous desert."

"Hakan Çelik," Delmonico says, "meet Ram Forrester. Ram, Hakan's the closest thing we have to a Muslim extremist, but he falls far short of the mark." His smile and wink give away the lightheartedness of his introduction.

"A pleasure to meet you, Mr. Çelik." He resembles a fire hydrant, with short, thick legs and arms, a domed head, big ears, and a squat torso. He even spits when speaking.

"I may strike you as an extremist, Archbishop, but I'm in the mainstream to my people in Ankara. Remember, Turkey has been under Sharia law for several years now."

Hakan pokes me in the stomach with his finger. "Mr. Forrester, tell your audience the Muslim view of this proceeding is that this is the final step to Allah's ultimate victory over the infidel. Only in this way will a one-hundred percent buy-in occur." He stomps off without waiting for a response, ready to join the front line of his upcoming battle.

Delmonico puts his cup down on a nearby table. "That's what I meant by agendas. Did you notice anything unusual about Hakan?"

"Other than his physique, you mean?"

"He doesn't speak English, you know. I assume you don't speak Turkish. Yet you both understood each other."

"He spoke plain English. I didn't even detect an accent. You heard him."

Delmonico smiles. "In this hall we speak and hear in our native tongues. It's as though we're equipped with internal translators. Step into the hallway and the effect is gone."

Bren's arrival distracts me from this revelation. In this crowd she's like the Aurora Borealis brightening the arctic night sky. Even so, the tension in her face sets off my alarm bells.

"Archbishop, if you'll excuse me, I need to speak to Brendali." He nods and I head toward her.

She hands me her cellphone. "I received this text while I drove here. Did you get it, too?"

The message is short, to the point. 'You and Forster will not escape eternal hellfire. God has our back, you should watch yours.'

This NITWIT group bugs me to no end. "I haven't checked my texts. Does Griff know about this?"

Bren leans toward me, speaks in a soft, low pitched voice only I can hear. "Not yet. These jerks don't scare me. From now on I'm taking my protection along." She pats her purse. "The waiting period ended. I picked up the gun on the way here from Sammy's funeral."

"I'm not thrilled, but with NITWIT on the loose and the *narco* threats, I understand why you need it."

"I learned my lessons growing up and in Mexico. Sometimes you have to shoot first, ask questions later."

"Is the guy who ambushed us the only one you've killed?"

Her eyes flash before she answers. "People hunt animals, right? That's what those bastards are, animals in human form. I only shoot in self-defense. I said prayers for that man's soul in church, confessed my sin and received absolution."

Yeah, like that makes it all better. "I'm glad we survived. So far, getting to know you has been quite a unique experience." I give her a broad smile.

She grins and taps my arm. "We're all unique, no? You think you're the brainy one, so I provide the security. And, sorry, but I'm the beautiful one, too." She winks, chuckles and walks away. Her little extra wiggle isn't lost on me.

Ram's Convocation Twitter Update: First impression, hope I'm wrong. This gathering looks like a heavy lift. #thereistime #gettowork

---

BRENDALI

Tuesday, November 16, 2027, Convention Center
After leaving Ram's side, the first person I approach is Asian, probably Korean. "Good afternoon, sir. I'm Brendali Santamaria with KJCR-TV. Would you mind answering a few—"

He turns and walks away, so I try again with a man in African clothing. "Sir, I'd like to ask for your thoughts about—"

"Perhaps later," he says, staring at the big screen. "I'm busy at the moment."

He's busy doing what—meditation? I move on to a Caucasian man. Maybe small-talk would work better. "Hi. May I ask what country you're from?"

"Russia. You're wasting your time if you want to know more." He won't even look me in the eyes. "Perhaps the Japanese Jew will talk to you." He stomps off toward the seats.

Why am I getting treated like an alien? I spot the Reverend Mother at a refreshment stand, introduce myself and ask to chat.

She peers at me over her glasses. "Your interview last week fascinated me. Why don't we sit and learn from each other?"

"Here, let me help." I take her fruit plate and offer my arm, but she prefers her cane.

Once seated, she places the cane against the chair with deliberation while balancing the food plate in her lap. Her peaceful, serene vibe is impressive. Never can I achieve that state of bliss. If only I could, my anger spells would disappear.

"What's on your mind, my dear?"

"At the moment so many things are running through my brain. I'm not sure where to start." I squirm in my seat, and move my braid so it hangs in front rather than down my back.

"As a rule, it's best not to speak unless doing so improves the silence."

Yes, except I'm here to ask questions, not gape at people. "What's your impression of the Convocation so far?"

"As the Surangama Sutra says, 'things are not as they appear, nor are they otherwise.'"

From men I get rejection, from her, riddles. What's she trying to tell me?

Her smile is disarming. "We have begun. Buddhists look neither backward nor forward. We strive to stay in the present." She moves her cane so the handle rests against her thigh.

This woman thinks in an interesting, different way, but I need more from her. Maybe I should ask closed-ended questions. "I understand you're on the steering committee?"

"I have that honor."

"What do you do in this role?"

"I dispense serenity, as and where needed." She uses a fork to stab an apple slice from her plate. "On occasion, copious amounts are required."

Her words make me smile. "What sorts of occasions require the copious amounts?"

"Oh, we have many strong opinions in this hall. Only rarely are they the same." She winks, grins and pops the apple slice into her mouth.

I'm glad we have someone like this attending the Convocation. "When the shape change occurred during God's interview, what did He look like to you?"

Her eyes close, as those she's trying to remember. "I did not observe any changes."

"No? The whole world saw them. How could you not?"

"Buddhists do not, in general, believe in Gods. This saying from the Sutta Nipata, one of our sacred texts, may explain our views:

In what is seen, there should be just the seen

In what is heard, there should be just the heard

In what is sensed, there should be just the sensed

In what is thought, there should be just the thought.

"You see, my dear, he whom you interviewed said viewers would see God as each individual perceives him. Buddhists do not perceive God, so we saw, heard and sensed only your guest."

I don't know anything about Buddhism. This is fascinating. "Does this mean a god won't fit into your belief system?"

"No, Buddhism is compatible with a god's existence, if indeed we have one. Your question brings to mind this story of the Buddha:

A Brahmin once asked The Blessed One:

'Are you a God?'

'No, Brahmin,' said The Blessed One.

'Are you a saint?'

'No, Brahmin,' said The Blessed One.

'Are you a magician?'

'No, Brahmin,' said The Blessed One.

'What are you, then?'

'I am awake.'

"This God you interviewed says he's the god of us all. That is good, if he is. Buddhism is more philosophy than religion. As Buddha said, 'see the truth, and you will see me.'"

"You're saying it doesn't matter to Buddhists whether a God is or isn't present?"

"Correct. We require no god. If there is one, our beliefs do not change. We stay in the moment, as always."

"You've given me a lot to think about, Reverend Mother. I came to you for information, and I received—" What do I call this?

"Buddhist revelations? You are a devout Catholic. We all must have our belief systems, mustn't we?"

Ram doesn't have one. Would he find Buddhism worthwhile?

"I suppose so." I reach out, clasp her hand. "When this Convocation is over, I would like to learn more about your beliefs. Can Ram and I do a feature on you for our show?"

"Of course." She covers my hand with hers. "Come to our temple. Visitors are always welcome. Call me, or simply show up. I will personally give you both a grand tour."

"I promise to get in touch. Thank you for your time and your wisdom. Excuse me, I need to go hunt down whatever else I can find that's newsworthy."

"Certainly, my dear. Until we meet again."

Brendali's Convocation Update: First full day at the Convocation. Met some invitees, had interesting conversations. Too soon for any real progress, people are getting acquainted. #hopeful #settlingin

---

BRENDALI

Wednesday, November 17, 2027, 8:50 p.m.
"To finish our show tonight," I tell our viewers, "Ram has two quick Convocation interviews to show you."

"I did them," he says, "to help familiarize you with some of the attendees, and get their views on the Convocation. This first one is Slomo Nakamura."

The interview comes up on screen. "Mr. Nakamura, please tell our audience what your role is on the Steering Committee and how you expect to help make the Convocation a success."

"I work with the Middle Eastern and Asian religions—Jews, Muslims, Zoroastrians, Hindus, Copts, Jains, Maronites, others—about a hundred people in all. Some of these faiths have fought each other on occasion. We, however, interact on a person-to-person basis. We're getting acquainted now so we can build friendships or working relationships."

"You've started an interfaith morning prayer session." Slomo's energetic nods confirm Ram's statement. "Has that helped bring people together?"

"Yes. It's open to all attendees. This morning about half of them showed up. Camaraderie is created when folks of different faiths pray together."

I speak up once the video ends. "Slomo's got the right idea."

"If his attitude prevails, the likelihood of success will improve. Others, such as Caleb Kimball, who's Evangelical, are cool to this gathering's purpose. Let's watch his interview."

"Mr. Kimball, I know it's early, but what's your impression of the Convocation and your faith's involvement in it?"

"Many in my faith resent our inclusion. We're not buying into this so-called new God. But for the example set by the beheaded mullah, we wouldn't have shown up."

"Though you're not here by choice, do you see anything positive about the gathering?"

"To spend time among this crowd, meet people from all over the world and discuss our religious viewpoints has its positives. But if I had my druthers, I'd stay home. My wife had to plead with me to attend. She didn't want to risk me losing my head."

"We don't have time to show more interviews," Ram says to our viewers, "but I can tell you that the motivations of our four hundred invitees are not aligned." Ram and I get a sign-off signal, so he adds a hasty final comment. "In addition to those here by compulsion, not choice, I found a lot of single issue attendees. If they get what they want, they'll likely go along with the majority. We'll find out soon enough. Good night, we look forward to seeing you tomorrow."

I arrive at Elena Rios' home at 9:45. She lives in a small, neat bungalow-style house in Silver Lake. Kate's already gone and Elena's saying goodbye to three others as I reach the door.

"My apologies for stopping by so late, but I wanted to help prop up your spirits. Also, Ram and I each made a $1,000 donation to your children's college education."

"Oh, how wonderful," she says. "Thank you! The ladies told me the account is up to $38,000. Please, come in. Would you like some coffee?"

"I'd prefer tea if you have some." We drink, chitchat and share cherry pie in her cozy living room until Elena excuses herself and returns with a large three-ring binder. She sits next to me with it in her lap.

"This isn't something I need to keep. I want you to have it. Kate said you're an experienced investigative journalist, so you can decide what to do with it."

"What's inside?" The white binder's about half-full and has no cover or spine title.

"Sammy never liked or trusted Allenby or Ken. This contains his research into them. I haven't opened or read it, so—" Her voice tapers off.

"Sammy did research? Why? What set him off? He struck me as an easy-going guy, not someone who'd investigate his boss or co-workers." I put my teacup down and push it away so I can pay full attention to Elena's story.

"He couldn't understand why Ken protected Allenby." Elena refreshes her cup of coffee. "As an Army vet, Sammy expected Ken to act like a captain. He thought Allenby should've been fired after that poor young boy died."

"What boy? I haven't heard about this. Fill me in." Is Allenby always drunk?

"Jack had his driver's license revoked about five years ago, so—" She shrugs and appears unsure about what to say next. "He drove through a red light, trampled an eight-year-old boy in a crosswalk and didn't stop. It upset Sammy that the station didn't fire or discipline him. He decided to find out why."

I bring my hands to my cheeks. "Oh God, how terrible! Wasn't Allenby prosecuted?"

"No. That shocked everyone. The license revocation amounted to a slap on the wrist."

"This kind of thing often occurs in Mexico, not here." I'm sitting straight up because something's fishy. A fatal hit-and-run that kills a little boy isn't prosecuted? Why?

"I don't know much about Mexico, my family's Guatemalan. Ken arranged Allenby's limo and driver. Sammy told me the station pays for it. He challenged Ken, who passed it off as a reward for Allenby's popularity and all the charity work his foundation does. That didn't sit right with Sammy or anyone else."

I wouldn't accept that explanation either. "Allenby has a charitable foundation?"

"This incident happened when Allenby drove home from a dinner event where he received a Man-of-the-Year award. I don't remember which organization he got it from, but it had religious ties." With her hand up and her head cocked to one side, I assume she's sorting out her memories.

"Yes, that's right," she finally says. "Sammy doubted the legitimacy of Allenby's foundation. Allenby claims it raises and distributes funds to churches in the area to support social programs." As Elena puts her cup down on the coffee table the binder almost slips off her lap. She manages to grab it in time without spilling anything.

"That miserable drunkard has a good side? Never can I believe that."

"I agree. When Sammy heard the foundation passes out tens of thousands of dollars a year, he decided to find out the truth."

"Where would Jack get that kind of money?"

Elena shrugs and taps the binder. "Whatever Sammy found is in here." She hands it to me. "This is his investigation."

I riffle through the pages. The first of the three sections has over a dozen separate account records from small local banks and a few credit unions. How'd Sammy get hold of these records? Why'd Allenby spread the money around like this?

"Maybe you can do something with it. Sammy thought those two were in some sort of conspiracy, that someone should see they don't get away with whatever scheme they hatched."

"Did Sammy mention any ideas or conclusions he'd reached?" A lightning bolt hits—Ken can access the station's finances. Hard to think Ken would help Allenby embezzle money to give to churches. He's not religious, or likely to engage in criminal behavior. Ram knows these guys better than I do. What will he say about this?

"No," Elena said in answer to my question. We look at each other for a good half minute. Her face is hard, serious. Whatever this story is or becomes, it begs for a voice. If something's wrong here, Ram and I can provide one.

18 | Burning Down The House

BRENDALI

November 21, 2027, 1:36 a.m., Alhambra

"Brendali, wake up. Leave without delay. Your life depends on it."

My eyes pop open and sleep drains away fast. Did I hear the new God's voice? Christ, what a weird dream.

I fell asleep on a clean, dry bed. Now the bedcover's wet and sticky. And the stench, *Meirda!* I throw it off and sink my feet into a soaked carpet.

What the hell? Someone poured gasoline in here while I slept? Skeleton Man. I freeze. He said NITWIT means to burn me to death.

The backdoor bangs closed. Whoever the intruder is, he's gone. But he's not far away.

I flip on the light, leaving a bloody fingerprint smear on the wall. I'm bleeding? How? I turn and hold my hand up to the overhead light.

"Mi Dios, no!" My breath catches. "Nooooooo!"

Jalapeno hangs by his paws from a leash tied to the ceiling fan, a kitchen knife stuck in his chest. His blood's splashed over the bedspread.

I fly out into the cool night air, snagging my purse from the table by the front door on the way. If this jerk's in the street I swear to God I'll kill him. I have my gun, my car, my bare hands. I'll make sure he feels my wrath. This *bastardo's* guts should cover the street. Let the rats feast on them!

With a big whoosh the house explodes into a fireball. I scream and run past my car, block after block, passing darkened but moonlit houses that stand mute like giant tombstones. Before long I'm out of breath, on my hands and knees on someone's lawn with my forehead resting against the moist grass. My tears do the watering.

Thank you, Lord, for that warning. Twice you've saved my life. You need me for the Convocation, I know. Tell me how to serve you. I'll do anything, whatever you need. Never will I let you down.

In slow motion I rise to my knees, intent on wiping Jalapeno's blood off my fingers and onto the grass. Instead, unable to keep the bile down, I puke.

I head back to the house. Papí always says no one crosses a Santamaria without paying a price. This guy better hope he doesn't meet me alone, *mano à mano.* He'll pay for what he's done. I'll make sure of it.

Sirens sound in the distance. Good, someone's called 911.

I bypass the small crowd gathered on my street. None look out of place. Curled up on the curb with my back against the car, the flames mesmerize me as they incinerate my childhood home. I'd pound the sidewalk in frustration if I could take my eyes off the spectacle and my nostrils weren't full of the smell of burnt memories.

Mamá, Papí, I beg your forgiveness. I've let you down. After all you've done for me, I owe you a new home. I swear it, I'll make it up to you.

A child's uncontrollable cries distract me. Yes, *pobrecito,* I know the fire's scary. Don't worry. God will sometimes test us in severe ways, but He knows best. Trust him, always.

"Mi querida niña?" The question's repeated three times before I gaze up at the old woman who asked. A shawl covers her gray hair and curlers peek out from underneath a pink net. "You're Miguel and Rosa's daughter, yes? Here, wear this." She's holding a thick flowery, if faded, green housecoat wide open like a shield.

"Why do I need that? I'm sweating from the heat without it."

"Por favor," she says, over louder sirens. "You're naked. Put this on before the firemen come." This is a demand, not a request. She makes that clear by violent shakes of the housecoat.

Mi Dios, I ran out without clothes? A look down reveals the tiny black thong I wore to bed, and nothing else. I hope no one in the crowd's taken pictures. Now that I'm known worldwide, they'll go viral.

The housecoat stays draped over my shoulders while I wiggle into it and button the tent-like garment. "Thank you. Sorry, I don't know your name. My folks never introduced us." I should've done that, I've visited home often enough. "I'm Brendali."

"Maria Alvarez, *mi querida,"* she says with a broad smile. "You're welcome to stay with my family tonight, if you need a place."

"You're so kind. I might, I don't know." Where will I stay, or go? "I'm sort of overwhelmed." I shudder, realizing I'm now homeless, even clothes-less.

Firetrucks arrive, followed by police cars.

"I understand, dear," Maria says, patting my shoulder. "I know it would trouble you to tell me what happened, so I won't ask. Tell these men. I'll leave my door unlocked. You'll find a blanket and pillow on the living room couch if you need it."

I want to thank her but choke on my words. While she walks away firemen bark orders to each other and unload their equipment.

Ram will help me. He has to. My hands shake so much I have trouble opening my purse. By putting it on the hood and leaning against the car because my legs won't support me, I manage to call him. Never would I manage to find his number if he wasn't on speed dial.

Endless rings. Ram, I'll keep calling until you pick up the phone. Do it!

At last, a groggy hello. *"Mi Dios,* Ram. Sorry to wake you. Can you come here right away? Please? I have no one else to ask. Please!" My voice sounds breathless and broken.

I need you to hold and comfort me, Ram. Don't you dare let me down.

"Brendali? What's the matter? What's wrong?"

"Oh God. I can't believe this. My house, Ram—" A long explanation isn't possible. I'm too choked up. "NITWIT tried to kill me. Again."

"I'm leaving right away."

God bless you, Ram. Of course, he can't hear my blessing, but God can.

"Excuse me, miss. Is this your home?" The question comes from the policeman standing behind me.

"Oh, I'm sorry, officer. This is my parents' place. I house-sit for them."

"Are you okay? Do you need medical assistance?"

Do I? I don't know. "My friend's coming. I'll, um, survive until he arrives. If you have some water, that'd help. I need to rinse my mouth out."

"I'll see if we can rustle some up." His tone and the compassion in his eyes show me he understands the hell I'm going through. "The fire department's arson investigator and I need to take your statement. If you don't mind, I'll call him over. You can talk to us together."

"That's kind of you. I'll tell you whatever you need to know."

They return minutes later with a water bottle. I take it, spit out several mouthfuls and splatter the rest over my reddened fingertips. It takes a long time to answer their detailed questions, explain about NITWIT and provide Griff's phone number.

By now the firemen have knocked the flames down. All that's left is a blackened pile of wood, pipes, family history and Jalapeno's charred bones.

Never will I forget the image of him hanging from the ceiling fan. The knife in his chest, his blood splashed all over the bedcover. The scene replays in my head like a video, inducing shudders, shakes, vertigo, tears, nausea. I stay upright only by gripping the car's side mirror.

I'm suddenly turned around, pulled close and surrounded by strong arms. I can't see him through my tears, but I recognize Ram from his cologne and the tone of his voice. Whatever he's saying sooths, his warmth and touch reassure.

I use all my strength to hold him tight. Don't let go of me, Ram. Don't you ever let go. If you do I'll spin away from the world. God forbid, I may never return.

19 | Trouble No More

Sunday, November 21, 2027, 2:15 a.m., Alhambra

As if Brendali's bare feet, hideous old green housecoat and disheveled loose hair aren't enough to signal her despair, the tears gushing down her face and her moans drive the point home. She returns my bear hug with surprising strength.

She's lost her childhood home. The memories, emotional ties and guilt must overwhelm her. She'll feel responsible for this, although she's not. I'm sorry for her, mad at NITWIT, upset at what she's going through—but I have to quash my emotions and comfort her.

I'm muttering every empty meaningless phrase that comes to mind—don't worry, everything'll turn out fine, I'm here for you, etc. These words don't provide much comfort. Brendali's bawling and probably not even hearing them.

Our embrace only ends when she pulls herself together enough to use the front of my flannel shirt to wipe tears from her face. "Ram, someone got in and poured gasoline everywhere. One lit match and poof, I'm burned alive like Jalapeno. He's—he's—he's—oh, God."

She shudders and embraces me again. I pull her close, encircling her waist with one arm while my hand gentles her head flush against my chest. Her hair smells of soot.

Brendali's been through so much already, for no reason. I'd

better not come face to face with the guy who did this. I might decide to fulfill her second golden rule.

"Jalapeno—that's your mom's dog?"

I can barely understand her muffled response. "Her adorable little baby." She sniffles. "Never ever will Mamá forgive me." Brendali lets go, rubs a hand across her nose, wipes it on my sleeve and drops to her knees. She pulls on my arm, a signal for me to do likewise. Once I've complied she makes the sign of the cross, bows and mumbles a Spanish prayer. I don't recognize the words except *perro,* which means dog. I get the gist and add my "amen" when she's done.

While still in a crouch I peek around the street and see no obvious threat. We get to our feet. "I want to hear everything, no detail omitted. But right now we need to get out of Dodge."

"What? We're not in a car."

"I meant we need to leave right away."

"*Mi Dios,* why?" She hugs me again, this time with less strength.

"Local media will show up soon. You don't want a viral video to circulate of you in your housecoat, distraught and victimized by an arsonist."

That straightens her up. She steps back. "You're right, but where can I go that's safe?" She waves at the gutted ranch-style house and wipes one last tear away. "I have nowhere to—"

"I have a spare bedroom and the building's high-security. You're staying at my place until these threats get resolved."

She takes both of my hands in hers. "I'm not too much of a burden?"

"Brendali, I came here for you." I gently put my arms around her shoulders and stare into her eyes. "I'll do anything for you, anything at all, except let NITWIT hurt you."

She gives my cheek a soft caress. "You're so wonderful. It's as though God sent you to me." Her gaze drifts to what's left of the house. She inclines her head, sighs and puts a hand over her eyes. A few seconds later our hands interlock. "I don't want to see this mess in the morning, or deal with reporters. Let's get out of the Chevy, like you said."

"It's not a—never mind. Do you need to take anything out of your car?"

"My gym bag has workout clothes and my iPad. I can get the rest of my clothes out of storage tomorrow."

"We'll do that together and come back for your car, too."

Once we're in my Mustang, I command the car to drive us home and send Griff a text alerting him to the fire. Brendali tries to reach her folks in Mexico but the calls don't go through. She smothers my hand with both of hers, pulls it into her lap and doesn't let go. Her head rests against my arm while she stares out the window with a forlorn, exhausted expression.

NITWIT should target me, not her. It's my show. I'm the devil atheist, she's a devout Catholic. How dare they do this to her? I continue to obsess about the situation until we reach a red light a mile from home. In frustration, I slam my free hand against the steering wheel and scream a four-letter word I rarely utter.

Brendali shifts in her seat and looks up at me. "Don't get upset, baby. I'm thankful you came for me." Her fingers tickle my hair, probably to calm me down.

She needs comforting more than I do. I'd put my arm around her but she's still holding my hand captive. "We'll get through this, Brendali. Together, no one can stop us." I see gratitude in her eyes and deliver a little peck to her forehead. She sighs and nuzzles my arm with her cheek.

This is nice, the two of us snuggling like this. If only the circumstances leant an air of romance. I sigh.

Once in my condo, Brendali downs two glasses of chardonnay while filling me in on the fire. I only notice the time when she finishes. "It's nearly four a.m., we should get some sleep. I'll show you the guest bedroom."

Seated at the edge of the queen bed, she slumps over with her head bowed. Her hands clasp and unclasp in her lap. In a remorseful tone she speaks more to herself than to me. "I'm a tough, proud woman. Santamaria strong, Papí says. But right now I'm a total mess."

Her watery eyes cue me to hand her the tissue box by the nightstand. She attacks the tissues like they might otherwise run away, balling a bunch up without using them.

"I'm terrified, Ram. I came this close to burning." She extends two fingers less than an inch apart. "I can't sleep alone in the dark tonight. It's impossible. I have to know I'm safe." The flat inflection to her hushed voice speaks volumes. She dabs her eyes, blows her nose, takes a few wobbly steps to me and wraps her arms around my waist. Her head settles against my chest.

Neither of us move a muscle for what feels like eternity. The smoky aroma from her hair doesn't obscure the fear in her heart. Eventually, with a soft childlike tone, her words interrupt the solitude of our embrace. "Tell me you'll hold me all night, like you're doing now."

She wants to sleep with me? I can't say no to that. "If you need me to do that, I will."

"Promise you won't take advantage. I mean, I'm sure you won't, but—"

"For you? I'd swear on a Bible if I had one."

"Wait." She leaves the room, returning moments later. "Use this."

"Your phone?"

"It's open to my Bible app. Put your fingers on the screen and swear."

This is silly, but whatever. "Brendali, by all the power vested in this app I swear to keep my hands to myself tonight." With the solemn oath taken, we move to my bedroom.

"I can't sleep in this heavy thing my neighbor gave me." She pinches the housecoat. "Do you have anything lighter that might fit me?"

After rummaging through my dresser I hold a white Dodgers

T-shirt against her shoulders. "That looks a little short, maybe. Let me find something longer."

"It's okay. I'll make do."

"Do you want to shower first? You'd get rid of the smoke smell." She nods. "I'll get you a few towels." I leave two on the bathroom sink, along with the T.

While Brendali washes the soot away I throw her gym outfit and a few of my things in the washer, clean the glass she drank from and refrigerate the wine bottle.

"Jalapeno, noooo!" Brendali's anguished scream reverberates through the bedroom as I change clothes. I hustle to the bathroom door in my boxers. "What's wrong? What's going on?" I rap hard on the door, but she doesn't respond. "I'm coming in unless you tell me you're all right." Once more, silence.

The door's unlocked, so I burst in. She's frozen in place, staring into the mirror. Her hands cling to the edge of the sink the way a mountain climber grabs a ledge lip a thousand feet above ground. Unlike a mountaineer, all she's wearing is a flimsy black thong, the rosary necklace I gave her and a towel around her hair.

I pry her hands from the sink, grab and turn her toward me. Her eyes are glassy, nonreactive. "Brendali, say something." She doesn't. "Bren, please!"

I'd better call 911. I don't know how to deal with this.

A single tear rolls down her cheek, which I wipe away with a finger before kissing her forehead. To my happy surprise, this focuses her on me. "Oh, Ram!" She lunges, throwing her arms around me.

I put my arms around her trembling body with care, so my oath isn't broken. "You scared the crap out of me, Brendali." Although her breasts aren't large, I'm very conscious of her nipples pressing against my chest. "What the hell happened?"

"I looked in the mirror and—and—and—" She takes a deep breath. "Poor Jalapeno. I couldn't move or look away. I waited to burn up with him."

Brendali breaks free, rushes to the toilet and raises the lid. On her knees, she vomits liquid—the wine, I suppose—into the bowl.

She lowers herself to the heated tile floor, her face chalky, and groans. Folded up—knees to chest, arms clasped around legs, back pressed against the white wall, forehead touching knees—she's despondent. Those groans break my heart.

I sit next to her and snake my arm around her bare shoulders. "What can I do to help you feel better?"

She unfolds, nestles her head against me and tilts onto her side. One leg crosses over mine. A hand reaches across my body to rest on my hip. "I don't know. I've never had flashbacks before, not even after seeing mass gravesites uncovered in Mexico." All this is said in a hushed, slow tone. "I'm glad you brought me here. You're my true *radiante caballero blanco.*" She plants a little kiss where her mouth is, inches below my shoulder.

Her words are electric in my ears. Maybe it's the whispered Spanish or how her body's posed. I shouldn't feel aroused, but can't help it. As a distraction, I grasp her rosary necklace. "Do you always wear this in the shower?"

"I love this. Never does it come off, even when I sleep. Whenever I see the necklace, it reminds me of you." A blush appears on her cheek. "I'm sorry to cause you all this trouble."

"Think nothing of it. Ask me for whatever you need, whenever the need arises. I'll make sure you get it."

"I'm so glad we met. The sooner I wipe that horrible scene from my memory, the better." She shivers and scans the bathroom, probably for tissues, but I'm not inclined to get them. "I have to accept what's happened, no? Somehow the fire is part of God's plan."

"Your absolute faith in him is humbling," I admit. "I don't have anything or anyone to inspire me that much."

"God's always given me inner strength." She sits up, gently turns my head with her hand so she can gaze intently into my eyes. "He'd do the same for you, if you'll let him. I can show you how to give yourself to him."

I can't accept the offer. "You're special, Bren." I use two fingers to brush her cheek. "You've gone through so much, yet you'd do this for me?"

"A gift, from my soul to yours." The sexiness of her whisper amazes me. Our eyes lock, inches from each other. I could stare into hers forever. Her lips move within an inch of mine. About to kiss me, she backs away. "Umm, do you have an extra toothbrush?"

"Sure." With regret I get one and put it by the sink, along with toothpaste and a bottle of mouthwash. I help Brendali stand and take a step toward the door to give her some privacy.

She grabs my wrist. "Don't leave. I don't want to frighten you again." That's not the real reason, of course. She's afraid of another flashback.

While she brushes her teeth and washes her face I lean against the doorframe, taking notice of all the things her body doesn't have. It's flawless—no piercings, tattoos, tan lines or blemishes.

"Sorry I'm staring, Bren. Your body, it's—" I should've stopped with the apology. I don't want her to feel uncomfortable.

"I'm used to it. Guys stare when I'm dressed, too. Sometimes I like the attention. It depends on the guy. God brought us together. Somehow we're necessary to his plan, so I don't mind you seeing me naked." She takes off the towel and dons the T.

"All I'll say is wow." I look away.

"Your boxers are wow, too. I saw a big bump in them earlier." She grins and gives my midsection a long look. "It's gone now. Too bad, I kind of liked it." Her come-hither look tests my oath, but I don't waver.

Once we're in bed she shimmies over to snuggle against me. Tipped on her side again, her head uses my shoulder as a pillow. Despite the T, a nipple tickles my skin.

Good luck falling asleep now, dude.

"This is comfortable for you, no?"

"I'm fine. Do you mind if I turn off the light?"

"No. Goodnight, *mi radiante caballero blanco.*" Her kiss lingers until it becomes a slow, tender but tired French kiss. If I take it further, I'll break my oath. Instead I reach my free arm over to toggle the lamp off.

If having Bren in my bed is part of God's plan, I'm totally on board.

RAM

Sunday, November 21, 2027, 10:15 a.m.

Underneath the covers, Bren's sprawled on top of me like I'm her mattress. Her hair blankets my face, her legs nuzzle the outside of my thighs and I've somehow slept with my arms wrapped around her waist. With most of the morning gone, I can't lay here until she wakes up.

Once I've finessed my way from underneath her and step out of bed, she curls into a fetal position. If angels can look angelic while asleep in a Dodgers T and a thong, she does. To keep her warm, I move the comforter up to her neck and turn the thermostat up a few degrees. On the way to the kitchen I move our washed clothes to the dryer so she'll have something to wear.

My cellphone pings while I fill the coffee brewer with water. "Hey, Griff, thanks for the callback. Yeah, we've had a new, ominous development. Brendali's parents' house burned—"

"You think I don't know that?" His loud voice makes me yank the phone away from my ear. "I'm no dummy. You didn't leave a stressed-out message at three a.m. to talk college football with your ol' bud Griff, right? Alhambra PD gave me the lowdown. Arson." He says that word like he's spit out something distasteful. "How's Brendali doin'?"

"She's unhurt, but emotionally fragile. She'll stay with me until NITWIT's dealt with."

"That arrangement has some, uhh, clear advantages." A pregnant pause ensues before he resumes. "I don't like what's happenin' one blasted iota. I need to see you both right away. Expect me around noon, after church."

"Maybe a little later? Bren needs to sleep. She's had a traumatic few days."

"Okay, two o'clock. Sheesh, you civilians are such softies." He ends the call.

I take out omelet fixings to prepare a breakfast Bren will enjoy. An unopened jar of jalapeno jelly gets tossed into the trash. Ginger-peach jam will work fine for the rye toast.

Midway through dicing veggies a hand touches my hip. A freshly perfumed female body presses against my back. Another hand reaches around to caress my chest. *"Buenos dias, mi radiante caballero blanco."* The sleepy tone enhances the sexiness of Bren's voice.

Oh, man, today she's a seductress? "Careful, I don't want to slice off my thumb." I put the knife aside. "You sound fantastic for someone who went through hell last night."

"It's a new day. Read Psalm 30."

Which one's that? I never could keep them straight back in my Bible study days.

"The words are 'weeping may endure for the night, but joy cometh in the morning.' I live by that motto." She turns me around so we're face-to-face, her arms around my waist, mine resting on her shoulders. "Last night you promised to provide whatever I need, remember? Today I need all the joy you can bring me."

Her eyes, focused on mine, have the same dreamy quality I saw in them at the hospital. "You're such a gallant man to help a damsel in distress in the middle of the night."

"Any guy would."

"Not the ones I've known."

I move my hands to her hips, over the Dodgers T. "You don't know the right men."

Her finger traces my cheek and jaw before coming to rest on my lower lip. "I know one, someone I've become a little bit intimate with. Someone I feel very close to." The sensuality in her voice is unmistakable.

I cover her hand with mine and move our intertwined fingers away from my face. "Are you trying to get me to break my oath?"

"You only took a one-night oath. And you said I'm wow."

"True." This is an invitation. "If we do what I think we're about to, things could get kind of complicated at work."

"God's wishes are more important, no?" On tip-toes, she uses both hands to bend my head so our lips are within kissing distance. "We can't disobey Him."

"We sure can't." I lift her up. She wraps her legs around my waist, whips off the T and coils her arms behind my neck. Our tongues share a long, hungry, passionate French kiss. Her sighs sound like music from heaven.

Brendali ends the kiss with a soft whisper. "Last night, asleep in your arms, God told me his plan for us." Her breath's like an intoxicating cool breeze, although it's only the aroma of my mint mouthwash. "I woke up happy. I want you to share my happiness."

"Mmmm, okay." I carry her to the living room and sit on the sofa. Brendali's seated on my lap, facing me, her arms still wrapped around my neck. The shampoo smell from her 4:00 a.m. shower wafts over me.

"My uncle Felipe believes that certain souls reconnect over many lives. When they first meet in a new life they feel a spark, a kind of— umm, that feels nice—instant recognition."

The fingertips of one of my hands have been gliding lightly up and down the curve of her spine as she spoke, while the other hand rests on her thigh. She leans into me, shivers and moans as our kisses continue. "Wait," she says breathlessly, "let me finish." She arches her upper body, her hands flush against my shoulders. "When we had dinner in Veracruz I realized Felipe spoke the truth. We've spent lifetimes together, I know we have. You felt the spark too, no?"

I hesitate, not wanting to answer in the negative. "The ambush might've distracted me. I knew I'd found my cohost and that you needed my company, some wine and dinner."

"God says I'm more a life partner than a show host."

From her tone I'm unsure if she's kidding me or criticizing my response, so I initiate another round of kissing. A short one is followed by more French kisses that continue until Bren pulls back for air.

"After we interviewed God, I asked him to help me find my angel. That's you, right?"

"I'm no angel, but God did bring us together to become lovers." She takes both of my hands in hers, interlocked. "We'll make love now, yes?"

"Hell yes, Angel." I struggle a bit but manage to stand up and carry her as I did before.

"God wants this very much," she says as we pass by the kitchen.

"He's not the only one." I'm in full agreement with God this time.

We're past the laundry room. "He chose and healed us, created a bond—no, a special communion. And he used NITWIT to move me into your bed, no?"

What we've been doing has reduced my capacity for rational thought. Besides, I'm uninterested in discussing theology at the moment.

I softly drop Brendali on the bed. We whip off what little remains of our clothing—her thong, my boxers—as she continues her monolog.

"I'm not usually like this. I flirt, play hard to get, make men chase me. I enjoy the game. Never will I play games with you, though. Except those you want me to play." That last sentence is delivered in her most husky tone, as she straddles my chest. "God's command is my desire," she whispers, bending to start another round of kisses.

We make love for two hours. Total exhaustion leaves us cuddled in each other's arms. Felipe's reincarnation beliefs aside, God's given me the one thing I want most—a life partner. Every day Bren's mine I'll thank him for bringing her to me. She's truly my angel.

Doesn't that mean God can take her away from me if this Convocation fails? How in the world can I make sure it won't?

21 | Mysterious Ways

RAM

Sunday, November 21, 2027, 1:35 p.m.

Brendali's head is on my chest, one hand outstretched to softly touch a crescent moon shaped scar on my right shoulder. "Baby, now that we're lovers I want to know all about your life before you became a *muy* big shot TV star."

I grin, charmed by the way she expresses herself. "Life as a local news anchor who does occasional movie voice-overs and used to play in a part-time band doesn't make me a celebrity."

"Don't give me your humble act. Tell me everything." She adjusts her position to plant little kisses on my forehead, nose and lips.

"It's not a real happy story." I sit up in a lotus position so we can hold hands. Her question's reasonable, but I don't want to get into this. "I grew up in a blue-collar suburb near Philadelphia. I've been told my father's side of the family traces back to the Welsh Quakers who settled the area, but I don't have proof of that boast."

"Anyway, I lost dad in a fatal factory accident at age five. Nick, my older brother, became my surrogate father. He died in Iraq. The army notified us on my twelfth birthday." I stop, hang my head and continue in a slow hushed monotone. "My mom became depressed, withdrawn, often drunk and abusive. She couldn't help me cope with my grief and I lacked the maturity to help with hers." My heavy sigh signals Bren that every uttered word hurts.

"*Mi Dios,* I had no idea. That's terrible!" She hugs me so hard I fall into a prone position.

"It toughened me up, I guess." My voice deserts me and my eyes lose focus. "I'm not proud of what I'm about to say. A day after my high school graduation, I—uh—well, I abandoned her. Packed a bag, ran away, never saw her again. By the time I grew up enough to realize what I'd done, the chance to explain or make it up to her had passed. She'd committed suicide—" I can't finish. The hurt, embarrassment and self-recriminations remain.

If I could admit it to her, I'd change 'not proud' to 'totally ashamed.' I mean, I walked out on my mom, compounding her losses. Plain and simple, I failed her.

Bren's 'how could you?' facial expression makes me stare at the ceiling, push air out and take a deep breath in. "I left a note so Mom would know I wasn't kidnapped."

"Did she look for you? Or ask law enforcement to find you?" Now Bren's face is etched with concern, but I can't tell whether that's for me or Mom.

"I have no idea. I spent a month on the streets. It wouldn't have been too difficult to find me. Angel, I can't talk about this. I can't. Maybe someday I'll get over it—"

Bren reaches over to grab my arm and stop me from pounding the bed, which I didn't know I'd been doing. "It's okay, *mi querido.* I understand. Blame it on your youth, no?" She wipes off a tear running down my cheek. "What happened to get you off the street?"

"I joined a seminary under an assumed name and left a year later."

"You studied to become a priest? You? An atheist?"

"Desperation makes people do strange things. Whenever we'd get drilled about the need to have faith, I'd ask why. I couldn't trust an unprovable concept. Still can't. I made a poor choice and compounded it by signing up with the army."

Bren's eyes burst wide open. "That's brave, considering what happened to Nick."

"No, it's dumb. Six months after I got posted to Afghanistan, shrapnel from a roadside IED explosion sent me to a military hospital in Germany. I learned my lesson. The scars on my left leg and right shoulder are constant reminders to me not to make impulsive, bad decisions."

Bren's choked up "oh baby" and her hug are comforting. "In the hospital I befriended an injured news reporter one bed over. He thought I had the voice and appearance for a television news career. It sounded good. Courtesy of the GI bill I enrolled at USC and earned a journalism degree. Ken hired me as a paid intern and offered me a job after graduation. From that point life improved until I got shot. The raised white spots you can see are where the bullets hit me. The more jagged ones are the surgical incisions."

"You've had a hard life, sweetie. Now you have me. I'm going to make it better." She taps her puckered lips to invite a kiss, so I oblige. "No, I want a sloppy long one."

The French kiss doesn't lead to anything. We're too spent to go further and Griff will arrive soon. I do gorge for a minute on the beauty of Bren's facial profile before going to the kitchen to get some snacks out for Griff's visit. Dressed in her silver-gray form-fitting gym leggings, a purple sports bra and nothing else, Bren soon joins me in the kitchen.

"You're the sexiest gym rat I've ever seen, Angel. Are you comfortable showing Griff so much of yourself?"

"I'd rather not, but I don't have a choice, do I?"

"I'll find you something." A search of my master closet results in selection of a casual blue denim shirt that reaches her knees. She models it for me, front and back.

"I like the fit. Does it work for you?"

"It'll do, but I need a belt." A brown braided leather belt I don't use much is the best option available. I tie a small bit of twine to it as a loop so the end doesn't flap around.

"Not perfect," I say, "but good enough." She's adorable in it.

The building intercom buzzes to let us know Griff's arrived. "I hope we'll hear the NITWIT investigation's making good progress," I say.

"We'd better or Griff gets no snacks." She heads for the living room while I hustle into some clothes.

Griff's impressive in his white three-piece suit, white dress shirt and the matching hat with a gray band. "Don't gawk," he says by way of greeting, "this is my church uniform."

We sit at the kitchen table, and Griff doffs the hat. "Would you like a late lunch, or something to drink?" Bren's on top of hosting. I didn't even think to ask.

"No, but thanks for offerin'. Let's get down to business, I can't stay long. LaTaunya expected me home an hour ago." Griff accepts a glass of orange juice from Bren. "NITWIT has no history in our archives. Either they're Evangelical radicals or lone wolf types who are harder to track. Religious fanatics aren't the most cooperative folks. Why God puts up with them smearin' his name is beyond me."

Griff looks upward, as though he expects God to explain. "You two can help. We have an angle you're better suited to look into than we are."

"Fill us in," I say as Bren pushes a snack platter toward Griff. "We'll get on it."

"Nah. Thought I'd raise the subject and leave. I'll mosey on home now." He stands, puts his hat on and steps toward the door.

"*Mi Dios,* you came to say you have nothing to tell us?"

I tap her hand. "Relax, Bren. He's kidding."

"I never kid." Griff takes his hat off and sits down again. "FBI agents are taught to stay serious, sober and narrow-minded at all times. Crack a smile, tell a joke, you get demoted, booted out or worse, sent to hell—a desk job at the CIA."

"Ha! Now I know you're joking."

"Anyway, KJCR-TV can supply leads." He puts a gruyere wedge on top of a cracker, and adds a pickle slice and a smattering of black and pimento olives to his plate.

"What makes you think so?" I dump a few items onto my plate, too.

"NITWIT's e-mail reached your boss on his company e-mail address, not the station's general in-box. Whoever called you both had your unlisted numbers. The guy who threatened Brendali downtown knew where to find her. The arsonist had her home address, although she's not the owner of record. The only place all this info comes together is KJCR-TV."

"Someone we work with is a NITWIT?" Puzzlement's clear on Bren's face.

"I can think of a few who've had their nit witty moments—" Like Ken, for example.

"Don't jump to conclusions," Griff says, "personal information isn't always secure. But if we can identify who's leakin' this info to our target, we're a step closer. Maybe a big step."

"Bren," I ask, "what time did Ken call to tell you to join the earthquake news team?"

She checks her cellphone. "A little before 9:30."

Griff's eyes roll up momentarily. "NITWIT had less than five hours to send Skeleton Man downtown with a press pass. That's not much time to plan an attempted murder. It also implies your boss's possible involvement. Follow these leads. Once we apply enough pressure, NITWIT will make a misstep somewhere along the way."

"Each incident involves a single individual," I say.

"Good thought," Griff says. "That's right."

"So maybe Skeleton Man's a lone dog, no?"

"You mean wolf, Brendali." Griff reaches for more snacks. "Or he may work with a few like-minded buddies. I'd like you to send me a detailed e-mail of your interaction with this guy, a complete physical description and a facial sketch. I can get you a sketch artist if necessary."

"Never will I forget that face, but I might need the artist's help to get the sketch right."

"If you don't mind me askin', how'd your parents take the fire news?"

"Phone reception's spotty in the part of Mexico they live in, and they don't have internet. I've tried to reach them several times but can't get through. I should try again. Excuse me."

Griff watches Bren scurry to the bedroom. "The fire's unfortunate, but it helps with security to have you both in one place." He wipes his mouth with a napkin. "LAPD promised to set up a watch around this buildin'. You won't notice. You and Brendali look cozy together. Is the men's shirt she's wearin' yours?"

"Yes. The only thing she has to wear at the moment is a workout outfit she had in her car. She put my shirt over it."

"She'll stay here until we neutralize this threat?"

"I think it's the safest alternative."

"I'll bet you do." An ever-so-slight smile crosses his face.

Bren returns. "I still can't reach them. I'll try again later."

"Text me their address and the message you want to send them. I'll see that local law enforcement in their town delivers it. Excuse me, I need to get home."

"I will, thanks." She grabs her phone but doesn't type anything.

Griff puts his hat on and pushes back from the table. "Ram says you're stayin' here until things settle down. Will that work for you?" He winks at me.

She gives us a sly smile and snakes an arm through mine. "Suits me. Ram has a nice place, no? Who knows, maybe I'll stick around forever."

22 | Suspicious Minds

BRENDALI

Monday, 11/22/27

Once Ram leaves for the Convocation I grab my iPad, select the Convocation app and open the message board on the host page. 'Show me whatever's happening that you think I might find newsworthy, or that I need to know about,' I ask the tech angels.

My screen goes dark before the host page's real-time viewer feature shows me four men in a small conference room. "We need to stop this nonsense," one says. He's younger than the others, handsome in an off-putting way with a goatee, beaked nose and thick eyebrows set over inset beady dark eyes.

"I suggest total noncooperation," an obese older man says. "Drag this out until the sixty day period ends. If no agreement is reached, this devil will leave us alone. Once he's gone—good riddance, I say— the real God can return."

"That course is dangerous, Gilbert." I recognize this third man as Caleb Kimball, the Evangelical Ram interviewed. I need to read his bio. "Remember what happened to that mullah? Any open resistance is dangerous. Passive resistance is better. Sometime before the sixty-day deadline, the other religions will ask us to negotiate. We'll listen, act as though we're interested or involved, but we won't say or do anything that binds us to any kind of commitment. Let them fight among themselves. Who knows, these groups may never even reach agreement. If they do ask us to sign one, we'll refuse. All we need to do is stay resolute. Spread the word."

The other men nod their agreement as my view of their meeting goes dark.

I can't believe this! How dare these *pinche estúpidos* not believe God is who he says he is? Their refusal to accept his orders means extinction, for God's sake! I slam my fist on the table. My iPad falls onto the carpet. I pick it up and send God a message. 'I've learned the Evangelicals don't intend to participate in good faith. What do you intend to do about it?'

The immediate response received, 'noted, under review,' doesn't tell me anything.

According to Kimball's bio he's a Vice-President of the Evangelicals United Coalition, sits on their Board of Directors and represents the EUC in the Global Evangelical Union. He's a professional public relations guru, too? *Mierda!* He'll influence his compadres to see things his way. Let's see, how many Evangelicals do we have? Thirty. No doubt they'll vote as a bloc.

'Ram,' I text, 'we have a big, big problem." The rest of my message fills him in.

He responds right away. "Thanks. I'll get together with the steering committee ASAP. Come join us. I'll text you to let you know where we are. We need to monitor these guys closely if God doesn't take care of this for us."

Will God do anything? He told us this Convocation's a test of our ability to solve problems without his help. What's the best way for us to deal with this one?

Turns out the security office is in the Convention Center's sub-basement. The cramped and overheated conference room is a tight fit for the five of us—Ram, me, the Archbishop, Slomo and Father Zeke. Due to her mobility limitations, the Reverend Mother's not with us.

"Fill us in, Bren," Ram says as we settle in.

"The Convocation app Ram and I have contains a host page you can't access. A message board allows us to exchange messages with God's tech angels. A real-time video tool allows me to listen in on the attendee's Convocation-related conversations. This morning I came across a troubling discussion between some Evangelicals. The tool has an auto-save feature, so let's watch it together."

"We have to decide what, if anything, we should do," Ram says once the video's been viewed. "We can't assume God will take care of this for us. Let's show him we don't need his help."

I chip in with "Ram and I can report on this during tonight's show, but should we?"

"One thing we should do is identify the three people we overheard and pay them some extra attention." That comes from the archbishop.

"I've done that already," I say. "We already know Caleb Kimball, the ringleader. Let me see if the tech angels have answered my request for the names." I check. "The obese guy is Gilbert Thibodaux, the third one's Jake Benveniste."

"Bren," Ram says while I look up the bios for these two men, "you know that as journalists we're obligated to make this development public. It's legitimate news."

"I knew you'd say that." I'm typing a message while I speak. "The tech angels will send you the bios for Thibodaux and Benveniste. Read them when you have a chance."

Slomo speaks. "The positive side to public disclosure is pretty clear, Ram."

"What in the name of God is that?" Zeke barks the question at Slomo.

"These three people won't have any idea how the word got out so quickly. They make their private decision today, and tonight its worldwide news."

Archbishop Delmonico grins and slaps Slomo on the back. "They'll immediately suspect each other. I like the way you think."

Of course! "We can also expect this group to feel some public pressure to make sure they don't follow through with their plan. It would destroy us, no?"

Ram's been typing something on his phone while we talk, and now looks up at us. "I'm going to pull Mr. Kimball aside and ask him if the news reports are true. He'll probably deny them, but I want to know how he reacts. We may have to confront him."

"God did say he'd take quick punitive action if attendees don't participate in good faith," I say. "The tech angels know about this, but no action's been taken yet. If we get a denial from Kimball—in other words a lie—maybe that'll trigger some activity from up above." I point skyward.

Our discussion continues but we reach no conclusions or action plans beyond agreeing to meet again if Kimball lies and God doesn't do anything about it. That's a start, but not an end.

RAM

Wednesday, 11/24/2027, Convention Center

Bren's disappeared somewhere in the crowd, doing the same thing I am—searching for news. I'm not having much luck. All I overhear is snatches of idle conversation.

"—dinner at Broken Spanish," one man says to another. "Good food, but I waited an hour for a table—"

"—no idea why I got selected." The voice comes from one out of a group of four younger men. "None. Wish I wasn't. I don't want to miss my baby girl's birth, she's due in two weeks—"

"—L.A. doesn't impress me," a priest dressed to give a sermon says. "Crowds, noise, terrible traffic. I should never have left my sleepy little island off the Irish coast—"

Isn't anyone focusing on the job at hand? This gathering wouldn't require sixty days if these people spent their time talking business.

The tense posture of two groups of men in a far corner draws my attention. I quicken my pace to check out what's going on, but on the way I bump into the one person I've been searching for the most.

"Mr. Kimball, do you have a moment?" He comes to a full stop. "A rumor's circulating that your group won't participate in good faith. Care to set the record straight for us?"

"I saw your show. What the members of my faith choose to do is our business."

Okay, he's taking the evasion route. "Does that mean you're confirming the rumor, or refuting it?"

"Neither," Kimball says with a smug smile. "Take my words as a no comment." He turns and walks away. It's tempting to pursue him but he's confirmed what Bren overheard, so I rush toward the argument.

"This general societal acceptance of sodomy is another sure sign of the imminent arrival of the Antichrist." I recognize the speaker immediately—Gilbert Thibodaux, in the florid flesh, spouting his views in a loud, insistent manner. Three men next to him voice fawning agreement.

"Are you of the opinion, sir, that we did not witness the Second Coming of Jesus?" That's Jake Benveniste. Is this an argument meant as a disruption? "Will you disregard our Lord's directions like that beheaded mullah did?" Benveniste's supporters stay silent.

The moment I snap Thibodaux's picture, the host page fills my cellphone screen with his bio profile. I didn't know the app does this, but now's not the time to read the bio.

The voice of Father Zeke, who reached the group when I did, overrides the din. "Y'all are loud enough to wake the dead. Even worse, you've drawn media attention." He points at me. "Aren't you familiar with the verse 'be ye all of one mind, having compassion one of another?'"

"My apologies, Father," Benveniste says. "Gilbert and I take the Word, as spoken by our Lord, with utmost seriousness, and yet—"

Crimson-faced, Gilbert outdoes Father Zeke's decibel level. "I cannot agree to shear the Great Book of all morality to better fit this immoral age. Such an act assigns victory to the forces of evil we valiantly fight to overcome, as did our right-thinking forebears. We—"

"Now, now," Zeke says in a soothing voice. "All of us strive to abide by God's laws. He didn't bring us together to throw away his wise counsel, but to find ways to marry his words to today's realities. For it is said: 'We shall all stand before the judgment seat of Christ.

Therefore, let us not judge one another anymore, but rather resolve this, not erect a stumbling block or a cause to fall in our brother's way.'"

Gilbert's fists clench and unclench while he peers at Zeke, Benveniste and the others nearby. I get the last and longest stare. "Sir, Mark states that from the beginning of creation God made us male and female. I shall never waver from upholding the Bible's natural laws. Nor shall I set my hand to any document that decrees man's acceptance of changes to those laws. I swear on the good book I would rather die than impugn my views."

He spins away, takes five steps and groans. His hand darts to his chest as he collapses and falls backward, his head smacking the floor with a loud thud.

He's either had a heart attack or a stroke. No one moves except me. My CPR training, learned years ago in the Army and never used, kicks in. His pulse is weak, but present. "Someone, call 911—tell them we have a medical emergency."

Again no one moves. "You," I say, pointing to Benveniste, "get to it!" He runs off. I text Johnny Ray with a simple message: 'Quick, bring me an AED.'

CPR protocol requires me to grab Gilbert's shoulders and shout his name. That garners no reaction. I unbutton Gilbert's shirt and start chest compression.

Press one, two, three. Repeat thirty times. Concentrate. Don't lose count. Follow with two rescue breaths.

It feels like no time has elapsed, but Johnny's sped through the crowd gathered around us. I keep the compressions going until he's ready to use the defibrillator. He begins by tearing Gilbert's undershirt with the AED's scissors.

Because I'm sweating, I move back. Johnny towels off Gilbert's skin, applies the pads and touches the analyze button. He starts CPR, so the AED must've told him not to apply shock. Either a steady pulse is back or it's gone.

Johnny and I take turns applying compressions until paramedics arrive. Once triage is done, Gilbert's loaded on a stretcher and taken away. One man in his group accompanies him.

I hear muted expressions of thanks and feel a few congratulatory slaps on my back, but acknowledge none of it as Johnny and I walk away.

"Glad you're here. Good work with the AED."

"Why, we practice so much, this here's like sliding backwards off a greasy log."

"Let's hope he pulls through." I give Johnny a rueful smile. "We could use a greasy log. I don't feel good about this gathering."

In the nearest restroom I dry off and check Gilbert's bio. Great, I've saved the life of someone whose opinions I totally oppose—a Louisiana preacher with reactionary, racist and homophobic views. He blogs, writes and is followed by far too many readers.

I switch to the message board, intending to ask why God selected someone like Gilbert to participate in this Convocation. However, I find this waiting for me: 'Take not life and death into your own hands.'

God wanted the guy to die? Oh, I get it. Gilbert swore he'd rather die than compromise. To God, that's a lack of good faith. I interfered with the imposition of immediate punishment.

A new message appears. 'Do you wish this man saved despite the Convocation rules?'

I respond. 'I won't take responsibility for that kind of decision. If you do save him, though, I hope he gains a more enlightened outlook on life.'

'Thy will shall guide us,' I read.

What the f--k? I send another message. 'I expressed an opinion, not my will.' The tech angels don't respond, so I take a moment to check my e-mails. This message gets my attention:

Forster, we haven't forgotten about you and your little Latina sidekick. We'll upload the attached video to the internet at 23:00 hours tonight unless you come <u>alone</u> **to**

this location one hour earlier and surrender yourself to us.

NITWIT's language and tech skills have improved. There's no sender's address. Maybe the use of military time is a clue Griff can exploit. The meet-up location's off the La Tuna Canyon Road exit from the 210 freeway, an area I don't know well.

The attached video shows Bren showering. This must've been taken at her folks' home the night it burned down. How else would NITWIT get it unless a member took it? This proves they're behind the arson.

Like a punch to the head, the full impact of the video hits me. The minute it's uploaded to the internet, the video will go viral. We'll never get it off the net, or deleted by anyone who downloads it. Bren will die of embarrassment.

I look around the empty restroom, punch the paper towel dispenser, bend over the sink and douse my face with water. "Shit!" The scream's involuntary. I clamp my jaws to prevent another, but bite my tongue instead. The sudden pain makes me punch the towel dispenser again. I spit into the sink to see if I've drawn blood. I haven't.

This is how NITWIT means to get their hands on me. What the heck should I do? I can't call Griff. He'll insist on seeing the video and sending FBI agents along. No way will I let him see Bren nude. Not Griff, not the rest of the FBI, not anyone. I've got to deal with this myself.

My angel doesn't deserve this. What'll happen when she finds out? She'll flip out in anger. I'm not telling her, simple as that. She's been through enough already.

In the video Bren's putting a black thong on, like the one she wore the night of the fire. If I ever meet this voyeur/arsonist my commitment to nonviolence will end. This video can't go out to the internet. I'll do whatever's necessary to prevent it.

Ram's Twitter Convocation Update: May have saved a man's life today. I know his Evangelical friends will pray for his survival. I hope he lives to rejoin us, remembering God's words about good faith and compromise. #LearnCPR #Savelives

BRENDALI

Wednesday, November 24, 2027 (con't)

I lost sight of Ram for most of the morning, until now. His gait's unsteady. He's sweating, too.

"Ram!" I repeat the call, louder this time. "Ram, what's going on? Are you ill?"

He enters the men's room before I can catch up to him. While waiting in the hallway, I open the Convocation app and click Slomo Nakamura's name on the invitee directory. The video finds him inside, engaged in cordial conversation with some Middle Eastern men. I mute the volume, not only because I don't understand Arabic but so that people walking by don't find out about the video feed.

Ram finally comes out, no longer sweaty but preoccupied. He doesn't even notice me.

"*Mi cariño,* are you okay? You look upset."

"I suppose I'm fine," he says in a strained tone.

"What's wrong?" I take his arm and stare into his eyes. He tells me what happened. "You saved a life. You should feel great about that."

"I should, yes, but—" He shrugs and taps my phone hard enough to make me drop it, though I don't. "You shouldn't spy on people. It's unethical, wrong."

"How else can I gather information? The men here won't talk to me." Why's he mad at me? "God wouldn't have given us a video feed if it's wrong. He did, we have it and—"

"I don't care. We're better reporters than that." He's got his hands on his hips, his upper body leaning toward me, his face reddening.

Are we about to have our first fight? If so, what are we fighting about? "Slomo's in a crowded public room, Ram. We're not intruding on some private moment."

"I don't care. This is plain wrong. It offends me."

I grab his hand with more force than intended. "Whatever's on your mind is messing with your judgment. Tell me what's wrong."

He looks at me, takes a few deep breaths. "I'm not real happy right now, that's all."

The hallway's empty. On tiptoes, I whisper into his ear. "We're a team in our work and our private lives, right? Let me help you feel better."

"Let's go do our job," he says in a gruff tone, and heads toward the hall.

"Baby, wait." I hurry up to join him, take his arm and give him my best mock-scowl.

He yanks it away. "We're here to cover this Convocation. When I work a crowd, I'm laser focused on what I need. If we split up, we'll cover more territory, speak to more people and get more information for our show."

We have the video feed because God anticipated that no one would talk to me. "Stay with me a little while, sweetie. I want to help you get over whatever's bothering you."

He sighs and shrugs. "Where do you want to go?"

"Let's see." Why can't I spot Slomo now? Oh, found him. He's on the other side of the hall, near the dais. The Muslim group's gone except for one man. I point him out to Ram, who responds with a 'lead on' gesture.

Before long we're close enough we overhear Slomo's conversation. "I understand, Hakan. But you know, our religions are in many ways alike."

I speak to Ram in a low voice. "Let's sit nearby and listen. They're so wrapped up in their conversation they haven't noticed us."

"Nonsense, Mr. Slomo." Hakan Çelik's close enough to spit in Slomo's face. "We have many fundamental differences."

"Allow me to prove my point," Slomo says with a broad smile. "If I do, you can join me for dinner and pay for the meal. If I lose, I'll pay."

"Consider it done, sir, if you'll pay for an expensive meal." Çelik folds his arms, his expression smug. "When a free meal is before me, I have five star tastes."

"Ram, I'd love to record this conversation, but the noise in here would drown it." Instead I open my Notes app and start using my version of shorthand.

"Okay, ten similarities," Slomo says to Çelik. "First, the most obvious one—Jews and Muslims each pray to the same God, though we've given him different names. We're both monotheistic, right?" Çelik nods. "However, Catholicism is tri-theistic with their Father, Son and Holy Spirit trinity."

Çelik's face beams. According to his bio, he's no fan of Catholicism or Judaism.

Slomo's wrong, though. Catholics believe in one God who takes three forms. Jesus is God's form on earth, the Holy Spirit is God's spirit in man, and God is otherwise himself. But this new god says earth's had multiple Gods, one after another. This complicates things, no?

"Our faiths both believe in the same angels," Slomo continues. "Gabriel, known as Jibril in the Koran. Mikail, called Michael in the Jewish faith. And Israfil, also named Raphael."

Çelik raises a hand, apparently to interject, but Slomo's on a roll. "Prophets are also common to both religions, Hakan. And Jerusalem's Holy City status is another shared belief."

"I begin to fear I will pay for your dinner tonight. Would you accept McDonald's?"

"They don't serve halal food," Slomo says with a grin. "Perhaps we can find a slightly more expensive spot that's halal and kosher."

"Ram, did you catch that? Slomo subtly referred to another similarity, the fifth so far—dietary restrictions." His eyes are fixed staring at the wall. I wish he'd tell me what's eating him.

Çelik unfolds a napkin, raises and waves it at Slomo. "I surrender, sir. You win. I shall finish the list. Strict adherents of both religions segregate men and women in our places of worship and pray several times a day—Muslims five times, Jews three. Our days start and end at sunset. We use lunar calendars. Last, men are circumcised and must wear a skull cap."

"Yes," Slomo says. "One head is uncovered soon after birth, the other stays covered throughout life." He laughs and slaps Celik's shoulder.

Celik's bark is delayed. He must've needed a moment to get the joke.

"That makes eleven similarities, by my count. Well done, sir." Çelik offers his hand, which Slomo shakes with enthusiasm. They walk away, talking like old friends.

"Ram, that conversation's worth the entire day. What a great story for the Convocation—a Jew and a Muslim find friendship and common religious ground."

"When I first met Çelik he sounded pretty aggressive. Slomo's won him over. If those two are willing to break bread together, we have reason to hope after all."

I look at him and decide to plunge in. "Tell me what made you unhappy earlier, baby."

He starts with "I got an e-mail," shakes his head, stops and goes quiet as he stares at me. When he resumes, he repeats what he told me about Gilbert Thibodaux and adds the messages he exchanged with the tech angels.

"That's why you're upset? God made the choice, didn't he? I don't get it."

"I shouldn't have made a suggestion. I should've left the decision in God's hands."

"Don't be too hard on yourself. God tested you the way he did with Job, Moses and Jonah."

"I don't belong with them. And this is a different God."

"You still have to live up to his expectations."

He reaches for my hands with both of his. "Angel, sorry, I'm not upset with you. I shouldn't have taken my emotions out on you. I'm thoughtless, sometimes."

I bring his hands to my lap. "I have a bad side too, baby. You've seen my temper tantrums but you insist I'm an angel. I've always been this way. Every day of my childhood I used to ask God why I have this cursed temper. Father Gonzalo, blessed be his memory, would hammer a message into my head. 'Brendalita,' he'd say, 'focus on piety, on prayer. If you do, in time, your tantrums will go away. Your troubled soul will find the peace it yearns for.' But my anger's never left. Maybe it never will."

"To me you're an angel," he says in a sweet voice. "I don't know why an angel can't have a temper. I mean, okay, in Hollywood they don't, but that's make-believe."

I want to kiss him for saying that, but the sadness I often feel after my anger spells descends. "Ram, I know you'll leave me at some point. I won't blame you when you do. You can call me Angel all you want, but I can't live up to that name until the hole in my soul is fixed."

He lifts my hand and kisses it. "Angel, if you can handle my occasional thoughtlessness, your angry moments won't drive me away. If any couple's a true match made in heaven, it's us."

He's right. My heart melts and I throw my arms around him although we're out in public. "I'm falling in love with you, baby," I whisper.

He grins. "I've already fallen for you. Hurry and catch up."

Is it too much to hope our love never leaves us?

Ram's mood continues throughout our nightly show. What bugged him earlier is still in his head, so once the show ends I accompany Ram to his dressing room to insist he tell me what's on his mind. Never have I been in here. The furniture's minimal—couch, chair, dressing table, mirror. Posters of famous rock guitarists fill the walls.

"I didn't know you have one of these here," I say, pointing to an old guitar in the corner.

"Sometimes I'll strum a tune or two before a show to calm down."

"Can you play me something?" Maybe that'll get him out of his funk.

He plays a few chords and puts the guitar down. "Sorry, Angel, I'm not feeling it."

Instead of changing clothes, Ram takes a guitar pick from his dressing table and flips it around his fingers while he leans against the table and stares at me. "Bren, I need to do something before I go home." He takes a deep breath, pushes the air out and drops the pick to the floor without picking it up. "I'd like to tell you about it, but I'm sort of sworn to secrecy."

What's that mean? Do I force him to tell me, or take him at his word? This conversation might define how much we can trust each other, so I don't push for information. "It's okay. Fill me in when you can." Both of us remain silent for way too long.

He draws me close. "You're such a wonderful angel." He sounds close to tears. This vibe's all wrong. I shouldn't let him go.

In silence we walk to my dressing room, one floor below his. At my door he stops and looks both ways down the empty hallway. I get a long, sweet kiss before he tramps away without saying goodbye. He's hunched over, his head down, withdrawn. It's all so unlike him that I want to run after him, help sort out his emotions. But I don't.

Why'd that feel like our last kiss?

Brendali's Twitter Convocation Update: Wonderful to see a Jew and a Muslim befriend each other. Maybe this can set an example for all faiths. #worldpeace #leadership

RAM

November 24, 2027, 9:45 p.m. (cont.)
With rain clouds low enough to hide the crests of the foothills, La Tuna Canyon Road eats moonlight like a black hole swallows starlight.

I've parked on a strip of dirt in between the road and the 210 freeway, which is to my right some twenty feet down below. Scrub brush dots the undeveloped hills to my left. My windows are rolled up against the night's coolness. Light rain sprinkles the windshield. The sounds made by semi-trucks and motorcycles that rumble by on the 210, interspersed with the occasional howls of wild animals somewhere nearby, are loud enough to pierce the glass.

It's hard to believe I'm in the midst of a sprawling metropolitan area. Chills ride up my spine. NITWIT's picked a perfect rendez-vous spot for a kidnapping or a murder and I didn't bring a weapon. How do I turn into Ram-bo without one?

A blinding light followed by a loud rap on my side window startles me. The NITWIT guy, positioned in the Mustang's blind spot, has effectively minimized his profile. All I can see is indistinct dark clothing. I crack the window open enough to communicate.

"Out of the car, Forster," he barks, flashing a handgun. His deep voice lacks inflection and accent. "Real slow. Keep your hands away from your body. Stare at your feet. Let's move."

I comply. "You think I care about the gun? I should've died

months ago, you know. I'm at peace with my mortality."

The man's too busy giving orders to respond. "Put your hands on the roof. Now." His rough frisk is meant to tell me who's in charge, as though his gun didn't already do that. He empties my pockets, tossing my cellphone, wallet, house keys and car fob on the wet hood.

"Clasp your hands behind your back." He jabs my back with the barrel of his gun.

"Not until you hand over the video."

"What makes you think I have it?"

Is this his idea of a joke? I want to see his facial expression but decide not to chance it. "Your message said you'd have it."

"You misread it, Forster. We said the video wouldn't get posted to social media, that's all. Go ahead, check for yourself. We're honorable people carrying out God's judgment."

Honorable people? Is he serious? I review the message. He's right. How can I get my hands on the video now? He must've brought it, I have to believe that. Do I have to fight him to find out where it is?

The muzzle of his gun taps the back of my head. "Put the phone back on the hood. Hands behind your back, let's go."

It's me and God against him and his gun. Who has the advantage? He does.

Once wrapped tight around my arms, the rope pinches. Double loops secure my wrists. Blindfolded, I squeeze into the small rear seat. Hopefully my stuff's no longer on the car hood. Moments after my door slams shut, I hear the trunk door open. A clanking noise lets me know something metallic is now inside it. The lid bangs closed.

Once behind the wheel the man executes a U-turn, the Mustang skidding on the wet pavement.

"You're not much of a kidnapper, you know." He doesn't respond. "In movies bad guys bind the victim's legs and arms. You only did the arms." More silence. "They also stuff the victim's mouth to prevent backtalk. You didn't. You've got a lot to learn."

My mouth versus his gun isn't a fair fight, but words are my only weapons. Maybe I can goad him into making a mistake.

After a quarter mile, at most, the car veers left onto a bumpy patch of dirt and stops. Does he intend to kill me for mouthing off?

My door opens. "Out of the car, Forster, we're taking a little hike."

I edge out inch by inch, without help. Cool air, and the moderate rainfall pelting me, heightens my senses. I hear the guy open and close the trunk.

"I'll take your blindfold off. Turn around, face the hill. Glance back once and you're dead where you stand."

To my left, streetlights illuminate the nearby entrance ramp to the eastbound lanes of the 210. We've driven from one side of the freeway to the other. Straight ahead four thick circular metal posts prevent vehicle entry onto a hiking trail that leads up into the Verdugo hills. The wild animal cries and vehicular noises are louder now that I'm out of the car.

The kidnapper jabs his gun into my back. "Get a move on, your eyes fixed on the ground. Follow the path. We're walking to the top."

The hill's steep and muddy. By the time we reach the crest I'm so winded my words come out in short bursts and gasps. "I've never understood you God-fearing evangelical types. The Bible teaches love, mercy, forgiveness. All you fanatics want is vengeance for imagined breaches of God's laws. The inconsistency takes my breath away."

I get the silent treatment again.

"No comment? How about this? Didn't Jesus say 'Put your sword back into its place, for all who take the sword will perish by the sword'? You know that passage, right?"

"Gunpowder is God power."

"Yeah, I get it. Power's what's important. If preaching your skewed views of the Bible won't convert people, you'll force a conversion or kill the nonbeliever, right?"

A whack to the back of my head makes my ears ring. I stumble and fall face first into a patch of mud. Rain's coming down in sheets now, so most of the mud washes off quickly.

"Get to your feet," I'm told.

I spit dirt from my lips as I respond. "I can't. Why should I, anyway? I know what you plan to do with that shovel you're carrying."

"I'll kill and bury you right here if you don't stand up."

"I can't pull myself up without help."

"Suit yourself." He sets the lantern on the ground, the beam pointed at me. He doesn't intend to shoot and miss.

He's behind the lantern. In silhouette his short, squat body is unlike Skeleton Man's. I can't see his facial features, which are hidden in darkness and covered by his hoodie.

I need to survive long enough to tell Griff NITWIT's got more than one member.

"Look around, Forster. Take ten seconds to pray, not that you will. Prepare to meet the maker you godless atheists deny."

"I already met him on my talk show, remember? That's what got your gang mad at me."

He widens his stance, levels his gun with both hands and takes aim.

I'm about to find out the truth about the afterlife. I'd love to see Nick, Mom and Dad. I gaze up at the sky. Thick clouds obscure God's view. Can he see what's happening and stop it?

I'll miss Bren. Wish we could say good-bye. Damn. God brought us together. He must've had something more than a short affair in mind, but I don't see a way to escape—

My body tenses as an impossibly loud gunshot rings out. At the same moment, a pack of coyotes leap over me, growling with fury. Five of the six head straight for the shooter. The other one tumbles and skids into the lantern, redirecting its light up to the heavens. That coyote doesn't move, having taken the bullet meant for me.

The frenzied animals barrel into the gunman, knocking him

over. He kneels, raises his arm and discharges a random second shot, missing me and the coyotes. One beast chomps down on the guy's wrist. He drops the gun with an anguished scream that echoes through the hills. The animals surround him. His arms flail as he falls to the ground.

Loud growls, pants and yips are mixed with terrified yells. The guy's getting mauled. I heard some serious suffering in the Middle East, but this is worse. "God, help me!" repeats with varying degrees of intensity, until replaced by whimpers.

As the next course on tonight's canine dinner menu, I'm the one in need of God's help. Tied up, I can't deal with a bunch of pissed off angry beasts alone. Nor can I get away from them. I'm white meat on a plate if the coyotes don't mind a little hemp with their meal.

The shooter goes silent, meeting his warped maker—or not. I manage to inch a few feet downhill, for whatever good that'll do me. The beasts encircle me, probably attracted by the smell of my fear. Snorts and low growls fill my ears. I close my eyes, play dead.

One animal sticks his snout in my face, ear and hair. His breath smells like a combination of skunk perfume and sewer gas. He sniffs, grunts and slobbers all over me. Another nibbles the rope near my elbow. A third does the same thing with the ropes around my wrist.

They scratch my skin but don't bite. My jacket and shirt sleeves rip but the ropes continue to bind. I open my eyes to gawk at the beasts. It's probably a trick of the meager light, but one appears to smile at me. Maybe I'm delirious, imagining this. He licks my face— his way of saying 'sorry, amigo, we tried. Adios.' They trot away.

I'm alone with whatever's left of a dead body. The storm's lessened a bit. Raindrops, when they strike my body, sound like a Taiko drum concert. I imbibe the cool air like snowflakes swallowed in flight. Van Gogh's famous painting, spread out above me, makes me free associate Don McLean's song. I sing-shout the first verse and stop, wishing I had my guitar. I love to play that tune.

I've never felt this alive, but don't understand. Stars don't actually resemble the ones Van Gogh painted, so why do these look that way? How can it keep raining if the sky's cloudless?

Without any help I can discern, I'm somehow lifted upright until my feet touch wet ground. The ropes unfurl in slow motion, falling away knot by knot, loop by loop, until I'm free.

This is bizarre. What in heaven's name is going on?

An indistinct hooded figure floats away downhill, flickering in and out of my peripheral vision. His loose brown robe and cane brings to mind Radagast, the animal kingdom's wizard. Of course I'm not in Middle Earth, but I do my best to follow him, hoping to find normality.

Why's this trek taking so long? This is a hill, not Mount Everest. Has my sense of time warped?

When I reach the metal posts I grab one, lean over and puke up the bile, suppressed stress, anxiety. I feel better afterward except for the cold, which my wet clothes enhance, and some light-headedness. The night's pitch black again, with a drizzle.

Who saved me, anyway? God? Bren? Radagast? Fortuity? What the hell did I experience up top? Jeez, no wonder I hate hiking.

A car pulls off the road, its bright lights aimed straight for me.

Oh, no—NITWIT has reinforcements? I try to hustle to my car, gain time to drive away, but tortoise-like waddling is my top speed. Upon reaching the car I get in and slam the door shut. My cellphone, wallet and iPad are here. The car fob's missing, which means this car won't move an inch. Does the dead guy have it, or is it in some random coyote's belly?

The other car stops less than a foot away, positioned to block the Mustang's non-existent forward motion. A young man exits from the passenger side. Griff slams his driver's side door shut, pulls my door open and slaps his hand hard against the roof.

"What in damnation brings you here, Ram?"

"How'd you know I'm here? Did you follow me?"

He stares at me, his face lacking any hint of his usual dry humor. "You think we're stuck in the 1950's? If so, you're watchin' too damn much film noir. We use modern technology. Ever hear of GPS trackin' devices? Wherever you are, we know. That's part of our gold-member service package for clients who don't tell us where they're goin', or why."

I force a weary smile. "Got a court order for that?"

"Step out, Ram. Like Ricky Ricardo used to tell Lucy, you got some 'splainin' to do."

After I do he eyeballs me, top to bottom. "You look like death warmed over, twice. And what's this?" He picks a hemp thread off my jacket. "Someone held a rodeo here tonight? Did you buck some wild bulls on these hills? Rope a bunch of steer in this storm?" I provide an edited version of what occurred, without mentioning the voyeur video.

"All right, we're makin' progress. Grab the duffel, Jimmy. Ram, how about you lead us up to the crime scene?"

"Under no circumstances will I ever go back up that hill again."

The younger man walks to the car to grab a bag. While he's out of earshot, Griff speaks in a low, firm voice. "This kind of thing's our job, not yours. You took a foolish, unnecessary risk comin' here alone. Do not repeat that error. Hungry coyotes might not rescue you next time. Get my drift?"

I nod and lean against the car, in no mood to argue. "I understand and agree."

They walk up the hill and fade into the darkness. Frantic, I look everywhere inside the cabin for the missing fob, but find nothing. I stand outside the car, look up at the sky and scream my frustration.

The dead guy took his shovel out of the trunk. Maybe that's where the fob is. Good idea, but I come up empty again. What'll I do now? Can't call Bren to pick me up—how would I explain why I'm here? I don't want to wait for Griff to come back down, that might take hours. Can't hitchhike home looking like a disheveled bum. Call Lyft? No. Tomorrow Bren would want to know why my car's missing.

The realization that I'm stranded is the last straw. Yeah, men aren't supposed to cry, but sometimes we can't help it. I lean over the trunk, fold and rest my arms on the lid, lay my head on them and let loose.

The tears stop when an animal nuzzles my leg. Make that two. Coyotes. One looks up at me, winks and lowers his snout. He's deposited my fob in the dirt.

I bend down, pick it up and cautiously pat his head. He woofs like a dog, which makes me smile. I put the object dropped by the second coyote in my jacket pocket and pat him, too. He barks in my ear, they woof in unison and run for the hills. At the big metal posts one turns in my direction and woofs again before chasing his buddy up the path.

Now I'm teary because the coyote encounter has touched my soul. I'll never forget it.

On La Tuna Canyon Road I drive past the spot where I'd parked earlier and bypass a 1960's era white lowrider parked on the opposite shoulder of the road. I'll put up 2-1 Vegas odds that it belongs to the kidnapper. Time to see if the guy lied when he said he didn't bring the video. If the damn thing's here I have to find and destroy it.

The car's locked. I stare into space, thinking through how to break in. To warm my hands I stuff them into my jacket pockets and come into contact with the object the second coyote delivered—the NITWIT guy's cellphone, a bit chewed up but functional.

The phone has no security code. I easily access his camera, find the videos he made of Bren and delete them. Wish I could tell her, but why give her something more to fret over?

Rather than trek up the hill or wait for Griff to come down, I'll find time to give him the phone tomorrow.

Back in my car, the heater blasting, I type Bren's name into every social media site I can think of. I don't find a hint of an uploaded video anywhere. While resting my head against the steering wheel I revert to my seminary days and thank God.

The upload threat's over. Bren and I both dodged bullets tonight.

Once again I almost died. If I'd been born a cat, I'd have six lives left. I'll use them all to keep my angel safe.

RAM

Thursday, November 25, 2027, after midnight

With NITWIT out and about Bren would never leave the front door of the condo unlocked, much less ajar. The sight of overturned furniture and clothes spread everywhere tells me she didn't. An intruder did.

"Bren? Are you here? Bren?" A hurried room-by-room search confirms that everything's here, except her. "Damn!"

I call Griff. "My place has been ransacked. Bren's gone. NITWIT's got her. Kidnap me, snatch her, it fits. I'm crazy worried. She might've died by now." I kick the kitchen chair into the living room. "What the hell happened to LAPD's security team?"

"Calm down, Ram. We'll find her. I'll personally ream whoever's responsible for the screw-up. Do you have any idea how they got away?"

"I don't have a clue."

"If they took her car, findin' them won't take long. We put a GPS tracker in it. Can you check that out?"

"Right away. I got her a parking spot in the garage. I'll text you."

Within minutes I let Griff know the car's missing. My next stop is the security guard's kiosk. "Has anything unusual happened to your security system since, oh, eight p.m.?"

The guard pulls his paperwork to show me. "We did lose the

video security system about an hour ago, but only for ten minutes. How'd you know? And what the hell happened to you?"

I race for the elevator without answering either question. Somehow NITWIT got in, sabotaged the video system and snatched Bren. She's definitely in trouble. I have to save her.

In the condo I grab Bren's purse and phone and head to my car. Once I've tossed both items on the passenger seat, I strum my fingers on the steering wheel, run them through my hair and tap the accelerator pedal. Each fidgety movement brings no solace. Every minute I check my cellphone for Griff's update, which never arrives. After ten minutes of silence I send him a text. 'I'll drive to wherever Bren's car turns up. Send me the address.'

I should've changed out of my dirty clothes when I had the chance, but can't spare the time now. The moment Griff texts me the address I'll double-time it to that location. In the meantime, maybe the dead guy's phone can provide some clues.

Under 'Lead-1' I find a text sent to the dead guy at 11:26 p.m., which is roughly when the building's video screens went down: "Target acquired. Confirm your end."

That message is over an hour old. What've they done with her? Should I pretend I'm the dead guy? Griff told me to butt out. I know his people are trained, but I can't sit on the sidelines this long with Bren's life at risk. Every minute matters.

I call Griff again, get no answer and leave a text. 'What the hell's going on? I need to hear from you, damn it!' Maybe Lead-1 will answer my texts. I use the dead guy's phone to send one. 'Job's done here.'

'Proof?'

'I have his cellphone, iPad.' The less I type, the better.

'Bring them.'

Crap. The dead guy knew where to go but I sure don't. How do I respond without tipping Lead-1 off? All I come up with is 'the usual place?' That might've blown this masquerade.

Time crawls. Each time the screen on the dead guy's phone goes dark, I refresh it. What the devil's taking so long?

'Yes. Victory.'

Is he referring to success or someplace on Victory Boulevard? Does this phone have a contact with a matching address?

In response to the blaring cellphone, my head bangs against the headrest. One thigh hits the underside of the steering wheel. My heartrate doubles. I let a finger hover over the "answer" button but don't touch it. At this time of night, who'd call except Griff? The incoming number's not his, though.

I use the dead guy's phone to send a text. 'Don't trust me? I told you, I have Forster's phone.' My phone goes quiet. Great! They've confirmed I'm dead.

The contact list has no entry for Lead-1. What now? It'll take forever but what choice do I have? An alphabetical search takes longer than I want, but Timba Restaurant's Victory Boulevard address in Burbank fits. A hurried scroll through the six remaining letters confirms that Timba is the only possibility.

It takes twenty minutes of crazed driving to reach the Cuban establishment at the corner of Victory and Western. With outdoor seating and palm fronds everywhere, and despite limited parking spots, the place looks nice enough—at least at 1:00 a.m.

I park in a loading zone space in front of the apartment building across the street. It provides a good vantage point for monitoring the apparently uninhabited restaurant. No one's likely to load anything at this time of night.

No sooner have I made myself comfortable than a not very gentle rap on my passenger door window diverts my attention from Timba. I unlock the door. Griff slides in.

"How'd you figure out you should come here, Ram?"

I don't want to talk to him right now. "The same question comes to mind about you."

He speaks to me in a drawn out cadence. "We found the coyote victim's car. His name's Hernan Mujica. The FBI's pretty skilled at information gatherin'. We learned he works here. The tracker on Brendali's Fiat, which is parked a block away, also led us here. When we add one and one together, nine times out of ten we get two. See? Now, answer my question."

"I came here to save Bren." I stare out into the distance. "She wouldn't need saving if your police buddies did their job."

He slaps his knee. "I'm told a bureaucratic snafu occurred. The order never went out. I chewed out the messenger and told him to relay my message to his boss verbatim, with passion and at full volume."

"I don't care whose error this is. The situation sucks and you damn well know it. Her life's in danger."

"This could get ugly enough to put yours at risk. We don't know who's inside, or what kind of firepower they've got. We're waitin' on police reinforcements and a search warrant. You need to leave. Let us handle this."

"Until Bren's safe I'm staying put."

"Ram, I have to insist. I'll keep you informed."

"The same way you've done that tonight?"

"I told you before. Leave this stuff to us." He gives me an 'I mean business' law enforcement glare. "You said you understood."

"Let me show you something." I pull a document out of my glove compartment. "See this press pass? It means I can hang around wherever newsworthy activity's taking place. The kidnap and hostage-taking of a journalist qualifies."

Griff sucks in a breath and opens the door with such force I'm surprised it doesn't fly away. "Make yourself invisible, got that?" He puts one leg outside and looks back at me. "Do not—I repeat, do not—interfere. Instead, wash up. The coyote aroma doesn't do a thing for you."

He slams the door and walks away.

Thanks, LAPD, for the shower I didn't get to take. I toss the press pass on the dashboard.

Over the next half hour a convoy of patrol cars from the Glendale and Burbank police departments pull up, park and mark off a perimeter. Anyone inside Timba isn't getting out. Except Bren, I hope.

An unfamiliar buzzing noise catches my attention, followed by vibrations in my pants pocket. It's Hernan's cellphone. Lead-1's trying to reach him.

His text message asks Hernan if he's nearby. I chance a short response. 'Yes.'

'Stay away, cops are everywhere.'

'I know.'

'They're not taking us alive, God willing.'

I type 'what about the girl' before changing the last word to *'chica.'* Once the text is sent I wait, my heart skipping beats until the response arrives.

'She's been taken care of.'

Oh no, they've killed Bren? I mean to pound the steering wheel but hit the horn hard by mistake. Damn! The beep's incredibly loud. Can't do that, dude. Maintain control!

'Gone to her maker?' Tell me she hasn't. Please.

'Not yet. We put her where the sacrificial lambs belong—in the meat freezer.'

'Okay.' At least she's alive—but for how much longer? Is she going to freeze to death? I exhale and text Griff to pass along what's at stake. Once more he doesn't answer. I leave an urgent voice-mail message too. This time I don't wait for a response.

While running across Western Avenue, I keep low to avoid attracting police attention and to stay out of NITWIT's sight. Good thing for my dark clothes, the cloud cover, the absence of moonlight. I have to avoid the streetlights, though.

The first police car I lean against is empty. So are the next two. The cops are getting ready to invade Cuba, while I want to save Mexico. I can't let them attack.

The fourth police car's also vacant. Instead of moving toward the restaurant, I'm farther away. The open driver's side window allows me to lean hard on the horn. That sets off a holy racket. I've forgotten that air horns in cop cars are damn near deafening.

Three cops run toward me. Good.

"Hands up!" They point drawn guns at me, so I comply. "Turn around. Hands on the roof, now!" one says. I'm spread-eagled against the car, none too gently. The rough frisk is the second I've undergone tonight. This kind of thing gets old fast.

They're amped, ready for battle. With my ripped dirty clothes, disheveled appearance and pungent smell, they don't recognize me and probably think I'm one of the bad guys.

An officer turns me around so I'm face to face with Sergeant O'Malley, according to his nametag. "I'm Ram Forrester. The TV guy. A press pass is in my car." I point to it. "Can I show you my ID?"

He does a double-take but allows me to take my driver's license out. He looks it over and apologizes for the rough treatment. "What's the meaning of standing on that horn, sir?"

"My cohost, Brendali Santamaria, is a kidnap victim and a hostage. Your command post needs to know they'll kill her if you barge in."

The officer who frisked me sticks his mug right up to me and tries his best interrogation voice. "Tell us how you came by that knowledge."

I ignore him and address the sergeant. "Time's wasting. Brendali's life is at risk. Get me to your command post right away."

O'Malley escorts me through the police cordon to a ring of cars at the far end of the alley. Griff and a captain, who are huddled with several other uniformed men and women, go mum when I reach them.

Griff tells me a hostage negotiator and paramedics are on the way. Over the next ten minutes I set out my concerns and brief the group on NITWIT and their activities.

Once the negotiator arrives, it's agreed he'll call Timba's landline phone. He'd overheard my statements on his radio. I stand by him in the unlikely event I can talk to Bren.

"Yo." I assume that's Lead-1's voice.

"This is the police. You're surrounded, sir. You cannot escape.

We have Hernan here with us, under arrest. He's told us everything. At a minimum you'll face criminal charges of kidnapping and murder. Resistance only makes things worse. Surrender peacefully and no harm will come to you. Under no circumstances should you hurt your hostage. Send her out first. After that exit one at a time with your hands held high, without weapons."

"We do God's work. Not yours."

"We know who your hostage is, why you have her. Surrender is your only option."

"God will grant us victory over the forces of evil. As men of faith, our fates are in the Lord's hands, not yours. We have no fear."

I whisper a Bible passage into the negotiator's ear.

"Who the forces of evil are is a matter of perspective," he tells Lead-1. "Doesn't the Bible say 'and they may come to their senses and escape from the snare of the devil, having been held captive by him to do his will?' You're captive to mistaken beliefs. We can help you achieve a true victory over evil."

"Spoken like the devil incarnate. This conversation's over."

The negotiator pockets his phone and turns to me. "We'll keep trying. Don't know that we'll talk him out here. This fella's more than a bit deluded."

"So what's the next step?"

"I'll make contact again soon, unless those guys have other plans." He inclines his head in the direction of the captain and Griff.

I rush toward them to repeat my question, but they move away.

Since I'm not part of the law enforcement fraternity I'm persona non grata, huh? Two can play that game. I absolutely must get Bren to safety. I return to my car, pull out Hernan's phone and call Lead-1.

"Yo."

"This is not Hernan," I say. "I have his phone. The hostage negotiator you spoke to minutes ago told you Hernan's under arrest. That's not true. He's dead."

"Who the f--k are you? Another police devil?"

"No. This is Ram Forrester."

"Yeah, right. He's dead and buried."

"Hernan tried to kill me, but he died from a coyote attack." I recount our text exchange after Bren's kidnapping, line by line. "Convinced yet?"

"You proved you have his phone. That's all."

Lead-1's deranged, but he's not stupid. "I'm going to let you take me hostage if you'll agree to release Brendali in exchange. When I show up at your door, you'll see this is no trick."

"Why on earth should I do that?"

"Because she's innocent. You know this Bible passage: 'From now on, when you lift up your hands in prayer, I will refuse to look. Even though you offer many prayers, I will not listen. For your hands are covered with the blood of your innocent victims.' That interview you're upset about? Ask Brendali. She had no idea it would occur. So why are you traumatizing her?"

"I refuse to believe you, devil."

"You probably wondered why we introduced God as our first guest." It's cold but I'm sweating now.

"That wasn't the real God, heathen."

"You're right." I put all the false sincerity I can manage into my voice. "Fox News saw through us. We staged a publicity stunt for ratings. I've no idea how they figured it out."

"You can't fool true believers." I hear what sounds like a chuckle.

"To keep Brendali's reaction real, I kept the guest's identity secret. She's a true believer, no different than you. You saw how she refused to accept the impersonator and kept insisting the guest wasn't God, didn't you? Her reaction after the show ended—I've never seen such an angry woman. Now you're punishing her for having the same reaction you had?"

There's no response. Maybe he's buying it.

"Look, Brendali's not at fault. I'm a more valuable hostage and no one but me is answerable for violating your God's laws. You didn't know any better when you indicted us. Now you do. I'm appealing to your Christian morality." Boy is that hard to say with conviction. "Do the right thing. Release her, take me."

"We will pray on this, pagan. You will hear from us soon."

I took my best shot. Have to hope it's enough.

The 7-11 a block away sells me a disposable razor, shaving cream and soap. In the restroom of a nearby gas station I clean up and toss my tattered coat into the trash bin.

On the way back my phone, not Hernan's, chirps with a new text message. I hold it in my hand and close my eyes. "God, please, let me save Bren." I shiver and check the message.

"Come to the door in exactly fifteen minutes, unarmed. Keep your hands visible and empty. We'll hold a gun to this little lady's head until your identity is confirmed. Any hint of trickery, the bullet won't miss."

Okay, we've cleared that hurdle. Now how do I get the police to go along?

Upon my return to the command post I steer the negotiator away. "I need your help. I got the NITWIT guy to release Brendali and take me hostage instead."

He stops short and places his hands on his hips. "This is my negotiation, not yours."

All you've done is make one phone call that went nowhere. "I know, but I'm afraid she won't get out alive."

The man runs fingers over his cropped white hair. "We know what we're doing. This process takes time and works best if only one person communicates with the hostage-taker. I'm trained to do this, and highly experienced."

True, but I need to get Bren out of that freezer, pronto. "Are you saying the police won't free Brendali because I made the breakthrough instead of you?"

The negotiator can't admit that to a member of the media. "I'll run this past the captain."

"Tell him I'll need a few minutes of front door access with no police interference until Brendali's safe."

"Doubtful he'll agree. He goes by the book. You're not in it." The negotiator pivots and stomps away.

Two minutes later Griff shows up, scowling. "The answer's no. Period. I told you not to interfere."

"That's not some anonymous victim inside. It's Bren. Your people put her life in danger."

"We've got everythin' handled."

Stay calm, collect your thoughts. Sound reasonable. "Out here you're in control, but they're inside. If you crash their party, I guarantee Bren won't survive."

"We have ways to force them out."

"If you mean tear gas, Bren's dead the moment the canister's unleashed. You get them out with one fatality too many."

"Ram, your idea's too dangerous. Too much can go wrong. The answer's no. It's out of the question." He strides off toward the command post.

I call out to him. "You and the captain have no choice but to agree, Griff."

He stops. In slow motion he turns in my direction. "Oh? Why's that?"

"If I'm not at the door in seven minutes, they'll consider that trickery and kill her." That's how I read their message, anyway. "Look, I'll show you." I hold my phone out for him.

He returns to check the text messages. "I don't like this one bit, Ram."

Is he reassessing the risks? I sure hope so. "Tell the captain I won't do anything stupid."

"I thought you're tryin' to talk me *into* this."

"Griff, do this for me, and—" And what? Where am I going with this? "I know you'll look good in a tux as a member of our wedding party." Where'd that come from? I haven't thought that far ahead.

He gives me a long hard stare. "Will you serve KC-style barbecue at the banquet?"

"All you can eat."

"I'll get you cleared." He walks away, grumbling. "Can't believe I'm doin' this for some freakin' ribs. LaTaunya always says I think with my stomach."

At the fifteen-minute mark I'm in front of Timba, waiting for Bren to come out. The police are stationed a watchful nonthreatening distance away.

She soon emerges shaking, her head downcast. She meanders toward me, as though she's drunk or disoriented. Her eyes are puffy, her complexion pale. The freezer must've been hell. Her hazel colored sweatpants are adequate, but the short white tee that ends a few stitches below her sports bra isn't conducive to frigid air.

She stops inches away from me. Her body stiffens as a fist taps one leg, not gently. "They taunted me about your death. I thought you died for me like all the others did. I see they got that wrong." She isn't screaming but her tone conveys anger, loud and clear.

I try to embrace her, but she backs away. "You said you'd protect me, remember? Why the hell didn't you, the first time I needed it?"

What's going on here? "Are you okay? Did they hurt you?"

As though she can't decide what to say first, her mouth opens and closes several times. She ends up speechless.

"Your purse and phone are in my car. Here's the key fob. Griff's here. He can show you where it's parked."

She snatches the fob and pushes me backward with both hands. "You had a little fling with that sex goddess Kate, didn't you? I hope you enjoyed her while I froze!"

"No, we didn't. I mean, I—" She knows Kate and I aren't civil to each other, so where's this crazy talk coming from? I try to embrace her again and get slapped hard across the face.

"Go in right away or they'll shoot us both." Without a single look back at me she wanders toward Griff, who's in front of a small group of cops by Western Avenue. When she reaches him, he grabs her. She collapses into his arms.

My arms should hold her, not his. How'd this happen, Bren? This is unbelievable. What did these bastards do to make you react like that? I can explain!

Someone manhandles me from behind and pulls me into the restaurant. I don't resist.

My captors seat me in the restaurant's kitchen, surrounded by three men. I recognize Skeleton Man from Bren's sketch drawing. He's outfitted in black and stands by the door. His voice gives away his Lead-1 handle. An obese woman leans against a fryer.

"Lord," Skeleton Man says, "we convene this tribunal to receive your judgment. Arch-sinner and blasphemer Ram Forster is here before you, already sentenced to death and eternal hellfire. A new charge is levied for the cold-blooded murder of our compatriot, Hernan, a fellow soldier of your gospel. May he rest forever in your arms. We await your sentence."

The others add amens, clasp hands, close their eyes and mutter a chant. The woman sings a hymn in a voice reminiscent of Mama Cass Elliott, but she sings "Words of Hate", not love.

Skeleton Man's gibberish continues for a good ten minutes, interspersed with occasional barks, yips and whistles. At one point a phone rings—probably the hostage negotiator. No one answers it. Twice Lead-1 stops and cocks his head, looking as though he's receiving instructions.

How bizarre. What a mockery of a trial.

"Yes, Lord. I see. We'll comply with your will." The others unclasp their hands and await the verdict. "You are declared guilty and sentenced to torture sufficient to lead to death."

He gestures to his accomplices. "Take him to the freezer while we confront the infidels outside. Prepare our defense. The nonbelievers will soon attack."

They won't kill me easily. "Doesn't your Lord know how Hernan died? Or did you not bother to tell him? Are actual facts irrelevant?"

"More blasphemy. Shut him up. Get him out of my sight."

I'm grabbed by the arms. Two men drag me away. "Hernan paid for his sins, the hideous way he died," are my last shouted words before we enter the freezer.

When the men lay me on an ice cold table I'm wishing I still wore that ruined jacket. A meat slicer's positioned inches from my feet. Several sides of beef hang nearby from metal hooks. I'm not fond of the symbolism. A humidifier, sink and a shelf containing large containers of various condiments are also in view. Everything else is hidden behind stainless steel refrigeration doors.

A man enters with the obese gal. He turns on the slicer while she puts a gun to my head and murmurs. "You'll cooperate with us, won't you, kitten?"

"What choice do I have?"

For the second time tonight I'm tied up, my arms and legs trussed like I'm a pig about to get roasted over a spit. The third man uses scissors to slice off a small section of a tablecloth. He stuffs it in my mouth and tapes my lips shut.

The three men leave. "Sleep well, kitten," I hear. "We'll return for you once we whip the devils." The door clangs shut and the room goes dark except for a garish green tint given off by the slicer's dim electric lighting.

I can't estimate how much time passes, but it's enough to make my teeth chatter and for one arm to go numb from lack of circulation or frostbite. I'm too wired to lay here with my thoughts. Although escape's impossible, I have to try. Can I cozy up to the slicer and cut the rope without slicing my skin? That's way too dangerous to try. Maybe I can fall off the table to a standing position instead? If I manage to do that, what's the next step?

I wiggle to the table's edge and pause to balance myself. Suddenly everything shakes and I'm thrown into the air. What the effing hell's going on? Earthquake? Aftershock?

I hit the concrete floor face-first. A cow haunch slams into my back, covering me like a frozen blanket. Pain explodes from the waist up. Blood oozes from one ear and flows freely from my nose. A blown eardrum. A broken nose. Maybe a concussion, too? It's hard to breathe with my mouth taped shut and blood interfering with air intake through my nostrils.

Calm down, dude. Take in whatever air you can.

What's that rustling sound? Mice? No. Radagast again. Huh? He flickers in and out of view, like last time. Why's he glowing? How is it I can see through him?

I'm delusional, I guess, but he's real enough to touch. If only I could. He pushes his hood back so I can see the contours of his face. Young. Real young. Not Radagast.

"Who are you?" I can hear my voice although I can't speak. Did I think out loud?

"Shhh." He stops the slicer's whir by pointing at it. The same gesture turns off the greenish light. He gives off a beacon's worth of light, while the rest of the room is black. The side of beef on top of me lifts, wafts over to the slicer table and drops onto it with a loud thump.

A finger of the ghost, or whatever he is, touches my lips. The tape falls off. A tong floats over and pulls the tablecloth piece out of my mouth. The barest touch of his fingers on either side of my nose, like a breeze passing by, improves my breathing and staunches the blood flow. I gulp mouthfuls of cold air while he repairs my ear and commands the ropes to become untied.

"Recognize me?" His voice sounds familiar, a little. A wind tunnel effect interferes with my attempt to pin it down. "I'm Nick."

My brother Nick? Have I died? Is this the afterlife? "I can't leave, Nick. I won't go, I refuse. Not the way Angel and I parted. I have to explain myself, make amends—"

"You must sleep." His fingers close my eyes. With my nerve receptors on hiatus, I'm no longer freezing. The throb of the cooling system is gone. So is Nick. Total darkness reigns.

27 | Sorry Seems to be the Hardest Word

BRENDALI

November 25, 2027 (cont.), 2:10 a.m.

Griff's hug reassures me that my nightmare's over. "You're ice cold, Brendali. Here, wear this." He takes off his suit jacket and wraps it around my frozen shoulders. "Glad you're free. Are you doin' okay?"

"I have no idea. I'm in a daze," I say through chattering teeth. With my body shaking, I pull his jacket tight to capture more warmth.

"Do you need medical attention?" I manage a whispered 'uh-uh' in response. "If you change your mind tell Officer Chi, here." He points to the officer next to him. "Paramedics are available. Otherwise, stay put. Things may get ugly. Officer, would you mind strollin' over to the paramedics to scrounge up a blanket for Ms. Santamaria?"

That request is directed at an officer behind us, who complies and soon brings back a green blanket with a Red Cross insignia. I throw it over Griff's jacket and wrap the blanket around me as Griff hurries away.

"Will these men get Ram out?"

Officer Chi, an Asian man probably in his late thirties, frowns. "The negotiator gave the kidnappers until 2:30 to surrender. They won't, I expect. We'll have to go in, arrest them and free Mr. Forrester."

I grab his arm. "They'll kill Ram if that happens."

"Ma'am, I'm sorry. I don't make these decisions. Mr. Hoosier and the others in command know what they're doing."

"Can I talk to them?"

"No, Ma'am. My orders are to keep you here until the operation ends."

God needs us for the Convocation. I whisper a prayer for Ram's safety and watch as a platoon gathers at the front door. They're armed with shields, guns, protective vests and helmets. A smaller group marches up the alley, probably to cover the rear door. A firetruck with a big ladder pulls into position on the street. Several ambulances park behind it.

A white-haired non-uniformed man steps forward and raises his megaphone. "This is your final chance to come out voluntarily, unarmed. Do not resist arrest. You have sixty seconds to obey this order."

I cross my fingers for the entire minute, but nothing happens.

An officer yanks the front door open, triggering an explosion that flings the heavy wood and glass door outward, into the squadron. The first man drops and doesn't move, his skull smashed. Three men behind him sink to the ground, too. Windows blow out. Fire rapidly spreads to the roof.

"Oh God, no!" My hands cover my mouth. I stop breathing.

Paramedics hustle to the four injured policemen. Emergency lights on the ambulance light up. The fire truck's giant ladder swings over the building. A fireman with a hose climbs to douse the flames. No officers go inside and no one comes out.

I tug on Officer Chi's arm. "We have to do something! Ram's in danger. He's probably hurt." Or dead, but I can't bring myself to say that. The knots in my stomach tighten.

"Ma'am, the matter's out of our hands. Our personnel train for these situations. They'll sort everything out soon."

Within minutes three injured officers are moved to ambulances that speed away, sirens roaring. The deceased officer's covered up, left in place. Once the fire's out, police rush inside.

Five minutes later an officer comes out, talking into his shoulder transmitter. His urgent wave is directed at the ambulances. That's not a good sign. Two paramedics hustle inside with a gurney. The overhead lights of an ambulance turn on and the rear door opens to receive the injured man.

My heart skips a beat. I kneel, pray, hold my breath and wait.

The paramedics soon wheel out an inert body. "No, no, no! Not Ram! No!" I run toward the gurney trailed by Officer Chi. Ram's face is alabaster white, like church statuary. His eyes are shut, the front of his shirt bloody. A few specks of dried blood are visible in one ear. I don't see obvious injuries. If he has internal ones, that's bad news.

Officer Chi pulls me back before I can throw myself over Ram. "Is he—" Again the 'D' word won't pass my lips.

"Let these men do their work, Ma'am. Mr. Hoosier wants us to wait. That's what we'll do. You need to undergo a debrief."

My face feels flushed as I answer, hands on my hips. "I'm going wherever they're taking Ram. He needs me. I have to know how injured he is. So do your debrief at the hospital."

"I'll check with Mr. Hoosier. We'll do what he allows."

Griff will let me go. He has a big heart. "Someone, please! Is he alive? Where are you taking him?" No one pays attention to me. "Damn it, tell me!"

After Ram's loaded into the ambulance, I pull a paramedic aside. "Ram and I work together. Can I ride in the ambulance with him?"

He looks me over. "I'll arrange it." He goes to speak to the driver while Officer Chi confirms Griff's agreement to have my debrief take place in the hospital ER. I accept the deal.

Once in the ambulance I hold Ram's hand and talk to him the whole way, ignoring the EMT guy seated with us who's monitoring Ram's condition. Ram's unconscious, so he doesn't respond. When we arrive he's wheeled into the St. Joseph's ER. I go to the waiting room.

A half hour later Officer Chi arrives and gets the debrief underway. "I'll try to keep this short, Ma'am, and contact you later if I need gaps filled in. First, how did your kidnapping occur?"

I don't want to relive this, especially now. But he needs to know. "I watched a movie called *The Shape of Water* while waiting for Ram to come home. A helicopter's loud whir drowned out the sound. Ram lives in the penthouse, a pad for copters is next to it. I give this no thought—once during the weekend another copter landed. It's infrequent, according to Ram. I turned up the volume and kept watching the movie."

I stop to take a deep breath. "The door burst open. Two men rushed in. I fought them until one flashed his gun. My cheese knife couldn't defend against that, so I gave up." Too bad I stored my gun in Ram's safe. The fight would've ended differently.

"The unarmed man began to tear the place apart to make it look like a robbery. The guy with the gun tied my hands and drove us to the restaurant in my car. The other guy must've flown the helicopter away. I never saw him again."

Officer Chi looked up from his notepad. "When you arrived at the restaurant, how many people did you see?"

"Five, counting the kidnapper and Skeleton Man. They—"

"Who's Skeleton Man?"

"Ask Griff, he can explain. I'm real worried about Ram. Do I have to tell you now?"

"If I need more detail, I'll contact you. Go ahead, continue."

"Aside from myself, the others included Skeleton Man, my kidnapper, one huge woman and two Latinos about my age. Skeleton Man did the talking, he's their leader. He told me I'd never—excuse me." I pull tissues from my purse and dab my eyes. "That *bastardo* said I'd never see Ram alive again because he'd been killed."

With pride Papi used to say 'none of my kids will ever break.' I need to remember that.

Officer Chi focuses his eyes down the hall, where Griff's hustling toward us. "My apologies, M'am, I know this is hard for you to discuss."

"That's okay. I'm an emotional wreck right now. It's been a rough night."

"You've been through a lot," he says as Griff sits next to me.

"All I can add is that Skeleton Man ordered his men to put me in the freezer. He said I'd get taken somewhere in the morning. They gave me a bunch of tablecloths to use as blankets, which didn't keep me warm. Later they released me, without explaining why."

"Thanks," the officer said. "Under the circumstances I don't have any more questions. Mr. Hoosier, do you?"

"Maybe, but they can wait. Copy me on your report, officer."

"Sure," Chi says. "M'am, I hope Mr. Forrester pulls through. I've enjoyed watching your show." He smiles, bows and departs with the Red Cross blanket since I'm warm enough in here with Griff's suit wrapped around my upper body.

I turn toward Griff, who's staring at me with a stern but dubious look on his face. Half a minute goes by before he speaks. "Can I ask you a question?"

I sigh. "Why not? This is a night for them, no?" I give him a wan smile.

"Maybe it's none of my business, but why'd you slap Ram outside Timba?"

He's too damn observant. "When I'm angry I do stupid things." I don't want to say more.

"Would you mind sharin' what Ram did to make you angry?"

"I'd rather not. It's between us, and unrelated to anything you're concerned about."

His law enforcement stare can intimidate without an uttered word. "I think I should tell you a few things I doubt you're aware of."

Griff details everything Ram did to take my place as a hostage, and how he escaped his own kidnap. The more he says the worse I feel, the smaller I grow. I bend over, gluing my gaze to the floor and using my hands to cover the rest of my face. His relentless words ring in my ears.

Ram put his life on the line to protect me. I owe him my life. No one's ever done anything like this for me. He really does love me, and I repaid him with a slap. I'm terrible, totally unworthy of him. From now on I'll trust and love him with all my soul, all my heart. Please, God, make sure he survives. I need him.

I retreat into my shame and sob in self-loathing. Griff's voice continues to buzz around me. The first of his words I recognize are 'your tears are ruinin' my suit jacket, you know.' That makes me laugh a little. I use a few tissues to dry my eyes and give him a tiny smile.

A doctor joins us. "You're here for Mr. Forrester, correct?"

We answer 'yes' at the same time.

"He's an interesting case," the doctor says. "He came in unconscious. We began to run a non-contrast MRI on him, but he woke up midway through, screamed bloody murder and tried to get out of the machine." The doctor chuckles. "First time that's happened in my twenty-three years of practice."

"Is he okay, doctor?" I ask.

"He's fine, despite the grade three concussion. That's another first for me. We did x-rays and a CT scan. They don't show any irregularities, so we're releasing him. As a precaution he shouldn't do anything strenuous, or drive, for at least the next forty-eight hours. He's quite fatigued and needs rest. Bring him back if he needs medical care or shows any of the symptoms on the discharge instructions he'll take home. He should come out soon."

"Thanks, doctor," I say. "I'm so relieved."

Griff stands after the doctor leaves us. "Based on the doctor's advice, I'll defer questioning Ram for now. Tell him I'll get in touch in a day or two." He prepares to go.

"You're not going to wait for him?"

He gives me another of his two-second smiles. "I'd like to, but I'm needed at Timba. I've got a lot to do before calling it a night."

Five minutes after Griff leaves, Ram and I hug like we've been separated for years. My face reddens and my mouth twitches. I cradle his cheeks in my hands and speak in a near-whisper. "I'm sorry, *mi cariño*. I'm so, so sorry. Never should I have gotten mad at you."

"Why apologize? We're together, safe. Nothing else matters."

"I said horrible things. I wasn't myself. You save me and I haul off and slap you? *Mi Dios!* Never again will I doubt you, I swear it. Tell me you forgive me, baby, please."

"Of course I do." He plants a sweet kiss on my lips and takes my hands. "Let's go home, Angel. I can tell you're exhausted."

Despite what he's gone through tonight, he's only concerned about me. That's the kind of man I can't let myself lose.

RAM

Monday, November 29, 2027, 8:15 p.m., KJCR-TV
"Our next guests are Archbishop Ricardo Delmonico, Rabbi Shlomo Nakamura and Hakan Çelik, the Muslim contingent's leader in the Convocation. We'll discuss how their respective faiths—known as the Abrahamic religions—might at last put aside their histories of religious violence."

"Let's give these men a generous welcome," Bren adds as she stands to greet them. I follow suit. Loud applause welcomes our guests as they stride across the stage to us. Hakan and Slomo sit to Bren's right, while the Archbishop takes the seat to my left.

"Since the Jewish faith is the oldest of the Abrahamic religions, let's start with Slomo," I suggest. "What's the historic, or scriptural, basis for religious violence in the Hebrew culture?"

"Back when the Jews escaped from Egypt and trudged across the Sinai Desert toward the land that would become Israel, the Amaleks, a Canaanite nation, attempted to destroy them." Slomo's so into this topic he's fidgeting up and down in his seat. "We prevailed. Our Torah reflects the impact of this war with two *mitzvahs,* or commandments from God. One calls upon us to obliterate the Amalek nation. The other is to never forget their evil deeds."

"Archbishop, does the Bible reflect these ancient battles?"

"Exodus 17:15 has been understood to mean that God, through

the Israelites, would permanently mandate war against the Amaleks and their descendants. In recent times this has come to mean the Palestinians, but that's incorrect." As usual Delmonico's casual demeanor is more measured than Slomo's. "1 Samuel makes it clear that God never issued a standing order to justify violence against anyone. Important Jewish Talmudic scholars, Maimonides for example, have said that the word Amalek refers to individuals or communities with a propensity toward violence, rather than a particular nation or society."

"Your comments raise an interesting thought," Bren says, leaning forward to talk around me to the Archbishop. "In Rome, where Catholicism started, its followers faced experiences not too different from what the Jews went through in the desert, no?"

"In a sense, that's true." Delmonico replies. "Roman Catholics, like the Jews before them, became victims of periodic religious persecution until Emperor Constantine's Edict of Milan in 313 decriminalized Catholicism throughout the Roman Empire."

"And from that point," I say in a more sarcastic tone than intended, "the Catholics became persecutors, isn't that right?"

Delmonico's raised eyebrow implies his surprise at my exclamation. "Not right away, but Catholics did later initiate and engage in the Crusades, the Inquisition, pogroms and other persecutions of Jews and Muslims. Jesus preached love, but the well of intolerance runs deep in my religion."

Bren turns toward Hakan, "Mr. Çelik, has this pattern of being the target of persecution, followed by becoming persecutors, also happened in the Muslim world?"

Hakan brings his hands to his lips and bows to us before responding, to our surprise, in English—which he doesn't speak. "In the time of Mohammed, God's final prophet, much opposition to him and his religion existed. He counseled his believers to exercise patience and prayer. Years later, tired of oppression, Mohammed revealed Qur'anic verses justifying violence against the oppressors. He called them infidels. Later generations mistook these verses to mean death to nonbelievers. Today some Islamic sects legitimize terrorism through these *hadiths.*"

"Is it fair," I ask, "to say that over the centuries the perception of the faithful within your religions changed God from one who fosters peace, tolerance and cooperation into a deity who promotes violence?"

The three men share reflective countenances until Slomo speaks up. "That's the hand we've been dealt by history, but going forward things can be different. Today's Muslims and Jews don't need to hate each other, but can't find the moral strength to cast their historic grudges aside. Today's Catholics aren't yesteryear's Crusaders, but anti-Semitism and hatred of Muslims is still high. We—"

The Archbishop interrupts. "Slomo, Hakan and I spent the weekend working up a statement or guideline that can provide a pathway to peace, or at least to tolerance, between our religions. At worst, the concepts we came up with provide a foundation for refinement with the same objective. Which of you have that sheet?"

"Brendali, please read it for us," Hakan says, handing her a sheet of yellow paper. "I can't read English." He speaks it here, though, like he does in the Convocation's main hall.

Bren scans the page before speaking. "Okay, these five points are listed:

1. Practitioners of the Abrahamic religions believe in one god whom they call by different names. To continue our conflicts would violate his moral code.
2. Holy wars, crusades or jihads contradict god's will and the true spirit of our religions. There is no justification for religious violence under any conceivable circumstance.
3. Each religious community should correct scriptural misinterpretations used to justify religious violence, teach these corrections and engage in intra-faith dialogue.

4. Historical, psychological and social narratives, as well as current-day tensions and unresolved issues, need attention. Resolution, wherever possible, should be reached. Mechanisms to address remaining issues should be created through a venue where impartial compromise solutions can be achieved.

5. A worldwide holiday to celebrate shared human dignity would highlight our progress and remind us of our inter-connectedness."

"That's impressive," Bren says, sharing my astonishment. "The three of you came up with this over a weekend?"

"Most of this comes from Slomo's Stanford doctoral thesis. We took his ideas and ran with them," Delmonico explains. "He's hosting Hakan at his home. They began their discussions before I joined in. I needed a half day to read through the thesis, but Slomo sold me on the overall concept pretty easily."

"He deserves some applause," I say, pointing at Slomo. "What do you folks in the audience think?"

They agree and shower him with praise. His face turns crimson. He pats his heart and bows.

I put a hand up to signal an end to the applause. "Gentlemen, do you plan to present this to your respective groups at the Convocation?"

"Yes," Delmonico answered. "I've asked Father Zeke to approach the Evangelicals, too. Despite their, umm, reluctance, he agrees we should try to bring them along."

Bren and I share a dubious look, but she speaks first. "Let's hope for the best."

I'm seated on Kate's dragon couch in Bren's dressing room while she changes into a dark red V-neck sweater, jeans and brown leather boots. "The Pew Research Center stats indicate a marked rise in religious violence over the last few years. With a few exceptions, the violence comes from followers of one Abrahamic religion against the others, or from governmental entities that favor one religion over the others."

"Think how much better this world can become if these three guys can get their agenda through and enacted by the Convocation." Bren dons a dark red and green Christmas sweater, giving her an early start on the holiday. "They'll need a miracle."

"Miracles are out of bounds. God's looking to us to solve this problem ourselves."

"That includes the still unresolved problem of the Evangelicals' unwillingness to play by God's rules. We need to do something about that."

Bren misunderstood that I meant mankind, not the two of us, but she's right.

"Yes we do," I say. "You and I can't let this Convocation fail. We have to get active, push the Evangelicals and everyone else across the finish line. If God doesn't find mankind worth keeping around, our lives together will end sooner than we'd like."

She comes over, sits on my lap and puts an arm around my shoulders. "Let's do what we did tonight—use our show not only to provide news updates, but to influence opinion. It's time all the attendees have a little fire lit under them, no?"

She's serious, and right. "We can try. And if that doesn't help, we'll get right into the steering committee's faces. If attendees can have agendas, we can, too."

A broad smile lights up her face. "That's my baby. We're going to win this fight."

Brendali's Twitter Convocation Update: We've learned that the Evangelical man who needed medical attention earlier has undergone major heart surgery. #Pray for good news #to health!

BRENDALI

Tuesday, November 30, 2027

Jimi freaking Hendrix at 7:30 a.m.? *Meirda!* "Ram, turn off the alarm—please!" I shove his shoulder a few times, to no effect.

The chilly bedroom air hits me once I toss off the quilt and bedcover. I silence Ram's alarm, get the hallway thermostat working and return to the bedroom. The idea that cool air on naked skin will wake him doesn't pan out—even with all the covers pulled off, Ram slumbers.

Upon checking the little yellow sticky pad I used to track our lovemaking last night, I find twelve O's for me and two for him. Six to one's about the right ratio, no? Poor baby, he wore himself out pleasuring me. With only three hours of sleep, no wonder he won't wake up.

After a half hour in the bathroom, I re-enter the warmer bedroom wearing only a towel wrapped around my damp hair. Ram hasn't moved. At this rate he'll sleep through the Convocation. I set his alarm to go off in five minutes and turn the volume to maximum.

In the kitchen I brew coffee, munch a blueberry bagel and wait for Ram to appear. A minute after the alarm blares he bumps into the door frame, bounces off and staggers in. He grabs the edge of the kitchen counter like a drunk and flops onto the seat next to me.

I sweeten my voice to show that innocent little me is unaware of his poor taste in alarm clock music. *"Buenas dias, mi torpe amor."*

"Boy, do I ache. But wow, what a night." He bends forward to kiss me and falls off the chair, onto his knees. This cracks us both up.

Ram tries to French kiss my belly button, but I push his head back. "You sacrificed for a good cause, *mi cariño.*" He rests his head in my lap, so I run a hand through his hair. "Mmm, baby. Does this make you feel better?"

He straightens up but doesn't stand. "I always feel better when I see you, especially *au natural.* How do I say that in Spanish?"

I pose to give him a close-up of every inch of me. "You say *sin ropa, tu niña traviesa.* That means 'without clothes, you naughty girl.' I want to teach you Spanish. It's the world's most romantic language, no?"

"Yes, but I won't retain your lesson until I wake up."

"El cafe esta listo." I point to the coffee machine, in case he doesn't get it. "I'll fix breakfast while you shower."

Ram gets to his feet, stretches and yawns. "Are you monitoring the Convocation today, or will you attend?"

"It's more productive if I stay here."

He pours black coffee into the largest cup he owns. "Okay. Fill me in if you find anything worthwhile." Ram retreats to the bathroom with his caffeine jolt. After forty-five minutes he's on his way to the Convocation, energized by my breakfast and a second cup of strong black coffee.

Once the gathering's underway I message the tech angels. 'Can you patch me into any newsworthy discussions taking place that involves the Evangelicals?'

Instead of a video feed I get a message. 'Nothing meets your criteria at the moment. After the lunch hour the Catholics and Evangelicals will meet to update the Ten Commandments.'

Oh, really? Now that's newsworthy. 'Please notify me when they begin so I can watch.'

I spend the morning focused on Sammy's binder. The Allenby Family Foundation's Articles of Incorporation and Bylaws are dense with legal mumbo jumbo I don't even try to understand. Board Minutes from only three meetings are included although the Foundation's been in existence for fourteen years. The latest Minutes are from a 2021 board meeting. A few tax records are here, too, though not all of them. The rest of the binder is filled with bank records that are above my pay grade to sort out. I try, though.

At lunchtime I realize the Ten Commandments meeting's already begun. I slap together a hurried turkey sandwich, sit down at the kitchen table and turn my iPad on.

Guilt about not covering this event in person pushes me to watch. Curiosity compels me to continue examining Sammy's binder. Which should I ignore? I touch the binder, my iPad, the binder, my iPad again—but not the sandwich.

This is ridiculous. Never am I indecisive.

The video feed gains my attention. A group of maybe fifty people are packed into a room a third the size of the main hall. A thin gray-haired man at the front of the room is speaking.

"We've made good progress by agreeing to drop the commandments that prohibit prayers to other Gods and forbid graven images. We'll retain those that respect parental honor and reject killing, adultery and stealing. If we finish the five remaining commandments today, tomorrow we can discuss whether to add new ones. Let's discuss the 'thou shalt not covet' commandment."

These are good decisions. Things are going well. What a surprise!

"All humans are greedy SOBs," someone yells. "Keep the commandment. Broaden it beyond 'thy neighbor.' Make it universal. We shouldn't covet near half what we do."

A higher-pitched voice chimes in. "I'm disgusted, personally. I agree, enlarge the commandment. Change 'covet' to 'avarice,' or 'greed'—some stronger word."

I join the cheers by clapping for the idea myself.

"Does anyone disagree?" The moderator looks around. No one speaks or gestures until a hand is raised off to my left.

An older man stands. "Greed, like other evils, is innate and cultural. We pursue all forms of it with abandon. A commandment to prohibit greed won't mean a thing."

No one reacts. He's probably right, but that shouldn't matter.

"I agree with Joseph," a man in the back of the room says. He gets to his feet and projects his scratchy voice. "The Vatican will never approve an expanded commandment. Over the centuries, no organization's been more rapacious than the goddamn Catholic Church and its tentacles, right down to local priests."

That's Jake Benveniste, the beady-eyed Evangelical I watched a week ago. He means to disrupt the discussion.

The whole group chatters. The moderator gestures and tries to talk through the outburst. His voice is drowned out as the noise level rises. I don't like this. They're screaming at each other now. Bits and pieces reach my ears.

"You Evangelicals can go to hell!"

"Ever since the Council of Trent, you Catholics have falsified the Gospel—"

"We need cooperation here, not name-calling."

"Who are you to tell us what we need? You're sellouts, all of you—"

"We're the ones who are saved, you're the ones who are lost—"

"Oh, yeah? I'll show you who's saved or lost!"

A fight breaks out. How can they tell who is Catholic, who is Evangelical? Oh, right—the color of their name tags. It's terrible, people hammering each other like this.

I push back from the table so fast my untouched sandwich is knocked to the floor. In my haste to leave I don't pick it up.

I pace around waiting for the elevator and use the time to text Ram. 'A huge fight's broken out in the Ten Commandments Reform meeting room. Get security and stop it!'

'Oh, shit!' is his eloquent reaction.

It'll take five minutes to reach the Convention Center if I run at top speed and the light at Figueroa Street's green. Once outside I bring up the video feed on my cellphone. The first thing I see is the moderator getting whacked in the head and collapsing.

Mierda, this is like a bar fight. Truly religious people don't act this way.

One guy swings the wooden leg of a broken chair at whoever comes near him. Toward the back of the room Benveniste's down. Blood seeps from his mouth and nose. Another man's dismantling an overturned collapsible table as people around him fight. If he pulls it apart the metal legs will become dangerous.

I type an urgent message while stopped at the Figueroa Street traffic light. 'God, angels, please, please help. This is scary and sickening.'

The instant response: 'We do not interfere in the exercise of human free will.'

'That's unacceptable. You brought these people together, forced them to spend two months doing something they don't want to do. You're not taking responsibility?'

No response, as usual.

As I hustle through the crosswalk Johnny Ray, another guard, Father Zeke and Ram are entering the conference room. The Archbishop's behind them. "God, please, make sure Ram doesn't get hurt." While scrambling across the Convention Center's parking lot I slow down to get ear buds out of my purse and into my ears.

"Everyone, listen up!" Father Zeke's trumpet-like voice is easy to recognize. "Stop this insanity! Y'all remember Galatians 5:15? 'If ye bite and devour one another, take heed that ye be not consumed one of another.' Control yourselves, for God's sake!"

Good luck with that approach, Zeke. None of the combatants are paying attention.

Johnny Ray and Zeke pull people apart and take a couple of punches themselves. The second security guard, a Latino, threatens to pepper spray anyone who doesn't calm down. He's ignored. Ram yells for whoever's in charge to take charge, but no one is.

We'll fail God's test acting this way.

The Archbishop, motionless, examines the battlefield with his arms crossed. Anger and sympathy alternately cross his face. He goes first to Benveniste, squats and checks on him. At least someone's concerned about the injured, no?

Johnny Ray marches people out the door, telling them to "skedaddle" and not show their faces again until they grow up.

As I enter the Convention Center, the man who took the table apart takes a run at Benveniste. A metal table leg with a hinged end is in his hand, a long screw extending out from the hinge. As the man swings his weapon the Archbishop flops over Benveniste to protect him. The hinge strikes Delmonico flush in his right cheek, the screw impaling his eye. The Archbishop's scream echoes around the half-empty room.

My scream does the same in the main lobby.

Everyone in the room stops to see what happened. People near me stare and walk away.

How uncaring these people are. Why on earth did God choose them? A jarring answer strikes me: he wants to know if the most uncooperative humans can become cooperative.

I watch Ram tackle the attacker, twisting the guy's arm until the table leg drops. They wrestle, each struggling to grab the weapon or prevent the other from reaching it. The Latino guard comes over, bends down and pepper sprays both of them flush in the face.

Ram's eyes are going to sting. I hope he doesn't rub them, that only makes the effects worse.

A man with a torn suit and bloody cheek directs me to the second floor. I speed up the stairs and enter the room right behind some paramedics. One calls for a second unit and a police presence. Only the injured remain, along with the two security guards. Father Zeke's gone, too.

Benveniste's unconscious. The moderator, on the floor but propped against a wall, is urging the paramedics to help the others. One goes to Benveniste, the other to the Archbishop. What's left of Delmonico's eye looks like scrambled egg whites in runny ketchup.

On the floor, Ram and the man he fought twitch and cough.

Ram's eyes are closed, his face red and puffy. I squat next to him. "I'm here, sweetie. Let's get you cleaned up."

"It stings. Jeez does it sting." He's rubbed his eyes, as I expected.

"I learned all about pepper spray in Mexico, baby, so listen to me. Force yourself to blink. Tears will help." Out of sympathy I brush his cheeks. "You'll need lots of water to wash the spray off your face and out of your eyes. Let's find you a faucet."

Johnny Ray and I pull Ram to his feet. "I can't see. Am I blind?" He sways back and forth as we leave the room.

I almost lose hold of him. "It's hard to keep you upright if you fidget. This is temporary, you're not blind. The Archbishop's the one with the real eye problem." That quiets him.

We approach the restroom. "Why, you cain't go in, Ma'm. That's only for men," Johnny Ray says.

"Too bad. Ram needs me."

He shrugs as we walk into the empty bathroom. I ask Johnny Ray to stay by the entrance and direct men elsewhere. At the largest sink, farthest from the urinals, Ram grabs the sides to stay upright while I take his shirt and pants off.

"Why bother with my clothes? The spray's in my eyes."

"Shush, sweetie. You rolled all over that floor. Your clothes have spray residue on them. I'll wipe off what I can. Keep one eye under running water for five minutes. Do the other when I tell you to switch."

I turn on the faucet, adjust the water temperature, wash my hands and push his head under the spray. "Make sure you can breathe, baby. Johnny, I need you!"

He does a double take when he sees Ram in his underwear.

"Men look like this when they're not completely dressed, you know?" That's meant as a joke, but sounds sarcastic to me. "Get me a large bunch of paper towels. I'm staying near Ram." He hustles to the dispensers, hands them over and returns to sentry duty.

The floor doesn't look dirty but I wet some towels and hand-wipe the nearby tiles before spreading Ram's shirt out across them. I use another wad to wash off the spray. Ram rinses the other eye while I clean his pants.

Once we've finished both eyes, I help Ram sit on the floor. His face is red and puffy.

"Mi cariño, do you feel better at all?"

"Wetter, yes. Better, no."

"Don't worry. You'll notice improvement soon." I kiss his wet forehead.

"Why the hell did Luis spray me?"

"I'm sure he didn't mean to." I wash my hands again.

"That doesn't make me any happier."

"God would want you to forgive him. You should." I bend down and put my hands around his neck. "Luis tried to help break you two up, no?" Ram shrugs and nods his grudging agreement. "Get dressed. You'll have to wear the clothes damp until you can change at home."

Johnny Ray and I guide him back to the conference room, which is totally empty except for Luis. He's putting chairs and desks back in order. "I'm real sorry about the pepper spray, Mr. Forrester," Luis says in a soft, hesitant voice. He stares at the floor, unable to look at Ram's flushed face. "The paramedics took the Archbishop and one other man to the hospital. The man who hurt them is under arrest."

Ram waves the apology away. "We'd better get to the station, Bren, and prepare for tonight's show. You'll have to drive."

"No kidding." I give him a wide-eyed 'duh.'

This is our first show in the large permanent studio the station built for us. The silver and black décor is modern and sleek. Instead of the typical talk show table and chair set up, we're seated around a large circular table with a liquor bar in view behind us. Ram wanted to have a *Cheers* type comedic waitress serve us drinks but Ken, the cheapskate, refused to pay for one.

Ram's vision is normal but stage makeup doesn't entirely hide the redness in his face. We begin with the Convocation segment of the show.

"Today some Evangelical invitees chose not to participate in good faith, contrary to God's dictates. God said that anyone who acts this way will face serious and immediate consequences, as will their followers."

"Casualties resulted," I add. "Before the show started I checked on the man who caused the melee. His injuries weren't fatal, but he died. God took his life as punishment."

"I helped break the fight up," Ram says, "and got pepper sprayed by mistake. Archbishop Delmonico sustained a serious eye injury while protecting an injured man and is hospitalized. We wish him a full and fast recovery. We're told his assailant has been arrested and jailed. No bail's been set."

"Ram and I don't want to see anything like this during the rest of the Convocation. We need a successful outcome. Our very existence depends on it."

"I expect God to express his displeasure soon," Ram says. "For anyone still skeptical of God's authenticity, pay attention. Over the next few days your skepticism will dissolve."

Brendali's Convocation Update: God's meted out more punishment for today's fight. Tonight Saddlebow Church, an Evangelical mega-church in Orange County, disappeared. Multiple eyewitnesses filmed it EVAPORATE. Deaths & injuries unknown. #Wild! #God'srevenge

---

BRENDALI

Wednesday, December 1, 2027

"Sorry to wake you, Griff. This can't wait."

"Who is this? Brendali?" His words are slurred. "Christ almighty, what blasted time is it, anyway?"

"3 a.m. I need your help."

"What's wrong? Did NITWIT kidnap your dreams and hold them for ransom?"

Okay, he's awake. "Very funny."

"What's so doggone urgent that you have to get me up in the middle of the night? Can't Ram help you?"

"No, he's asleep. I tried to wake him, but couldn't."

"So you don't mind deprivin' your good buddy Griff of some hard-earned shut-eye, is that it? Law enforcement personnel need beauty sleep more than media celebs do."

"I'm sorry, Griff. Would you like to know how NITWIT is funded?"

He won't nod off now. A subdued response comes through. "Are you tellin' me you have that information?"

"Maybe." I launch into a quick explanation of Sammy's binder. "I've reviewed financial documents from at least twenty bank accounts. Math wasn't my best subject in school, and this many numbers makes my head swim. But its possible Jack Allenby's laundering money for NITWIT and others through his charitable foundation."

He snorts, loud and clear. "I hear 'maybe' and 'possible,' not 'definitely.' Spend a few more hours figurin' this out until you reach a non-speculative conclusion. When you're done, call me when I'm awake, functional and at my office. If there's criminal activity goin' on at a high enough level, the FBI would investigate."

"I can't do the accounting, Griff. Someone who can needs to look this material over, trace the money coming in, going out. My intuition tells me—"

"Women's intuition won't stand up in court. You know that."

"That's why I'm calling you." Because I woke him up he's not willing to help? What a grump! "My journalism experience in Mexico, where the aroma of corruption stinks more than the air pollution, honed my intuition. That smell is all over these pages."

"You woke me up because some pages stink? Good thing I like Ram. Next time you consider callin' at this hour, make damn sure a dead body's nearby." I sit through a long moment of silence. "Let's assume you've got somethin' here. Hang on a sec."

Two minutes later he's back on the phone. "Show up at my office at 10 a.m. Bring your stinky binder. And by God, girl, get yourself some blasted shut-eye!"

He gives me the address and disconnects. Good, we're getting somewhere. Griff will fall back asleep, but I can learn more from this binder if I put my tired mind to it.

This FBI office is spooky. Every face is ultra-serious. Gray's the dominant color. It's on tables, carpets, chairs, walls, the artwork on the walls, people's clothing. The shades vary, but everything's gray.

I'm deposited into a gray conference room by a gray-haired woman celebrating her thirtieth anniversary in the office. I want to ask how she could stand it that long, but congratulate her instead. One legal pad with gray paper and a light gray colored pen is on the table. The pen's probably filled with gray ink. A glance out the window shows me that our sunny morning's turned overcast and gray.

After fifteen minutes Griff waltzes in, accompanied by a super-fit blond man with a broad, toothless smile and muscles on top of other muscles. "Good mornin'!" Griff's voice is full of the energy I lack. "Brendali, Jorma here will help us work through the issue you called about."

The man squeezes my hand hard enough to break all five fingers. "Jorma Jokipakka at your service, Ma'm." I can't place his slight accent.

"You must not follow hockey or you'd know Jorma on sight," Griff says. "He's the first Finnish-born Harvard grad to play in the NHL. He retired from the Kings several years ago, joined the FBI and has become our main number cruncher."

"Math puzzles cause less wear-and-tear on the body than punches to the head or pucks to the face," Jorma says. "I enjoy solving math puzzles I can sink my teeth into."

"Ah, so that's where they went?" Griff's question makes me smile.

Jorma winks but his neutral expression is unchanged. "Mr. Hoosier says you have something of interest to sort out." His attentiveness to my backstory recital is shown by occasional questions and frequent requests for clarification. "What specifically is it about this," Jorma taps the binder on my lap, "that makes you think underhanded activity has taken place?"

"How many drunkard racists do you know who have charitable foundations that hand out tens of thousands of dollars a year? I can't figure out where all the money comes from, what these accounts are for, where the money goes. But I can tell something's wrong."

"You've looked over all the records?" Griff bends forward and reaches for the binder.

"I keep careful records for my tiny little bank accounts. I'd expect a CPA to at least match my detail level. These records are hopeless."

"We'll see about that," Jorma says, taking the binder. "The IRS carefully regulates non-profits." He flips through pages as he speaks. "Under the Tax Reform Act of 2022, all 501(c) organizations, including this one, must maintain specific detailed financial information on donors and recipients. The idea is to simplify tracing illegal money transfers, including those that support terrorist activities."

"Do these records meet the IRS criteria for specificity?" Griff barked the question out.

"Not by a long shot." Jorma leans back. His body shakes without making a sound. Maybe the FBI forbids laughter while on duty. "Are these the only records?" They look at me, Griff with a poker face, Jorma with a quizzical raised eye.

"How would I know? This is all I have. Someone else did the legwork."

Jorma closes the binder. "Let's input all the documentation, organize it and see where that takes us. We'll also look up the foundation, check its quarterly IRS reports and see if they jive with these records."

"That'll take a couple of days, no?"

"Give us an hour," Jorma says.

Wow, such speed! I give them a big, appreciative smile. "Thanks so much for doing this."

Jorma grabs the binder, steps toward the door and turns back. "Griffith, if you can assign someone to run a trace on the foundation, that'll help. Let me write the name down for you, with the TIN." He does that and continues. "I'll get this organized by account, contributor, date, deposit, outlay and recipient. We'll resume at 1 p.m. with our starting line in place."

"The Allenby Family Foundation for Socio-Religious Growth, huh?" Griff reads Jorma's note, written in blue rather than gray ink. "Sounds fishy to me, but once you've worked here long enough, everythin' does." He gives me an exaggerated shrug and his usual half-second smile.

At the nearby Coffee Bean & Tea Leaf, I order a double-shot latte and sort through the latest news until people recognize me and stop to chat. One man asks for an autograph, like I'm a real celebrity. No one ever did that in Mexico. Another man asks for a date, which I laugh off. I lose track of time, so I'm surprised when Griff calls before noon.

"Brendali, you don't need to stick around."

They must not want to get involved. "Thanks anyway. Should I stop by to pick up the binder?"

"Why on God's green earth would you do that?" The abrupt growl in Griff's tone causes me to knock my nearly empty cup to the floor.

"I thought you meant the FBI has no interest in the binder." I pick the cup up and toss it into the trash.

"We're initiatin' a formal investigation. Glad you brought this to us."

I want to exult, but keep it to a smile. "You're welcome." Ram will love this!

"If the investigation plays out like it might, you're in line for a sizeable reward under the FBI's 'Informer Enticement' program."

"Give it to Elena Rios. The binder belongs to her deceased husband. She and her kids can use the money."

"If you insist. Keep this under wraps, though, please."

When it comes to corruption, my intuition's never wrong. Allenby's foundation finances are in good hands. I wonder, though—is Ken involved?

Brendali's Convocation Update: The Saddleback Church REAPPEARED this morning, about an hour ago, as a six-screen movie theater. The Pastor did not and is assumed dead.
#God'swrath #CooperateEvangelicals

BRENDALI

Tuesday, December 14, 2027, KJCR-TV

Our studio audience gives Archbishop Delmonico a standing ovation. He bows several times in response. I give him a big hug, thrilled he's doing better.

Ram shakes his hand and points at Delmonico's face. "Thanks for visiting. The eye patch fits you."

"Sure it does." The archbishop takes his seat at our bar table. "If I want to switch careers from religion to piracy, I'm set."

"Will you have to wear that your whole life?" I ask.

"I'm told I won't." He looks from me to Ram. "I brought someone along who can explain why. Can she join us?"

"Of course. Let's hear all about it."

"Before I ask her to come out, may I provide some late breaking news?" He grins, probably in response to the surprised look on Ram's face.

"Go right ahead," I say.

"An hour ago Pope Francis III informed me that if I submit a recommendation on Biblical changes to the Vatican, he'll get it approved and adopted as official church doctrine."

The bombshell receives a standing ovation.

"This'll supercharge the discussions at the Convocation," Ram says. "The Evangelicals will go bonkers, though."

Delmonico's grin comes and goes at the speed of Griff's smile. "The pope follows the Convocation closely, and not only through your show. I send him daily updates. He wants to it to succeed."

I lean forward to make eye contact. "Did the pope consult the church's traditionalists before making this announcement?"

"Not to my knowledge." The Archbishop shrugs.

"If he didn't, won't this news ignite a thunderstorm of international criticism?"

"I've known Francis for a long time. We went through seminary school together. He won't care about criticism. He's putting his stamp on his prelacy."

"I'd love to discuss this with you in more detail," Ram says. "But you have someone to introduce, and our time's limited."

"Yes. Dr. Tatiana Kucherova, please join us," he says in a loud voice. "Folks, you're about to meet the finest eye surgeon in Southern California, if not America."

Ram and I stand to greet her. A tall blonde, the doctor joins us in a white medical smock over ordinary clothing. She's without rings or other jewelry and has brown eyes that are large for her pleasant, if kind of mannish, face. A pixie haircut emphasizes her unisex look.

We shake hands. Her grip's strong. She takes the empty seat to the Archbishop's left.

"I saw the Archbishop's eye when the paramedics arrived." I incline my head toward the doctor. "Gross is the only word I can use to describe it. How'd you fix him up so fast?"

"I've seen worse, actually. No matter, we always strive to provide the best treatment."

Wow, she has a deep voice. "I don't know how you could possibly save that eye."

"She didn't," Delmonico says.

"Oh." So why'd he call her the greatest eye surgeon around?

Dr. Kucherova glances at Delmonico. "We had to enucleate his eye, meaning remove it, without injuring the muscles and orbital contents. The next step, an ocular implant, has occurred. Once swelling reduces enough to proceed with the final step, we would in normal cases insert an ocular prosthesis."

"You mean a glass eye," Ram says.

"Yes. Sorry about the medspeak. A good ocularist can create an identical eye that moves in the orbit like the original did." She looks at each of us in turn, apparently to make sure we understand. "Of course, that doesn't restore vision."

"You said 'in normal cases,' Ram points out. "Is something abnormal about the archbishop's care?"

"The Archbishop won't need a prosthesis." She gives Delmonico a warm smile. "Shall I tell them, or would you like to?"

"That's why we're here. You're the surgeon. You'll explain better than I can."

She nods and pauses. "For implants I prefer a hydroxyapatite composite, a natural mineral found in human bones and dental enamel, over other available options."

"But eyeballs aren't made of bone." Isn't that right? Now I'm unsure. "I've always thought they were made of something more, uh, squishy."

"You're correct." She smiles at my poor word choice. "Eyeballs are mostly made of collagen fibers. The orbit itself, or eye socket, is bone. It's part of the skull. Anyway, here's the thing." She leans toward us like she's about to tell a secret. "We inserted the implant and sent the Archbishop back to his hospital room. I visited him the next morning, and you'll never guess—"

"Mi Dios, don't tell me!"

Dr. Kucherova's eyes widen. "Excuse me?"

"When the U.S. Bank Tower collapsed, I underwent emergency surgery to set my broken bones and address a serious head wound." I pause a moment to keep my emotions in check. "The next morning the doctors examined me and found no trace of any injuries. I called it a miracle, an undeserved one. I'm unworthy, but so happy it happened."

"I heard her doctors deliver the news," Ram says. "Most everyone who knows me is aware of my atheism. My outlook changed that morning, because I couldn't explain Brendali's overnight recovery. I call it a miracle, too. No other word fits."

Dr. Kucherova sits back, taking this in. The Archbishop's good eye is focused on his lap. I'm too wrapped up in my emotions to guess theirs.

Delmonico puts his folded hands on the table and looks at me. "God doesn't judge people by what they deserve or their worth. He bestows miracles to serve his needs." His hand moves to my forearm. "Brendali, I'm sure your miracle relates to the Convocation. I'd like to think mine does, too."

"Your miracle?" The question is Ram's.

The doctor's subdued voice is barely picked up by her microphone. "As a physician, I'm not supposed to believe in the supernatural. However, from time to time we see things science can't explain." She sighs and lowers her voice another notch. "My personal experience confirms this. Not long ago, a sex change could only happen in science fiction. Now it's routine. If we're honest, we'd admit that miracles can and do occur."

"But tell us," Ram asks again. "What's your miracle, Archbishop?"

Delmonico's grip tightens on my arm. He's unable to answer.

"The hydroxyapatite composite is softening." Dr. Kucherova's normal medical voice is back. "An iris, a pupil and nerves are forming. Muscles are attaching to a new sclera. The composite's differentiating into the necessary optical components. As a functional eye takes shape, we track his progress. Somehow the Archbishop is growing a brand new eye."

The audience's collective gasp is probably repeated throughout the world. The Archbishop blinks his good eye several times and, with a finger, wipes away a tear. Ram's eyes are moist, mine watery. Only Dr. Kucherova's eyes remain dry.

Wonderful, we're about to have a group cry on worldwide television. I pull myself together enough to keep the conversation going. "God also saved Ram after his shooting. The doctors called his recovery a miracle. They got that right. Archbishop, welcome to the club. The three of us are living testaments to miracles. We're additional proof our new God exists, because all three miracles are his."

Delmonico and Dr. Kucherova look at Ram. He's not ready to converse so I continue.

"It's up to us to speak for our new God, no? Ram predicted God would soon convince the remaining doubters that He's the real thing. We all have good eyes, so why not accept what they show us? I say to the doubters, put your skepticism aside. God wants mankind to survive. Never would a God want anything else. We have to make sure He finds us worthy."

The unplanned speech gets a rousing round of applause from the audience. I blush.

Archbishop Delmonico applauds, too. "I couldn't have said that better, Brendali. God has truly blessed you."

"No doubt." Ram's arms encircle my shoulders and pull me toward him. "I'm convinced she's an actual angel." The entire world watches him plant a passionate kiss on my lips.

It's a big surprise, but I love him and kiss back. Damn the consequences.

After the show Ram and I meet Ken in the conference room closest to our studio. His hostile stare focuses on me. "What's the big idea, Brendali?"

"Did I do something wrong?" Is he objecting to our kiss?

"Who are you to speak for this so-called God? Your contract says you're a talk show host and an occasional news reporter. That's all. I'm not interested in having you mouth-off about this phony. I've been plenty lenient, but this nonsense will stop right now."

"What do you mean?" My face flushes. "You've been on my case since I came here, for no reason. I want to know why."

"Ken," Ram says, "Brendali's right, you've been much tougher on her than anyone else. You—"

"Don't you take her side," Ken raises his voice and leans in toward Ram. "So she's your newest love interest? Big deal. Another will come along and you'll drop her."

"What?" Ram and I react in unison.

Ken slams his hand on the table. The sound's loud, like a bullet's discharge. "I'll help you out, Brendali. You don't like the way you're treated? Fine. You're fired."

"Huh?" I'm stunned.

"If Brendali's fired I resign," Ram says. "KJCR-TV sunk a lot of money into our show's new studio. We're getting global attention. You're taking a loss because you don't like her?"

"We'll find another use for the stage," he says.

"What about God? You insist he's fake but he's proved otherwise, no? God chose us to bring the Convocation to everyone. If there's no show, God might get very upset."

"Oh, I'm real scared now," Ken says in a sarcastic tone. "Like Ram used to believe until he fell under your spell, plain and simple, Gods don't exist." He pounds the table and stands. "Brendali, the last day of this so-called Convocation is your last day of work here."

He leaves in a hurry, slamming the door behind him.

Ram and I stare at each other for several seconds, until Ram takes my hand. "I don't know why he treats you this way, but I won't stand for it. We'll do the Convocation together here. After that, we'll contact competitors. One of them will pick us up. What do you say?"

All I can do is nod. I've never been fired before. Does this have anything to do with my work on Allenby's foundation? How would Ken know about that?

My phone signals an incoming call, but I ignore it. Only later, while Ram drives us home, do I remember to check the unknown caller's voice message.

"We have bigger fish to fry than you and your boyfriend," it says.

"Your Convocation will fail. Judgment Day will arrive at last. Amen."

I forward the voice message to Griff before playing it for Ram. He shakes his head in disgust. I can only mutter one question. "What are those *bastardos* up to now?"

Brendali's Convocation Update: Our big secret's out. Yes, folks, Ram and I are a couple. We didn't plan the kiss. Hope you enjoyed our show! #Spontaneous #Truelove

---

32 | Church (Part of Someone)

RAM

Saturday, December 25, 2027

"A good afternoon greeting isn't appropriate on this saddest Christmas Day in Los Angeles' history. I'm Ram Forrester. In the absence of Jack Allenby, who's under the weather, I'm here to anchor this special newscast."

Jack's had too much egg nog, but that's nothing new. "A historic local church, an important institution beloved by the Latino community since the city's founding, has been destroyed. We don't have numbers yet, but the loss of life is considerable. No one's claimed responsibility."

It's impossible to hide my dismay, though I try. The NITWIT caller said he had 'bigger fish to fry.' He must've meant this. How'd they pull it off? If they can accomplish this, they're a much more serious threat than I thought.

"Brendali Santamaria is with us from Olvera Street. Fill us in, Brendali."

The camera catches the somber look in her eyes. She stays silent long enough for me to suspect she didn't hear the cue. When she does speak her cadence is slow, soft and melancholic.

"I'm near *La Reina de Los Ángeles Iglesia*—The Queen of the Angels Church." She raises a hand to cover her mouth. We hear a heavy sigh.

"This morning's Christmas church service held an overflow crowd. They showed up not only to celebrate our sacred holiday, but to attend a special sermon given by Mexico City's beloved bishop, Cuauhtemoc Olin. His body hasn't been found yet. The explosion occurred—uhh, excuse me." She turns away, flicks a finger against her cheek and gathers herself.

"The injuries, the fatalities—dozens of each. Men, women, little ones." Her voice cracks. "I'm heartbroken." Her eyes close.

Before I decide to end the report, she speaks with a firmer voice. "Let me finish, Ram, please." Her next breath is so deep her entire upper body heaves. "I walked past this blood-smeared Maria doll lying on the ground earlier." She holds the bloody doll against her white blouse for the camera.

"For those who don't know, these doll figures are indigenous children dressed in their tribe's styles. This one's a girl from my tribe, Nahua, dressed in a tiny *huipil.*" She puts the doll in a baggy without appearing to realize her top is smeared with blood.

Ken's voice rings in my ear buds from the control room. "Pull her. Brendali's not giving us a report. All we're getting is emotion."

Bren's hard at work despite hurting so much. I'll damn well let her finish. With the screen focused on her, I emphatically shake my head to refuse his order.

"I thought about the cute little *niná* who brought this doll to church, dressed in her holiday best. Is the doll's blood hers? Is she gone, so soon? Who took her life? Are her parents grieving, hurt or dead?"

She puts a hand over her eyes and goes silent. "We expect to hear from Archbishop Delmonico soon. As compassionate as he is, we must ask him how God could let this happen to these innocents on the day we celebrate Jesus' birth. We need an explanation."

With no signoff she walks away. The camera gives us an unobstructed view of a ruined church reduced to a mess of wood, pipes and plaster. The building, built in the mid-1860s, is leveled. We segue to a commercial as the image fades from view, but not from our memory.

The victims share Bren's faith and culture. She would've been among them if she'd arrived fifteen minutes earlier. Did NITWIT mean to kill her? I don't want to bring up that idea—she'll feel guilty, that all the victims died for her. I remember our first show, her evident pride when she walked on stage in that stunning white *huipil.* The doll must've triggered that memory and others, too—childhood, her cousin Lilia, the funeral her folks didn't attend.

I need to comfort her, not sit here with my heart breaking.

"We'll come back to Brendali soon," I tell our viewers once the commercials end. "We have Kate Chung in the area, speaking to some of the survivors. Let's watch."

While her interviews play on screen I review a faxed document a staff member hands me. I can't believe what I'm reading, including the post-it with Ken's spiky handwriting.

Back on camera, I introduce this breaking news. "We've received a claim of responsibility. Management wants me to read it to you, verbatim. Every word you'll hear is typed on this page." I hold it up. "Not one word represents the work or opinion of this station. KJCR-TV and I refute and reject this screed in the strongest possible terms."

We, devoted members of the Evangelical community, as righteous followers of the Lord, our God, on this glorious day commemorate the anniversary of the miraculous appearance of his Son, Jesus Christ, on earth. Chosen by Him to enforce his dictates as stated in the Holy Book, we hereby sayeth:

First.   As His appointed agents of societal transformation, it is our unique task to, with diligence, meet and quash any and all threats to His Word.

Second. We who are called to practice the gospel discipline also preach the gospel glory and teach the gospel enactment. We cannot stand idly by when those who claim the mantle of the Lord's appointed leaders act contrary to His inerrant principles and guidance.

Third.   We therefore demand that the Catholic Pope, who hath stated his willingness to revise the Bible, resign forthwith. We have today demonstrated forcefully our intention to see him do so. Also, Archbishop Delmonico must withdraw from the so-called Convocation and swear on the Bible to submit no list of biblical changes to the Vatican.

Any refusal to these demands shall bring about Judgment Day, so sayeth the Lord, our God.

I lean forward. "A fringe group called the National Institute for Teaching Western Inspirational Theology—NITWIT, for short—wrote this piece and claims responsibility for the bombing. Cult experts will slice and dice this statement, but in my unvarnished opinion nothing justifies or excuses a church bombing. No God worthy of our faith would ever reward those who engage in the wholesale indiscriminate murder of his devoted worshipers."

It's not easy to calm down. "Enough said. I understand Archbishop Delmonico has arrived at the scene at Olvera Street. Brendali Santamaria, do you have more on this?"

Despite a little puffiness around the eyes she appears to have regained control of her emotions. "Ram, the Archbishop's approaching to speak to us. Let's hear what he has to say."

The camera pans past a throng of reporters awaiting the Archbishop. Accompanied by several LAPD officers he trudges toward the group, shoulders slumped. His eye patch is visible. An aide runs up and touches his arm. They stop for a brief conversation.

Delmonico nods and moves in front of the crowd.

"I'd like to start with a short prayer for those who have died or been injured, for their families, friends and all who hurt and grieve over this horrific event." Delmonico's voice, normally casual, has a solemn tone. "Our hearts may cry, our pain may sting, but we are not alone and we will persevere."

With clasped hands in front of his lips, the Archbishop bows his head and speaks in a loud, clear, defiant voice. "Grant eternal rest unto them, O Lord. Let perpetual light shine upon them. May the souls of the faithful departed, through the mercy of God, rest in peace. Amen."

He turns toward the remains of the church, makes the sign of the cross in its direction, drops to his knees and bows. His forehead rests on the ground as his arms stretch as though to reach for the injured or deceased. He doesn't move for a full minute.

Several reporters mimic Delmonico's pose. Others remain upright with bowed heads and hands over their hearts. The camera angle doesn't show us this, but even among that typically cynical group, I'm sure tears flow.

Delmonico stands, faces the group and waits for them to gather themselves.

"I'm told Ram Forrester read a statement of responsibility from an Evangelical group called the nitwits—an apt name for religious terrorists. I call upon the leaders of all faiths to immediately make clear your opinions about this atrocity, using every available social media avenue. I especially hope to hear loud and clear rebukes from the many Evangelical faiths."

On Twitter denunciations already abound from Evangelical and other Protestant pastors, Catholic priests, rabbis, Islamic clerics and regular folks. No tweets support the bombing.

The Archbishop looks at the gathered media throng with indecision etched on his face about what to say next. "I want this understood by all. I will not discontinue my work with the Convocation. To the contrary, I am even more motivated to see it succeed. I hope the other invitees share my reaction. After all, we're all brothers and sisters before God.

"Let's remember the Bible is the product of societal conventions long departed, not an unalterable truth. These texts have been revised many times over the centuries. What some of us insist is the literal written word of God at best approximates whatever he originally said."

A shout interrupts him. "Does this mean you believe the Bible contains errors?"

The Archbishop turns toward the questioner. "I will not take questions, but will answer yours. We must regard the Bible not as a tool for hewing to a single ironclad interpretation but as a living document, responsive to and anticipating changes in our increasingly complex and dynamic society. The idea of periodic revising of the text, within reason, to better fit our needs and those of generations to come makes eminent sense. Several years ago I wrote a proposed Canonical on this. The Vatican rejected it, of course." He gives the questioner a slight smile.

More questions are shouted out. Delmonico puts both hands up to cut them off. "I said I won't take questions, but one person may pose a question. I'm sure she's extremely upset by what's happened." He shields his good eye to scan the gathered crowd. "Brendali Santamaria, if you're here, do you have a question?"

"Yes I do, and thank you," she shouts. He turns in the direction of her voice and waits. "I have in mind Psalm 85:16: 'But you, O Lord, are a God merciful and gracious, slow to anger and abounding in steadfast love and faithfulness.' How does such a God allow this bombing to occur?" The camera shows her pointing to the demolished church.

"That's an excellent question, Brendali. Romans 11:33-36, in part, states 'how unsearchable are His judgments and unfathomable His ways.' That is truly all we have to hold on to, along with our faith that a greater good will somehow come out of this sad event. I believe the Convocation's success will become that greater good."

Reporters immediately start to shout out more questions. Delmonico signals for quiet.

"Folks, keep in mind that we have a new god. His ways are not necessarily those of the New Testament God. He did say, without elaboration, that he has different expectations. As imperfect beings, we must trust this God's ways. In your most trying moments, do you not tell yourself to trust God? I urge you all—find the strength to do so again."

No one in the media throng speaks up for at least ten seconds. The silence ends with another cacophony of questions.

"My apologies, but I have to keep this short. Many parishioners are in dire need of my attention. I must go minister to them." He begins to walk away but comes back.

"I will say one more thing." He brings his hands together in a pose that suggests he's considering his words carefully. "I call upon Pope Francis III to disregard the demand that he resign. The Vatican should stand strong. I fully support and follow the pope's lead. I'm confident he will guide us toward a new era of Christianity."

He leaves. The camera cuts back to Bren as the media disperse. "The Archbishop's statements covered the points we needed to hear from him, but—"

I lose track of Bren's words. The distraction is a man who happens to walk behind her, dressed in a security guard outfit. He resembles God and, at the periphery of the camera's view, disappears in a white-yellow flash of light. No one in the vicinity seems to notice, including Bren. Did I really see that? Or did I imagine it?

Ram's Convocation Update: Convocation members, when you reconvene Monday, expect to address the church bombing and issue a statement on it. #prepare #disavow

---

33 | God Only Knows

BRENDALI

Saturday, December 25, 2027 (cont.)

How can I celebrate Christmas now? With soot on my skin, hair and clothes, I'm washing this miserable holiday away while Ram makes dinner. He's a great cook, but salad, baked chicken and potatoes instead of a holiday dinner with Griff, his wife and their new baby girl? It's a letdown.

Thank God for this tubful of hot water, though. Soaked up to my chin, my eyes shut to the world's ugliness, Jenny & the Mexicats thumping out a Latin rock beat through my ear buds—ah, nice! A bubble bath would make this even better, but a girl can't have everything, no?

Despite closed eyelids the flash registers, rousing me out of my stupor. What's happened? Why did all the lights burn out? I open the curtain to step out.

"Mierda!" It takes only seconds to recognize the security guard and yank the curtain closed. *Mi Dios,* I've exposed myself to God. Full frontal, too. "What are you doing in here?"

"My apologies, Brendali. A slight miscalculation. I meant to materialize in your living room. I shall rectify that error now."

After a yellow-white flash reflects off the wall's marble tiles. I check to make sure he's really gone, dry off and wrap the towel around me. "Ram, I'll need a minute before you start."

I hear "we'll wait" as I close the bedroom door.

What should I wear for our special visitor? Who cares, he's here for a reason. I wiggle into my favorite light blue sweats. Should I offer coffee, tea, cookies? We don't have any sacramental wine. Would he make do with Rosé or the Pinot Grigio Ram bought last week? Does God even eat or drink?

In the living room I snuggle up to Ram on the couch while God paces around without acknowledging me. "This Convocation is far behind schedule," he says. "At this rate the required tasks will not come to fruition in the allotted time period. The prior God favored the Abrahamic religions over all others, but I most assuredly do not favor the Evangelicals. Their inflexibility and intransigence is holding up progress and endangering all of humanity."

"Bren and I are getting involved. We intend to push the deliberations forward."

"Fine, do that. But reserve a place for me on your show Monday night. I shall reinforce my prior message and impress upon these invitees the need for haste. You two shall facilitate and support this communication."

Never will Ken appreciate God's second appearance or his message, but I have other concerns. "God, you let so many people die, including little ones. Those poor souls went to church, prayed to you every Sunday for mercy, penitence, love. Yet you allowed these deluded nuts to still their voices. Churches are sanctuaries, no? Sacred ground, now violated. I don't want you on our show until you explain your inaction."

God brings his hands together in front of his mouth and gives us a slight bow. "All who died shall reasonably soon return newborn if the Convocation succeeds. Death and rebirth are intrinsic to the cycle of life on this planet."

I can't sit and listen to such cold-hearted words. Ram tries to keep me with him but I fling his hand away, jump up, get right in God's face and point an accusing finger at him.

"Those you let die came here to escape poverty, crime, corruption.

They took any job, put up with prejudice and family separations. Despite these hardships they considered themselves lucky because in America, this most promised land, they could raise their children and live a better life. God granted them extraordinary favor, as they saw it. But no, you let these deranged terrorists dispatch them like they're so many squashed ants."

I stop, bury my face in my hands and shake hard enough to fall over. Damn it, this hurts. The anguish reaches to the deepest parts of my soul.

Ram pulls me close to him. "We'll arrange Monday's interview, as you ask," Ram says while I grieve. "Promise Bren you'll tell the world why these victims had to die."

"I feel your pain, Brendali," God says in a somber tone. "My appointed task is to restore this wayward world to an acceptable operational level. Everything I do is intended to achieve that objective."

"I didn't hear you respond to Ram." We return to the couch, Ram still holding me.

"I shall say what your world must hear," God says. "I make no promises to earthlings, not even the select few I choose to protect. But I do sympathize, and will help you. Lean back and close your eyes, please."

A feeling seeps in like the effect of hot water in my bath, which relaxed every muscle in my body. This, however, eases my subconscious. No actual voice mouths the words "we shall resume our discussion Monday night," but they imprint onto my brain anyway.

I open my eyes sometime later to an unmistakable smell. Our Christmas tree, a seven foot tall Douglas fir, has somehow sprouted red roses from top to bottom. The 'his and her' stockings we hung by the chimney as a goof are full of white ones.

God's gone. Ram's eyes remain closed. His neck has sunk into the sofa cushion, his face pointed at the ceiling. His arms lay limp at his side.

Love overwhelms me. For Ram? God? Everyone? I don't know, but Ram's the only one here. I express my love by sitting on his lap and planting a tender kiss on his lips. He doesn't react. I repeat it, this time with gentle caresses of his cheeks. When his lips meet mine they part to let my tongue in. It tickles his, so he tickles mine while remaining asleep.

Nose to nose, I stare at his closed eyes. *"Mi cariño,* I love you. I always will." Never have I meant those simple words more. For a moment I'm not sure he heard, but his arms draw me against him.

"Angel, I love you, too." The words slur, like he's sleep-talking. "With my heart and soul. Forever." Only the words matter, not the enunciation.

Our tongues search for ways to wrap around each other. I know he's awake when his tongue ramps up the urgency. Our intimacy wants nothing more than to remain unchanged. This feels like eternal bliss.

I press against him, my head at rest on his shoulder, my chest pressing against his. It's perfect, how our bodies fit together. "Baby, you still owe me a few O's," I whisper.

"Would you like them now, before dinner?" He pulls my sweatshirt off to fondle my breasts.

"Mmm, not so fast. My O's accrue interest at 100% per week. I'm owed six. At midnight the week will end. You'll owe me twelve."

He smiles. "Fine, we have all night."

That's true, but the aroma coming from the kitchen signals that dinner's ready. "First we eat. After, you work off your debt."

Ram stands, gently plops me onto the couch, and goes to check on dinner. A moment later he calls over to me. "Check this out, Angel. God left us a Christmas gift."

Once I'm in the kitchen he points to the main course he's pulled from the oven. "You saw me put a whole chicken in, with cut up potatoes, right?" I nod. He puts his arms around my bare shoulders. "Now we have chateaubriand, with bercy sauce and chateau potatoes, the way the best French restaurants make it.

Look at the salad bowl, too—green beans almondine."

"Let's eat, baby. We can delay dessert until our bedroom business is finished."

At the dining room table I pray to thank God for his bounty. I'm no longer angry with him or anyone else. With his gift and Ram to keep me happy, secure and loved, what can possibly upset me now?

34 | Que Sera Sera (Whatever Will Be, Will Be)

BRENDALI

Monday, 12/27/27, KJCR-TV

"Everybody, please stand and welcome back Earth's only true deity, our Lord of many names." Ram's next few words are drowned out by raucous claps, hoots and hollers.

After the usual bright white flash, God materializes on stage about two feet from us. The shocked audience goes quiet for a second or two. Sustained applause follows. He bows to the crowd and stands by the empty seat next to Ram. "Thank you both for allowing me to return."

"Lord, Ram and I would like your thoughts on the progress of the Convocation so far, and on the Christmas Day church bombing. Which do you prefer to discuss first?"

"The bombing." God moves a few feet away. "We shall require a screen." In empty air He traces a thin black rectangular outline with his index finger, reaches into a pocket of his pants and blows white powder from a small vial into the center of the outlined space. It spreads like liquid, creating a flimsy blank sheet that hangs in place unsupported. As though he's shaking water away, God flicks his fingers at the thing. It thickens and enlarges into a projection screen.

Enthusiastic applause follows the magic trick.

God positions himself midway between us and the screen. "I

shall now explain how a tiny fringe group can give the entire Evangelical faith a bad name and earn my wrath."

Head shots of sixteen men come up on the screen, arranged below the word NITWIT. Skeleton Man's photo is in the top row. Does that mean he's a leader? I hope Griff's watching.

"Have you any idea," God asks Ram, "how many Evangelicals live in the U.S. alone?"

Ram shrugs. "I don't have a clue."

"Rounded off, 65 million at present. These sixteen people committed mass murder in the name of Evangelism, without the knowledge, consent or approval of these many millions of worshipers. Church leaders have rightfully condemned the attack."

A diagonal block appears, superimposed in red over the head shots: $16 \neq 65,000,000$.

"I caution everyone not to judge or define a religion, whether Evangelical, Muslim, or any other, by its fringe actors," God says. "One must maintain perspective and proportion. Ignore social media distortions and slanted, therefore fake, news reports. Fanatics are by definition outside the mainstream."

"I agree," Ram says. "Groups such as NITWIT invoke their version of God to parade as though they're religious. They do that to justify or rationalize wrongful, immoral, blatantly nonreligious acts. None of us should buy into that nonsense."

A fat paintbrush that appears in mid-air erases the photo. "Evangelism is one example of strict Biblical interpretation," God says. "Fringe Christian groups do not differ from those in the Islamic fringe. Ultra-strict interpretations warp scripture, thereby falsifying it."

"Let's get back to the bombing," I say. "I'm still waiting for you to explain why you didn't protect those poor people who lost their lives."

"Deities do not interfere with acts of free will by planetary inhabitants except in limited circumstances. In the same way that trees burn in a fire but their seeds sprout and grow again, humans die but their souls are soon reborn. This tragedy should motivate the attendees to work together, whereas my interference would lessen motivation by betraying the idea of free will.

"This chart is my limited exception. I am exposing the members of this group so that no further hijinks of this sort occur. I trust the FBI will round them up in due course and that your legal processes will impose appropriate penalties."

Ram and I exchange a glance. I'm positive we're thinking the same thing. "You've tied your decision not to interfere to the Convocation, so let's discuss that. What's your opinion of its progress to date?"

"The Evangelicals attending the Convocation should under-stand that I have begun to mete out punishment in response to their passive resistance to the aims of this gathering. This will continue unless they henceforth act with the absolute utmost good faith. They will feel my wrath if their conduct remains obstructive."

The words of that last sentence bounce off the walls and reverberate around the studio. Once the echoes end, God continues. "My invitations to attendees identified these objectives, shown here in abbreviated form." He flicks his hand at the screen, which now shows this:

1) Acceptance of the free unfettered practice of all religions, or of none.

2) Release of all historical and current religious disputes without compensation.

3) Development of mechanisms to resolve future religious disputes by nonviolent means.

4) Updating the holy books and traditions of every religion to meet current and future societal needs.

"The small steps taken to date to address these goals are inadequate. Over the last thousand years religions have functioned as a brake on moral advancement. These objectives are meant to reposition them to serve as a force for advancement of human society."

God may not realize that berating humans will seldom make them work harder, or better. "Surely you have something positive to say about the Convocation, no?"

He steps over to the screen and snaps his fingers. "Satisfactory work has been done on item 4. No serious discussion about items 2 or 3 has occurred. Lip service, at best, has been given to item 1. The invitees have wasted weeks on end."

"They have another month," someone in the audience yells.

The paintbrush reappears and erases the list. "I think you should meet someone."

A baby's bedroom appears on the screen. Panned in slow motion, we're shown walls decorated with depictions of a wooly mammoth, dodo, Tasmanian tiger and a giant tortoise—extinct animals, all. Who decorates a nursery this way?

A dark green wooden crib sits in a corner. The top half of a mobile attached to the crib is visible. Papier maché animals hang from the narrow threads. We peek over the side of the crib's wall to find a chubby baby who gives us a wide-eyed, curious, happy smile.

"Her name is Choden Lama-Sherpa," God says. "Her birth occurred during my previous interview. She has two paths ahead of her in life. The outcome of this Convocation will determine which path she follows."

As if on cue, the baby starts to cry.

"Choden is a stand-in for every living soul, including the invitees. These millions of paths forward also depend on the outcome of the Convocation."

A woman about my age enters Choden's room wearing a Woods Hole Oceanographic Institute T-shirt and sweat pants. She scoops her daughter up, takes her to a nearby rocking chair and nurses her.

Cries are replaced by slurps as mom tells Choden about the Jason/Medea ROV, a deep sea submersible she works on.

The mother hugs her baby as God waves at the screen. "Watch and you shall now see Choden as her life proceeds if the Convocation achieves success."

We're going to see a video of the future? *Mi Dios!* How?

At five years old Choden runs happily after a ball. She receives an award in her elementary school at about age twelve. A few years later she delivers a valedictorian address at her high school. Harvard bestows a Master's Degree in History at age twenty-four. A son is born during her thirtieth year. Five years later Choden is a professor of history, blogger and small-scale celebrity. A televised interview she gives on a talk show in Boston comes up next.

God speaks over the rest of the video. "This is the successful Choden, who lives the adult life you would want for her. Many others of her generation can succeed if given the chance. I can show you a quite different life Choden will live if the Convocation fails, but will spare you the pain. To summarize that sad alternative, I will say only this: in that life, when Choden dies, humans join the ranks of the animals you see on her wall."

If this doesn't drive the attendees to action, nothing will.

"Tomorrow," Ram says, "I'll ask some pointed questions to whoever I encounter at the Convention Center. Attendees, prepare to tell me what you'll do for Choden, the others of her generation and those who come later. Our viewers and I will expect substantive answers."

"I will listen to those responses with interest." God squeezes the sides of the screen to thin it. Applying pressure to the top and bottom shrinks it to the size of a large speck of white dust. A final pinch causes it to self-destruct, but the matchstick-sized flare is lost in the flash of bright white light of God's disappearance. The audience gasps. Ram and I exchange glances. I remember that God looked like my Tia Juanita back when we first interviewed him. Like her, he prefers dramatic entrances and exits.

Brendali's Convocation Update: NITWIT has issued a statement in response to God's interview, denying Her (or His) authenticity and promising retaliation. #neverfear #moderationwilltriumph

BRENDALI

Tuesday, 12/28/17, KJCR-TV

'Ram, fyi, Ken needs me to anchor the morning news team's special report on the protests taking place worldwide. I don't have a choice. Work on the attendee interview video montage has to wait.'

I peek at his response to my text while a report plays from our sister station in Nashville, where one of the more raucous protests is occurring. His text asks what's happening, so I fill him in. 'Protests, some violent, have broken out wherever a sizeable Evangelical community exists. God made it crystal clear that mainstream Evangelicals weren't to blame for the Christmas Day bombing. The protesters don't care.'

Once the afternoon team takes over the newscast I skip lunch to catch up on my video preparation. I'm no masochist, but my next text to Ram invites more work. 'How about interviewing the attendees for their reactions to the protests?" His agreement means I'll have to splice those interviews into a second video montage once I finish the first one.

Griff texts me a few minutes before 3:00 p.m. 'FYI, a hold has been placed on all the Allenby Family Trust accounts. Stay alert, you may get some blowback.' I'm too busy to even acknowledge the message, much less give his words a second's thought.

I skip dinner. In the ten minutes before we go live I've managed to finish the second video segment, gotten dressed and made up. I reach my seat on stage as the 'on air' sign lights up. Never have I felt this rushed, out of breath or fatigued, not to mention hungry.

"Good evening, world." Ram mutes his usual enthusiastic greeting but the audience hoots back 'Hey, Ram!' for the first time ever. He beams at them but keeps his smile to a minimum.

Why are these people so enthusiastic? Don't they know or care about the protests?

We start with the montage of Ram's interviews of attendees, who are asked what they'll do for the recently born and as yet unborn generations. We hear first from a Hindu woman named Abha, dressed in traditional Indian clothing. "I will do everything I can for Choden, others of her generation and their children. I want them to have long, happy lives, the good life our gods have given us."

That's all we get—a vague statement with no specifics. And this is one of the better ones.

Hakan Çelik, wearing a business suit with a red-checked *keffiyeh,* is next. Lots of Americans will see the headgear and feel repulsed, associating it with Muslim terrorists. He probably wore the *keffiyeh,* which he hasn't worn here before, for that reason.

His statement to Ram is blunt: "Allah speaks of a day of reckoning, when the seas pour forth, hills turn to dust, mountains blow away, clouds are rent asunder and the moon splits apart. The Christian God also says a day like this will come. Let it, I say."

The audience jeers. As Çelik spoke I wrote a quick note to Ram: 'The standard negative response for balance, but it is disappointing.' Ram's penned response is 'no worries, these folks will get over it.'

Xaio Lin Chang, a demure Chinese woman, provides a soft but firm comment. "We who practice Tao believe every person is allotted a specified amount of *ch'i,* our energy or life-force. Every person must strengthen, control and manage this to live a long life. I would teach the exercises that help accomplish this to Choden and all who come with and after her."

Again, no substance. I felt disheartened listening to all the insipid responses, and now, with this montage airing, the feeling's returned.

Jamison Jensen, a tall, beefy man with close-cropped graying hair, wears the bolo tie common to New Mexico. He delivers his comment in a deep, slow monotone. "As Mormons, we believe each person contains a spirit that resides with God before birth. The Exalted decides when to give that spirit a physical body and an earthbound existence, to gain experience and prove his or her worth. To Choden and her peers I say God has birthed you and provided a set of unique challenges. Show strength, do good works and prevail to earn a place with Him."

As he's speaking, I give Ram another note. 'Didn't anyone you interviewed get it? You should've asked what they'd do for Choden in their capacity as Convocation attendees.' He draws me an apology emoji.

A dissolve replaces Jensen with the Reverend Mother Verma. She leans on her cane and speaks in her usual circular manner. "I say to Choden that the Way is not in the sky, but in the heart. She who is greatest in battle is not the one who conquers a multitude, but who conquers herself. I counsel Choden and all youngsters to find and stay true to themselves, and continue to learn. Do that and in time all will turn out well."

The studio audience whistles and cheers when the video ends. Can't these people hear how superficial these responses are?

Ram peers around at the audience, confusion on his face. "The answers we received have a common denominator. Not once did anyone link his or her participation in the Convocation with the aim of assisting Choden, her generation and the following generations. I have to tell you, I expected better from each person I interviewed." That shuts up the in-studio crowd.

"All these interviews miss God's point, Ram. Attendees, you have responsibilities—to yourselves, your families and humanity. God chose you to cooperate and deliver results. He didn't select you to mouth meaningless blather—"

I clear my throat and take a deep breath. If I don't hold my tongue I'll regret my words. "Let's move on. Everyone must've heard of today's riots and demonstrations. The destruction, injuries, all the deaths—it's saddening, no?"

"Hell no," someone in the crowd shouts. "F—k 'em!"

If I could figure out whose words those are I'd have him removed. "God's first objective for the Convocation requires us to agree to embrace the free practice of all religions, or none, by everyone. Ram asked several attendees when they'll discuss this objective, and for their own opinions of it. Let's see what they told him."

First is Dion Shannon, the Irish moderator who got whacked in the head during the Ten Commandments group melee. He's fully recovered, thank God. "In response to today's riots I'd like to see the Convocation come together, address this issue and resolve it. This one's not hard to reach agreement on, in my opinion."

Shannon is followed by the Cao Dai Pope, Binh Huu Li, an elderly Vietnamese man. "God founded Cao Dai specifically to harmonize our many religions. They are not so different, one from another, for each has God's love in common. How we follow and praise God may vary, but if he can accept our various devotions, why can't we do the same?"

I've scribbled a quick note to Ram. 'These Cao Dai guys should take charge of this objective. They have experience with it. Most religions find nonbelievers inferior. It's short-sighted, no?' He nods his agreement.

Up next is Slomo Nakamura and his usual staccato. "Of course we should come together. This is a yes or no issue. What needs debate? Accept some religions but reject others? We've grown past this. Any religion can accept any other. We all attend to our spiritual needs according to our heritages and cultures. Let's praise our diversity, not divide ourselves by it."

Johnny Ray gets a few seconds of worldwide fame, too. "Why, I reckon we all should aim to go back on our raisin' and mend some fences. Dang, this here ain't like we have to go 'round our elbows to reach our thumbs, you know?"

"Common sense, delivered with a Southern drawl," Ram whispers to me.

Hewson Ricketts, a young Jamaican Rastafarian, finishes the video. "True everliving Rastas will never say 'you and I.' We say 'I and I' to emphasize the oneness that exists between humans and Jah, who you call God. We practice livity, a balanced, natural lifestyle. With this philosophy, how can we reject joining with others to rejoice in Jah? Come, smoke with us, share our ganja. Let us bring religions together and celebrate."

The audience cheers like crazy. Maybe they shared his ganja before the show began.

"I interviewed about twenty people," Ram says. "Each expressed willingness to accept this objective. When I told Slomo, he moved to call the Convocation's first caucus to vote. The steering committee seconded his motion."

Ram stopped speaking, likely to let that sink in. The room quiets until he begins again.

"After the vote, we discussed when to release the results. Archbishop Delmonico told us that Pope Francis III, who leaves for South and Central America tomorrow, wants to attend a session of the Convocation next week if God will allow him in. Some wanted the announcement held for the pope's arrival, but the majority chose not to wait given today's violent riots.

"Are you ready to hear it?" Ram's milking the moment for all its worth. The studio's awash in applause and hoots. "God," he looks up as though at the sky and hesitates to build suspense. "The first objective passed by unanimous vote of the Convocation attendees."

A standing ovation shakes the studio with applause. It's wonderful, but we'll need a miracle to get to unanimity with the remaining objectives.

Brendali's Convocation Update: Big doings today, good and bad. Build on the positive momentum, attendees—you have five weeks to pass God's test. That's doable. #Getitdone! #rootingforyou

RAM

Tuesday, 12/28/17 (cont.)

After the show Bren and I walk a few short blocks to Porto's Bakery. We chow down on a late but scrumptious Cuban dinner— empanadas, meat pies, potato balls, chorizo pies and tamales. Way too much for two famished talk show hosts.

"I almost forgot," Bren says, handing me her phone. "You need to see this." It's Griff's text about the FBI freezing the accounts of Jack Allenby's foundation. "What do you think Griff means by blowback?"

"Jack and I have worked together for over a decade." I don't have the mental energy to give Griff's words much attention. "He's not an outgoing, sociable sort of guy. Kind of secretive—maybe now we know why—but harmless. We might get some kind of verbal confrontation when Jack's drunk, but that's probably about it."

We head back to the station in a calorie induced stupor. Overeating didn't improve Bren's fatigue. She's quiet, yawns after every few steps and leans into me the entire way.

I don't stay to write my usual post-show critique notes. The memo I intend to send Ken, asking for budget approval to hire a fulltime videographer, can wait until tomorrow. Bren creates top notch video montages, but freeing her from the drudgery of doing them is a priority.

We're in my office only long enough for me to put our excess Cuban food in the fridge, and to send the video of our show to my home computer. I'll critique it in the morning, with fresh eyes.

In the elevator Bren cuddles against me until we reach the lobby. "It's kind of spooky here this late," she says. "The building feels deserted."

"Yeah, the vibe's different. Look." I point to the empty security desk.

"Security doesn't work after 10:00 p.m.?"

"They must," I say. "Maybe the guard's doing his rounds or using the restroom."

"No, I don't think so." She points to the video screen. "The cameras are turned off. Is this how Ken squeezes costs and improve profits?"

That's too much, even for Ken. "I doubt it. How about if I drive us home tonight?"

She hands me the keys to her Fiat. "Thanks, you should."

We enter the garage and go up to the roof. Bren's car is the only one in sight, parked in a corner next to a stairway. We hold hands and walk in silence.

Halfway to the car I tap the key fob to unlock the doors. The tail lights blink on and off as usual. Jack Allenby popping up from the space between the car and the stairway wall is unusual.

"What'd ya know, it's our cute couple." The mocking tone's clearer than the slur of his words. "This little Chiquita's sure got you by the short hairs, Rammer."

"Jack, aren't you usually in a bar somewhere at this time of night?" I try to walk past him to open the passenger door for Bren but he blocks the way. "Excuse us, please."

He shoves me, hard. "Who the hell're you to interfere with my business?" He wants to start a fight? He pushes me farther away from Bren. "Stay f'ing outta my life, hear me?"

"I'm not in it. You're imagining things." Blowback. If I engage, headlines will scream 'KJCR-TV celebrities duke it out in empty

RAM

garage.' That isn't good for any of us, or the station. "What are you talking about?"

Behind Jack, Bren puts her purse on the trunk and opens it. Her facial expression's dead serious. I hope she keeps her cool, especially if she's reaching for her gun.

"My family foud—fount—foundation," Jack says. "Goverment f'ers froze the accounts. Ken told me you collab—collab—dealt with the FBI."

Like a fullback plowing into linemen, Jack barrels into me. I'm pushed back several more steps. I've heard of aggressive drunks, but this is ridiculous.

"You've jumped to an incorrect conclusion, Jack, like you did when you called Brendali a wetback. She's born and raised here—a U.S. citizen. You insulted her again tonight. Give her a sincere apology and we'll both forget about what's going on here and head home."

His forehead furrows as he sways back and forth. "What's the deal, Rammer?" He gives me an unfocused stare. "You want'cher old anchor seat back, is at it? Sorry, it's mine now." He pulls out a gun and waves it at me. "This's a warning. Back the fug off—"

He stopped talking because the nozzle of Bren's pistol is pressed against the back of his head. Her hold is steady. She's in full control of her emotions despite her scowl.

"Never again will you point a weapon at my man." She moves the gun behind his ear. "Shut up and listen, or I swear it, I'll scatter your 100-proof brains all over the floor. Put your hands down, this second."

Jack's only reaction is a wobble. She pushes the nozzle into his earlobe.

I hope we don't have a double-murder—Allenby shoots me, Bren shoots him. "Do as Brendali says, Jack. She knows how to use a gun. Don't make her prove it."

He points the weapon at the ground.

I exhale. "Put your gun on the ground and take three steps back from it."

He doesn't respond or move.

"You heard Ram, asshole," Bren says, poking his rear end with her pistol.

Jack's body jerks a step in my direction, his eyes widening in surprise. He complies with my demand. I pick up the gun. He doesn't need to know I'd only use it to protect Bren.

She circles around Allenby, motioning to him to move to the Fiat. He complies. "Frisk him, baby." Good choice. She won't hesitate to use the gun if necessary. I would.

Allenby puts his hands on the trunk of the Fiat and spreads his legs.

"Remember this, bastardo. I never miss my target unless I mean to." Good idea, if Bren's trying to distract Allenby while I frisk him.

I'd better not call the police. We don't need an incident report. All that would do is document this for the newspapers and our competitors.

"Threaten Ram again and I'll come after you until we settle the score, you and I. A *narco* gangster in Mexico died from my bullet. I had to defend myself, one of us had to go and I didn't volunteer. He went to the devil, that *malhechor. Comprende?*"

I turn him around. "He has no other weapons, Bren."

She points her gun at his ashen face.

Allenby looks at her, me, the ground. He leans to one side and takes a deep breath. "Bitch, you haven't heard the last from me." His slur's gone—how interesting.

He takes two steps in my direction, his arm out like he means to fight me for his gun. A shot rings out. He drops to the ground.

Jack's not dead or writhing in pain. He's quivering, though, face down on concrete.

Bren presses one foot against his back, between the shoulder blades. Her pistol points at the back of his head. He turns a cheek to stare up at her with one wide open eye.

"You're not listening to me, *pelotudo.*"

He blinks and makes no effort to escape. His cheek's dark red now.

"Never will I let someone call me a wetback or a *Chiquita* and get away with it. I don't make exceptions for a sorry excuse for a human like you, either. I have no idea what your personal issues are, but right now you're my problem. You'll get up when I let you and walk away without a single backward glance. Do anything else and I'll put you out of your misery, guaranteed. *¿Comprende?*"

"Yes," he whispers.

"Say that louder, in Spanish."

"*Sí!*" he yells. He repeats it at lower volume, his voice choking at the end.

She moves in front of me, as if to provide protection. In slow motion Jack gets to his feet and turns away from us. After he adjusts his clothing, Jack trudges in a straight line toward the elevator, head down with slow movements, his drunkenness gone. He leaves a wet spot on the ramp floor.

Bren notches the safety off and stuffs the pistol into her purse. "About time I got in some shooting practice. This gun fits snug in my hand. I'm glad I bought it." She puts her arms around me and stares into my eyes. "Are you okay?"

"I'm fine." She amazes me. "Angel, remind me to never get on your bad side."

Her voice is a whisper. "Never before have I controlled my anger this well. I'd have wild emotion, then regret whatever stupid thing I did. This's better, not that I want to get mad all the time." She quiets, her anxiety subsiding, and lifts her face toward mine.

Her eyes tell me what to do next, so I provide the tender kiss she wants. "I love you." We don't move. With our bodies together, our hearts beat in tandem. After a while I open the passenger door for her. "Now we know what Griff meant. Let's go home."

A dirty towel in Bren's trunk comes in handy. I check the safety on Allenby's gun and learn Jack never released it. I wipe my fingerprints away. His too, no doubt.

Bren stays silent during the drive, clutching my hand the whole way home.

Jack's a hopeless drunk, but I bet he didn't imbibe a drop of alcohol tonight. Has he acted drunk before? Maybe he's feigned all the drunkenness? No, at times I've smelled liquor on his breath, so he's a legit drunk sometimes. I didn't smell any tonight.

No security guard, no working cameras. Perhaps this whole thing's a set up? Jack intended to scare me, if not do harm, but didn't expect Bren to have a gun.

"Angel, about the security situation tonight," I glance over at her but she's too deep into some kind of internal discourse to respond. I go silent, too, until a car blows a red light, nearly collides with us and keeps going. The same kind of car Allenby drives. My loud curse brings Bren out of her reverie.

"Sorry." I'm going to do a show on hazardous urban driving, first chance I get. "Would you look up Allenby's bio? Tell me whatever you find about his family."

Five minutes later she gives me the scoop. "He's never married but had a child out of wedlock who died young. No brothers, sisters, other relatives. Parents deceased. He's alone."

"So why does he have a family foundation?"

We don't have the answer, but know who can find out. "Angel, call Griff right now, would you? Tell him what's happened with Allenby. Let him know we have Jack's gun. Griff can have it if he wants. Suggest that whatever's going on here might involve Ken. He always covers for Jack."

She looks at me, breaks out in a big smile. "Technology makes investigative reporting easy. Let's see where this leads."

BRENDALI

Monday, 1/10/28, 10:00 a.m., Convention Center
An air of anxious excitement hangs over the Convocation. I get fewer cold shoulders than usual. Some attendees greet me by name, others express eagerness to see Pope Francis III in the flesh. No work's getting done but the morale boost is huge.

Our casual chats end when Ram strolls up to the lectern. "Good morning! I know some of you have worried that Pope Francis' plane might bypass L.A. rather than try to land during this so-called hundred-year storm we're experiencing. I have good news—the plane carrying him has landed."

Ram waits out the cheers. "He'll travel first to the Cathedral for lunch with the local priesthood. After that he'll come speak to us. We'll expect the pope to arrive around 2 p.m., but let's give him a hearty welcome whenever he arrives."

Ram walks away, beckoning me to follow him. I don't need my intuition to know something's wrong. His face shows concern, not anticipation.

In the empty hallway he checks to make sure no one's within eavesdropping distance. "Delmonico says the pope's people think he might've pulled a muscle or two in the turbulence the plane flew through. The Archdiocese's doctor will check him out. His speech may not take place, although Francis insists on doing it."

"Let's hope that's all it is." I want him here, but most of all I want him healthy.

Ram glances at the ceiling. "Maybe lunch, the company of local clergy and some painkillers will get him through the day."

"I suppose. I'll watch him like a hawk when he gets here. Johnny Ray should stand by with the best paramedics available." We can't take chances. This pope's too important, too vital to the Church and the world.

"Good idea. I'll go find him."

Despite the storm Pope Francis shows up on time, entering the building through a delivery entrance that offers the most protection from the pounding rain.

The steering committee, Ram and I are on hand to welcome him. Francis usually takes pride in his upright bearing, a holdover from his days in the Canadian army when folks knew him as Chaplin Girard Toussaint. Today, with slumped shoulders, he's a fatigued 55-year-old man. Is this wear-and-tear from his trip, or is he ill?

He's dressed the customary way for a public event. A zucchetto covers his head, a white mozetta cape does the same for his clothes. Across his chest hangs a large gold pectoral cross.

"Mi Dios!" I pull Ram's arm to get his attention and point to the pope. "Is that the papal Fisherman's Ring on his finger? Popes never wear them in public anymore."

Ram squints to get a good look. "When he gets closer we'll see it better. I know each new pope gets his own ring. Look for his name inscribed around the border."

Might Francis let me kiss his ring? If he does, I swear it, never will I wear lipstick again.

We've formed a receiving line—Father Zeke, Reverend Mother Verma, Slomo, me, Ram last. Archbishop Delmonico trails His Holiness, followed by the usual retinue.

Is the pope all right? Will he bless me? Can I kiss his ring? "Ram, our first meeting with God shocked me, but this wait is anxiety provoking. I'm flushed, sweaty. Something's wrong with me, no?" This is silly. I last felt like this as a teenager pining to meet Enrique Iglesias. That never came close to happening, but this will.

He chuckles. "You've met your share of celebrities, Angel. Treat him like any other."

I take Ram's arm to stay upright, rooted to my spot. "The pope's more than a celebrity. He's the Vicar of Christ, the supreme leader of my Church."

I have to restrain myself from running up to Francis, who's shaking hands with Father Zeke. I'd love to take that picture. The pope's a quiet introvert, Zeke's a loud extrovert. Zeke's baritone voice reciting Biblical verse is loud and clear while the pope's words, if he's saying anything, don't reach us.

Ram leans in and whispers. "Watch his left hand. Francis is massaging his chest. The pulled muscle, maybe?"

The pope's hand is against the mozetta cape, to the left of the pectoral cross. Twice in rapid succession he presses his chest like he's in pain. "Let's hope it's nothing worse."

"I'll alert Johnny Ray." Ram sends a text and gets an immediate response. "Paramedics are here and ready. Good."

Pope Francis meets the Reverend Mother. I didn't see him bless Zeke but he can't do that with her, she's not Christian. I can't imagine their conversation. Her circular Buddhist sayings don't fit his plainspoken way of talking. They don't spend much time together. She's probably given him a headache trying to figure out what she means.

He's with Slomo now. "Ram, I'm next. What should I say? I've never been this nervous meeting someone. I'm shaking, for God's sake."

"Relax, he puts on his pants no differently than we do."

"That's a visual I don't need right now, *mi cariño.*" He grins.

I tune out the hallway noise to concentrate on the pope's words.

"I've heard much about you from Archbishop Delmonico, Rabbi. Positive things. He is quite taken by you."

"That's kind of him, Your Holiness. It's a truly extraordinary honor to know him and meet you."

"The pleasure's mine, I assure you." Again the pope massages his chest, wincing this time. "A man who has studied Judaism and Islam and holds a doctorate in comparative religions from Stanford has achieved much. Without doubt you will have continued success. I would consider it a privilege to read your doctoral thesis."

"I'll send it to you. If you would allow me, Holy Father, though I'm not Catholic I humbly wish to show you the respect your office deserves." He graces Francis with a broad smile. "May I kiss the image of the Jewish apostle you wear on your finger?"

The pope holds the Fisherman's Ring out for him to kiss St. Peter. Camera shutters click like crazy. I'll probably spill tears if I get the same chance.

"You have been blessed by our Lord," Francis says. "God will look after you and hold you dear." Slomo, stock-still with the same huge smile, says nothing.

My turn. Oh God, don't pass out. I'll always, always, always remember this moment. The Pope, inches away from me!

"The lovely Miss Santamaria," he says. "From the moment you barged across my television screen in the middle of the night, my lady, I have watched you with great interest."

He's watched me? "I, I—" For Christ's sake say something! "Your Holiness, I don't know what to say. Speechlessness is a rare thing for me."

His hand clasping mine transports me to heaven. "You have become the voice, even the face, of Catholicism throughout the world. Your nightly show, your demonstrations of faith, the example you set for young girls everywhere, you are a bright beacon of light for the world."

Mamá would have such pride if she heard this. The pope winces once more but I'm so taken by his words, it hardly registers. "I'm only a reporter, Your Holiness. God placed me here. It's not my doing. I hope in some small way to help this Convocation succeed. As is said in Mexico, he who does not speak, God does not hear."

He turns to the Archbishop. "Yes, she is humble, too, as you said. Perhaps she is indeed an angel, as suggested during that marvelous interview she did with you." The Archbishop smiles, but I see concern on his face.

"If it pleases you, Holy Father." I'm overheated. His compliments are going to my head. I can't bring myself to ask him to let me kiss the ring.

He understands, turns back to face me and holds his hand out. I take it but can't make out his next words. Is this what an out-of-body experience feels like? He sounds far away, muffled, slow. His lips will soon meet St. Peter's imprint, his breath warm on the gold.

I try not to topple over.

"—so, Miss Santamaria, you have my most sincere appreciation. God is with you, He shines through you. On his behalf, I bless—ahh."

His hand tightens around my fingers. Pain marks his face. He falls forward, against me. I encircle him with my arms but he's much too heavy.

"Help! Help me, please! I can't drop him, he's the Pope! He's having a heart attack!"

Chaos ensues—shouts, gasps, moans, wails. By the time Slomo, Archbishop Delmonico and his people lay the pope on the floor, Ram's called Johnny Ray. I'm on my knees beside Francis, my hand still in his tight grasp. His eyes, open but distant, look into my watery ones.

"Tell them all—for me," his voice wavers. "They are all blessed—by the God of their religions—if this gathering succeeds. This—is what—I came to say—a benediction—for all."

His eyes close. He lets go of my hand. God, please, that's not a death rattle, is it?

Paramedics ask me to move away. I take a few steps back and collapse in Ram's arms.

I'm in shock but can't cry. Ram's speechless, holding me like I'm a sack of groceries, not a woman who needs his strength, his comfort. I look up at his impassive, this-is-business face. He's using his cellphone to film everything for our show.

Never, never, never will I watch that video. Why should I? Forever I'll remember this meeting, for all the wrong reasons.

Brendali's Convocation Update: Pope Francis III collapsed in my arms. Pray to God for him, everyone. We need him here on earth.
#Survive #Godbemerciful

BRENDALI

Monday, 1/17/28, 8:15 a.m.

I'm at my devotional table in our guest bedroom, about to light some aromatic candles and pray for the pope to heal. I've done this daily since his heart attack last week. A puzzling envelope from the Archbishop's office leaning against the framed picture of Jesus distracts me. I open it.

My Dear Brendali,

Ram told me how much you care for Francis, how upset and concerned you are about his health. Please rest assured he's receiving the best care possible. I'm overseeing it and can attest that he improves daily.

Francis can now see a limited number of visitors. (This is off the record, please.) He specifically asked for you and Ram to come by.

I understand you stop in at the Cathedral twice a day to say prayers for the Pope's wellbeing. When you're next here, ask for Father Pedro. He'll make the necessary arrangements.

Ricardo Delmonico

"Ram! Ram!" He's asleep so I jump on the bed and slobber kisses all over him until his eyes open. "The pope's doing better and wants to see us," I say before he's fully awake. "What fantastic news!"

"I know." A big yawn interrupts his words. "The Archbishop told me. I wanted to show you his message last night but couldn't rouse you. I understand why you've started to take sleeping pills, but I wish you wouldn't. Anyway, I put the note where you'd find it."

"I'm leaving right this minute to make the arrangements."

"Shouldn't you dress first?"

He doesn't really think I'd go to church in a flimsy red teddy, does he? He turns over and goes back to sleep. I'm gone before he wakes up.

I don't know what the equipment in this Cardiac Care Unit room does, but I'm sure every measurement helps the Pope recover.

"Good afternoon, Your Holiness," I say. "The Archbishop told us you're doing better."

"Somewhat," he says in a low voice. Ram and I move closer to hear him. He offers his ringless hand. I take, kiss and release it.

"I've prayed for you every morning and night. I'm so worried I've hardly eaten."

"That's true," Ram says. "For Bren's birthday on Saturday, we went out for an expensive dinner to celebrate. She moped and left her food untouched. I've made dinner for us every other night, same thing. Bren worries about you, I worry about her."

"My dear, I know your prayers hold a special place in God's heart. Thank you for being so concerned, but you mustn't feel so strongly for me."

"I can't help myself, Father. The Church and the Convocation need you."

"I am with you in body and spirit, even if my heart balks. Stop worrying." A grimace flicks across his face. Oh, no, is he about to have another attack? His features return to normal after a few seconds, and he addresses Ram. "We didn't have the chance to meet. Now we can."

"It's my pleasure, Pope Francis."

"You're the former seminarian?" Ram nods. "Not all men find the seminary suitable. You have found your own path in life, however."

"I tried, Your Holiness. You and Brendali can surrender to unquestioned faith. I can't."

"In time, perhaps, you may manage it," he says, closing his eyes. "No need to rush. You have a long life ahead, and God is with you." He doesn't reopen his eyes for long enough that Ram and I look at each other, wondering whether we should leave or call for a nurse. Francis stirs before we act on our concerns.

"Come closer, please," he says, gesturing. I obey. "I have a special prayer for you. Give me your hands, please." His feel clammy when he grasps mine.

His tired eyes meet mine. "You are a woman with a God-given place and purpose." His voice is stronger. I bite my lip, finding it hard to breathe. "God has blessed you, such that any blessing I may impart is unnecessary and inferior." He tries to smile, but grimaces again. "By the power of my office I bless you, Brendali Santamaria, and ask God to grant you continual success in life, love and all your endeavors." He closes his eyes and frees my hands.

Now I'm sure. Ram and I will always have each other. I give him a tender look. He must've read my thoughts, because he takes a knee and reaches for my hand.

"Angel, I didn't come here with this in mind. Although it's early in our relationship, sometimes people simply know the right time to make a commitment. You're so radiant right now, so happy. I want you stay this way and never mope again." His voice, so thick and emotional, doesn't sound like him. "I hope what I'm about to ask will keep that beautiful smile on your face."

Never can I believe this. I forget to breathe.

Ram goes quiet as his hands search his pockets. "I don't have anything resembling a ring, so, umm—"

Pope Francis interrupts. "Use mine. It's on the shelf behind you." He inclines his head in the direction of the window. Ram retrieves it, takes my hand again and kneels a second time.

"With the Pope's Fisherman ring, Angel, I solemnly ask for your hand. Will you marry me?"

The world screeches to a halt, except for beeps from medical equipment and the hiss of air escaping from somewhere. I'm speechless, breathless, choked up. It's not that I can't speak, but this is unreal. Never did I expect this question to come to me in a hospital room, in front of a pope, with his ring about to go around my finger. My free hand grabs the bed rail, in case I faint.

"Yes." Despite using all my strength, my voice is a whisper.

"Pope Francis, did you hear the answer?" He doesn't respond, so Ram asks again. "My dear, my love, please. Will you marry me?"

I repeat my answer, louder this time. "I will. Yes. Of course." My voice cracks on the last two words. He heard me and slips the pope's ring on my finger. It's way too big, but who cares?

Joyful tears fall as I lift it to my eyes. I get a hazy view before Ram's arms surround me. This is my future husband's embrace, and it will stay that way forever. We keep our kiss chaste, our eyes locked on each other.

A familiar voice pipes up behind us. "Ram, Brendali, since I arranged it, I whole-heartedly approve your union. Congratulations."

The wonderment in the pope's voice is clear. "Is that who I think it is? Thank God you two are witnessing this. Otherwise, I would've thought I'd arrived at St. Peter's Gate." The Pope stares straight at God, his eyes sparkling, his mouth wide open.

"Please, Lord," I say, "do for the Pope what you did for me, Ram and the Archbishop."

God shakes his head. "No miracle is required. His heart is mending. He needs only proper medical assistance and to pay attention to simple things. Change your diet, Pope Francis. Eat less starch. No pasta or bread means less of the pesto you love, but try it on chicken and in a tomato salad. Trust me, you'll like it. Also exercise more, stress less. Moderate your workload."

"That's easier for you to say than for me to do, my Lord." The pope tries to sit up as he speaks. "As head of your church, I have responsibilities I cannot delegate to others."

Ram raises the pope's bed to help him into a more upright sitting position. "I'm sure God didn't show up to chat about diets," he says. "Do you want to discuss something with us?"

"Of course." God walks over to the CCU equipment and checks the readouts. "Your doctors will discharge you within three days, Francis. We shall discuss the Convocation."

"What do you suggest, Lord?" The question's mine.

"My words fell on deaf ears. You, Ephraim, the pope if he is interested, and the members of your steering committee must come up with your own ideas."

Ram sits on the edge of the pope's bed, apparently unconcerned about whether he should. "None of us have moved the group forward."

"Try a different approach," the pope says, his voice louder. This meeting with God and his prognosis are helping him recover.

"Do you have suggestions, your Holiness?"

He points a hand at himself. "I will speak to your Convocation, but not alone. I have in mind a few influential speakers who can perhaps appear on short notice. Friday, shall we say?"

"We'll clear our calendar for you," Ram says.

"Televise the speech live, worldwide. I'll urge your viewers to rise up, become vocal and pressure the attendees to cooperate. We require positive results before the upcoming deadline, and will accept nothing less."

"What a wonderful idea," I say. "We can mobilize social media, hear everyone's voices. But we need some heavenly help." I look over at God.

"Yes," Pope Francis says. "Lord, you may have to help with the other speakers. They will participate remotely."

"I will do what is necessary," God says. "Who shall you invite?"

"Leave that to me. I'll tell you in my prayers."

Ram turns toward God. "Can the main hall's message board play a continuous feed of viewer messages?"

"Of course," God says. "Would you like short videos?"

"How can you do that?" The question is from Pope Francis.

"You would not understand the engineering. The spoken words shall also translate into the language of each attendee. Ram, instruct your viewers to state their name, city, country and a message urging the Convocation members to complete their tasks. Limit each message to a minute or less. The vignettes will play in the main hall every day, for all to see and hear."

"This is amazing." I laugh. Loud noises from the hallway distract me. A nurse comes in. I turn in God's direction, but he's disappeared. "Uh, Ram, maybe we'd better go."

We say hurried goodbyes. The pope's ring is placed back on its shelf as we walk out of the room, engaged. I'm in a blissful daze all day.

Brendali's Convocation Update: God's dissatisfied with the pace of the Convocation. Ram and I will turn up the heat on the attendees. #Staytuned #Letsgetthisdone

---

BRENDALI

Friday, 1/21/28

Ram's face beams from his seat on the dais now that he's fulfilled the tough job of introducing the pope.

Francis runs through his obligatory thank-you list. My heart flutters when he mentions me. It's funny to hear him say he appreciates the opportunity to address the Convocation when this was his idea. He should thank himself.

"I shall speak candidly about the task God set for you," he begins, "and introduce a few speakers who will appear remotely, on screen." He points toward the big screen.

"In September, 2006, Pope Benedict XVI gave a speech in which he suggested that Islam is a religion of violence. Before he apologized, and spurred on by Benedict's unfortunate comment, the Muslim community issued a most remarkable response entitled 'A Common Word Between Us and You.' This document made worldwide news. You can easily find it on the internet now, and I suggest that each member of an Abrahamic religion read it. I will here recite only the first two paragraphs:

"Muslims and Christians together make up well over half of the world's population. Without peace and justice between these two religious communities, there can be no meaningful peace in the world. The future of the world depends on peace between Muslims and Christians.

"The basis for this peace and understanding already exists. It is part of the very foundational principles of both faiths: love of the One God, and love of the neighbor. These principles are found over and over again in the sacred texts of Islam and Christianity. The Unity of God, the necessity of love for Him, and the necessity of love of the neighbor is common ground between Islam and Christianity."

The screen goes blank. "I'm sure you know this plea for peace had no appreciable effect upon relations between the Muslims, Christians and Jews," Pope Francis says. "If anything, relations have since worsened. Today it is more likely that all-out war will occur than that peace will reign. Much of that worry has a political and economic basis, but resolving the conflicts of the Abrahamic religions will do much to ease the problems.

"Those here who belong to these faiths can set a tone for this Convocation. Show the world how to put politics aside. Accept the commonality of your religions and that you are all one in God's eyes despite your differences in worshiping him. Let peace begin here, in this hall, and spread outward throughout the globe."

The audience response is restrained. The pope, perhaps realizing this, continues. "Not long ago the Dalai Lama wrote an article entitled 'The Global Community.' His idea, that our worldwide community consists of brothers and sisters, is stated as follows:

"Today's world requires that we accept the oneness of humanity. In the past, isolated communities could afford to think of one another as fundamentally separate and even existed in total isolation. Nowadays, however, events in one part of the world eventually affect the entire planet. Therefore we have to treat each major local problem as a global concern from the moment it begins. We can no longer invoke the national, racial or ideological barriers that separate us without destructive repercussions. In the context of our new interdependence, considering the interests of others is clearly the best form of self-interest.

"The necessity for cooperation can only strengthen mankind, because it helps us recognize that the most secure foundation for the new world order is not simply broader political and economic alliances, but rather each individual's genuine practice of love and compassion. For a better, happier, more stable and civilized future, each of us must develop a sincere, warm-hearted feeling of brother and sisterhood."

The pope slowly scans the hall. "Your group consists of many different cultures and faiths, but you are all of one species. You are brothers and sisters on a genetic level, sharing physical traits and spiritual aspirations. Do not let your differences overwhelm your similarities as you gather to make common cause in this Convocation."

He pauses for a sip of water and looks around, as though he's gauging the audience's apparent lack of interest. "In 1960 the possibility of Senator John Kennedy becoming America's first Catholic president created considerable controversy. Imagine that!" The Pope feigns shock and gets a few scattered laughs. "He addressed that concern head-on. This part of his speech should speak to you today." The big screen shows Kennedy in HD clarity.

I am not the Catholic candidate for president. I am the Democratic Party's candidate for president, who happens also to be a Catholic. I do not speak for my church on public matters, and the church does not speak for me.

Whatever issue may come before me as president, I will

make my decision in accordance with these views, in accordance with what my conscience tells me to be the national interest, and without regard to outside religious pressures or dictates. No power or threat of punishment could cause me to decide otherwise.

If the time should ever come, and I do not concede it will, when my office would require me to either violate my conscience or the national interest, I would resign the office. I hope any conscientious public servant would do the same.

"At this Convocation each of you must recognize your positions as conscientious public servants. Take a moment to reflect. Your February 4 deadline is weeks away. God's remaining objectives await your attention and agreement. Do not feel compelled to speak for your religion. Do only what is best for the public interest.

"If any of you feel incapable of fulfilling your roles because you cannot disregard outside pressures or qualms of conscience, I have good news. God has conveyed to me that you may leave this Convocation, without penalty or recourse to you or your fellow worshipers, if you do that before I resume my speech." The pope steps away for a brief chat with Ram out of range of their mics.

Why didn't God share this news with me or Ram? Is this his way of dealing with the Evangelicals?

About half of the Muslim attendees leave. None of the Evangelicals do.

Slomo rises and leans over to whisper something to Ram. Upon finishing, he speaks into his microphone. "I request that Hakan Çelik join me in an effort to bring back those who left. Excuse us, please." As they leave together, Ram tells the Pope something we don't hear.

"I am sorry to see our Muslim friends depart," Francis says to the crowd. "I wish the two men leaving persuade them to return, and applaud the rest of you for choosing to stay.

"Let's now go to Chicago in the year 1893. The Bengali Swami Vivikananda, a Hindu, gave a short but powerful speech to the first-ever World Parliament of Religions. Today that organization is at the forefront of the laudable interfaith movement. Here is the Swami, thirty years old at the time:

> I am proud to belong to a religion which has taught the world both tolerance and universal acceptance. We believe not only in universal toleration, but accept all religions as true. I am proud to belong to a nation which has sheltered the persecuted and the refugees of all religions and all nations of the earth . . . I will quote to you, brethren, a few lines from a hymn I repeated from my earliest boyhood, and which is every day repeated by millions of human beings: 'As the different streams have their sources in different paths which men take through different tendencies, various though they appear, crooked or straight, all lead to Thee.'

Television and HD clarity videos didn't exist in 1893, so this speech couldn't have been filmed. Did color TV exist in 1960 when President Kennedy gave his speech? Is God somehow showing us these speeches as they occurred?

"You also should have pride," Francis says. He points to himself with both hands. "You are listening to this old man prattle on about religious tolerance. God asked you to declare an era of religious tolerance, and you have done it. You will forever more accept views that are not your own and refrain from passing judgment on other perspectives. I applaud that achievement."

The pope peers downward, as though reflecting. He stays silent for a good long while before raising his head. "Nonetheless, your work is not done. In the time that remains, work like you've never worked before. This is a moment of vast historical importance."

Less applause is received than before. Some attendees don't clap at all.

"Thank you for your exuberance," Francis says, perhaps sarcastically. "I want to remind you that in the Kennedy decade, in the midst of widespread unrest due to the Vietnam War and civil rights demonstrations, one man of God stood out. This orator, a famous Baptist minister who remains a beloved historical figure today, made a famous prophesy. He promised us that the day would come when the glory of the Lord would be revealed in such a way that all of mankind would see it."

Francis grasps the sides of the podium and leans in, close to the microphone. "This prediction came true when the entire world saw God reveal himself to us on Ram Forrester's show. This minister also foresaw that when that day of glory came, men would work and pray, struggle and stand together." He looks around. "Here in this hall, you're doing exactly that. This is the predicted time. You embody that minister's vision."

"Only together will we see all God's children—every religion represented in this room and any that are not—say as one voice: we are free of the threat of extinction, free to remake this world as our new God intends, free to attain new heights, generation after generation, as humanity has done for several thousand years.

"That's what's on the line. All of mankind expects no less of you than diligence, a good faith effort and success."

The room is silent. Pope Francis gazes up at the ceiling, as though to the heavens. "I will leave you with one last word. With this new God's technological help, one-minute vignettes collected from people all over the world will play on this screen in a continuous loop, one after another, until your job is done and this Convocation ends. In this way people will express to you their hopes for mankind's future."

He's pointing to the big screen. "I am sure these mini-testimonials will move you. They convey the dreams, desires, wishes and good cheer of humanity, and reinforce the fact that the world is paying attention. Do what God asks of you for yourselves, your families, those who share your faith and those who do not. May God bless you all."

Pope Francis steps away from the podium and shakes hands with Ram, who raises the pope's hand like he's won a boxing match. Francis waves with his free hand, glowing in the accolades the crowd's giving him. He gives Ram a quick hug and walks away, throwing kisses to the audience.

I loved the speech, but will it change the minds of the Evangelicals? They're the ones who most need to take the pope's words to heart, but they don't hold him or his church in high esteem. I have no reason to feel encouraged.

Brendali's Convocation Update: Pope Francis' powerful speech today gave the attendees a real shot in the arm. May they carry his message into action and succeed. #Getitdone #theworld'swatching

---

RAM

Friday, 1/21/28 (con't)

"Bren, I'm going after them. I want Çelik to bring his people back. If half the Muslim contingent leaves, that'll leave the perception they didn't really agree to anything. We need a bullet-proof agreement."

"I'm surprised he didn't walk out with the others. Let me get the message board up, maybe it can help you find them." She opens her phone to do that as I leave.

Outside, everywhere I look people in purple and gold are arriving for tonight's Lakers game against the Celtics. I can find Çelik by searching for his red *keffiyah*.

I call Bren. "Are you with me, Angel?"

"Yes. The message board's up. This is kind of cool. The tech angels posted a street map. It shows that Slomo and Çelik are together."

"Good, where do I go?"

"You're on Figueroa at Pico. They're crossing Chick Hearn Court, moving north toward Olympic Boulevard."

"I'm one long block away, passing the Nokia Theatre. Hang on, I'm going to run."

I hoof it past Lindsay Plaza and get caught up in the Staples Center foot traffic at Chick Hearn Court. A red light stops my pursuit. All the folks bunched up on the opposite sidewalk obstruct my view farther up the street.

"Where are they now?"

"At the corner of Figueroa and Olympic. They're not moving for some reason, probably a long light. Maybe I can get a visual—"

The 'walk' sign illuminates. I run through the crosswalk and pay no attention to whoever shouted "hey, isn't that Ram Forrester?" Fan interaction can wait. I see Çelik now, his arm stabbing the air several times, pointed west. Slomo's not reacting. "Found them, Angel. Thanks for the help." We disconnect.

I'm soon close enough to hear Slomo and Çelik's intense conversation in Arabic. They're oblivious to their surroundings. I open the message board on my cell phone, ask to use the universal translation tool and receive directions to activate it. Once my ear bud's in place, I interrupt.

"Excuse me, guys. Nice night for an argument, isn't it?" Slomo translates for Çelik.

"You see? I was right," Çelik says. "If we bicker long enough over where to have dinner, the media will say we're arguing."

"He'll need you to interpret my English, but I understand him perfectly," I tell Slomo. He doesn't ask how I know Arabic. "Didn't the two of you leave to try to bring back the men who left the Convocation?"

"Hakan assures me his people will do whatever he asks. We let them go. He's hankering for Rosa Mexicano down the street. That cuisine's unavailable in Ankara. I prefer Boca, right there." He points across Olympic. "Better Spanish food than you'll find in Spain, especially the paella. It's heavenly."

"If you're hungry for Mexican food you can join me," Çelik says to me, spraying my shirt with his saliva. "Or you and Slomo can enjoy Boca together."

I caught up with them to convince Çelik to bring his group back. Although that's apparently no longer an issue, I side with him. Slomo shrugs and joins us.

"I respect your group's decision to walk out, Mr. Çelik. May I ask why they made that choice?"

"You have no experience with the Muslim world, Mr. Forrester. Many Muslims are unwilling to sign an agreement with Jews, on principle." He looks at and spits on Slomo with the next few words. "Forgive me, my friend."

"I understand and take no offense."

"Remember, you agreed to travel to Ankara to visit next summer. I hope what occurred won't change those plans."

"As penance, you have to host me for an extra week."

Çelik gives Slomo a brief grin. "That gives me enough time to show you all the sights of the city—both of them."

"I'm glad you two get along well," I say. "That's a wonderful symbol for the world to see. Would you guys consider coming on my show to talk about your friendship?" I rethink that. "I suppose that's not such a great idea if what Hakan said applies to friendships, too."

"Sadly, you are correct." Çelik shrugs and picks up the pace. "When you and I first met, Archbishop Delmonico called me our token Muslim extremist. I played along, but you see, as the west has its biases, my people do, too."

"Perhaps one day we'll get past these things," Slomo says, with an undertone of frustration.

"Until we do, I don't foresee Allah's followers tolerating our friendship. All Muslims are proud to host guests, even Jews. But friendship's forbidden. It does happen, as it has with us, my friend. I can push boundaries, but some require more work than others."

"I suppose something extraordinary has to occur to change those attitudes," I say. "Such as signing off on the Convocation agreement and explaining why over and over until the message sinks in. Think you're up for the challenge?"

Çelik's outpacing us now. With horns blowing on the street, he probably didn't hear my comment, as translated.

"He's really hungry," Slomo says. He chuckles and shrugs. "I am, too. Let's wait until dessert to talk shop. Hakan's open-minded if we pay for his meal."

Next to us the eastbound traffic on Olympic has come to a

complete stop. Despite the street noise, we hear a passenger in a black Chevy truck scream "Go home, Arab scum!"

The truck's in the lane nearest the curb, so we can also see something metallic pointed at Çelik. Slomo reacts faster than I do, by running toward Çelik. I yell "Duck, Hakan! Drop to the ground!" He's startled, but doesn't comprehend my warning or the situation.

Slomo tackles Çelik, covering him at the same time two loud gunshots ring out. I can't tell if they've been hit. I'm frozen in place, watching this happen too fast to grasp. People in the vicinity scream, hit the ground or run.

Two more shots tear into Slomo. His body jerks. My jaw drops, my brain unable to process what I'm seeing.

The truck steers onto the sidewalk, aimed right at me. I run into the street. The driver behind the Chevy saves me by keeping his car in place.

Another shot spurts out of the shooter's gun, but I can't track it. I use my phone to take a quick video of the rear of the truck as it rolls down the sidewalk, trampling a woman twenty feet or so away who'd dropped to the concrete for safety.

Thank god for my journalism skills. If I can get this video to law enforcement, they can use it to find the bastards in that truck.

I hustle over to Slomo. "How is he?"

The man tending to Slomo looks up at me. "I'm an orthopedic resident at UCLA Medical Center, sir. This fellow's gone. My girlfriend's calling 911. I'll check the other man and get over to that poor girl."

I grab Slomo's wrist for a pulse and, finding none, turn him over. Profuse bleeding from his mid-section and chest and his vacant eyes tell me God can't perform another miracle here.

Such a brilliant guy. An unlimited future cut short way too soon, for no reason. I'm too amped to tear up. God, why couldn't you save him?

Çelik's *keffiyeh* is blood spattered. He's not moving. At first I think he's been shot in the head, but that's wrong. He stirs, trying to sit up. The blood is Slomo's.

Multiple sirens sound while I try to text Griff. My jumpy fingers miss some of the correct letters but the message gets sent, along with the truck video. I don't have the heart to fill Bren in. I'd lose what little is left of my composure.

"This fellow's okay," the resident says about Hakan. "A separated shoulder, no gunshot injury. Paramedics will take care of him. Excuse me, I'm needed down the street."

I look around, numb. The crowd around us gawks at Slomo's body. I catch the eye of a woman decked out in Lakers' gear and a ton of jewelry.

"Oh, honey," she says, wrapping me in her arms. "It's all right. You're out of danger."

A stranger's embrace is all I need to lose it. "You don't understand," I try to say with a choked up voice, and maybe I manage it. "My friend's dead." I can't internalize my emotions. Tears roll down my cheeks.

A second woman also embraces me. They try to console me. I hear voices, not words.

"I'm sorry." I want to break their holds, but they don't let go. "I'm okay, I'm okay."

"You sure aren't, baby," the second woman says.

I picture Bren when I hear 'baby.' I'll have to tell her what's happened in person, not by phone, once I get my emotions in check.

Çelik kneels and places both of his hands on Slomo's cheeks. He bends over, kisses Slomo's forehead and hugs him. I leave the ladies and pull Çelik off Slomo. The front of his clothing's bloody, so when he stands and hugs me, some of Slomo's blood soaks my shirt.

"God has him, Hakan." He won't understand, so I take the ear bud off, give it to him, and motion for him to put it on. When he does, I repeat my words.

He nods and gives the ear bud back. "He saved me, gave his life for me." Çelik's eyes are glassy. He inhales deeply. "I will force my people to sign the Convocation agreement if I must. In that way I will honor my dear friend."

Is that why God let Slomo die? The price is too high.

"Doesn't that—" Again, we have to exchange the ear bud. "Doesn't that mean you'll sign your life away?"

When the bud's back with me, he looks into my eyes and puts a hand on my shoulder. "What does it matter? We all go sometime. You heard Slomo wish that we get past this one day. Allah, the merciful, has granted me more time on earth. He must mean for me to help make Slomo's last words come true."

"You can count on my assistance." I forgot to give him the ear bud. He doesn't understand, but nods anyway and reaches over Slomo's body to hug me again.

With Slomo prone between us, his blood pooled around our shoes, we remain stationary until two police officers gently break us apart.

Ram's Convocation Update: I want to commend Pope Francis' powerful speech tonight, but I can't. The Convocation, indeed the world, has lost a great man tonight. Shlomo Nakamura, RIP.
#heavyheart #gonetoosoon

RAM

Saturday, January 22, 2028

Bren and I couldn't sleep a wink last night. We didn't even try. We discussed Slomo's passing and mourned all night long. She did finally nod off on the couch about an hour ago, so do I wake her or carry her to bed?

"Angel, sorry, but I need you to wake up." I'm shaking her. "Griff called from downstairs. He's coming up."

Her eyes open and she yawns while focusing her gaze on the wall clock. *"Mierda,* at 6:30? Why?"

"We'll know soon enough. Go throw on some clothes. I'll brew the coffee."

Only minutes later we're huddled with Griff in the kitchen around our largest cups of strong hot coffee and the donuts he's brought along.

"Sorry to wake you both so early. Ram, we ran the license plate on the video you sent me. Remember I predicted a mistake would occur we could capitalize on? Your video captured it. Bystanders have confirmed it."

"NITWIT murdered Slomo, no?" Bren's eyes are bleary but her mind's sharp.

"We haven't made the connection yet," he says, "but we might later today."

I grab the only chocolate-covered donut in the bunch. "Are you talking about the murder, or the mole at the station?"

"Both, I expect." Griff puts his coffee mug down and doesn't elaborate.

"First tell me who the mole is," Bren says. "I'll give that *cholo* a piece of my mind."

"No, you won't. We don't want the mole tipped off." Griff breaks a sugared donut apart and dips one end into his coffee. "Here's what we know. As listed on the DMV registration documents, the Chevy's owner is a certain family foundation we've had some recent interest in. The person who lives at the owner's listed address is the foundation's sole employee."

Bren's fist pounds the table hard enough that a little of my coffee spills. "Allenby's foundation!"

"Right. This guy is Allenby's nephew."

"Wait, Allenby doesn't have a family," I say. "We looked him up. That's what we read."

"His older step-sister has a different last name. Their connection's not obvious." He twirls his coffee cup in slow motion, as though something's on his mind. "This employee's the child of her first marriage."

Bren looks at me. "I don't think Allenby has access to personal info—"

"I didn't say he's the mole," Griff says as I refill his cup. "Brendali, you need to know who this lady's second husband is to find that out."

He's toying with us, but Bren's no dummy. "OMG, don't tell me—"

"Ken's wife is Allenby's step-sister?" I ask. "You're kidding me, right?"

"Think about how well the pieces fit," Griff says. "We knew the personal information came from KJCR-TV. Ken can call up all the Human Resources data, correct?"

"Of course." Bren and I say in unison.

"The first NITWIT message came up on Ken's computer. Maybe he sent it to himself or had Allenby's nephew do that. We'll find out. Ken called you at 9:30, Brendali, to send you to cover the earthquake. Skeleton Man showed up, knowing you would, too. It's not much of a jump to think Ken, directly or through Allenby, tipped NITWIT and gave them your other personal data."

"No wonder he's so supportive," Bren says. "Jack's his brother-in-law."

"I'm not done," Griff says. "Ram, I wondered why the Chevy's driver tried to run you over. I mean, okay, his passenger screams an epithet at a Muslim on the street and gunshots follow. Random violence by bigots is common these days, which is unfortunate. But the driver steered his vehicle at you, a white guy, not Mr. Çelik. All night I've asked myself why."

"Did you come up with an answer?" I'm at full attention.

"We rousted Allenby's nephew from bed an hour ago. That's why I'm here so early. LAPD's taken him in for an interview as a person of interest. I do have an idea about why this happened. It's only an educated guess. I hope the guy will confirm it."

"Tell us," I say.

"The pope's speech is on television, right? So these guys knew your location. They'd have no problem positionin' a man between the Convention Center and your condo. It's easy walkin' distance close. However, early Friday night means traffic's a mess with the Lakers game and the workweek endin'. The two men in the truck are runnin' late, they're out of position, but The Force is with them. You're out of your expected path, headin' right toward them."

"It's feasible, no?" Bren searches my face for confirmation. I'm doubtful.

Griff continues. "They improvise, which is the mistake. The passenger yells a slur at Çelik as cover, and shoots at him to divert Ram's attention. They intend to run Ram over but the whole thing goes wrong. Çelik lives, Slomo dies, Ram's unhurt. Frazzled, the driver runs over a girl in his haste to escape."

He looks satisfied, neither proud nor gloating. "Today's interview should clarify things, put us on course to wrap this masquerade up, but—" His phone rings. "Excuse me for a moment."

We hear "uh huh" "okay" and "ten to fifteen minutes." After a grunt the call ends with "see you soon." He puts the phone in his pocket and stands. "I need to get down to LAPD to watch this guy's interrogation. Thanks for the coffee."

"Take me along," I say. "Maybe I can confirm that this nephew's your man. I would've seen him at Timba. You'd have a criminal action to threaten him with. That can prod his cooperation."

Griff's eyes roll up. "I'm impressed. You've watched your police procedurals. I'll discuss that with the LAPD on the way to their HQ and let you know if we need you."

4:00 p.m.

In response to a text from Griff I'm seated across from him at a large oblong table in the main conference room at his FBI office. Bren, who's out shopping for a bridal gown, isn't with me. A pull-down projection screen is in front of us, ready for use.

"With this arrest," Griff says, "all the NITWIT group members shown on God's chart have been rounded up except Piotr Krol, aka Skeleton Man." He checks his notepad. "We have his history, residence address and vehicle ownership. We don't have him."

"Fill me in."

"Mr. Krol emigrated here from Poland in his youth, with his parents. He became a brilliant engineer and designer. In fact he lives off the royalty payments on his patents. Seven years ago he survived a car accident but sustained serious head injuries, among many others. He found religion during his recovery and his personality changed. He lost his job and family, disappeared and over time took on a few aliases."

"I get the picture. You'll arrest him soon?"

Griff nods. "He's good at vanishin' and has probably left SoCal.

We've put him on our most wanted and no fly lists and taken our other usual steps. Unless he's in a cave somewhere we'll nab him before long."

"Bren and I will feel better once you do."

"Her binder got us off to a good start. It documents the Allenby family foundation's revenue stream." Griff taps a few buttons on a console situated between us as he speaks. "We'd begun to trace the sources when Mr. Nakamura's murder occurred. The confession by Allenby's nephew this mornin' sped up the process. A lot of money came to the Foundation from drug cartels and the black market for illegal weapons in Central America. The foundation's basically a money launderin' operation."

"Allenby's a money launderer? I've got to hear more. This astonishes me."

"What a little coward this nephew is." Griff smirks. "But he's useful. His surname's Ochoa and his father's Mexican, high up in the Boca Del Rio drug cartel. I'll show you part of his interview. LAPD's going to send out a press release on this case any time now, if they haven't already.

"Let's see if I can get this to play." He pauses to work the console. "Here we go."

On the screen Ochoa, who looks about Bren's age, is seated in a small room. With no distinguishing facial features, he's an average Latino in a light blue polo shirt, with thin gold-framed glasses. His gaze is focused on the interviewer, who's not visible.

"My father called me right after this bogus new God interview ended," he's saying.

The interrogator's deep baritone voice booms. "Who's your dad?"

"He's in a Mexican cartel hit hard by this TV lady—what's her name again?" The name isn't provided, but we know its Bren. "They want her dead in the worst way. My father knew she left the country but didn't know where she'd gone until he saw the interview."

Bren's not safe, even in L.A. I'd better tell her. "You know that's been a constant worry," I tell Griff. He nods.

I return my attention to Ochoa's confession. "Dad suggested that I arrange to kidnap this gal and bring her to Tijuana alive. The captors would get $100,000. I'd receive $25,000 for making the arrangements. That's where she would've gone, but Piotr chickened out at the last moment and let her go."

"Do you know what your dad intended to do with the captive once he got her?"

"They'd probably do their usual thing," Ochoa says with a shrug. "By that I mean rape, torture, murder, followed by burial somewhere in the desert."

A chill runs up my spine. This bastard doesn't give a damn. I glance at Griff. "If you hadn't traced Bren to Timba, she wouldn't have survived." Bren will faint or explode when she hears this. Should I tell her? I'd better, but I'll need to pick the moment carefully.

"Explain how you arranged the kidnap," the interviewer says.

"Piotr and I co-founded this little group to, uh, agitate. God's insulted when people abuse him and fail to follow the dictates of his Bible. We're his enforcers."

"This is NITWIT, right?"

"Yes." Ochoa's face lights up with a cocky, or maybe proud, expression.

"So what did you do once your father offered that money?"

"I called my uncle to discuss the offer. He's not my uncle, actually, but I've called him that all my life. He's Jack Allenby, the TV news anchor. Jack agreed to have his foundation front NITWIT's upfront costs in exchange for a 50/50 share of the reward. So I called Piotr. The deal got done when Jack accepted a 60/40 split. He suggested I e-mail Ken Wise to kick the effort off, which I did."

"Jack Allenby supports domestic terrorists." I can feel my jaw open, my eyes pop. "I can't get my head around this."

Griff smiles as he puts the Ochoa video on pause. "Allenby's family foundation sent about half its outgoing funds to religious organizations. NITWIT got a start-up share. I assume Allenby supports them to help Ochoa, who strikes me as a zealot. However, if what Ochoa said is accurate, it shows Allenby's awareness of the nature of NITWIT's business."

"Is Ken involved in this, too?" My mind may as well get blown all the way. I'd never expect him to do anything like this.

"He's on the foundation's Board of Directors but Ochoa told us he does no oversight. Prosecutors can decide whether to pursue a case, but as a board member Ken's exposed to potential culpability for money launderin', among other things."

I look down and shake my head a few times while thinking this through. "Uh, can you tell me one more thing?"

"Depends on what you're askin'."

I hesitate but decide to plow ahead. "Ken's a good friend of Allenby's. Do you have a feel for whether any of the money Jack's foundation received came from KJCR-TV?"

He gives me his long intense law enforcement stare. "I didn't plan on bringin' this up but the answer's yes—a steady flow, though not a lot at any one time. Some embezzlement happened. We don't yet know that Ken's the embezzler, although that makes sense. Ochoa did say your station paid the rental fees for the helicopter and pilot who kidnapped Brendali."

I'm amazed—at this, and at Krol handing Bren back to take me as a hostage. If he lives on patent royalties his one-fifth share of $60,000, which pencils out to $12,000, might not have meant much to him. I convinced him she's innocent of the sins he thought she'd committed, so he chose not to hand her over. Even with a cockeyed understanding of the Bible, does this mean he maintains a shred of morality or decency? Hard to believe it, but I'd rather not find out.

RAM

Monday, January 24, 2028

Upon arriving at the Convention Center I sit down for a private chat with Father Zeke. "What will get the Evangelicals to cooperate? We know what they're up to, but how do we get them to change?"

"Twenty men are hard-and-fast holdouts. I met them on Friday, quoted Proverbs 29.1 and Luke 12:47, but it did no good. These people refuse to believe the new God's authentic."

"Do you think they'd listen to reason, whether based on the Bible or common sense?"

Zeke leans back in his chair, looks up and clasps his hands together. "I've talked to them until I turned blue in the face, which is hard for a guy of my ethnicity to do." His chuckle's louder than his words. "If you have any ideas, spout 'em."

"Let's meet with them at 1:00 p.m., in this room. I'll figure something out."

I summarize the situation in a message to the tech angels. For once their response is immediate: 'This afternoon, check the news for developments you may wish to mention.' I ask for clarification but, as usual, get none.

By checking the attendee bio for Gilbert Thibodaux, the influential Evangelical heart attack victim who hasn't returned to the Convocation, I learn that he's recuperating with his wife's relatives in Arcadia. At my request the tech angels provide his phone number.

I send Bren, who's monitoring the Convocation from home, a text. 'Would you mind calling Mr. Thibodaux for me? I saved his life, so hopefully he'll do me a favor. Sound him out. If he's healthy enough and willing to come speak to his friends, I could use his help getting them to start participating in good faith. Get him here for a 1:00 p.m. meeting, if you can.'

She responds a half hour later: 'He'll show up. I will, too.'

The meeting occurs in the same conference room where the fight over the Ten Commandments took place. The twenty men are seated in fold-up chairs behind long brown fold-up tables. Zeke and I face them in similar seats.

Zeke calls the meeting to order. "Lord, hear me. You hand-picked the men in this room to participate in this Convocation. They're good God-fearing gentlemen, doing their best to achieve righteousness in all things. Perhaps this is why you selected them.

"These men, Lord, yearn to do God's bidding at all times, in every way. Yet they face a moral quandary. They insist upon following the Bible's dictates but perceive your instructions for this Convocation as contrary to those principles.

"They know Romans 2:5-6: 'Because you are stubborn and refuse to turn from your sin, you are storing up terrible punishment for yourself. A day of anger is coming, when God's righteous judgment will be revealed. He will judge everyone according to what they have done.'

"These men want to know whether you will judge them by their lifelong adherence to your dictates. Or will one act, the well-intentioned and principled rejection of your remaining objectives for this Convocation, bring terrible punishment upon them?"

No answer comes from God. No reactions come from the men in the room.

I didn't expect Zeke to take this tack, but he's expressing how they feel. Fine, maybe I can work this into my comments.

Zeke points at me. "You know Ram Forrester, you've seen his show, heard his reports, maybe looked at his Twitter posts. He has a few words for you."

I stand and dive into my spiel. "Gentlemen, I understand your concerns as Zeke explains them. I'm no pastor or religious expert. I did Bible study and attended seminary for a year in my youth. I learned a few Bible passages that stuck with me and come to mind today.

"One, Proverbs 3:5-7, says 'trust in the Lord with all your heart, and do not rely on your own understanding. Acknowledge him in all your ways, and he will make your paths straight.' I take this to mean that if God tells you to undertake a particular act, you should.

"James 2:18 also speaks to this. That passage says 'But someone will say you have faith and I have works. Show me your faith apart from your works, and I will show you my faith by my works.'

"Each of you has faith. Our new God will show you his faith by his works—the many things he plans to do to help us fix earth's problems—if we show him our work, meaning a successful Convocation. We can't finish this work unless you join our efforts."

I wait for their response, but the group remains mum. That's not a good sign, so I change gears and hope our guest will make an impact. "I want you to hear from someone you know. I'll probably have a few additional comments after his speech. Please welcome back your compatriot, Gilbert Thibodaux."

Bren strolls over to the door and calls Gilbert in. Much thinner now, he hugs me, whispers a thank-you and turns to face his peers. He gets the silent treatment, too.

"Hi, y'all," Gilbert says. "That I can see y'all again—heck, that I'm here today—is a testament to God's mercy. He chose me to attend this Convocation so Mr. Forrester could extend my life.

"Friends, I am burdened and wish to make a public confession." He stops to draw a deep breath. "Since my near death I've reflected upon my life, works and beliefs. All I see is failures, a constant display of sin, pride and arrogance. I served only my ego, not God, for decades.

"You've read my words. The many times I urged you to remain steadfast in the face of licentiousness, my calls to y'all to honor our 'superior religious faith' over others, my advice that you consider women and the non-white races as inferiors." He sighs, shakes his head and stares at the floor.

"I wrote from weakness," he says in a soft voice. "From ignorance. From fear. I confess. Before you, as God is my judge, I reject those words and attitudes. I failed you, myself and our Lord. I take solace from 1 John 1:9—'If we confess our sins, he is faithful and just and will forgive us our sins and purify us from all unrighteousness.'"

Gilbert breaks down, sobbing. Bren goes to him, embraces him and says a few soothing words. When he can, Gilbert continues. "I've been blessed with some additional time on earth. I will use it to atone for my grievous errors. To that end, I urge y'all to make this gathering succeed. Let our new God know we are with him, ready to help achieve his goals. Your cooperation will make this happen."

He sits to complete silence from his former followers.

I deliver a few final words. "I know a lot of you had a personal relationship with the prior God. Mine is with the new one. In fact, I received a message from his angels earlier today, suggesting I check the news this afternoon. While Gilbert spoke to you, I did."

I bring my cellphone up close enough to read the screen. "This comes from Fox News, which many of you follow. Check it yourselves. Apparently the Museum of Biblical Creation and the Good Book Museum have disappeared. You may recall this also happened at the Saddlebow Church last week."

I look around at their stunned expressions. A few people do check their phones.

"If you continue to obstruct progress you can expect more of this type of thing, or worse. God knows you have not heeded his demands. What angers Him is your refusal to negotiate in good faith, as his invitations require. His retribution has begun with these acts. You, and all who follow the Evangelical faiths, are in imminent danger. To ward off further punishment, you must participate in a meaningful manner for the Convocation's eight remaining days."

Now everyone's eyes are rapt, focused on their phones, their faces stony.

"Sound reasons exist to change your perspective on this Convocation. Think of this—you are in position to become the religion that saves mankind. That has obvious proselytizing advantages I need not spell out for you. Please pray on this. Humanity needs your cooperation."

The meeting ends with the group walking out in silence. Some look thoughtful, others mad. I can't read the other expressions. None of them stop to chat with Gilbert. I thank him for his words, and congratulate him for the improvement in his worldview.

My approach needs work, I guess, but these Evangelicals must change their attitudes. If they don't, the morning after the Convocation ends we'll wake up to God's Judgment Day, if we wake up at all.

Ram's Convocation Update: Met today with the Evangelical attendees, but did it matter? Whether the Convocation succeeds or fails depends on this group's decisions. #lookbeyondyourselves #prayforguidance

---

RAM

Monday, January 31, 2028

I wake up to find Bren gone, but she left a text message: *'Buenos dias, mi cariño!* Overnight, God told me where to go and what to do today. I may arrive late to the CC. Don't worry about me, baby.' The message makes me smile.

Before breakfast I ask the tech angels to update the disappearance of the Evangelical museums. A prompt response comes back. 'The buildings are permanently gone. Of the ninety-eight people in the two buildings, all will return except two. Their fate has not been decided.'

'Are they hostages? Or sacrifices if the Convocation fails? Where are they?'

'All ninety-eight have been deprogrammed and are free of their religious blinders.'

'Can I use this information in today's meeting with the Evangelicals?' The question goes unanswered.

In the same small conference room we used in our last meeting, most of the twenty Evangelicals stare at me with hostile expressions. A man in the back row pretends he's asleep. The others sit with slouched postures.

Bren walks in with Gilbert Thibodaux and takes the seat between me and Zeke. Gilbert sits with his former peers, who shun him.

I get the meeting started. "Gentlemen, I want to understand why your group opposes God's remaining objectives. He's only asking us to resolve existing religious conflicts and create an infrastructure to deal with future problems. Why isn't this acceptable?"

Caleb Kimball, who I interviewed many weeks ago, stands to answer. "First, aside from our unfortunate recent scrum with the Catholics, many of the Evangelical faiths don't have a history of violent conflicts with other religions. These issues aren't our concern. The more important reason for our inaction is this so-called God. Our allegiance belongs to Jesus Christ and no one else. It's impossible for me to overlook who is asking. This imposter's a devil. We refuse to cooperate with his efforts."

Bren gives me a note. 'God told me what to do. I'll take it from here,' it says.

Okay, so this is her show. Maybe she can make progress. Zeke and I sure haven't. "Brendali has a few words she wants to share with you."

Upon taking my seat, I notice that my message board now reads 'approved.'

"Every so often this new God you don't believe in speaks to me in my sleep." Bren leans casually against our table as she faces the men. Her voice is reasonable, relaxed. "Last night, in addition to asking me to bring Gilbert here, he told me to have you set your cell phone cameras to the video function."

No one does.

"Sir," Bren says, pointing to a bald older man in the front row wearing a black T-shirt with "God rules" emblazoned in red across his chest. "Why are you refusing to do as God asks?"

"For the reasons Caleb mentioned."

Bren glances at the floor, nods once and straightens her posture.

"This God has done all sorts of unexplainable things to authenticate his claim. Remember the earthquake he predicted and caused? Ram, the archbishop and I also received miracles. How can you deny who he is?"

"He admitted he's not the New Testament God. That's all we need to know." The man has taken off his glasses and is about to clean them with a handkerchief when he disappears. The glasses drop to the floor.

Bren and Gilbert are unperturbed, but the man's sudden absence brings yells, curses, banging on tables and other noise from the nineteen remaining men. I've knocked my cellphone to the floor. Zeke's spilled coffee over his suit and dress shirt.

Everyone opens their phones. I guess this is how God proves his authenticity and administers discipline to this group.

"Touch 'play' and watch the video," Bren says. "The entire world, including the other Convocation members, should do likewise."

Two men and one woman appear on our screens in identical shapeless, unadorned royal blue robes. They're seated behind an irregularly shaped table made of some sort of rock, on a couch covered by what looks like a green tarp. A blank white wall is behind them.

The blue-eyed redhead in the center seat speaks first. "We're coming to you from the moon's All-Souls Transfer Station. I'm Joshua. Some of you may know me as the pastor of the Saddlebow Church." He points to the blonde woman next to him. "This is Sarah, who oversees the Museum of Biblical Creation." He nods at the bald bearded man seated to his right. "Luke has the same position at the Good Book Museum. Soon after those buildings disappeared, we arrived here."

What the hell? Everyone in the room expresses disbelief in their individual ways, by voice, facial expression, gesture or some combination. Only Caleb Kimball isn't devoting full attention to his screen. He's found something of greater interest to stare at on the ceiling tiles.

All three rise as Joshua continues to speak. "The angels we've met told us we'll return to our physical bodies and lives if God wills it. Meanwhile, we look like this." Their robes fall. I can feel my eyes enlarge and my jaw drop. Their heads are unattached to bodies.

Every voice in the room exclaims "oh my god!" or "Jesus!" except for Bren's *"Mi Dios!"* and my "what the f—k?"

The screen shows Sarah, close-up. Her pleasant face is all business. "Excuse my butting in, Joshua. Until now we've been ardent Evangelicals. An orientation course on the afterlife has rendered us nonreligious. Before we get into that, however, we ask for a volunteer from the Convocation's Evangelicals to join us."

She has no takers, of course, but Zeke's bark takes care of that. "Each of you, write your names on a piece of paper. Fold them up and bring the pages to me. We'll pick the volunteer at random." He hands out blank paper from a notebook he has with him. Only Gilbert complies.

The man who faked sleep disappears. The others react the way they did when this happened to the older man.

"Gilbert, you know everyone, right?" Zeke's loud voice bounces off the walls and ceiling. Gilbert nods. "Please do what I asked for your colleagues."

Once Gilbert hands over eighteen folded pages, Zeke turns to Bren. "Please select one." She spreads them out on Zeke's table, picks a page from the middle of the bunch and hands it to him. He opens it. "Gilbert's our volunteer."

Gilbert stands, with a broad smile. "I will accept whatever comes, my friends. May God confer His blessings on each of you."

He, too, disappears. This time the room remains silent. Bren and I exchange glances.

Luke, who appears older than Joshua and Sarah, finally speaks. "The angels told us that at death, our souls arrive here to transfer to their next stage of life. Most undergo rebirth, arbitrarily becoming men, women or non-binary sexes, this race or ethnicity or that one, the children of poor or rich families, etc.

"A few souls return to their present lives and share what they call their near death experiences. When they die again, they repeat the journey. We hope that happens to us.

"Other paths exist," Joshua adds. "For example, morally bankrupt souls are banished forever to Saturn's moon, Titan. The common concept of hell isn't wrong, but its location is inaccurate and admission to that nefarious place is much more exclusive than we all believe."

Sarah chimes in. "This transfer station is like an airport without amenities. Souls arrive here and take a tram to heaven, which is nearby. They can watch their funerals on video feeds if they wish, receive counselling if needed, review the good and bad things they did in their lives and prepare to move along their designated spiritual paths to their next life once their memories of the last life are erased. What we call heaven is an assembly line, not an eternity."

If what they've said is true, we all have some serious rethinking to do. I have to defer it, though, because getting the Evangelicals to participate is more important than anything else at this moment.

"Gilbert has arrived and will join us," Joshua says.

In a blue robe similar to those the others no longer wear, Gilbert sits next to Luke. "So I've died, huh? I didn't feel a thing. The guys who disappeared before me probably didn't, either. This sure isn't Earth, though, is it?"

Luke interrupts. "All of mankind needs to understand that if humanity ceases to exist, so do our spiritual paths. No judgment day, no rebirths, not even any heaven. The angels will eject our billions of bodiless souls into the void of deep space to wander for eternity in dark, cold, airless space."

The men's faces run the gamut from thoughtful to stunned, but everyone's paying attention, including Kimball.

"I don't buy this malarkey," a man in a seat nearest the hallway yells. "You all can go stuff it." He blesses us with two middle fingers.

Instead of disappearing, he elevates out of his chair in slow motion and is slammed backwards as if by a tornado-strength wind.

He topples over once and, upside down, hits the rear wall. His body explodes, turning that area into a bloody, bony mess.

Everyone yells, including Bren, who also grabs my arm with all her strength. Zeke's eyes bug out. I would've fallen to the floor but for Bren's intercession. A blood-spattered man in the last row throws up.

The Evangelical contingent is reduced to seventeen shaken men.

As happened during the Convocation's opening day, we hear a disembodied voice so loud it envelops our senses and vibrates inside our bodies. "Stand, Mr. Kimball." The man complies with insouciant slowness.

"You truly refuse to believe I am your God?" The voice, if anything, is louder.

"Yes, I do." He puffs up his chest, locking eyes with me as though he's answering my question.

"The voice of God belongs to your God and no other."

"I don't recognize you as our God."

"You will stake the lives of sixty-five million Evangelicals on that opinion?"

"Absolutely. I know you can't, or won't, follow through. You may make a building disappear, or a person for that matter, but our entire faith? That's mass genocide. No one worthy of godliness would do that. Only a devil would."

Bren's voice comes to my attention. "Mr. Kimball, God's trying to give your group every possible chance to cooperate. If you won't, he'll punish each—what the hell?"

I'm in a trance, unable to speak, but I know my nerves are intact because my head has knocked a ceiling tile off its perch.

"Mi Dios! What's going on, Ram? You're—huge. And you're on fire!"

Despite the heat from my knees down I can't stop staring at Kimball. Nor can he tear his eyes from mine.

God's voice thunders. "What would prove my bona fides to you, sir?"

"I doubt anything would." Kimball remains calm.

"How does this suit you?" God shuts my eyes and moves my hands in front of my lips as though I'm praying. For over a minute I'm mouthing incomprehensible words in a language I've never heard before.

In response to my chant Gilbert reappears, fully clothed, in the same chair he sat in before. His body falls over and is caught by the man next to him. He eases Gilbert to the floor.

I'm completely oblivious to the room's reaction. I can see Gilbert only because his chair is situated between me and Kimball.

Another man rushes to Gilbert, bends and grabs his wrist. Gilbert grasps the man's arm while his eyes flutter open and his mouth gasps for breath.

"Oh my God," Gilbert says in a weak voice. "I've had such an amazing dream."

"No, you didn't," God says through me in a lower, conversational tone while the second man helps Gilbert sit up. "You disappeared, spoke to us from the moon and reappeared. That is what you dreamed, correct?"

Gilbert shakes his head to indicate agreement. "My friends, God's spirit is with us, channeled through Ram." These words are uttered in a halting, amazed voice. Gilbert glances at the others nearby. "I suggest you fulfill his demands."

"Sound advice," God says, in my voice. "So you will no longer question my authenticity, I leave you with one more demonstration."

I repeat the chant that brought Gilbert back. This time Joshua materializes, naked, on the floor in front of me. A man spreads his jacket over Joshua to cover him below the waist.

"I have chosen to bring you back, sir," God says. "You will have to find your own way to Orange County, though."

"Thank you, Lord," is all he can muster. His eyes watery, Joshua tries to take all this in but is overcome with emotion. "What about Sarah and Luke?"

"They are rejoicing in their return. Fox News will televise their arrivals, and yours. It will make quite a splash in the news cycle, I expect."

Several men grab their cellphones, presumably to watch the about-to-break news.

Joshua doesn't try to hide his tears. "I need to call my wife." A phone is handed to him. He blubbers as he hears her voice.

"Oh, Jesus," competes with "God have mercy" and other similar exclamations, all uttered by the men watching the news broadcast.

"Mr. Kimball," God says, once more in his authoritative voice, "does what you have witnessed change your perspective at all?"

"I'll have to give this some serious thought."

"Good," God says. "That is an improvement." The video connection to the transfer station disconnects.

Aside from the whispers of Joshua's conversation with his wife, the room is quiet. A hundred thoughts run through my head as I feel myself return to my normal size.

I'm wiped out. Brendali fixates on my lower limbs, which are free of any hint of fire although my pant legs, shoes and socks are singed. Most of the Evangelicals are mute, perhaps engaged in silent prayers. Zeke leans in my direction and bellows at me from two feet away. "How in God's name did you do that?"

I can't even manage a shrug. "God spoke through me, for the second time."

I gather enough strength to stand and lean against my table. "Mr. Kimball, your group should meet without Brendali, Zeke or myself for the rest of the morning." I need time to recover my senses. They probably do, too. "Talk things through. If you decide to remain uncooperative I'll announce deadlock, closure and lack of success at the end of the day since continuing the Convocation would serve no purpose. Think long and hard about your choices and what they mean for mankind and Evangelicalism."

I sit again because my legs feel weak. "If your group agrees to participate, we can get the remaining objectives done by Friday's deadline. Let's meet here after lunch, at 1:00 p.m. Call or text Father Zeke if necessary."

"I'll leave you my number," Zeke says, scribbling it on one of the pages Gilbert gave him. An odd look crosses Zeke's face. He unfolds all of them, one by one and waves the pages as he stands. "Gentlemen, so you'll know, these are the names Gilbert wrote on these pages." He reads each page aloud, repeating 'Gilbert Thibodaux' every time. "I hope you'll now show Gilbert a bit more respect."

I lean on Bren and Zeke as we head out the door. I've placed the fate of humanity in the hands of seventeen men determined not to accept our new reality. Maybe I've screwed this up.

RAM

Monday, January 31, 2028 (cont.)

Bren's inside the L.A. Cathedral, praying that the Evangelicals will come to their senses. I'm in the plaza outside, waiting for her and desperate to locate anything I can find online that'll come in handy when we reconvene.

A call from the 212 area code takes me away from my Google searches. "Good morning, Ram. Carson Freeman here."

I straighten up. Our corporate CEO's calling? I know what this's about. "Good morning to you, too, Mr. Freeman."

"Call me Carson, please. I trust you've heard the news?"

"What news is that?"

"Ken Wise and Jack Allenby have been arrested. They're suspended, pending the outcome of the legal proceedings."

Okay, he means the NITWIT funding situation. I'm not too surprised.

"We need to fill their positions until the situation clarifies, Ram. "You're a natural for Allenby's slot but I'm calling to let you know someone else will take it. I don't want you to feel slighted."

"I appreciate the courtesy. I'm fine with your decision. I'll concentrate on my talk show."

"We'd like to offer you Ken's GM slot on an interim basis, initially. We'll make the added responsibility worth your time."

Me succeed Ken, even on a temporary basis? That could get dicey. If we can finish the Convocation first that'd help, but do I want Ken's headaches? "I'm honored, and stunned. I've never considered this. I need to think it over."

"Of course. All of us here in New York think you're the right guy for the job. Get back to me tonight so we can work out compensation and other details if you're onboard."

"I will. Thanks for the confidence vote. Can you tell me who Jack's replacement is?"

"Kate Chung. She subbed for Jack several times before you returned from disability leave, did well and deserves the opportunity."

What a turn of events. "I'm happy for her, but you should know something. Kate and I had a three-year relationship that didn't end well. I don't know how receptive she is to having me as her boss, even for a day. You should check that out while I consider your offer. If this would make her uncomfortable, I'll pass."

"Thanks for the heads-up. I'll talk to her. We can discuss it tonight."

The call ends. I stare at the phone, disbelieving the words I heard, when it rings again. This call's local.

"Ram, Caleb Kimball told me his group will participate in negotiations but won't commit in advance to accept an agreement," Zeke says. "I've cancelled the 1:00 p.m. meeting."

We've taken a half-step in the right direction. "Did Kimball specify any terms the Evangelicals want before they'd sign?" I wave to Brendali, who's walking toward me.

"No. The conversation didn't last long. He mentioned they're divided over agreeing to participate."

"Is Gilbert helping them?"

"They excluded him. You'd think they'd show him some gratitude after his selflessness this morning, but no." Zeke's disgust comes through loud and clear.

I guess forgiveness isn't a high priority for this group. "Can you spread the word to the entire Convocation that a general meeting will take place in the main hall at 2:00 p.m.?" He agrees and we sign off.

I update Bren on both calls while we head back to the Convention Center. Her reaction to the news from New York surprises me. "Carson wants you to take Ken's job, no?"

"How'd you figure that out? I had no idea."

"Who else would they make an offer to? Aside from Jack, you have the most seniority. Either it's you or they bring someone in from another station. Why do that when you're already here and you know the market?"

"Smart-ass. Kate's replacing Jack."

"That I didn't expect. Good for her. Did you tell Carson you'll accept?"

"No, I said I'd consider it. I need to get back to him tonight. How do you feel about it?"

"I know you won't fire me."

"True. You're cohosting my life, Angel."

In the 2:00 p.m. meeting, each religious faith agrees to huddle separately and designate one person to participate in a joint meeting where all faiths will hammer out an agreement for God's last two objectives. The chosen representative will relay our talks to his or her group, get their feedback and bring it back. We'll repeat the process until terms of agreement are reached.

Two hours later we're in the conference room nearest the security guard station. We've got thirty-seven attendees plus Brendali and myself. The representatives include the four surviving members of the Steering Committee, representing their respective faiths, Caleb Kimball for the Evangelicals, and Hakan Çelik for the Muslims.

Johnny Ray had set up a projector for us, which is now turned on and focused on a pull-down screen.

"I'll start," I tell the assembled group, "with a statement of purpose and principles from URI, the United Religions Initiative. I like this group's approach. They do a good job of laying the groundwork for what we're here to do. Here's how they frame it:

We [URI] seeks to promote enduring, daily interfaith cooperation, end religiously motivated violence and create cultures of peace, justice and healing for the Earth and all living beings.

"Go to their website—Brendali, if you don't mind, please project it onto our screen so everyone here can read URI's entire preamble, purpose and principles. I hope you'll agree that these principles provide a good starting point for us." Bren reads a few of them aloud:

Respect the differences among religions.

Listen and speak with respect to deepen mutual understanding and trust.

Practice healing and reconciliation to resolve conflicts without resorting to violence.

Seek and offer cooperation with other interfaith efforts.

Deliberations and decisions shall be made at every level by bodies and methods that fairly represent the diversity of affected interests and are not dominated by any.

I stay silent for a few minutes so everyone can review the full URI statement. "We'll close today at 5:00 p.m. as usual, so let's start to formulate an agreement that covers God's objectives and is acceptable to our many faiths. Go back to your groups and get your discussion underway. Come back tomorrow at 8:00 a.m. so we can get an early start integrating everyone's feedback. The other attendees can show up an hour later, at nine."

Thursday afternoon, February 3, 2028, 3:30 p.m.

The steering committee and I gather near the security guards' station to take stock of where our groups are.

"Over the last few days," I say, "our conceptual plan has worked. The attending religions, other than you-know-who, have agreed to forgive past historical inter-faith or intra-faith grievances. For current and future grievances, we've settled on a quasi-judicial process that starts with mediation. If necessary, arbitration or a bench trial conducted by a panel of clerical judges would follow. Up to two levels of appellate judges will hear appeals in trial cases only, with case precedent developed to guide future proceedings. Does anyone disagree with that summary?"

No one does. "Are there any details your groups want to offer that haven't been raised, discussed or accepted over the last few days?"

Archbishop Delmonico speaks first. "The Pope asks for creation of a global judicial structure independent of organizations such as the U.N. or the Hague."

The Reverend Mother adds her feedback. "My Buddhists want the jurists assigned to each trial or arbitration to belong to faiths other than those involved in the dispute."

I chip in what I've heard. "Çelik told me the Muslims want to impose mandatory monetary penalties for the losing side. That strikes me as harsh. However, we're making progress. These details can get worked out."

Father Zeke's been quiet until now. "Kimball's Evangelicals refuse to sign off on the concept or explain what their issues with it are."

We all have the same incredulous reaction. As the Reverend Mother puts it, "We've come to a dead stop at the edge of a cliff."

"Let's go talk to them," Bren says. "We need to address this right away."

The five of us march into the room where the Evangelicals are huddled. I nod to Gilbert, who gives me an unenthusiastic wave in return.

"I understand there are some issues your group has with the agreement under discussion," I say. "Mr. Kimball, can you fill us in?"

Something in his posture as he stands conveys an arrogance I find disheartening. "Until Monday we regarded this security guard as a devil. But when we witnessed him work through you to raise Gilbert, Luke and the others from the dead, we realized that he's Jesus. His return signifies that the Day of Judgment is upon us. Therefore, this Convocation must fail. The seventeen of us are proud to bring this day about. God's judgments will exalt our righteousness and speed us into eternal heaven."

That's certainly a unique take on things. Bren's hand covers her eyes. Her head's tilted toward the floor and her body shakes gently. I can't tell whether she's laughing or crying. If it's the former, the reaction's wrong although she is trying to cover it up.

Zeke speaks up. "Consider Romans 2:5-11: 'Because of your stubbornness and unrepentant heart you are storing up wrath for yourself in the day of wrath and revelation of the righteous judgment of God, who will render to each person according to his deeds.'"

"That is your opinion, but we who have God's ear do not share it," Kimball says in a smug tone.

"Let's not get fight over bible quotes right now," I say. "We need a reality check."

A bright white light flashes around the room. God reappears a foot away from me in his security guard attire. "I have followed your discussion, gentlemen," he says. "Mr. Kimball, you consider yourself an earnest believer in the words of the Bible as you and your brethren interpret it, correct?"

"Yes, of course." His self-satisfied smirk makes me want to smack him.

"Is it accurate to say that the central premise to your

interpretations is that the Bible contains the actual words of the New Testament God and his apostles?"

"Absolutely, yes."

"What if your premise is false?"

"That is impossible, so we have not considered it."

"I can prove your premise is erroneous, sir. Take Acts, for example. The earliest known version of it comes from a Greek codex written in the first or second century, many decades after your Jesus walked the Earth. Centuries later the Greek original was translated into Latin. Much later that version was re-translated into Old English. Several more revisions took place over recent centuries. The same thing happened with the rest of the Bible. The New Testament God's words, if any remain, are indistinguishable from the verbiage added at various later dates."

"We do not agree with you."

Bren whispers in my ear. "Bingo. Watch what happens."

"You have decided that I am Jesus, yet you are unwilling to accept my word?" Kimball, knocked to the floor by the physical force behind God's spoken words, must surely get the message. His hypocrisy is so obvious, yet he can't see it.

Kimball gets to his feet, his face red with either anger or embarrassment.

If the room had windows, God's voice would shatter the glass. As it is, his next words actually blow the room's two doors off their hinges. "You are willing to jeopardize the continuity of your species based on an unproven and incorrect assumption that the present version of the Bible contains the literal words of God? Your attitude is obstinate and unprincipled. My wrath will pale in comparison to that of the followers of other religions, indeed of the entire world, if this Convocation fails because of your insistence on following these flawed views."

The rigidity of Kimball's thought process astounds me. What is it in him that makes him incapable of accepting this God's words?

God lowers his voice to a normal, though edgy, tone. "You mentioned mass genocide several days ago, ascribing it to me. You are the one who will truly end the reign of humanity, however, if you persist in obstructing this Convocation."

Kimball and God stare at each other for what seems like forever, but is probably a half-minute. "I shall now pass judgment on you and your followers," God says.

The man next to Kimball pulls on his arm, causing the two to briefly converse. Kimball speaks once the discussion ends. "My group wishes to consult with me."

"I shall wait," God says. Kimball and his peers, including Gilbert, engage in energetic though whispered conversation. God turns toward us, with a wink.

At length Kimball turns toward us. "Out of the seventeen of us, nine choose to accept judgment. We expect to receive exaltation and eternal life as the Bible promises. The other eight agree to accept the Convocation's final agreement."

If God intends to punish anyone, the math will turn in our favor if he limits the punishment to two stubborn men. I hope he'll spare the overall Evangelical community.

I hear God's words in my head. 'You are wise and compassionate, Ephraim.'

Kimball doesn't flinch at God's prolonged stare. "The nine of you who wish to receive judgment shall stand. Mr. Kimball, you shall receive judgment first."

The other eight men get to their feet and interlock arms with Kimball.

"Caleb Kimball, you have no faith," God says.

"Of course I have faith. I—"

"You are certain you possess the absolute truth, Mr. Kimball. Individuals like you do not need faith, because certainty eliminates the doubt from which faith springs. You are guilty of many sins, notably those of stubbornness, inflexibility and obstinacy. Your nonexistent faith will condemn the billions alive to death and abort the lives of untold generations to come. This is nothing less than genocide, sir. You shall not receive exaltation, but I will grant you the eternity you seek—on Saturn's moon, Triton, which you call hell."

Kimball puffs his chest up for only a moment before he disappears. Yells of astonishment fill the room.

God turns to the eight remaining men. "Do any among you, having heard my judgment of Mr. Kimball, wish to reconsider your opinions of this Convocation?"

One of the men, clearly the youngest, raises his hand. "I will join my brothers who choose to support the agreement."

God's voice once again comes inside my head. 'You see? I only had to punish one man, not two or 65 million.'

God's next words are directed at the Evangelicals. "Those of you willing to pledge support to the agreement created at this Convocation, please stand. Any who still seek judgment may form a line to my left and receive it." Everyone stands. No Judgment Day line forms.

"We have a unanimous quorum," God says. "Continue your work." In a flash he's gone.

Bren seizes my hand and squeezes it to signal her happiness. I give her a hesitant smile, believing we'll accomplish success only when we have a fully executed agreement.

"Gentlemen," I say. "Thank you for reconsidering. I think the entire Evangelical community will benefit from your decision. If you'll excuse us, I'll announce your concurrence to the Convocation at large."

We leave. In the hallway I turn to the others. "Bren and I have to prepare for our show tonight. While we're gone I'd like you to start drafting an agreement we can present for a vote tomorrow. Maybe bring in a lawyer to help, if you have one you trust. I'll rejoin you no later than 10:00 p.m. if you're still working on it."

"We can do this at the Cathedral," Delmonico says. "I have the perfect attorney for this work. I'll invite her to meet us. Ram, can either you or Brendali miss your show tonight to help us with the drafting? I'd like to have you both, but I know the show must go on."

Bren responds. "Go with them, Ram. I'll handle the show."

The Reverend Mother adds her comment. "I have watched you throughout this ordeal, Mr. Forrester. I'm reminded of a Buddhist saying: 'A man is not called wise because he talks and talks again; but if he is peaceful, loving and fearless he is in truth called wise.' You are all these things. Your wisdom will help us tonight, I'm sure."

Zeke doesn't express an opinion but from his face I can see he wants me present.

"I guess I'll find my two cents to add," I say. "I have to make a call to someone in New York before I can join you, but go ahead, get started."

45 | Signed Sealed Delivered

RAM

Friday, February 4, 2028

Bren and I slide into our seats on the dais. "We're all looking bright-eyed this morning, aren't we?" My question's a gentle tease, prompted by the sleepy appearance of the others.

Compared to day one, the invitees' attitudes have completely changed. That day's quiet has given way to boisterous chatter. I bring the big screen's Convocation icon to Bren's attention, as it's no longer a bare tree near death in a raging thunder storm. Now the apple tree is thriving. Oranges, lemons, peaches and all sorts of other fruit grow on it. One man and one woman, both naked, are reaching up for their choice of nourishment.

"We know who those two are, don't we?" I ask Bren.

"Yes. I'm glad God didn't choose us as models," she answers.

"Let's get this session started," I suggest to everyone. Heads nod, which is better than having them nod off. "Bren, would you do the honors?"

She gets up, goes to the lectern and taps the mic a few times. The pings don't catch everyone's attention so she speaks up. "Quiet please, everyone. We're ready to begin, thank you!" She has to repeat herself twice more before silence reigns.

"It's not a good morning, it's a great one!" she says, sounding more chipper than she is. "This final session of the 2027-2028

World Religions Convocation is televised live, everywhere, courtesy of Earth's New God and his tech angels."

We're televising not only to let everyone know we've accomplished our mission, but to keep pressure on the Evangelicals not to renege.

"This is our last gathering," Bren says, "and it's been a long haul. Let's get it done!" That prospect prompts loud prolonged cheers.

"The six of us up here did an all-nighter, pretty much, drafting the agreement we call A Proclamation to End Religious Violence. We posted it on the Convocation's website, but you might not have seen it unless you've been awake since 4:00 a.m. Take some time to read it over." Bren's hard copy of the document is in front of her. "We got bleary-eyed, so please help us find any typos or unclear verbiage we may have missed. If you have questions, ask."

Pointing to the new gal on the dais, Bren continues. "Elaine Knutsson, here, is the lawyer who helped us draft this document." Elaine waves to the crowd. "The two of us will be seated at the folding table we've set up to my right." Bren points to the table. "Come see us with your questions or proposed changes."

Over the next hour we get the feedback we wanted—no changes other than typos and a few word choice improvements. Bren makes real-time changes to the version and posts them on the website. She also prints a final agreement, using the printer I brought from home.

I step up to the lectern at exactly 10:00 a.m. The attendees want to leave, as do we. They'll accept whatever we put in front of them. "Gentlemen and ladies," I say, "are you ready to vote on and sign the Proclamation?"

My question gets an enthusiastic response, but the few dissident Evangelicals in my line of sight aren't clapping. I hope that doesn't mean they've changed their minds.

"God asked for a unanimous 'yes' vote, and it's my understanding we've reached unanimity. As I call for each faith's vote, I'd like the representative to stand and say yes, you will sign. Follow a 'yes' vote by going to Brendali's table to sign the Proclamation. The

Catholics and Buddhists, who are represented by the Archbishop and the Reverend Mother, have already voted yes. They'll sign when called."

"Any questions?" I see no hands raised. "I'm doing this in alphabetical order. If you care to make a statement when you announce your vote, feel free but keep it short, please. The first group to vote and sign is Aladura. How do you vote?

The representative, a short older man, stands and shouts his message. "Our religion believes in healing and salvation. We vote 'yes' to heal our world." He walks to Bren's table.

"Atheists?"

Their man resembles a Hell's Angel biker, or maybe he is one. He stands. "Whether or not a god exists, only humans can help each other solve the world's problems. To us, voting 'yes' is the only option."

"The Baha'i faith?"

A frail Indian man of indeterminate age stands. "Our faith, formed in 1863, works for social justice and equality. Religious tolerance is essential to our outlook. We vote 'yes!'"

"Bon?"

"We are but a small Tibetan faith focused on meditation and enlightenment," an Asian woman says. "Our 'yes' vote is consistent with our values."

"Buddhists—Reverend Mother, you can go sign." Elaine escorts her across the dais as I continue the roll call. "Let's see. Next is Cao Dai."

A Vietnamese gentleman jumps to his feet. "Founded in Vietnam in 1926, Cao Dai preaches peace and harmony in each person and the world. We vote 'yes.'"

"Chinese folk religions?"

An elegantly dressed woman rises. "We are 400 million strong not counting our revered ancestors, who today look down upon us with approval and honor. We vote 'Shi!' 'Yes!'"

"Christian Science?"

A young man dressed in a suit and tie struggles out of his wheelchair. "Our credo is to spread the word that life, truth, and love must be understood and demonstrated as supreme over all, while we work to destroy sin, sickness and death. Count us in— 'yes.'"

"Catholicism. Archbishop, please go and sign. Confucianism?"

A stout, bald Chinese man stands. "Our teachings assert that each person's role in society is the fulfillment of propriety, honor and loyalty. This proclamation is in alignment. We vote 'Shi', too."

"Druze?"

No one reacts until a Middle Eastern man decides to take the lead. "We believe favorable reincarnation requires a life lived in moderation and spirituality. 'Yes', we are with you."

"The Evangelical faiths?" Let's hope nothing's changed since yesterday.

Gilbert stands, a good sign. "Our four core beliefs are conversionism, activism, Biblicism and crucicentrism, but the word 'evangelical' is from the Greek 'euangelion,' meaning the good news, or the gospel. We have been reluctant to accept the tasks assigned to this Convocation, but our eyes have opened. So our good news is this: we, too, say 'yes.'"

I wasn't sure where his statement would lead but he's on record. A smattering of applause accompanies him as he heads toward the signing table.

We're good from here on out, no surprises, all the way to the Zoroastrians.

"To all our members present, I thank each of you for your cooperation. We have a unanimous vote on each of God's objectives, and a Proclamation signed by representatives of each participating religious group. Ladies and gentlemen, prepare for humanity to prosper into the indefinite future."

Everyone rises to shake hands, slap each other on the back, and exult. Even a few of the reluctant Evangelicals join in.

"I now announce this Convocation ended," I say to the crowd, none of whom are listening. "Have a safe trip home, everyone."

I spot Brendali gathering her papers, including the original signed Proclamation. She puts them in her briefcase, looks up at me with a radiant smile and sends a long distance smooch.

That's not enough for me. I head toward her, bypassing the Archbishop and Father Zeke. "We did it, Angel."

"With God's help it worked out," she says. "My prayers came true."

I take her in my arms, bend her backward and deliver a long kiss, knowing now that we'll share many more of them during our long future together.

Ram's Convocation Update: The Convocation is a success. God will include us in his planetary turnaround plan, but let's not give Him cause to rethink this. #cooperate #toabetterEarth

---

RAM

Sunday, February 6, 2028, Cambria

Brendali and I lucked into the guest cottage at Fog's End B&B, a mere seven miles from Hearst Castle. Yesterday, despite the winter season, we marveled at the opulence on display and enjoyed the grounds and gardens.

After we dawdled over the B&B's breakfast, we're about to check out. The B&B's owner, Joe Bellinger, greets us. "I hope you two enjoyed your stay and our hospitality. We're honored to have you here."

"Your place is wonderful! We only wish we could stay longer," Bren says. "Can you give us some advice? We'd like to do more touring before we head home. Where should we go?"

"Do you have anything special in mind?"

"We've ruled out the wineries. I don't want Ram to drink and drive."

"With the Convocation over," I say, "we need to find neat little vignettes to feature on our show. Do you remember Huell Howser's show, *California Gold*? Ours is a 21st century version—this God thing we got caught up in came as a total surprise. That's over. We'd love any leads you know of on places folks don't know about, or have a unique or funky back story."

Bellinger slaps the desk in front of him for emphasis. "What you're looking for is six minutes up the road, but I can't recommend it. The place is called Nitt Witt Ridge, also known as the 'poor man's Hearst Castle.' It's a dilapidated, ramshackle property with a state historical landmark designation."

Bren and I respond at the same time. "That's not the kind of place we'd have an interest in," she says with finality. At the same time I react with "Really? Tell me more."

No doubt due to our divergent reactions, Bellinger hesitates momentarily. "Back in the 1940s Arthur Beal, a garbage collector in Cambria, bought the land undeveloped. He built his home out of garbage he collected—beer cans, washer drums, bits of tile, car parts, old stoves, abalone shells, whatever he could pick up from the nearby pine forests and beaches. He included a few things from Hearst Castle because he did some maintenance work on the property."

"This is intriguing, whether or not we follow it up," I say.

Bren rolls her eyes and vehemently shakes her head. "I'm going to pack up. Nice to meet you, Mr. Bellinger. We'll come back sometime." She leaves in a huff.

"Maybe I shouldn't have mentioned this," Joe says, sounding mystified. I assure him we're fine, and he continues. "Beal passed away in 1992. His ashes are spread around a redwood tree on the property. The house is architecturally unique. I might have an old brochure somewhere—as I said, I don't recommend the place."

He returns after a while and hands me the brochure. The photos show what looks like three single-level homes stacked haphazardly on top of each other under one roof. Abundant shrubbery peeks over the top of rock walls abutting the street. Four rock-strewn Roman-arch columns support the two upper levels and further hide the lowest. The ad hoc, whimsical build tells me Mr. Beal wasn't an architect. Even so, I'm impressed he did all the construction work.

"I see fencing up all around. Is that a no trespassing sign?"

"Yes, but the photo's a few years old. The owners who bought the property from Beal's estate put up the fencing but also ran tours for a nominal contribution. They sold the place two years ago. The fencing might've come down. I haven't been over that way in a good long while."

"Does the current owner do tours, too?"

"He's an absentee. To my knowledge no one's ever seen him."

"Can I keep this? I'd like to show my staff, work up a feature."

"It's clutter to me, so consider it yours."

I put the pamphlet in my pocket. "Great tip, thanks. I'm going to talk Bren into steering past the place on our way to wherever we decide to go."

Back in our room, Bren's packing consists of hurling our clothes into the luggage while giving me an angry stare. "We're not going anywhere near any place named Nitwit, Ram. I refuse. That's final. Don't you dare try to change my mind!"

"I've got to at least eyeball the place. It's nearby. I'll run over, check the property out and come right back. The building's fenced up, see?" I show her the photo and the pamphlet. "I shouldn't need much time to look around."

"Call Lyft if you want a ride. The Fiat stays here with me."

The fence around Nitt Witt Ridge hasn't been removed but the gate's slightly ajar. Although curious, I resist trespassing. Instead I take photos of the exterior at different angles from the street. Only when I'm finished do I realize the Lyft driver's gone.

"Angel, the place is deserted and my driver abandoned me. Can you pick me up?" I get a torrent of objections and Spanish curses, but she agrees.

Instead of waiting around on the street, I slip through the gate since the owner's not local and the building's uninhabitable. I snap a picture of the plaque that explains the property's landmark designation, and hustle up the stairway to the backyard.

The stairs have risers made of large abalone shells arranged next to each other. The landers consist of cut stone pavers, while piping forms the handrails. The backyard, spacious but unkempt, has grown back to its natural state.

I stop at what someone might charitably call an avant-garde sculpture, made of three thick truck tires laid sideways and stacked on each other. The largest serves as a foundation. The smallest is next, with the mid-sized tire on top. Dirt and crushed stone are inside all three. The top layer consists of a copper wire in the form of a human, a carved wooden Chihuahua and a store-bought cat and rooster figurine.

I photograph the sculpture and keep moving. The second floor corridor features rock and mortar plastered all over the walls, beams, arches and half-walls. The illusion is of a cave carved to allow casual furniture and shelves to fill empty nooks and crannies. Everything here has seen better days, but the overall effect is natural and cozy.

I don't have time to explore the kitchen before Bren gets here, so I snap more photos and bypass it. The bathroom doesn't make me linger despite the odd presence of side-by-side His-and-Her toilets. The bedroom's unremarkable, but the fresh sheets and bedding make me do a double-take.

Someone's living here—the owner? A homeless vagrant?

I return to the kitchen, open the fridge and find it full of new canned food tins. The electricity's turned off, so the fridge is basically a cabinet. Plates that fill the sink show telltale signs of food eaten within the last day or two—the ketchup stains haven't dried yet. Water service isn't on, either.

Bren announces her arrival by repeatedly honking the Fiat's horn. I whip out my phone to text her. 'I'll come right down. Sorry. Couldn't resist. This place is deserted but fascinating.'

Five angry emoji faces show up as her response.

I pocket the phone, turn toward the door and find Skeleton Man blocking my exit, his gun pointed at me.

"Mr. Forster." His sick grin isn't reassuring. "Welcome to my humble bolt hole. You're trespassing, you know. Another violation of God's will. You are indeed hopeless."

Of all people, he owns this place? Oh, sure—his patent royalties. He must've been upstairs, on the third floor, while I poked around. I don't say a word in response to his goading, but my facial expression is probably eloquent enough.

"We're going out into the garden, Mr. Forster. Your blood can water my thirsty flora while your last moments are spent in the bright California sunshine of a February day." A hideous smile crosses his face. "Would you like your ashes spread around the redwood tree? Mr. Beal might like some company. A little dismemberment, plus some coal to burn your remains down to ash in the fire pit, will easily accommodate him."

The man's sick, but I don't doubt he means every word. How the hell do I deal with this?

We traipse up the stairs into the backyard, stopping at the tire sculpture. "Have a seat," Mr. Krol says, pointing to the top of a rock and abalone shell half-wall that separates us from a mannequin poised on a wooden platform. The figure, seated on the closed top cover of a toilet, has one hand raised in a perpetual wave to pedestrians on the street below.

"We're going to take care of God's business right now," Skeleton Man says with a smirk. A loud click readies his pistol for use.

"May I ask one question before you shoot?" Skeleton Man nods. "Why'd you decide to let Brendali go instead of sending her to the *narcos* and collecting the cash?"

"I don't care about money, Mr. Forster. God's blessed me with enough. I can do His will until the day He brings me home, but God would look askance if I surrendered your girlfriend to whatever degradations those heathens south of the border would inflict upon her. I agree with you, she's an innocent bystander to your violation of God's laws. You're the one who must suffer for your grave sins."

He actually has some Christian morality, according to his own lights. How astonishing.

"Prepare to die, Mr. Forster." He leans over the tire statue and assumes a shooters stance.

"Don't you dare fire that gun, bastard." Bren says from behind him, near the stairway. Her pistol's pointed at him, her purse deposited on the wall beside her.

He whirls in her direction. The sound I hear is loud enough for two guns because each of them discharged their weapons at the same moment.

His bullet missed her but rifled through her purse, which topples to the ground.

Skeleton Man's doubled over, his empty hand covering his midsection. The other hand, having knocked over the cat figurine, hangs onto the top of Beal's statue. I can't see his face but his groans say enough. His shaky gun arm rises, aimed at Bren, but he falls to his knees. I barrel into him from his right side as the shot discharges.

He's stretched out flat on the ground, affording me a quick glance to check whether Brendali's been hit. Another miss, thank God. I step on the guy's wrist and apply my full weight.

"Drop the gun immediately." My command sounds frantic, not assured. Blood seeps from underneath him, darkening the rock pavers he's splayed across. His face is chalky, the grimace severe, but the malevolence in his one good eye is undimmed.

"Bren, call 911. Tell them to get police and an ambu—" A third shot sounds. Skeleton Man's gun, at ground level, has discharged while pointed away from us. He would've only hit a squirrel or rabbit if one happened to pass by.

She pulls a stun gun out of her purse. Before she can use it we hear a groan, followed by a death rattle. Skeleton Man's gun hand loosens, his weapon rendered useless. His good eye dims, loses luster and focus. He's reuniting with his God—or with ours.

"I didn't mean to kill him," Bren says in a slow, hushed tone. "I only wanted to stop him from shooting at you." She looks at me. "We can't leave him here."

"We'll do the honorable thing," I say with a shrug. "I'll call Griff and tell him what happened—by coincidence we found Skeleton Man. He shot at us twice. In self-defense we shot back, killing him.

I'll ask him to contact the local police for us. He can talk their language and explain things so they'll understand. We'll await their arrival, go through the whole story and hope they don't arrest us."

She sighs. "At least we're finished with the Convocation and the death threats. God doesn't need us anymore. We can make the show into what you envisioned. Best of all, we're finally free of violence."

"One thing we need to do is set a date for our wedding." I put my arms around her, give her a short 'kiss your troubles away' kind of smooch and go off to call Griff while Bren does a last rights prayer for Mr. Krol's soul.

Down at Bren's car, we await a hopefully friendly visit from the local cops.

BRENDALI

Saturday, April 1, 2028, the L.A. Cathedral

"Before I pronounce you man and wife, you may say your wedding vows." A priest is translating Archbishop Delmonico's words into Spanish for my extended family. "Which of you wishes to go first?"

I turn to face Ram. "I will." We hold hands. His eyes are soft, loving and a little glassy. But his smile is wide. I've never loved a man so much. Now if I can only say my vow the way I've rehearsed it.

"My dear, dearest Ram," I say, breathless as I try to fight off the emotions threatening to overwhelm me. "You are the man I dreamed of as a child, the man I never thought I'd meet, much less marry. You are the dream I've clung to, the one who could fix my nightmares, including those I lived through when I wasn't asleep. You replaced my deep-seated anger with never-ending joy. I vow to love you, only you, not only until the day I die but forever afterward, from heaven. And I swear to teach you Spanish!"

Everyone laughs, including Ram, at that improvised last line.

He coughs to clear his throat and starts his vow. "Brendali, I call you Angel not only because God sent you to me, but because you are one. You have healed the pain I've held inside since childhood, extracted the insecurities I've carried for far too long, and replaced those evils with unending waves of love. In my world I hear no sweeter sound than your voice, see nothing more beautiful than your smile and receive no love more sacred than yours. You have the strength of will I lack, the depth of emotion I bottle up, the devotion to God I don't exercise. I vow to cherish you, empathize when you're sad and tease you out of your anger. I will never remove you from the pedestal I have placed you on. I will complete you as you complete me. Forever, we're one in two bodies."

The guests applaud as we turn toward the Archbishop. I can't breathe because Ram's vow touched me to my soul. I have to focus on what comes next, the most important seven words of the entire ceremony.

Delmonico's silence makes me think he's having second thoughts about performing the wedding. "I now pronounce you man and wife," he finally says. "You may kiss the bride."

Ram gives me his most tender look as we hold hands again. We stare at each other for only seconds, though they feel like minutes.

"Are you ready for your kiss?" he asks in a near whisper. I nod because I'm too overtaken by emotion to give him my usual smart-ass reply. He releases my hands, pulls me to him, bends me backward and plants The Wedding Kiss on my lips. I don't want it to end, but of course it does. We turn around to face the crowd.

Once again I'm awestruck by the setting—row upon row of pews, far more than our small group needs. A mass of organ pipes off to my left. Glass-covered mosaics spread the light coming through the windows. Spanish limestone paving stones line the floor. Twenty-five Communion of Saints tapestries hang on walls made of Turkish marble.

It's all so stunning. Never did I expect to marry in such a marvelous place of worship.

I look at my family as Ram and I bask in praise. Mamá's crying. Papi beams with pride. Julian has one arm around his wife, Rosie, the other around his oldest daughter, Socorro. Both are teary. Lobo's bouncing his youngest girl on his lap. His two pre-teen daughters, seated between him and Linda, his wife, pay no attention to the beauty around them. They're fixated by whatever's on their phones. This is the family Ram has adopted.

Griff, who is Ram's best man, is stoic. His wife, LaTaunya, is trying to quiet their adorable little baby girl, who's all lungs. Lorena, my bridesmaid and friend from Veracruz, gives me a wide smile when I look her way.

My many Mexican relatives, Johnny Ray, Father Zeke, the Reverend Mother Verma, Gilbert Thibodaux and even Hakan Çelik, who to our surprise made the trip here from Ankara with his wife, round out the crowd. Kate wasn't invited, of course. I wish Elena Rios could've come, but it's her son's birthday. Ram's wish, to have had Slomo Nakamura with us, goes unfulfilled though he is with us in spirit.

No offense intended to the Archbishop, but it would've been nice if Pope Francis III had performed the ceremony. He offered, but his balky heart won't let him travel.

"We're lucky to marry on April Fool's Day," I whisper in Ram's ear. "Now we'll give each other funny April Fool's anniversary gifts for decades, no?" He grins.

Our wedding party takes place at the Trans-Pacific Diner restaurant, an actual train dining car converted into a posh dining spot. The train's windows are beveled, the chairs are dark wood with green velvet seats and backing, and the walls and ceiling are mahogany. A green and blue tartan rug covers the floor.

We rented the whole place for the wedding party. It's expensive, but you only get married once. Griff chows down on the all-you-can-eat KC-style barbeque, ignoring LaTaunya's scowls from the third plate on.

I like her. She's funny enough for both of them, which is good since Griff claims to have no sense of humor. LaTaunya and I will probably become close friends unless the FBI moves Griff out of town. Once Griff's eaten his fill, and before the cake is served, they leave early because the baby's freaked out by all the noise.

Lobo's band provides the night's musical accompaniment. Ram sits in on guitar once or twice—in particular, when he takes a knee in front of me and sings a calmed-down version of the Bleachers' "Let's Get Married." I melt, overcome with joy. Lobo's band mostly plays Mexican tunes ranging from Latin rock to *Norténo* music to *Cumbia* and even a bit of Bolero. They throw in a few of their own songs every once in a while.

The Archbishop shows his informal side after several glasses of wine. I love his story about meeting the first Pope Francis before he became pope. It's amazing how much significance a chance encounter can have on someone's life, no? I promise Ricardo (we're on a first name basis now) I'll keep volunteering and praying at the Cathedral. I think he'll remain a friend, too, at least until he becomes Pope.

Çelik and his wife, Bersin, greet us. Hakan's muttering *"Tebrikler, gözünüz aydın"* over and over. We don't have a translation tool anymore, so Bersin interprets. The words mean "congratulations, I'm happy for you." Through her we express our appreciation for their attendance, and graciously accept their offer to visit them in Ankara.

Many of my relatives congratulate me on forming Friends of the Queen of the Angels Church, a fundraising nonprofit dedicated to rebuilding and restoring that important church. Our wedding invitations asked our guests to make monetary contributions to the foundation instead of giving us wedding presents, so I'm sure they've enriched the coffers.

'Friends' should keep me busy for the next several years. I'll run it better than Allenby did with his foundation, which I suppose goes without saying. Maybe I'll stay involved in community affairs after the church is rebuilt, but never can we know what the future brings.

To have Mamá and Papi here for the two weeks before the wedding has been wonderful. They got to see the progress being made to rebuild their house. Papi, who worked on framing and other construction trades his entire life, asked the workers a lot of probing questions and declared himself satisfied with their responses.

Mamá insisted that Ram give her male grandchildren. Ram promised her three babies, with gender the luck of the draw. But if we have a girl, he said, she'll be named Rosa, for her. Mamá's been in heaven ever since.

No one asked me if I want to deliver three little ones, but no matter. However many children I have, I'll cherish them to the day I die. And spoil them daily.

My brothers accepted Ram right away, especially Lobo. They bonded immediately over their musical talents. At our place earlier this week Lobo showed Ram some Latin grooves and introduced him to *Nortéño* music on Spotify, including his band's songs. Ram showed off and played his Clapton guitar for my family. Lobo invited him to bring it to Tucson so they can jam with the band in his recording studio. Ram's super excited about doing that.

We cut the cake and drink more champagne than necessary. When we leave to get into our limo, God's white-light appearance brings oohs and aahs from the wedding group behind us. Johnny Ray's exclamation "why, butter my butt and call me a biscuit!" cracks everyone up.

God ignores the others and focuses on us. "Congratulations, lovebirds."

"Thank you, Lord," I say, trying not to slur my words. "You brought us together and kept us safe. Please, have some of our wedding cake."

He gives me a skeptical look. "You are more than a bit tipsy, my dear. I am stopping by to bestow a special gift on you both." God snaps his fingers. A large manila envelope materializes in his hand, to the astonishment of the wedding guests and restaurant staff nearby.

Ram takes the envelope since my hands aren't free—I'm carrying a large bouquet of roses the *maître d'* gave me on behalf of the restaurant.

"Open this once you get inside the limousine," God says.

"I can't thank you enough for bringing this angel to me," Ram says as he wraps an arm around me. "I'm forever indebted." He extends a hand to God. His muttered "oh, right," means he's belatedly remembered that God's untouchable. He bows instead, and would've fallen over if he wasn't holding on to me.

I laugh, along with some people behind us. Father Zeke, called upon for a Bible quote, declines to provide one. Instead of a Buddhist saying, the Reverend Mother mutters, "I'm sure somewhere or other Buddha declared that one can be heedless at his own wedding." That draws more laughter and a "bravo" from a passerby.

"Ram," God says, "we shall not mention your indebtedness again. I wish you both a wonderful Tahitian honeymoon. Rest up. You will hear from me once you return."

That sobers us up. "What now?" I ask.

"The details can wait. I am loath to spoil your only honeymoon. Ta ta." God vanishes to a mixture of applause and astonishment.

Inside the limousine Ram opens the envelope. His eyes go wide as he reads the two pages. He hands me one, a bullet-point outline of God's turnaround plan. The page turns to ash in my hand as the limo pulls away, but doesn't smear my wedding dress.

The second page lists baby names. We're asked to tell God how many children we want, their chosen names, birth order and gender.

I point to two listed names. "This one first, followed by this next, okay?"

"Fine," Ram says. "I'm in no hurry to figure out the third one's name and gender."

We share a long kiss, sure that baby Rosa will have at least one younger brother, Nick. A sister will follow if I have anything to say about it.

THE END

| Acknowledgments

Any project that is four years in the making will involve a lot of input from a wealth of people. *First Second Coming* is no exception. Many people willingly provided their thoughts, comments and suggestions to improve the novel. I will invariably miss some of them in this acknowledgment, and hope no one feels slighted by the inadvertent omission.

The "author's best friend" prize goes to Marianne Robin-Tani, followed closely by Sharon MaHarry, both of whom were vital members of a weekly critique group Marianne and I founded. Their encouragement, insights and interest in this story helped make it happen. Others in the critique group who provided useful commentary and feedback are Margaret Tsubakiyama and Liana English. Thank you, ladies, for your contributions.

Speaking of critique groups, the monthly one I joined after FSC was well-developed also helped with edits, ideas and probing questions about character motivations and plot development. To my Pasadena Area Writers' Society (PAWS) friends Tony Chiarchiaro, Willow Healy, Gil Roscoe, Candy Avila, Jay Brakensiak, Cynthia Kumanchik and Yvonne Ruiz, many thanks!

Because Brendali is a Latina and I am neither female nor Latino, I asked Gloria Sol, who I had the great pleasure to work with in my lawyering days, to act as a sensitivity reader. She was a great help, making sure I didn't stereotype Bren and that my use of Spanish was passable. Another Latina friend, Silvia Santana, has not only cut what's left of my hair for decades now, but gracefully continued to do so after she learned I'd bestowed her speech pattern on Bren.

Laura Perkins, an editor extraordinaire, provided her thoughtful edits on all facets of the story. I doubt FSC would have been published without Laura's guidance. My deep appreciation also goes to YA romance author Ara Grigorian, who is as much a mentor to me as anyone. Ara's suggestion that I do a writing exercise eventually turned into a solid Chapter 1 that replaced fifteen weaker versions of that chapter and got the story off to a solid start. He is mentioned, along with his excellent more recent Young Adult romance *15 Days With You,* in Chapter 2.

Jasmin Iolani Hakes brought the Parliament of World Religions to my attention. I attended the 2018 parliament in Toronto and gained a wealth of insights into the many religions represented there and the interfaith movement as a whole. The hundred or so attendees I spoke with, out of about 8,000 who attended, also gave me very positive feedback on my story and confirmed that they constitute a ready-made market for it. I also came across URI—the United Religions Initiative—in Toronto. With their permission, excerpts from their "Preamble, Purpose and Principles" are included in *FSC*.

Holly Kammier, who co-founded Acorn Publishing LLC, is an award winning author in her own right. She offered to publish *FSC*. I didn't immediately say yes but she waited patiently and got my assent. She's had faith in me and in the story, and her editing and overall help in the prepublication phase was essential to turning my manuscript into a full-fledged published novel.

Many of those mentioned above have affiliations with SCWC—the Southern California Writers' Conference. Marianne and Sharon introduced me to this group, who are now my "tribe." I met Jasmin, Laura and Holly there, too. Like magic, every time I've attended this conference something positive has occurred to move my book toward publishing. I heartily recommend SCWC to any budding authors living on or near the west coast, or willing to trek there in February or September to learn the ropes, make friends and, perhaps, find an agent or publisher.

Regarding permissions, I greatly appreciate having received the following ones:

- The Dalai Lama's staff has approved inclusion of the excerpt from one of his articles.

- The United Religions Initiative ("URI") agreed to allow the excerpts from its Preamble Purpose and Principles to appear.

- The owners of Fog's End Bed & Breakfast in Cambria, California graciously permitted my use of their business. If you are interested in a B&B in Cambria, reserve a room at fogsend.com.

- Approval to place the funeral scene situated at and outside of St. Theresa of Avila Catholic Church.

- The owners of Nitt Witt Ridge, also in Cambria, didn't know they'd be selling the historical landmark in 2025 to Skeleton Man until I told them. They nonetheless assented to using the property's name in my book. If you're visiting Cambria and interested in taking a tour of the property, contact the O'Malleys through their website at nitwitridge.com (yes, only two 't's) to make arrangements. There is no fee for tours but donations are gladly accepted.

To my Beta readers—Jenny Knutsson, Lorin Petrazilka and Liana English, thank you for your time reading the manuscript and your feedback about it. Jenny, also a lawyer/writer, in particular provided some exceptional feedback that helped strengthen the story. Thanks also to four people whose gracious testimonials are found in the front pages—Mark Moses, Adena Bernstein Astrowsky, Tony Harrison and Tony Chiarchiaro.

The story contains excerpts from the following public domain sources:

- "A Common Word Between Us and You" was an open letter dated October 13, 2007, from leaders of the Islamic religion to leaders of the Christian religion following some unfortunate commentary from Pope Benedict WVI the prior year. The pope later apologized for his remarks.

- A 1960 speech given by then-Senator and soon to be president, John Kennedy, addressed his Catholic religion. At the time this became a political issue since no prior U.S. president was Catholic.

- In 1893, Bengali Swami Vivikananda gave a speech at the opening of the first World Parliament of Religions which is excerpted in Chapter 39.

- The five principles proposed to bring peace to the Abrahamic religions, found in Chapter 29, come from a 2008 Special Report put out by the United States Institute of Peace. The report is entitled Abrahamic Alternatives to War: Jewish, Christian and Muslim Perspectives on Just Peacemaking.

| About the Author

Jeff Pollak, the author of *First Second Coming* and sequels to come, was raised in the Riverdale section of the Bronx by a single mom and two grandparents who lived eight floors up.

After graduating from college in Buffalo, Jeff headed west to Los Angeles for law school and spent his entire legal career in and around civil litigation. Now retired, writing fiction is Jeff's new passion.

Made in the USA
Middletown, DE
09 September 2020